A CHERISHED MOTHER

"Mother, you are the most brilliant woman in all of London," Letty giggled. "I hope someday I may learn to be as clever as you."

—"Motherly Advice" by Sheila Rabe
in *A Mother's Delight*

* * *

Such loving words of praise would cheer any mother, whether she is a Regency-era heroine or a modern-day reader. For what mother isn't happy to hear of the love and admiration a daughter holds in her heart?

Yet, such sentiments should be spoken aloud, particularly on a day when we take time to thank mothers and show them our love and appreciation. And what better present to offer at this celebration than the delightful stories of a Regency-era motherhood from the skilled pen of six treasured Zebra authors. So while away the time with Monique Ellis, Violet Hamilton, Isobel Linton, Sheila Rabe, Jeanne Savery, and Lois Stewart, and let them take you to a time of proper manners and impassioned hearts where love is first felt in a mother's arms and found forever in a hero's embrace.

ZEBRA'S REGENCY ROMANCES
DAZZLE AND DELIGHT

A BEGUILING INTRIGUE (4441, $3.99)
by Olivia Sumner

Pretty as a picture Justine Riggs cared nothing for propriety. She dressed as a boy, sat on her horse like a jockey, and pondered the stars like a scientist. But when she tried to best the handsome Quenton Fletcher, Marquess of Devon, by proving that she was the better equestrian, he would try to prove Justine's antics were pure folly. The game he had in mind was seduction — never imagining that he might lose his heart in the process!

AN INCONVENIENT ENGAGEMENT (4442, $3.99)
by Joy Reed

Rebecca Wentworth was furious when she saw her betrothed waltzing with another. So she decides to make him jealous by flirting with the handsomest man at the ball, John Collinwood, Earl of Stanford. The "wicked" nobleman knew exactly what the enticing miss was up to — and he was only too happy to play along. But as Rebecca gazed into his magnificent eyes, her errant fiancé was soon utterly forgotten!

SCANDAL'S LADY (4472, $3.99)
by Mary Kingsley

Cassandra was shocked to learn that the new Earl of Lynton was her childhood friend, Nicholas St. John. After years at sea and mixed feelings Nicholas had come home to take the family title. And although Cassandra knew her place as a governess, she could not help the thrill that went through her each time he was near. Nicholas was pleased to find that his old friend Cassandra was his new next door neighbor, but after being near her, he wondered if mere friendship would be enough . . .

HIS LORDSHIP'S REWARD (4473, $3.99)
by Carola Dunn

As the daughter of a seasoned soldier, Fanny Ingram was accustomed to the vagaries of military life and cared not a whit about matters of rank and social standing. So she certainly never foresaw her *tendre* for handsome Viscount Roworth of Kent with whom she was forced to share lodgings, while he carried out his clandestine activities on behalf of the British Army. And though good sense told Roworth to keep his distance, he couldn't stop from taking Fanny in his arms for a kiss that made all hearts equal!

Available wherever paperbacks are sold, or order direct from the Publisher. Send cover price plus 50¢ per copy for mailing and handling to Penguin USA, P.O. Box 999, c/o Dept. 17109, Bergenfield, NJ 07621. Residents of New York and Tennessee must include sales tax. DO NOT SEND CASH.

A Mother's Delight

**Monique Ellis, Violet Hamilton, Isobel Linton
Sheila Rabe, Jeanne Savery, Lois Stewart**

**ZEBRA BOOKS
KENSINGTON PUBLISHING CORP.**

CONTENTS

Lady Charlotte Contrives

by
Monique Ellis

December, 1811

White's was hushed that icy late-December evening, its famous bow window empty and painted with frost. The lamps were lit. Fires burned cheerily on every grate. Seasonal greenery adorned each mantel and doorway, the spicy tang of pine mingling with the aromas of tobacco, brandy, punch, and good food. A smattering of determined wagerers huddled at the gaming tables, faces pale or flushed according to their degree of inebriation and their fortunes at play. One, faring particularly poorly, had just reversed his coat for luck, its brilliant scarlet lining unintentionally adding to the festive decor. It being yuletide, London was thin of company, entertainments rare. Those who gathered at White's famous club on St. James's Street were there more by default than by choice.

In the far corner of the dining room, two men lingered over their port, moderate shirt points crisp against firm jaws, neckcloths notable for their precise folds, fastidious evening dress unforgivingly formfitting. The younger of the pair—stern-faced, hawk-nosed, of medium height and somewhat stocky, with a lingering air of the country about him—smiled slightly at his taller companion as he lifted his glass in mocking salute.

"To this joyous season," he said "Where shall you be spending the great day, Jamie?"

"Alone, if I have my way about it," James Debenham, Duke of Rawdon, returned. "With my aunt, if I don't. And I won't. She'd be glad to include you, you know. Why not join us, Ned, at least for dinner? Better than rattling around in that musty mausoleum of yours across the square."

"I prefer my own company," Edward Connardsleigh, Viscount Connard, shrugged. "Or maybe it's that I know better than to inflict myself on others at this season. Certainly I'd have little to offer in the way of jollity or wit."

He scowled into his glass, unwelcome thoughts of Connard Manor intruding like malicious devils on this pleasant evening with an old friend: his stepmother in self-important control of the household; his grandmother keeping to her apartments; his sixteen-year-old half brother, Artie, roaming the estate, shooting at anything that moved.

Not that he grudged the lad the entertainment! Far from it. Artie reminded him of what their father must have been at the same age, angular and tall and never quite certain what to do with his excess of elbows and knees. Bumbling, good-hearted, not overly intelligent, but with a core of sound common sense for a boy that age. A worthy and an excellent heir. He'd just received another bill from Weston for five rig-outs and a shooting jacket. The boy was growing at an alarming rate. *He'd* seemed to stop when he reached his fifteenth year, just after his mother died . . . There'd probably be a bill from Hoby as well in the next week. The leather it took to cover the boy's feet!

Very carefully the thirty-four-year-old Connard tried to avoid thinking of the other child at the manor, home from her Yorkshire boarding school for the holidays.

Eleven, she was now. He'd never set eyes on her. He never intended to. He knew her name only because his grandmother insisted on raising it in conversation. Enough that he'd given the chit his name and permitted her to be raised at his expense. As his stepmother said, that was more than the baseborn brat deserved, no matter what his grandmother claimed about his faithless wife's innocence.

What a fool he'd been at twenty-two—a raw lieutenant,

recently come into his majority and in possession of a comfortable independence from his mother. And far from home, lonely, ill, still feeling betrayed by his father's remarriage four years earlier and cursed with a half brother in leading strings who either puked or howled or both.

The disaster had begun during the Holland invasion close by Texel. They'd planned to seize the Dutch fleet, then strike at France through Flanders. What a farce . . .

Ripe for the plucking, that's what he'd been. And plucked he had been—by a sixteen-year-old vixen with the face of an angel and the soul of a devil who'd played him false before her vows were even spoken. He could still see her, bursting into his quarters, sobbing out that her army-surgeon father, John Morecamb, had just succumbed to the same fever that had laid him low. What could a man do then but offer every possible comfort? Especially if he already loved the engaging minx to distraction?

Sixteen—that's all she'd been when her father died, sixteen! The same age Artie was now. And when she'd betrayed him? *Still* sixteen . . .

"Anything new on Christo?" he asked to change the subject around which his thoughts writhed in familiar fury and desolation.

Rawdon scowled, deep gray eyes scanning the room. A pair of flunkies was clearing the covers from a table across the way. In his customary corner the portly, retired General Maitland nodded over congealed roast capon and mushroom fritters, his broad waistcoat liberally sprinkled with onion sauce and claret and snuff. But for those three, the room was empty. It seemed safe enough.

"A little," he admitted in a guarded tone. "Wellesley's taken an interest, and the Horse Guards've become involved. They're little use—more punctilio than perspicacity—but I've my own men on the trail. We think there's been another incident. I'll let you know."

Christo Debenham, Rawdon's younger brother, had been

killed on the chaotic retreat to Corunna in '09. Official military reports claimed French *tirailleurs*. Rawdon insisted he had evidence of murder. The duke had been quietly following lead upon lead ever since, pursuing long-delayed justice for his brother's sake. That Connard was aware of the situation was a tribute to their many years of friendship. The issue was potentially too explosive for casual dissemination.

"Cheerful pair, aren't we?" Rawdon now commented wryly, well aware that his companion was remembering the days of '99 and '00, Texel, and a chestnut-haired damsel with hazel eyes as changeable as her affections. "A joyous Christmas to you, Ned, and a better new year to the both of us than the last few have been!"

"Bother, Christmas! A deal more trouble than it's worth. I'm well out of it here, with Artie playing master at the manor. Good practice for the boy."

"And the girl?" Rawdon inquired hesitantly.

"I've no idea, nor do I care. Alive, I suppose—since I've not been informed otherwise—and there as usual at my blasted grandmother's insistence. Why d'you suppose I'm here?"

Connard signaled for another bottle of port, settled himself more comfortably in his chair, stretching powerful legs into the room.

"Wretched winter we've been having," he grumbled, then grinned. "Listen to me! Forced to resort to the weather, *faute de mieux!* Let's discuss Wellesley's chances come spring, or Brummell's latest insult to Prinny, or even that colonial jackanapes, Madison. What is it about short men? Madison over there, Napoleon on the Continent? At least Wellesley's of a decent stature, thank the Lord!"

Rawdon chuckled as a pair of lackeys appeared at his London neighbor's elbow, one to deliver the wine, the other bearing a silver salver on which reposed a folded sheet of heavy cream vellum addressed to the viscount in an awkward hand.

Connard's brows soared in inquiry as he glanced at the second man.

"Delivered by an indiwidual claiming the name of Stubbs, my lord, some time ago," the red-nosed flunky enunciated carefully in an unctuous whisper. "He insisted the matter is urgent, or I would not have presumed to disturb you even now. While you and his grace were at dinner? Impossible, as I informed him most firmly, my lord!"

"Blast! Next time disturb me, please. Stubbs still here?"

"No, my lord. He said to inform you he was returning to Kent on the instant."

"Odd . . ." Connard commented, his eyes flicking to Rawdon. "You remember Toby Stubbs, my head groom at the manor? What business he'd have in London—"

Connard handed the bowing man a crown and unfolded the message, scowling as he attempted to make it out. He cursed softly under his breath at the hastily scrawled words. Then for several moments there was silence. At last he looked up, his expression bleak.

"It's my grandmother," he answered the concern in Rawdon's eyes. "She's suffered some sort of seizure."

"How serious?"

"I'm summoned home. Artie says something about hoping I'll arrive in time. Dear God—I always thought the old baggage was immortal! She's been there, standing beside us all, through everything." Connard glanced about in apparent confusion, his hand running distractedly through his crisp brown hair, then surged to his feet. "My apologies, Jamie, but I must be off. I can get there tonight. It's a matter of only a few hours with a good pair, even at this time of year."

"At night? In December? Without a moon, and with most of the journey on country lanes? Don't be a fool! If highwaymen don't get you, the ruts will." Rawdon stood, signaling the waiters to begin clearing their table. "I'll drive you down in the morning. In the meantime, I'll bear you company."

Connard's eyes snapped defiantly at his much-taller friend. "I am leaving tonight," he said with the precision of one greatly perturbed. "To be exact," he consulted his pocket watch, "I shall be well on my way in less than one hour—by midnight at the latest—so long as my valet moves his stumps. If he doesn't, I'll still be on my way. No need for your escort. I may not be the top-sawyer you are, but my cattle're every bit as prime and I've yet to overturn myself."

"You have clothes enough in Kent," Rawdon returned firmly. "If you insist on leaving tonight, I'll have myself and my blacks at your door in half an hour. Dress warmly. Since you want speed, we'll take my new racing curricle."

The road into Kent proved every bit as glacial as Rawdon had predicted, and every bit as treacherous. An Arctic wind whipped the barren branches and scurried through the hedgerows, sending the remains of the last summer's leaves scuttling before it. There was no need of highwaymen to delay them. A patch of black ice did for the curricle in the second hour. The horses, miraculously unlamed, lasted another, protesting all the while at being ridden, Rawdon's mount suffering the added indignity of his hastily packed cloak bag jouncing on its rump. Rawdon's prized blacks, tethered to a fence that leaned drunkenly into the wind, were now done for as well, their heads hanging low, their sides heaving as their labored breaths clouded the icy air.

Dawn—long in coming—and a burly farmer on his way to market found the two frozen and irritable lords hunched by the side of the track, noses red and running, fingers pinched with cold, tempers not at their best. He jovially offered them transportation between piles of turnips, carrots, and cabbages. They accepted with sincere gratitude, tying the blacks to follow, and so inched their way from village to village, cadging lifts from carters and farmers and even an emaciated curate on his way home from a deathbed—an unfortunate reminder to the anxious Ned Connardsleigh of what he was facing upon his arrival at the manor.

They munched on coarse bread with equal gratitude, consumed hard cheese and pungent pickled onions and bitter home-brewed ale, wrapped heavy woolen scarves more tightly around their necks and shivered in their stylish, many-caped greatcoats, their curly-brimmed beavers pulled low over smarting eyes. Nowhere along the road was there an inn offering rigs, or even nags, for hire. Rawdon consigned his blacks to the mercies of an ancient gap-toothed ostler at the first establishment they happened upon. So close to the holiday, all even remotely acceptable transportation was spoken for.

Their purses depleted and tempers soured by anxiety and adversity, disheveled and bleary-eyed and with their beards forming dark shadows along their jaws, the two men at last arrived at the manor atop a load of provisions—flour, sugar, spices, currants, and sugared fruits intended for last-minute Christmas baking.

Connard stared almost uncomprehendingly at the front of his ancestral home, its facade starkly crisp in the cold winter sunshine, like something seen through the wrong end of a spyglass. The red brick Tudor house with its white stone trim, flanking wings, and myriad twisted chimneys seemed a mirage conjured by an unpleasantly humored genie. He shook himself. Then, with a sigh, he trudged across the gravel and up the sweeping stone steps. The shivering Rawdon trailed behind him, clutching his cloak bag with a death grip.

Connard tried the door. Eleven in the morning it might be, but the door was still firmly bolted.

"There's no hatchment," Rawdon croaked.

Connard nodded. He had noticed that too. They were in time. He tugged on the ancient bellpull. He pounded the oaken doors with his fists. He shouted with a voice so hoarse, it barely rose above a squeak, cracking like a pubescent boy's. He gave the bellpull one last despairing jerk, then glanced at

Rawdon. Had both men not been beyond exhaustion, they would never have attempted it. As it was, Rawdon nodded, dropped his bag, and duke and viscount charged the door like bulls in springtime. It fell open before them. They crashed into the astonished butler, skidded across the gleaming floorboards, arms flapping, coattails flying, to tumble in an unceremonious heap at the foot of the dark oak stairway leading to the gallery and the upper floors.

"My lords?" Parsons gasped, recognizing his master and his master's old friend despite their disreputable appearances, then righted himself with as much dignity as he could muster, resettling his powdered wig and adjusting his brocaded waistcoat. "Welcome home, my lord," he intoned, "and welcome to Connard Manor, Your Grace."

Rawdon rolled on his back, propping himself against the first tread on his elbows.

"Hallo, yourself" he chuckled. "Close the door, will you, Parsons? It's a might chilly out there, and we've had all the chilliness we desire."

Quivering at the injustice of being called to book—even a superior butler had the right to be nonplused once in a while—Parsons shut out the bitter December wind.

"You—you were not expected, my lord," he protested.

"I wasn't? Well, I damn well should've been!" Connard snapped, scrambling to his feet. "What kind of unprincipled monster d'you take me for?"

Of course, Parsons knew to the inch precisely what sort of unprincipled monster he was. Parsons knew about the frog in Cousin Amelia's bed. He knew about the beheaded roses. He knew about the trout hung to smoke in his father's study chimney. He knew all about the heartbroken boy mourning his mother's untimely death, the proud young soldier returned from the wars with his child-bride, the embittered barely older cuckold locked away in his study with a brandy bottle for comfort, the banished wife, the bastard child.

"I—I don't know, my lord," Parsons protested feebly.

"Yes, you do!" Connard snarled, courtesy forgotten. "Where's my grandmother?"

"At this hour, my lord? Lady Connardsleigh is in her apartments, of course."

"How is she, dammit?"

"As well as can be expected," Parsons acknowledged in puzzlement. "Her ladyship's hip pains her from time to time when the wind's in the east, but—"

"I don't give a tinker's dam about her rheumatics! Where's the doctor?"

"Doctor, my lord?"

"Oh, hell—see to His Grace, will you? He needs a meal, a bath, and a bed—in any order he prefers. I'll find out how she is for myself."

"And the younger Lady Connardsleigh, my lord?"

"Leave my stepmother be," Connard scowled, shrugging out of his greatcoat, "but have Artie informed. He's the one who summoned me home, after all!"

Connard tossed the filthy rumpled coat to his bemused butler, tore up the stairs three at a time, and pelted down the central corridor, up the separate flight leading to the west wing housing his grandmother's apartments and down another interminable corridor, skidding to a halt on the tacked-down drugget.

Her door was closed. Well, what did he expect? He stood staring at its blank surface for a moment, perplexed by the sound of laughter. Then, no longer quite certain *what* he should fear, Connard turned the curved brass handle and eased the door open.

He didn't see any of them directly—one couldn't from that angle—only their reflections caught in the huge dressing-table mirror. They were four: his grandmother, Artie; a diminutive silver-haired lady dressed in flowing pink whom he remembered vaguely having met in London while his mother was still alive, and a scrawny, flaxen-haired girl. The bed curtains were drawn back, the room bathed in liquid winter sunlight.

A half-played game of backgammon stood on a tray by the bed. A gateleg table held another tray loaded with Christmas comfits, breakfast buns and wigs, pots of tea and coffee and chocolate.

He registered it all automatically without truly noticing any of it.

What caught his attention was his grandmother, rosy-cheeked and dimpling as she reclined against her lace-covered pillows, holding court in the grand manner—his grandmother, and the girl chattering of a schoolroom triumph and some dried-up stick of a schoolmistress named Miss Moore. Beside the mirror over his grandmother's dressing table hung a portrait he hadn't seen in years—not since his father married Adelle Parkins. It was reputed to have captured his mother as a young girl to perfection. The delicate features, the eager expression, the vibrant eyes and flaxen hair, even the sprinkling of freckles across the high-bridged nose matched the unknown girl's so closely they might have been twins, except for his mother's elegant antiquated clothes of brocaded silk and fragile lace, and, in contrast, the girl's shapeless gray stuff gown with its careful darns and blotted stains. Even the lowliest of his scullery maids was better dressed.

His head spinning, and unwilling to consider any of it—the girl, the portrait, his grandmother's apparently excellent health—in his exhausted, frozen state, he attempted to ease the door closed. Lady Charlotte's eyes flew up, meeting his in the mirror.

"Ned?" she called. "Ned, is that you? Whatever are you doing here?"

Groaning, running an embarrassed hand over his darkly stubbled jaw and glancing in despair at his muddied Hessians and travel-grimed leathers, Connard eased reluctantly into the bedchamber. Then, befuddled though he was, he glared across the room at Artie.

"What d'you have to say for yourself, you young make-bate?" he growled, but the growl came out as more of a croak.

Artie flushed, his mouth opening and closing like a panting hound's.

"Never mind about Artie," Lady Charlotte caroled. "What are *you* doing here, Ned? And in *such* a condition? In *my* apartments! Have you *no* sense of decorum? Why, you look as if you've spent the night carousing in the lowest of stews!"

Lord Edward Connardsleigh could have sworn he heard the elderly lady in the chair by his grandmother's bed chuckle, but the whispered words "That's it, Charlotte—always attack!" *must* have been an hallucination. He ignored the shamefaced Artie. He ignored the diminutive old lady with the familiar face. He ignored the flaxen-haired girl staring at him with a mixture of awe and fear and longing. He hadn't achieved the rank of lieutenant, commanded men many years his senior, suffered through bouts of lice, fleas, dysentery, and barracks fever for nothing! If he had learned one thing during his four interminable years of military service, it was to recognize the enemy.

"Grandmother, *what* is going on here?" he barked. "Who *are* these people?"

"Why, this is your half brother, the Honorable Arthur William Percival Connardsleigh," she said with very evidence of innocent bewilderment. "I *thought* you were acquainted. Artie, the Viscount Connard, head of the family and formerly an officer in His Majesty's service, now something of an agricultural reformer."

"Blast it, Grandmother—"

"And this is an old and *dear* friend, Lady Daphne Cheltenham, Dowager Countess of Stoker, come to bear us company over the holidays. Daphne, may I present my grandson, Lord Edward Connardsleigh, Viscount Connard?"

"Naturally you may! A well-set-up young man, and not a *total* fool from the looks of him," Lady Cheltenham smiled, gazing directly at the infuriated, frustrated viscount, *"and* not customarily given to these indecorous, ill-tempered starts, I would imagine. I trust you had a pleasant journey from town, my lord?" she inquired graciously of him.

"Tolerable. Madam," he said with an abbreviated bow, "your servant. Welcome to Connard Manor—I think. *Grand-mother*—"

"And *this*," Lady Charlotte continued, ignoring the interruption as she gestured towards the flaxen-haired girl, "is your daughter, the Honorable Lucinda Mary Morecamb Connardsleigh." She stared pointedly from the girl to the portrait of her first daughter-in-law as a child. Connard followed her eyes, his jaws grimly clenched. "Make your curtsy to your father, Lucinda."

The girl bobbed nervously. Connard gave her a curt nod, his eyes averted.

"I believe you were ill, Grandmother?" he said in a dangerously level voice.

"Oh, I was! *I was!* Buttered crab—a surfeit of buttered crab. You know what buttered crab does to me, Ned. *Most* unpleasant. Mal de mer is nothing to it. One not only suspects one will die. One wishes quite sincerely to do so, and as *quickly* as possible!" She turned to Artie, her eyes twinkling. "And you alerted your poor brother because of my gustatory intemperance? Shame on you! *What* must he have thought?"

"Precisely what you intended, I imagine," Connard muttered. Outflanked, outgunned, and outmaneuvered. And he was too damnably tired to deal with it at the moment, or the girl, or any of it.

"Pardon me, Ned! What did you say? You must speak up if you expect these ancient ears to catch your drift."

"Nothing, Grandmother, nothing. What, er—" He floundered desperately. "What are you all doing here?"

"Catching up on the children's activities, and having a most welcome morning 'tea.' Once I recover, I'm *always* famished. You appear rather fagged yourself, not to say— What was that dreadful bit of cant you favored as a boy? Gut-foundered?

You appear positively *gut-foundered,* Ned! Would you care for some chocolate or tea? There's coffee, too, if you prefer, and buns and sweets. But then, I suppose everything's dried out or cold by now, so probably you wouldn't. Care for anything, I mean.

"I am *so* sorry Artie notified you, my dear. What a to-do over nothing! But I suppose he thought matters more grave than they were. The dear Lord knows, I complained bitterly enough at the time, *besides* throwing everyone in a tizzy because dear Dr. Thorne was nowhere to be found. Where *did* you finally locate him, Artie?"

"I—um—ah—"

"Well, no matter. You found him, and he prescribed my usual tonic, and scolded me as well—also *quite* as usual!—but I *do* so love buttered crab that I tend to ignore the inconvenience occasionally, just as one does when it comes to having children. They can be *quite* as inconvenient as buttered crab, you know, and *equally* indigestible, but well worth the troubles they cause nevertheless—again, like buttered crab. Dearest Marianne was used to say much the same of life—that sometimes it was *not enough,* and sometimes it was *too much*—but *I* find buttered crab more particularly applicable to children. Even *you,* dear Ned, for all your faults, have always been *quite* worth the effort and inconvenience."

"Blast it, Grandmama—"

Lady Daphne ducked her head, hiding a smile. Artie backed away, not watching where he was going as he shifted uneasily from foot to foot, knocking the backgammon set to the floor. And Lucinda? She blanched—which was difficult for a child already so pale to do. Then she flushed, kneeling to help Artie retrieve the men that had rolled all over Lady Charlotte's bedchamber.

As for Connard, he took three determined steps toward his grandmother's raised bed—which was a good thing, as he had barely cleared the doorway when a brassily blond, plump

female garbed in cherry red charged past him, her eyes flashing.

"Oh, Lord," he muttered, easing farther from harm's way
as he sketched a reluctant bow in his stepmother's direction,
"it needed only this!"

"What is going on here?" the new arrival stormed, not
noticing him as she snatched Lucinda to her feet and delivered a pair of stinging blows to the girl's face. Artie lunged
between his mother and the ashen-faced, trembling girl.
Adelle knocked him away, grabbed the girl's arm, and jerked
her viciously to the side. Artie lurched into the gateleg table.
Tray, pots, platters, plates, cups, crashed to the floor. "Now
see what you've caused, Miss Charity-Child! You were supposed to be confined to the nursery. Isn't there *anyone* in this
demented household I can trust?"

"I thought—Great-grandmama requested—" the girl quavered, attempting to back away, tears welling in her eyes as
she nursed her assaulted cheeks.

"When I want to hear your puling voice, I'll tell you so!
Lady Charlotte has been ill. She requires seclusion and rest.
I gave *strictest* instructions you were to be kept behind locked
doors, and in this house it's *my* instructions that count! Who
released you?"

The girl ducked her head, her eyes on worn, scuffed boots
as Artie placed a reassuring hand on her shoulder. Connard's
eyes flew from his defiant half brother to the trembling child
at the lad's side, then to his grandmother's grimly smiling
face.

"Really, Adelle, this is *most* unnecessary," Lady Charlotte
interposed with immense satisfaction. Piqued, repiqued, and
capotted! The hand was playing out better than even she could
have anticipated, and she had anticipated a great deal. The
look on Ned's face was priceless, and Adelle hadn't even
noticed him yet! "Such a low-bred fracas before her ladyship," she continued blithely, indicating Lady Cheltenham.
"I requested the child's presence myself, Adelle. Artie

brought her to me on *my* instructions. Why, I haven't seen my darling great-granddaughter in *months,* thanks to you!"

"His name is Arthur William! And I'll deal with *you* later," Lady Adelle spat out, whirling first on her son with a rich rustle of silk skirts, then turning to confront Lucinda. "As for *you,* Lady Charlotte doesn't need you to give her a re-relapse," Adelle continued in high dudgeon. "An ungrateful little hoyden, that's what you are, with no more idea of the respect due your betters than a leg of mutton! Ungrateful, and the bane of my existence! It's time and more Lord Edward came to his senses and packed you off to the workhouse, where you belong, my girl! I'll be discussing the matter with him as soon as he returns—of *that* you may be sure! Now, off with you!"

Damn, but he was tired, and this was like nothing so much as a bad farce—only it was real, and he had to deal with it somehow, the sooner the better.

"Good day, Adelle." Connard's words dropped into the sudden silence like gunshots in a ballroom. "How have you been keeping—or need I ask?"

His stepmother froze, then slowly turned, her eyes rising as she dropped Lucinda's arm and automatically settled her silk skirts. *"Edward?* Dear me! Whatever are you doing here—not that you aren't *always* welcome," she appended with a mixture of defiance and consternation, patting her curls and producing a sycophantic simper.

"Standing in my grandmother's bedchamber," he replied, taking the easy way out as the children knelt to gather up the detritus of Artie's second accident. "I trust that does not discommode you?"

"That's not what I mean, and you know it! What*ever* are you doing at the manor? The by-blow is here. We agreed it wasn't wise for you to permit her in your presence. Some might interpret that as acknowledgment that she might have some loose claim on you, which would reduce dear Arthur William's—"

"I don't care about that!" Artie protested, pausing in the midst of sopping up puddles of cold coffee and tea from the highly polished oak floor.

"No? Once a fool, always a fool!" his mother spat.

"And as to claims, hers is better'n mine!"

"Really, Adelle!" Lady Charlotte interposed silkily. "Your breeding is showing. Or should I say your *lack* of breeding? We'd all be considerably more comfortable lacking your presence, if you'd like the truth with no bark on it."

"A claim?" Connard reluctantly glanced at the girl once more. The waif was now sheltered by a determined Artie. Following his grandmother's lead, he then glanced pointedly from the portrait hanging by the dressing table—Damn, but the resemblance was uncanny!—to Adelle. Even if it were meaningless, her treatment of the child passed all bounds of decency. "Interesting you should mention such a possibility after all these years."

"There is none! I have never been so insulted in all my life," Adelle fumed. "If his lordship were only alive—"

"Well, he isn't. I'm 'his lordship' now, and have been for a dozen years," Connard returned coldly. "Perhaps you should take that into your calculations on occasion. Ignoring the fact does you no service."

"How you can expose evidence of such harshness and ill manners toward your mama in the presence of an elevated guest—"

"You are not my mother, for which I thank the Lord," he growled. "Why did you strike the child? She'd done nothing deserving of such treatment."

" 'Tis all the creature understands or deserves at *any* time!"

"I doubt that most sincerely." His customarily warm brown eyes hardened to agate. "There will be no recurrence. Do I make myself clear?"

"Perfectly clear, *my lord*. Well, *you* discipline the chit in the future, then! I wish you joy of the attempt, for a more incorrigible, thieving, ill-begotten, ill-favored, brazen brat I've never known! I accepted the rearing of her only as a favor to you, and look at the thanks you give me."

She attempted to sweep past him, her head held high. Connard caught her arm in a determined grip.

"I think it's time we had a little chat," he continued as if she hadn't spoken, resigning himself to more exhaustion. He seemed to hear distant music—full symphonies and complete concertos, playing only for him somewhere deep inside his head. "D'you think you young people might raid the kitchens," he inquired, turning to Artie and Lucinda, "or gather pine boughs and mistletoe, or whatever it is you traditionally do in celebration of the season?

"In other words," he said with a slight softening of his features, "you're both least wanted at this juncture. And, Artie, see if you can find some beefsteak for the gir—for her cheeks. And—and, Lucinda—" He started to extend his hand, then dropped it to his side. "I'll see you later, if you'll let me," he finished helplessly.

It was the first time he had ever spoken his daughter's name.

The child nodded, her eyes wide, more filled with hope now than fear.

The diminutive Lady Cheltenham smiled conspiratorially at her old friend, then rose and swiftly followed the young people from the room, casting a searching look at Connard along the way. Charlotte had always claimed he wasn't really a bad sort, only wild as a youth, and impetuous and foolish, and often too ready to leap to conclusions without carefully examining the evidence. If that were a hanging offense, half the *ton* would be swinging at the crossroads.

The "little chat" proved quite a bit more.

A defiant Adelle by turns protested her own innocent good

intentions and maintained her stepdaughter-in-law's perfidy and Lucinda's baseborn status. She named Connard every kind of a fool. She played on his sympathies, his prejudices, his family pride. She invoked his father's honor and his grandmother's antecedents (which were distinguished). She detailed with blistering fidelity the scene at the Lame Swan in Chauntleigh Minor twelve years before, reviewed the contents of the damning correspondence found scattered among Marianne's nightrails with an accuracy that hinted she might almost have composed it herself. She listed the witnesses by name—barmaid and ostler and landlord—who put paid to the slut's pretense of respectability. She attempted regality, tears, palpitations that had more of Drury Lane than reality to them, declaring with heaving bosom and reddened face that no baseborn brat was going to filch so much as a farthing of her dear Arthur William's inheritance.

Through it all Connard persisted grimly, questions spewing rapid-fire from his lips like a cannonade against which the woman could muster no viable defenses. Old grievances were aired in passing, old hatreds and jealousies and insecurities. He was reminded once more of how deeply he detested this upstart who trapped his father into a hasty marriage, then swept into the still-mourning household to set father against son and servant against master.

The first year had been hellish. No wonder he'd pleaded for a pair of colors upon the advent of the puny, squalling infant who was his new half brother, born but six months following the hurried wedding ceremony. No matter how much Connard had despised the grinding boredom of army service, its petty jealousies and mind-numbing routines, it had been infinitely preferable to life at the manor. No wonder, either, that his father had become an irritable, intemperate, exacting parent, by turns retreating to his shooting box in Hampshire and his fishing lodge in Scotland—where he caught the chill that descended to his lungs, felling him in his prime at the time of the Texel business.

Connard had arrived at the family town house on Grosvenor Square following the muddled early-October evacuation, child-bride in mourning for her father on his arm, to find his own father two weeks' buried and Lady Charlotte established in London. In Kent, his grandmother informed him, Adelle had proclaimed his demise on foreign soil a certainty and four-year-old Artie heir to his father's titles and estates, mandating the lad forthwith be addressed as "my lord."

Connard had hurriedly sold out, returning to Kent on a bleak November day to wrest the reins of family governance from his stepmother's clutching fingers and the title from his confused little half brother. He then banished the highly vocal Adelle and her bewildered son to the dower house.

As if a festering wound had been lanced, some semblance of the manor as it had been in his mother's time leapt into being under Marianne's direction.

Years of following the drum with her father had taught her to create havens of warmth and peace in the most unlikely of places. Now it was as if a fresh breeze had blown through the manor. Neighbors, servants, all sincerely wished him happy, and knew him to be. That Christmas of 1799 was one of deep contentment despite their double bereavement. When, in February, Marianne blushingly admitted her suspicions of a child on the way, his joy had seemed complete.

And then had come March with its brutal disillusion.

Not until May, self-indulgent in his bitterness, had he set aside the brandy bottle and taken pen in hand to inform his grandmother of what had transpired.

Lady Charlotte descended on them within a day of receiving his letter, taking up residence in her old apartments and badgering him through locked doors. He was a fool and an idiot and deserved to be horsewhipped, she'd informed him at every opportunity, ignoring her reentrenched daughter-in-law's barbs and his mawkish self-pity. Then she vanished for two weeks in September, reappearing with a whimpering infant she claimed was his. He had refused to see either of them. Dammit, what could anyone expect? Wisdom? From a twenty-two-year-old who'd just had his world crumble about his ears?

But he wasn't twenty-two any longer.

And there was the unnerving possibility that his grandmother might have been right all along. Maybe he *had* deserved to be horsewhipped twelve years ago. At least he could've consented to see Marianne, but Adelle kept insisting his "wife" didn't deserve an interview, and it was easier to agree. He'd dreaded seeing her, afraid he would forgive her the moment she came through the door and unwilling to risk yet another blow to his pride. That had been cowardly of him.

Now he studied his stepmother's petulant features, frowning slightly.

Over the past hour Adelle had lost her customary bandbox appearance. Inappropriate jejune curls stiff with sugar water straggled around her blotched face. Her plump fingers twisted among the tangled puce ribbons binding her bodice, fear lurking at the back of her pale, protruding eyes. He realized with a touch of compassion that the determinedly girlish Adelle had passed her prime. Mere vapid prettiness did not age well. Marianne Morecamb, on the other hand, had possessed a beauty that neither vicissitude nor time could ever tarnish. . . .

"Where was Marianne sent?" he demanded for what seemed the thousandth time. "Where is she now? What has become of her? She *is* the child's mother, after all."

"Why keep asking questions I can't answer? Repetition won't change the fact that I neither know nor care—nor should you! Enough the matter was seen to."

He scowled in disgust, mind churning through the revelations and half revelations to which his stepmother had been treating him.

"How came you to be aware of her involvement with Cecil

Packham?" he inquired suddenly, abandoning subjects that seemed to lead nowhere.

"Everyone knew!" Adelle protested. *"Everyone!"*

"Except me. Odd, that. We lived in each other's pockets. How did she find time or opportunity? Where did they become acquainted?"

"How should I know? London, perhaps? Enough they quite clearly were!"

"Packham was at *point-non-plus,* and Marianne's allowance was modest, to say the least. What had either of them to gain from such an association?"

"You *are* rather dull, you know," Adelle sneered, "and always have been. Say what you will about Cecil—*he* was never dull! How should I know what they wanted, unless it was the fun of courting danger? There's always amusement to be gained from diddling a fool."

"But what became of her? Where did you send her?" he persisted, returning to familiar territory, uneasy with where this new line of questions might lead.

"What *possible* reason can you have for asking at this late date? You were glad enough to leave things to me at the time!"

"Apparently a grievous error. There was an allowance. I saw to it myself. What became of it?"

"It hasn't been collected in donkey's years," Adelle asserted defiantly, "not since eight months after her brat was born."

"It's never been stopped."

"Well, I had it forwarded to *me*—for Arthur William," she added at Connard's threatening scowl. "That bit of muslin didn't deserve such generosity, and *my* allowance has *never* been sufficient for my needs. I've asked you to increase it often enough!"

"And so you left Marianne with nothing?"

"Which was no more than the doxy deserved. *You* didn't care! What's done," she spat out, throwing a furious glance at Lady Charlotte, "is done, and you can't undo it, so don't think you can. Oh, I can see your fine mind churning. The resemblance to your mother is meaningless—a common face with common features. The brat might as well have been officially declared a bastard. She's welcome *nowhere*—I've seen to that! So whatever the truth may have been, it doesn't matter anymore."

"The truth always matters," he insisted, unease returning.

"And you're still a pompous fool! Truth is what people believe it to be. As for your trollop, she disappeared years ago, when *you* had her chased from the manor. I may have given the word, but it was on *your* orders, my fine lord, and all the district knows it! If you try to change things, you'll be deemed fit for Bedlam by anyone who counts. I wouldn't risk that, not if I were you."

"No," he returned with sudden comprehension, "you did it for yourself and perhaps for Artie. The last I can forgive a little, but your treatment of my wife—"

"Some wife for a viscount! Miss Nobody of Nowhere? What loving mother would permit her only child to be robbed of his rightful inheritance for the sake of a nameless hussy's whelp? Why, poor Arthur William would have been forced to hang on your sleeve for the rest of his life! His father's will was a disgrace. Arthur William deserved better of him, and so did I!"

"And could have had it without all this," Connard sighed, glancing from the portrait of his mother to his grandmother's enigmatic face. "I was prepared to make settlements on you both, provide you with a separate establishment—anything you wanted within reason. The papers deeding the property in Hampshire to Artie when he came of age were drawn before I ever returned to Kent."

"A shooting box? You expected me to be content with a *shooting box?* And to wait for it when all this"—her sweeping gesture included the manor, the surrounding countryside, even the position of Viscountess Connard—"was rightfully *mine? You are* fit for Bedlam!" She surged to her feet, her

eyes flashing. "Just remember—you appointed me the chit's guardian. She's mine now to deal with as I wish, and don't you forget it!"

On that Parthian note she swept from the room, her head high, her chin thrust before her like a battleship's prow.

Seconds stretched into minutes. Connard moved uncomfortably about his grandmother's bedchamber in the thundering silence, as if trying to put some distance between himself and the old lady's bright, too-observant blue eyes.

He fetched up at last before the western bank of tall windows giving on park and game preserve, wearily leaning his arm on the deep frame, his forehead resting against the smooth Bath superfine of his coat sleeve, his powerful fingers balled in a fist. He barely noticed the sere lawns sliding like frozen brown ocean swells toward the gray-black tracery of the home wood, Chauntleigh's Creek stitching its verge with a dull pewter sheen. His gaze shifted upward, absently following a hawk circling high in the thin blue sky. The bird, at least, was unfettered. Fortunate hawk! No guilt or doubts or remorse in its small, purposeful brain. No sense of descending from a nightmare in which it was innocent victim into one far worse in which it bore the dual burdens of ineffable horror and crushing culpability. Most fortunate hawk, indeed! If only he were out there with it, circling free in the sky, only a quivering rabbit and a quick hot kill to consider. . . .

Dear Lord, but he was tired! Too tired for all this, too mind-numbed. His face was hot and dry, his skin tight with exhaustion. His burning, gritty eyes felt twice their normal size. His Hessians pinched unmercifully thanks to swollen feet, another minor theme in the symphony of his misery. The ephemeral music still haunted him—phantom waltzes now rather than concertos, and country dances and mazurkas and jigs, and the occasional raucous military march. Everything appeared too bright, too loud, too rough or too smooth. He wanted nothing so much as his bed, and undemanding oblivion.

"Say it, Grandmother!" he finally pleaded. "You'll explode if you don't."

"Really, Ned! Such an *indelicate* turn of phrase," the old lady responded, a lingering twinkle in the depths of her eyes. "At least you're finally asking questions!"

Twelve years it had taken! She had never been certain the proof she required would materialize. She could have attempted the thing without it, but the risk would have been too great—to Lucinda, to herself, to any hope of peace and happiness and harmony being reestablished in this most unpeaceful, unhappy, inharmonious household.

"Well?" Connard broke in on her wandering thoughts.

"Well, yourself," she retorted. "I said all I had to say when Lucinda was born."

"She's my daughter," he admitted leadenly. "There's no doubt."

"Do *you* have any?"

"No, I don't think so. Not now. Not anymore."

"It was always there, if you'd only been willing to see the child."

"But I wasn't. I *couldn't!* Don't think too harshly to me. I was little more than a boy when she was born, dash it!"

"You believed yourself old enough to marry and take on the responsibility of a wife and father a child," she responded, her tone biting. "You were old enough to command men in battle and run the estate. How 'young' could you truly have been? It's such a convenient excuse—youth! And such an overworked one. The point is not whether I think harshly of you, but how *you* view yourself."

"With greater disgust than you will ever appreciate," he admitted bitterly. "Adelle has made that poor child's life a living hell, hasn't she. No matter whose she is, she didn't deserve that."

"What do you think? Lucinda, legitimate and accepted by

you, posed a threat to her darling Arthur William's precious pockets. The next child might have been a boy, and 'robbed' him of the title as well."

"Artie's a good sort," Connard protested. "He doesn't figure in this."

"Of course he doesn't," his grandmother agreed, "or only in the very best of ways. He adored Lucinda from the moment he set eyes on her—and she wasn't very adorable, believe me, and of no use at all as companion to a rambunctious five-year-old. Sickly, frail, fretful—it took a great heart to understand the needy vulnerability of an unloved, unwanted newborn rejected by its father, and offer it unconditional love and protection. Of course, he understood her situation only too well. Neglected by his mother except when she wanted to impress others, unmercifully snubbed by you—who better to champion Lucinda, even if he couldn't put words to it in those days?"

"I don't show very well in all this, do I," he sighed.

"No, you don't," she agreed without compromise or concession.

"And I believed I was evidencing such great nobility, permitting the child to be raised at my expense!"

"Well, you did have some assistance in reaching that conclusion."

"From a harridan I'd always despised?" he snorted. "That doesn't shed a particularly favorable light on my intelligence! As for compassion—"

"No, it doesn't, but don't turn bathetic on me, for pity's sake. Wallowing in guilt will serve no one, least of all Lucinda. She deserves a strong, kind, level-headed, loving father with some backbone to him, not a self-indulgent jellyfish."

"Which is all I've been till now . . ."

"If the coat fits, wear it!"

He sighed, his eyes still following the hawk. Perhaps it wasn't hunting after all, merely riding the wind for the sheer joy of it. And when was the last time he had done something for the sheer joy of it? Dear Lord—he couldn't remember! But, yes, he could, and couldn't bear the memory. It had been the day he presented Marianne with the damnable cart and pony to carry her about the estate until the child was born. Two weeks later he was cast-away in his study, and she was cast out in the cold of a dark March night. He had no more idea what had become of beast and conveyance than he did of his wife.

"Marianne—she was only sixteen," he said hesitantly. "A child, like Artie."

"So you think if Lucinda is yours, then—"

"No! The evidence of my cuckolding was overwhelming, Grandmother," he bit out coldly, "in all its degrading detail. No one could believe her innocent—even you. Had she been, horsewhipping would be too good for me. But *sixteen!* She was in a scrape—a bad one, I'll grant you—and I let her down. There had to be *some* explanation! Besides, after so many years, what does guilt or innocence matter?"

"It would matter a great deal to her, I should think. Eyes can be deceived, you know, if there's something to be gained by the deceiving."

"It was Marianne, Grandmother—naked as a jaybird and drunk as a lord—sprawled on Packham's bed. I saw her with my own eyes. The pony cart was tethered in front of the inn as if she didn't care who found her out."

"Not very sensible for a girl of Marianne's intelligence," his grandmother retorted. "Had she been there by choice, I doubt she'd have been so rash as to give no consideration to having her presence discovered. Exposure is rarely the goal of an erring wife. Besides, the Lame Swan?" she added with contempt. "In Chauntleigh Minor? Come, now! The lanes are so ill marked and twisting, I get lost half the time myself when I try to find the village, and I've lived in this neighborhood, girl and woman, for more years than you're likely to see! Think on that, if you must think on anything."

"It was Marianne," he insisted.

"Oh, of that I've not the least doubt. And naked as the day she was born, I'll grant that as well. It was a nice touch, enough to send any full-blooded young husband into the boughs. But *cast-away?* A girl who wouldn't touch so much as a drop of ratafia, let alone anything stronger? How unusual! How convenient! How infinitely clever! So jug-bitten, I've been told, she had no idea where she was or how she came there. So jug-bitten she was beyond coherent speech. Now, *that* was pure genius. And Packham with his neckcloth only slightly loosened and not a hair out of place! Oh, yes, I've made my own inquiries. Tell me, Ned—who stood to benefit if your marriage was destroyed and your unborn child declared a bastard before it ever saw the light of day?"

"I could never believe such evil of anyone," he protested.

"No? Preferable to believe your wife an adulteress and yourself a cuckold? Strange choice."

"If I believed for one instant there was the slightest possibility," he ground out, "I'd kill the bitch with my own hands!"

"Better you not believe it, then. I've no desire to see you swing on Tyburn Hill."

Winter 1811-1812

The Christmas of 1811 was a joyous time for almost all at Connard Manor.

Pine sprigged with holly and bound with bright red bows festooned doorway and mantel. Kissing boughs of mistletoe fashioned by the deft fingers of Lady Daphne and Lady Charlotte hung in spots both traditional and odd. The yule log was duly searched out in the home wood by Connard and Rawdon—an enormous chunk of oak the men could barely compass with their arms—and dragged home with much ceremony. Never had the holiday baking been more aromatic, the pudding stirred in turn by each member of the household plummier. Goose and duck turned on spits, golden skins crackling and running with rich juices while larded venison haunches stuffed with spicy forcemeat roasted slowly and mince pies marched along pantry shelves, awaiting the great day.

A panicked Lord Connardsleigh conferred with his grandmother as soon as he woke from a much-needed nap that first day of his return. He had provided gifts for Artie and the rest of the family before he departed for London. The customary lengths of goods and trinkets and purses for indoor and outdoor staff, baskets for tenants and parish poor—those had been seen to as well. But he had nothing—*Nothing!*—to place for Lucinda beneath the fir they would decorate in the German manner on Christmas Eve. He was all for dashing post-haste to London, buying out every toy shop and emporium.

"Don't be foolish," Lady Charlotte laughed. "Tie yourself

up with a big red bow and sit under the tree," she suggested. "A father is the best gift the child could receive."

He told *her* not to be foolish, at which she smiled a little and shook her head. Then, with a mysterious look, she opened the jewel chest on her dressing table, rummaging among the pearls and diamonds and sapphires.

"If you don't think a father's a good enough gift, you might consider this," she said, disentangling an antique gold locket that had once been his mother's. "I've been saving it for Lucinda for quite some time."

He glanced from the locket to his grandmother in puzzlement. She well knew his opinion of the atrocious bauble.

"Open it," she prodded.

He did, and blanched. The locket had originally contained a portrait of himself as an infant: sausage rolls of fat wreathing compressed adult features, golden curls haloing his head as if he were a simpering Rubens cherub. The obnoxious thing was gone. In its place was an exquisite miniature of Marianne, but not as he had known her. The haunted face was pale and thin and careworn, the bloom faded, the once-sparkling eyes dulled by sorrow and illness and pain.

"Dear God! When was this likeness taken?" he asked at last.

"Two weeks before your daughter's birth," his grandmother replied, watching him. "An interesting token, don't you think? The artist softened it as best he could, but he hadn't much to work with."

"Dear God," he repeated quietly, then after a time gently closed it and slipped it into his waistcoat pocket, his face blank. "How did you come by it?"

"It was with Lucinda when I fetched her home."

He organized a hurried expedition to Broughton, the nearest market town, with Artie (who knew Lucinda's tastes and interests) and Rawdon (cursed or blessed—he had never been sure which—with numerous godchildren, and supposedly knowledgeable regarding young people in general) as advisers.

This netted him a haughty-faced doll of the mannequin variety resplendent in purple velvet carriage costume complete to fur rug, sable hat, and muff. Its gold-beaded reticule even contained a miniature handkerchief, vinaigrette, and Book of Devotions.

A chair in the Egyptian style for the doll followed, then a silver porringer and mug, a coral necklace, and a pagoda sunshade. A carnelian ring, the stone circled by pearls, was unearthed at a small jeweler's. Three natural history tomes, which to Connard seemed unbearably dry but which Artie insisted would entrance Lucinda, were next. Then came a butterfly net, a Mozart sonata too complex for any child but an infant Mozart to master, and a hoop.

A set of fine Reeves and Woodyar embossed watercolor cakes complete with mahogany case, charcoal, porcelain palette, and assorted brushes and lead pencils was discovered languishing on the top shelf of one shop, a maroon leather portfolio filled with sheets of the best heavy watercolor paper at the rear of another.

A Radcliffe novel, a prayer book bound in ivory, a squirrel muff, a pair of ice skates, a length of fine burgundy merino, another of palest blue kerseymere, a third of finest sprigged India muslin, and an assortment of trim and ribbons—some for the child's hair, some for the new garments to be fashioned from the luxurious fabrics—were painstakingly selected. Connard also found two dresses already made up at the same establishment, one in deep green wool trimmed with delicate bone-colored lace and knots of ribbon, the other in soft old rose. They would do temporarily. At least they were better than the horror she was sporting when he arrived.

This bounty appeared under the tree, wrapped in bright papers and tied with brighter ribbons by shopkeepers eager to please. Of the locket containing Marianne's likeness there was no sign.

Also under the tree appeared eight clumsy parcels bearing the viscount's name, several in paper so old it crumbled at the first touch, one bandbox-fresh and precise to a pin. Connard glanced in puzzlement at his grandmother when Artie deposited this booty at his feet. Lady Charlotte merely smiled the enigmatic smile he was coming to dread, and suggested he open them starting with the most decrepit. Within layer upon layer of tarnished silver tissue reposed a lock of silver-white baby-fine hair clumsily braided into the semblance of a watch fob.

"Grandmama!" Lucinda protested. "You said you'd given that to Papa when I made it! You said he liked it very much!"

"I lied," Lady Charlotte replied unrepentantly. "He wouldn't've appreciated it. He wouldn't've appreciated a one of them, but I waited and hoped. Now"—with a meaningful glance in Connard's direction—"perhaps he will."

The parcels contained, in chronological order, the watch fob, the imprint of a child's hands in hardened dough, a framed butterfly dancing above pressed flowers and leaves, a crooked sampler, an intricate rendering of his name in pen and ink illuminated with blotches of red and gold and lapis blue and circled by an uneven Celtic-style border, a livid green wool knitted scarf with the Connard crest worked into the stitches, twelve monogrammed handkerchiefs sporting the occasional rusty dot, the fey portrait of a long-nosed girl with flaxen hair in a frame composed of seashells, and a leather-bound diary containing exquisitely penned quotations for each day of the year embellished with appropriate tiny drawings touched with watercolors.

"It wasn't necessarily wise to so unman him," Lady Daphne later cautioned her old friend. "Oh, your point was well taken, and the ploy was *brilliant.* Given the opportunity, I might well have been tempted to do the same, but *still*— Ah, well, what's done is done. The child *was* pleased in the end, but the compounding of guilts you heap on Connard's head may have *quite* an opposite effect from the one you intend. The soul can bear only so much before it rebels."

"You think so?" Lady Charlotte chuckled. "Rest easy! I've been planning this for years, every detail of it. Ned's ripe for the plucking, and I'm going to see he's well and fairly plucked!"

Lucinda proved everything a proud father could desire, except cloyingly sweet and vacuously pretty. She possessed intelligence. She possessed acumen. She possessed an inquiring mind. She possessed spontaneity. She possessed a surprising, puckish wit. She possessed a tartness—once her initial awe in the presence of this mysterious and magnificent person who was her father wore off—that was as refreshing in a young girl as it was unusual, and reminded him not only of his deceased mother and his very-much-living grandmother, but of his missing wife. With all these attributes in her favor, who could reasonably demand a flawless complexion, lustrous hair in the precise hue declared de rigueur by the *ton,* a plump feminine form, or delicate features in the current doll-like style? He was delighted with his coltish, trusting daughter.

Connard kept Lucinda constantly at his side, at first bearing her prattle of school matters—endless tales that revealed far more concerning the unpleasant nature of the Broward Academy than the child realized, and in which the inestimable Miss Moore invariably played a major role as *dea ex machina* and lovingly compassionate champion of oppressed youth— with amazing fortitude and not a little curiosity. He was, after all, attempting to absorb the events of eleven years in barely more days.

He listened approvingly to the first assaults on the Mozart sonata.

He discussed the wonders of the natural history volumes with aplomb.

He took tea with "Miss Moore," the doll in the elegant carriage robe, and cursed himself for not providing an appropriate miniature tea service.

He attempted the hoop with deplorable clumsiness, and admitted the butterfly net and sunshade more appropriate to July.

He sat for his likeness, carried the handkerchiefs, wore the scarf, displayed the self-portrait and the butterfly and the infant hands and the sampler and his illuminated name in prominent locations in drawing room and library and bedchamber.

He placed the diary on the desk in his study, signaling its uncommon virtues and skilled decoration to any neighbor who happened to call.

When they attended the parish church, he ushered Lucinda into the padded family pew with all the punctilio he would have employed had she been Queen of England, ignoring the technically greater claims of his grandmother and the dowager countess of Stoker. After services he introduced Lucinda to all who approached, ignoring the starts and stares, the sidelong glances, the whispered comments. To each invitation he received for himself, his family, and elevated London guests, he responded they would be delighted—if his daughter were equally welcome. Those who displayed any degree of cordiality he assured of their attendance. To those who dithered, he responded with a shrug and the back of his head.

Not to put too fine a point upon it, Viscount Connard was besotted.

Through it all his grandmother maintained a commendable restraint, content to play a minor part now that two of the principals had entered upon the stage. As she put it to Lady Daphne, "He's going on so well, it would be idiotish of me to meddle!"

Rawdon, observing in silent approval, provided his undisputed cachet for the girl whenever possible. While the sycophantic deference his lofty title and extreme wealth were accorded within the beau monde might customarily grate on him—for the forthright duke despised toad-eaters—this once it was proving useful. As the final touch, he tooled the girl about the countryside, passing her the reins and initiating her in the handling of a mettlesome pair once their first exuberance had worn off.

And Artie?

Artie basked. Artie gloated. Artie reveled. Artie preened himself in delight, and all but said "I told you so!" to his adored half brother.

This, as he informed Tobias Stubbs, head groom at the manor, was more like! And all the more satisfying for taking so many years to come about. Justification of faith was a wonderful thing, though he could never have put it so aptly.

The manor, helter-skelter during the years of Adelle's erratic governance, miraculously assumed that same gracious calm instituted by Marianne Connardsleigh during her brief tenure as viscountess. That this had nothing to do with Lucinda or Lady Charlotte, and much to do with the indefatigable Lady Daphne, never occurred to the outraged Adelle. Thwarted and ignored, self-consequence insulted, she took refuge in her apartments and indulged in a glorious fit of the sulks.

Even Nature cooperated, providing a fine dusting of snow on Christmas Eve and melting it two days later.

Only the absence of a thick layer of ice on the trout hatching pond gave the least inconvenience. Lucinda perforce consigned her new skates to the back of a nursery cupboard while assuring both her father and Artie that next year would do quite as well, and instead basked in Connard's approval and His Grace's attentions. Most miraculous of all, she was now housed in a true bedchamber instead of the nursery cubby to which her step-grandmother consigned her eleven years before. This change of venue—windows from which one could see the park while wriggling one's toes in thick Aubusson carpets rather than peeping through a barred lancet while teetering atop a rickety stool—had worked a wonderful change in the child. It symbolized, in the clearest manner possible, her transformation from despised outsider to cherished daughter.

For Lucinda, however, not all was perfection. To the pointed questions she posed her great-grandmother concerning her mother (if her status had changed, then so should her mysterious mother's) no answers were forthcoming beyond the ones she had heard from earliest childhood: that Marianne Connardsleigh had been a beautiful lady of great character and immense charm; that she had been falsely accused of nefarious deeds and banished from the manor through the agency of Adelle; that nothing Adelle had ever claimed was to be believed; that her father still loved his wife dearly and would one day openly acknowledge the fact; that, most tragically, this lovely lady had vanished some months following Lucinda's birth.

With that Lucinda was forced to be content, though she did wonder at the rather self-satisfied expression that often suffused her great-grandmother's features. But the adult world was unfathomable. She decided the silent patience recommended by Lady Charlotte was indeed her only option and, in the manner of most children, accepted that which she could not change even as she privately protested it.

For Connard also, the bitter came with the sweet. Beneath his delight in his newly acknowledged daughter, his success at playing lord bountiful, lurked deep mortification. He had always considered himself a rational, reasonable, just man. The illusion had been shattered. Basically straightforward and honorable, he found unbelievable the actions and motivations Lady Charlotte imputed to her daughter-in-law. But, guilty or innocent, only the situation as he could accept it mattered. His young bride had been in desperate need of his assistance. He had turned his back on her. That, with the wisdom granted by maturity, he found unpardonable. Days were meaningless when considering the years that had passed, however. Beyond seeking Rawdon's advice as to how one instituted a search for a person long vanished, he did nothing immediate.

As for Lady Daphne and Rawdon, the one lingered because she had always intended to, the other because this rather informal country Christmas reminded him of simpler days, when responsibilities were fewer and goals less grim. And here was that niggling imp, Curiosity, dancing at the back of their minds: How would the game play itself out?

On the third day following the New Year—after summoning the local family solicitors, the family's customary physician, and the parish constable—Adelle Connardsleigh emerged from her apartments and descended the stairs, her chin thrust forward, ready to do battle. She ejected Artie, Rawdon, and Lucinda from Connard's study, interrupting a spirited game of skittles. She had Messrs. Horace Coldbottom and Eustace Penworthy, Ichabod Thorne, and Constable Puffy Toper shown in. She appropriated Connard's desk, settled her heliotrope skirts, patted her yellow curls, and proceeded to open her budget.

She had permitted her stepson, she informed the local worthies, to play his lunatic game over the holidays. It was, after all, a time for charity and forbearance. But eccentricity could be carried too far!

The bastard foisted on them by Lady Charlotte had been permitted to mingle with family and countryside. Why, she had actually been welcomed by respectable people who should know better than to tolerate such nonsense! She had been indulged in every caprice, even to endangering a duke, and everyone else in the vicinity, by driving a pair of half-wild horses.

She had steadfastly refused to sanction these solecisms, demonstrating her horror by conscientious withdrawal from all social activities. The Morecamb girl, however, Adelle informed her avid audience—calling Lucinda by her mother's maiden name to stress her baseborn status—was *her* legal charge. Would Messrs. Coldbottom and Penworthy produce the papers they had been instructed to bring in proof of the fact?

They did so. She surged from the desk and descended on Connard, waving a sheaf of documents in his face.

"The game is over," she snapped. "I'll *not* be demeaned by that by-blow's presence under my roof one day more, nor have her jeopardize Arthur William's position. The necessary arrangements have been made. She goes to the workhouse today!"

"I suggest we conduct this discussion privately, madam," Connard protested with a mildness of tone at great variance with his hardened eyes and firmed jaw, waving the documents aside. "Such family matters are not for general dissemination. Gentlemen, I apologize for any inconvenience, and thank you for your patience. If you would be so good as to show yourselves out, and request Parsons to—"

"And forego my witnesses? What sort of idiot do you think me? They stay!"

Connard eyed her with distaste. "Then might I examine those papers? I'm not certain I recognize them," he returned, wresting the sheaf from her with a resigned shrug. If exposure was what the harridan wanted, exposure she would have. The tale of her malevolence would travel, doing Lucinda nothing but good in the process.

He glanced at the documents, tore them in half, and tossed them on the grate, where they dissolved in a curling black mass.

"The aberration of a moment of weakness," he said with pretended indifference. "So ends your ill-conducted supervision of my daughter. No court would uphold those. Do you have any questions, gentlemen?" he inquired of the four goggling men.

They had none.

He then turned on the sputtering Adelle.

"As you find you cannot share a home with my daughter and maintain your equanimity, you will remove yourself—to Bath or Tunbridge Wells—and form your own establishment. Beneath my roof you shall not remain, for it is her roof as well. In the process you will relinquish your son to my guardianship. He is welcome to remain with us at the manor for as long as he desires."

Adelle swelled with indignation. Connard raised a hand in admonition.

"There will be no discussion," he continued quietly. "There will be no argument. Bath or Tunbridge Wells—which is it to be? I would have your decision now."

"Now?" she shrieked. "You see, gentlemen? He's mad! He's a monster!"

The men shrugged.

"He's fit for Bedlam! Arrest him! Incarcerate him! This is my home, not his!"

"I see no madness here," Thorne offered hesitantly, "only sound common sense."

"No law I know of been broken, m'um," Toper added. "Can't h'arrest 'im."

"But he's attempting to rob my son of his rightful inheritance for the sake of a nameless brat," she spluttered, "and deny me my rights! He forces us both to associate with baseborn scum! All the world knows what that girl is! It's neither right nor just!"

Penworthy and Coldbottom ducked their heads and made flapping motions with their hands, as if she were an enraged goose and they attempting to shoo her away.

"Madam, you purposely ignore the conditions of my father's will." Connard smiled—if such a cold and bitter expression could be termed a smile. "He named me my brother's sole guardian. I am resuming control of my household—that is all. Should Artie desire to remove with you, he may do so. It's merely that I do not believe he will."

"My son's name is *Arthur William!* I forbid you to use that tasteless diminutive!"

"Arthur William, then. The fact remains—the choice is his. You will be gone in three days' time. My traveling coach will carry you to one of the two destinations I have specified, and one of those only—if you desire to retain the allowance I make you above your jointure. Do I make myself clear?"

"You've never liked me," she spat. "You've been all that is unfilial and cruel—after all my devoted efforts on your behalf! Now you're revenging yourself on me because your father cared more for me and Arthur William than he did for you or your *saintly* mother!" She whirled furiously on their avid, flustered audience. "This is *my* home! All this is *mine!* I am the dowager Viscountess Connard! My son is the future viscount! He has no right to do this—no right at all!"

They shrugged, shook their heads, tugged at cuffs and waistcoats.

"Head of the family," Penworthy mumbled.

"Every right, custom, and law," Coldbottom concurred.

Lady Adelle stared wildly from Connard to his four traitorous supporters. This was not how the scene was supposed to play itself out. Disaster stared her in the face.

"I'm but a poor widow, abandoned and alone in this pitiless world," she sobbed, dramatically casting herself to her knees, essaying a new tactic, "with only my child—the future viscount and heir to all patronage tied to these lands—for protection, and he is underage, unable to defend me and too innocent to see the necessity!" She extended her arms, facile tears streaming from her eyes. "This heartless monster would cast us upon the highroad to starve for the sake of a whore's get! Gentlemen—save us!"

They shook their heads once more, turned with little bows to the viscount, and silently departed. This would make wonderful telling—at the Lame Swan in Chauntleigh Minor, at the King's Fancy in Connard Village, even at the Laughing Maid in Broughton. Pints all around for weeks!

"It's your duty to support me and thwart him," she shrieked after them. "I'm a defenseless widow! Have pity on a fatherless boy and his mother!"

"You make yourself ridiculous," Connard said with contempt as the door closed behind the four men. "You'd best stand or you'll crease your skirts, and I know your gowns are of utmost importance to you. Lord knows, you spend enough on 'em."

"Varlet! Scoundrel! Blockhead! Ingrate! You begrudge me the very clothes on my back! Well, aren't you going to assist me?" she demanded, her heel catching in her hem.

"Hardly. If you could kneel, then you can rise."

Rigid with fury, Lady Adelle struggled to disentangle herself, finally clambering gracelessly to her feet to the sharp crack of tearing silk.

"You, a gentleman? Ha!" she hissed. "But I'll bring you low yet, my fine lord, just you wait and see! And you'll pay! Oh, how you'll pay! No one will receive you when I'm done, and as for that ill-begotten brat—"

"Leave my daughter out of it! But for this exhibition, I might have attempted to retain you beneath my roof for form's sake. As it is, you've overplayed your hand, and have only yourself to thank." He winced at the venomous glance she threw him, straightened his shoulders. "Now, tell me—how did Marianne come to be at the Lame Swan that day in such a state? I want the truth this time, and not a farrago of inventions even a simpleton would recognize as such."

"I've already told you, I remember nothing," she snarled, moving toward the door. "Too much time has passed. Besides, why this sudden great interest in the doings of a whore and a gamester? I'm not the fool you take me for!"

Connard blocked her way, his arms folded across his broad chest, his powerful hands balled into fists, his eyes murderous.

"The truth, this time," he said softly. "All of it! It shall make no difference in the allowance I make you, that I swear—unless you treat me to still more lies, and I do have the intelligence to recognize any fabrications, madam. Yours are invariably blatant."

"I'll have that assurance in writing, if you please," she demanded after eyeing him narrowly, "and an increase in my allowance! Then we'll see."

Connard strode swiftly to his desk, scratched a few words on a sheet of paper, signed it, sanded it, and handed it to her. "Above all," he said with deadly calm, "how did *you* happen by there?"

A slow smile of victory spread across Adelle Connard-sleigh's plump features as she examined the informal pledge, folded it, and tucked it within her tight bodice.

"How d'you think? I took her there myself, nodcock, once she couldn't protest!" She laughed at the appalled expression on his face. "Oh, you were easy to gull, you were. You saw precisely what you were intended to see, and concluded precisely what you were intended to conclude. Such a cooperative stepson! I almost liked you that day. . . . She's dead by now, or worse. Any road, she's dead to you, and that's all that matters. Arthur William's position is secure, for you'll never marry again—I'll see to that!—and you won't live forever. I'd watch my back if I was you, Edward *dear.*"

With a toss of brassy curls and a swirl of silken skirts she was gone.

Lady Adelle Connardsleigh had more assistance than she needed—or desired—in preparing her removal. And far more oversight on the part of housekeeper and maids—despite her protests that housekeeper and maids had far more important matters to occupy their time.

The missing Connard emeralds, discovered tucked between layers of nightrails and undergarments, were returned to the safe in the viscount's study along with his mother's personal jewelry. A precious small Rembrandt appeared in the bottom of one trunk, a full set of plates bearing the family crest in another. A Sèvres dinner service, three priceless Oriental carpets from his father's rooms, even draperies and wall hangings had found their way into Adelle's more intimate belongings.

Word spread quickly through the district: The reign of Adelle Connardsleigh was over. Lady Daphne chuckled and busied herself with menus and curious morning callers. Lady Charlotte sniffed knowingly, descending repeatedly on Adelle's apartments on forays of inspection under the guise of rendering assistance to her despised daughter-in-law. Lucinda, resplendent in one of her new gowns, shadowed either Lady Daphne or her great-grandmother, the wary look of a hunted animal slowly vanishing from her eyes. And Connard? He retreated to his study in relief accompanied by Rawdon and a mortified Artie.

"I don't care what you say," Artie insisted. "I know the law says she's my mother and the parish register agrees, and I know it ain't the thing to admit it, but there's not a particle of love lost between us. She's never wanted me about except when it suited her to play devoted parent, and then she stuffed me in velvet and lace and fawned over me like I was Prince of Whales! The rest of the time, the farther away I kept myself, the better. I was just her way of sinking her claws into our father, don't y'see. It's no use scowling at me, Ned! I'm no scholar, but I ain't stupid. Servants think you don't understand things when you're little, but you've got ears, and you remember, and you figure it out. Why, half of 'em don't believe I'm more than your *stepbrother!*"

"Don't be nonsensical," Connard protested. "You resemble our father more than I do! There isn't an ounce—" But Artie gave a disgusted snort, half laugh, half groan.

"I know what I know," he said simply, "and one thing I *do* know is she was nothing but a tradesman's daughter in Broughton before she joined a pack of travelin' players and acquired airs. I've called on m'grandfather a few times, unbeknownst to Mama. He's a decent sort, and kinder than she ever deserved. . . . As for Lucinda, Mama hates her, and she's never had more to do with either of us than she could help—except to scold and carp, and birch Lucinda every chance she got. I tried to stop her, but—"

Connard gave up protesting Artie's assessment of his mother, her lack of affection, the reason for his existence. How could he? The boy had it more or less right.

They discussed school, the possibility of either university or the army (Artie preferred the notion of breeding hunters to either), the necessity for Artie to learn estate management (which interested him not at all), the possibility of his spending some time in London to acquire a little town bronze (which interested the boy even less). Connard proposed an abbreviated grand tour—some areas of the Continent remained accessible despite the scourge of Napoleon. Artie countered with the American colonies as a far more interesting destination. Indians! Encountering them would be something like! The sole conclusion they reached was that at no time would Artie be forced to reside under his mother's roof. An annual week-long visit to Bath would satisfy the proprieties.

The morning of Adelle's departure, the baggage wagons were loaded before dawn as flaming torches lit the drive, catching on hurrying figures and beaming faces. Ever watchful, Parsons examined each item as it passed him. Not one chair, one rug, one table, would go with his former mistress unless she had a clear right to it. When Tobias Stubbs emerged toting the florid portrait of her ladyship that had graced the drawing room, even Parsons forgot himself so far as to smile slightly as he waved the head groom on—for willing hands were many that morning.

Traveling coach and baggage wagons slowly rumbled and creaked their way down the drive at last under leaden skies, Adelle raining curses on Connard's head and swearing revenge.

* * *

Those days prior to his stepmother's departure were Connard's time for private conferences with the junior members of his family. The one with Lucinda proved no more satisfactory than that with the customarily eager-to-please and generally malleable Artie. The child, abused though she had been—or perhaps for that very reason—had a core of steel nothing could bend. Contrary to her father's wishes, Lucinda insisted on a return to the Broward Academy to finish out the school year. Even a puppy, a kitten, and a promised pony were insufficient inducement to remain at the manor.

"Dear Miss Moore has been so kind to me," she explained two days following Adelle's downfall as she perched on a small tabouret at her father's knee beside the study fire. "When I first arrived at school, Papa, I was so lost. And I missed Great-Grandmama and Artie dreadfully, and it was so uncomfortable in the dormitory—girls everywhere, and some of them not very nice, especially the older ones, who seemed to make an art of spitefulness. And it was so cold, and the food was ghastly, and—

"Well," she sighed, "darling Miss Moore made all the difference, you see, like a much older sister, or an exceptionally kind aunt. She dried my tears when the bigger girls pinched at me and helped themselves to what few treasures I'd brought, and explained that I could make the next few years a torment, or I could profit from them. She did it with all us new little ones, and there were two even younger than I—if you will credit it, poor things, for I was but barely seven and they were not yet six. Parents shouldn't have children unless they truly want them, for I presume they've some choice in the matter if only they will make it," she finished sternly.

Connard had the grace to flush as he meekly agreed that children should indeed be wanted, or else "not had."

"It's Miss Moore who's seen to it I have instruction in drawing and watercolors and learned to play upon the pianoforte,"

Lucinda continued determinedly, "though Great-Grandmama did provide the funds. It caused Miss Moore a deal of trouble, what with Miss Broward arguing that she should have the money to use for more deserving girls (which meant she'd pocket it for treats for herself), and making Miss Moore's life most unpleasant! Why, what would she think if I simply didn't reappear, without an explanation of some sort?"

"That your life has changed for the better, and be grateful for your sake," Connard snapped irritably. "Enough of Miss Moore! You owe her nothing."

"I owe her far more than you can ever appreciate, Papa," she protested. "I *must* go back, if only to thank her properly and say good-bye, and once there, why not stay? It's not so long until spring, and I do enjoy my studies. And then there are my friends. I have some, you know, however unlikely that may seem," she added with a smile.

"Notes all around would more than suffice," he insisted. "As for Miss Moore, I can add some modest remuneration for her care of you, and there's an end to the matter!" The viscount was becoming heartily sick of Miss Moore.

"You can't repay such kindness with money! Besides, Miss Moore wouldn't accept anything from you," Lucinda returned wisely, "though I'd dearly love to see her in a pretty dress just once! Or, if she did, she'd spend it all on a treat for the younger ones. They never understand why they've been sent to such a place, and are in great need of being reminded they've an intrinsic worth."

"More of your Miss Moore's golden words? Then she's not the paragon you make her out to be," he countered with no small satisfaction, "but only an utter fool!"

"I beg to differ, Papa. Miss Moore isn't a fool. She's just a very proud lady."

"She can't be all that proud if she teaches in the hellhole you've described," he snapped. "Any teacher worth her hire wouldn't endure such conditions above a week! Forget the woman."

"You don't understand, Papa. Miss Moore says if one's explanation of something isn't understood, it's one's own fault, and one must try again until one gets it right. You'll allow me a moment to consider?" Lucinda pleaded, gazing up beseechingly at her father. He nodded, summoning up patience from he was not sure what source.

She frowned into the fire, its ruddy glow catching like golden spangles in her fair hair. Connard smiled at her intent air, silently blessing his grandmother for her interference. Only the ruse of her imminent demise would have dragged him back to the manor at this season. How stubbornly he had cheated himself over the years, and of how much! As for what he had done to Marianne, what he had done to them both in his youthful arrogance . . .

"Imagine you are lost on a desert in deepest Araby," Lucinda broke in on his uncomfortable ruminations, "nothing but sand everywhere, and the sun beating down with the force of a thousand hammers, and you come across an oasis—all palm trees, and clear pools of cool water, and wonderful shade. That's what my Miss Moore is like."

"What do you know about 'deepest Araby,' " he chuckled, passing a gentle hand over her glowing hair, thankful for the distraction, "a child like you?"

"Miss Moore's father was there once when he was a young man. He described it to her, and she described it to us—how hot it was, and how desolate, and how your skin feels dry as dust and the sand scratches till you think you'll go mad, and you see things that aren't there called 'mirages' because of the brightness of the sun, which is like a furnace in a Midlands manufactory—and how her father felt when he came upon an oasis. Well," she concluded seriously, "that's how I've always felt about Miss Moore: If the school is a desert, she's the oasis. Miss Broward, however," she chuckled with an impish glance at her father's stern face, "is a quite formidable lioness, only not so kind. A lioness at least sees her cubs have enough to eat. Miss Broward only sees *she* has enough to eat!"

"I knew a lady once whose father had spent time in the deserts of Araby. His descriptions bear a striking resemblance to yours."

"They do? Then now you understand about my Miss Moore."

"Well, we'll see," Connard agreed reluctantly. "I truly do not approve of your returning to that pestilential place."

"It isn't a bit pestilential! Merely dark and cold and damp and sometimes rather depressing to the spirits."

"A governess at the manor under your great-grandmother's supervision would be far more suitable," he countered, then at the naked plea in her eyes, conceded reluctantly, "but I'll discuss the matter with Grandmama."

That conference proved even less satisfactory than the ones with Lucinda and Artie. Connard protested an unwholesome attachment to this unknown Moore female—at least as great an objection to the school as its remote location and oppressive atmosphere. Lady Charlotte acidly retorted that the instructress had earned Lucinda's love and loyalty twice over during the time he refused to so much as set eyes on his own child. Now that he found the girl acceptable, he resented the teacher's influence—fair neither to the teacher Lucinda adored, nor to Lucinda herself.

"Jealousy is never attractive," Lady Charlotte concluded tartly. "In a man your age it's ludicrous, however understandable it may be. What will you do when it comes time for Lucinda to marry—chase every potential suitor from the house because he might have the effrontery to appropriate a little of her affections to himself?"

"She refers to the blasted female as an oasis, for pity's sake! She fawns on her. She dotes on her. She *idolizes* the creature! The cases are in no way similar. Besides, it will be many years before Lucinda—"

"No? They are in *every way* similar. What view would you have a young lady take of her prospective husband? Certainly a little affection, a little 'idolization,' will be in order! Miss Moore has earned Lucinda's devotion while you spent her childhood sulking. Unwholesome affection? Come, now!"

"Such a relationship should come to a natural and desirable end," he protested.

"Natural and desirable to whom? To you? It's time to place the needs and desires of others above your own selfish whims. No, hear me out," Lady Charlotte continued firmly as Connard turned on her in righteous indignation. "First, you will be searching for Marianne. Oh, yes—you've said nothing, but I'm well aware you've discussed the matter with Rawdon. High time, but it means you'll be gone unless you expect others to perform the task that is properly yours.

"Secondly, the services of a governess have yet to be sought. Not just anyone will do for Lucinda. The child is superlatively intelligent, and possesses a most creative, original mind—characteristics that have been fostered by her Miss Moore." She laughed merrily at his look of surprise. "Naturally I have been in communication with the dear lady since Lucinda was first packed off to Broward. *Constant* communication. A tutor might be far more fitting than a governess, come to that. At best, it will take considerable time and effort to locate a suitable female. In the interim, why interrupt the child's schooling? She enjoys Broward, for all its abysmal location and worse conditions. Observe all you admire and, yes, love, in your daughter. Behind her stands a devoted lady who deserves the majority of the credit!"

"But we don't even know the woman's antecedents," Connard broke in, "or if she's a proper influence. As for the school, it sounds a veritable cesspool!"

"Pish-tosh! That didn't bother you when you left for London, nor has it concerned you for the past five years. Stop attempting to wield a heavy hand, Ned. It doesn't become you, and Lucinda will resent it—with justification, I might add!"

"Well, it bothers me now," he protested. "Everything has changed."

"Reality hasn't changed, merely your perspectives. Would an unsuitable female have raised your daughter to be the delightful girl she is? Ponder that, if you will!

"As for the deplorable conditions under which the child has existed for the past five years, you can change that with a handful of guineas and a letter to the headmistress. I had not the option in the usual way, given Adelle's instructions, but special food, special uniforms, special housing are all available—for a price. Most people who send girls there don't bother. It's a repository for the unwanted and the unloved. The most I could manage was art and music instruction—for which I had to pay double, given that Miss Moore had to grease Broward's palm before she would permit such a thing!"

"You seem remarkably well informed on the place."

"I made it my business to be. Lucinda is, after all, my great-granddaughter. Who d'you think left the notices lying about for Adelle to find—and then insisted the place was totally unsatisfactory to ensure the child be sent there? Better an evil one knows than one that one doesn't! It was the best of a bad bargain. . . ."

Lady Charlotte sighed, a rueful light in her eyes. "Stop thinking of just yourself, Ned," she continued reasonably, "or else think a bit more rationally. There's a final consideration, however little you may like it. Miss Moore has offered the only security in Lucinda's life since she was barely seven. Brutally separating the child from the teacher she loves would do far more harm than good. She would rightly resent such high-handed interference, especially given the reason for it. As of the moment you are her knight on a white charger, complete with shining armor and escutcheoned shield. Do this, and you will deservedly lose her trust. It won't be easily re-won—I'll see to that."

"Are you indulging in blackmail?" he demanded incredulously.

"Perhaps . . . Or perhaps I'm just trying to ensure you don't make the second-worst mistake of your life."

And so, contrary to her disgruntled father's wishes, Lucinda returned to Yorkshire, carnelian ring on her finger, coral necklace clasped about her slender neck, watercolors in a special parcel at her side.

This time the journey was performed in the comfort of her father's traveling chaise rather than by common stage, and with regular stops at the best posting houses. Warm chambers boasting vermin-free beds awaited her, and private parlors and sumptuous meals. Outriders and a brace of abigails and a footman and Tobias Stubbs, head groom from the manor, took the place of the single scullery maid Adelle Connardsleigh customarily allotted her. She was dressed in a fur-lined cloak, a winter carriage costume, and new bonnet. Hot bricks covered with straw warmed her feet while fur rugs kept any potential chill at bay and the precious squirrel muff ensured toasty hands. Picnic hampers contained every possible delicacy from the manor's kitchens. The trip, despite the inconveniences and delays of winter travel, seemed to pass in an instant.

When the crested chaise with its steaming team drew up to the stark stone porch of Broward House deep in a moorland glen some fifteen miles from York, Miss Mary Moore, instructress *extraordinaire,* was standing at the window of an upstairs classroom watching and waiting as she had, when possible, for two days.

The woman's thin, sweet face paled as her hands clenched among the stiff folds of the brown apron covering her black bombazine dress, her troubled hazel eyes scanning those exiting from the luxurious private carriage with alert wariness. Finally she sighed. It was all right—this time. Next time? Who knew . . .

She tucked a wandering wisp of chestnut hair back into her severe bun, still watching as another conveyance—this the gig from the inn at Winthorp in which Lucinda normally arrived—drew up, depositing two little girls dressed in similar dull brown costumes on the steps along with their bundles and boxes. There was a small joyous reunion below that caused the teacher to smile tenderly.

Then, with an involuntary shiver, she left the icy classroom and descended the slick, worn stairs to the equally frigid entry hall, a smile of greeting firmly in place.

This would be the last time she would welcome Lucinda Connardsleigh upon her return to Yorkshire, of that Miss Moore was certain. Given the crested carriage, the time had come, and much sooner than she had expected. Indeed, she was not certain she had ever truly believed it would, no matter what Lady Charlotte claimed. A miracle had occurred, or a curse been fulfilled—she wasn't sure which.

"Well, girls—pleasant holidays and comfortable journeys?" she inquired as the trio pelted through the heavy main door, skidding to a halt as they spied her.

Beyond the girls, servants from Connard Manor toted parcels and bandboxes and Lucinda's small trunk into the austere, inhospitable building and trudged up the narrow, steep stairs. Staying well in the shadows, the self-contained teacher ignored their bustle, her eyes determinedly fastened on her exuberant charges.

"In-cred-ible!" Lucinda caroled, her face wreathed with a smile as she ducked a curtsy. "Darling Miss Moore, you won't credit what has occurred! I've had to pinch myself every day to make sure I'm not dreaming."

"There do appear to be a few changes," Miss Moore twinkled in agreement, smiling at the other two girls. "Welcome back, Sarah and Emily. Your uncle fares well? And his wife and children?"

"Hello, Miss Moore," the diminutive twins chorused, dropping quick curtsies of their own. "They're blooming, every one, though not best pleased to see us. Duty is such an ugly word. Isn't it wonderful about Lucinda? She has a home now. She's wanted!"

Miss Moore smiled her habitual calm smile, forced her hands into their habitual calm clasp at her waist, and glanced around the barren stone entry of the barren moorland stone house that served as temporary perch for so many unwanted sparrows.

"Lucinda has a home?" she queried. "How delightful for her!"

"It was like a fairly tale," Lucinda agreed, giving her teacher a hug, then yielding a place to the other girls as she whirled across the gray stone flags, her arms outflung. "The best fairy tale that could ever be! You'll *never* guess—not in a *million* years! My father, the viscount? Great-Grandmama told him she was sick so he'd come home—only she wasn't, of course, as she's *never* ill—and somehow we became friends. It had to do with a painting, but Papa says I must wait a few years before he explains it all to me. He likes me, Miss Moore! My father *likes* me!"

"Decorum, Lucinda, if you please," Miss Moore protested. "A breath between statements, and an opportunity for others to speak if they wish. You rattle on so, it's exhausting."

"Oh, Lucinda's tale is much more interesting than anything we have to relate," Emily laughed. "We'd only bore you with unheated garrets and meals in nurseries and obnoxious little cousins—who *are* obnoxious, no matter what you've taught us to say in polite company—and would displease you no end!"

"Much better," Sarah agreed, eyes shining. "We can only dream of a real home, for there's no one in the world to rescue us. But for Lucinda the dreaming's over! She claims the reality's even better than any of us can imagine—to be loved and wanted."

"Can you believe a room all to one's self?" Emily chimed in. "And so many gifts she couldn't count them?"

"And, a duke," Sarah sighed, "with a pair of coal-black horses, and gray eyes that laughed—though Lucinda says they held the saddest, most wistful expression sometimes when he thought no one was looking."

"Highly intriguing," Miss Moore chuckled. "Are you certain it wasn't indigestion or hunger which troubled his grace?"

"Oh, *Miss Moore . . . !* But the duke wasn't the best of all, though I suppose it's improper to show satisfaction about it," Lucinda burbled on, coming to a brief rest before her teacher and seizing that lady's hands to twirl her about. "My step-grandmother? She's gone! Gone! Gone! Gone! Gone to Bath forever! I don't quite know why—Great-Grandmama says I'm only a child, and not to be made privy to certain things for years, which is most unfair as I'm so dreadfully curious, and it does concern me, after all—only that there was a fearful row, but Papa told me not to worry, for she can never hurt me again.

"And, there *was* a duke—and a very nice, extremely handsome one too, though quite old, like Papa—and he let me drive his horses, and just look at the ring Papa gave me for Christmas! And the necklace! And these new clothes—can you imagine? And there's more!" Lucinda danced about the hall, kid boots flashing in the dull light. "New clothes no one's ever worn but me! Can you credit it? New clothes! And there's two dresses I had made a little small on purpose. I think, if we try very hard, they can be made over for Sarah and Emily."

"How lovely," Miss Moore murmured, her eyes blank and her smile filled with sympathetic delight for her exuberant charge.

"Isn't it? But even that isn't the best part. Papa's gifts—you do remember all the gifts you helped me make? He loved them! Every one! Even the scarf, and it was particularly hideous. I despise knitting! And he wore it. To church on Christmas Eve, with the whole village there! That is love, for the thing's preposterous."

"Yes, I suppose it was," Miss Moore agreed, "but you did the best you could. After all, you were only a moppet of eight, and it was so cold, your fingers were numb, and then there were the chilblains."

"And you unpicked the worst parts and repaired my faults every night after I'd gone to sleep. I know you did! I told Papa so, too. He said you were most kind, but that you shouldn't've bothered. He said he loved the blots! And he says in the spring I'm to go home to stay forever and have a governess and a pony and a kitten and a dog and whatever else my heart desires—at least until I marry. Great-Grand-mama said that." She cocked her head, studying her inestimable preceptress as her face fell. "You don't appear as pleased as I thought you'd be, Miss Moore," she said.

"Of course I'm pleased, dear child. It's only rather sudden."

"Sudden? It's taken an eternity! Almost five whole years if you count one way, and eleven if you count another. That's how old I am, you know, so it's taken my entire lifetime. Lady Adelle made it an eternity!"

"To me, you first arrived only yesterday." Miss Moore smiled. "You do recall our discussions concerning the relative measures of time?"

"Remember? Of course I do! 'Time is a finite and immutable absolute when viewed from the scientific perspective, and an eternal flow from God's, but expands or contracts for the individual according to his circumstances.'

"The only thing wrong is you won't be there, dear Miss Moore, but everything else will be perfect, so why not that as well? The only reason I came back at all was you"—Lucinda dimpled almost shyly—"for Papa wanted me to stay at the manor, but I said I couldn't—not without saying a proper goodbye, only why should I have to say good-bye at all? That wouldn't be sensible. Papa said we'd see. When he says that, it means he'll discuss it with Great-Grandmama and do as she recommends, and so I discussed it with her myself to save time, and she said yes, if you were willing come spring, which of course you will be, for why shouldn't you? Isn't Great-Grandmama a darling to consider my wishes of importance, for many grown-ups wouldn't, you know."

"Unfortunately it's not possible, my dear. My life is here," Miss Moore informed her would-be employer firmly, "among children who need me. No one needs me at Connard Manor."

"I do! The manor is much nicer than Broward now that my step-grandmother is gone, and you should see the library, Miss Moore," Lucinda cajoled. "Books—books everywhere, and then more books! In all kinds of languages. So many books, you couldn't read them all in a lifetime, and Papa says I may read anything I can reach without using the ladders so long as I treat them with respect. Isn't that kind?"

"Respect for ladders? A novel concept!"

"You know what I mean." Lucinda grinned in appreciation of the correction and its small pun. "You'd love it, Miss Moore! You'll simply have to reconsider. You'd be so much happier there than here!"

"For a time, perhaps, but a governess's term of employment is by its very nature limited." Miss Moore smiled gently. "One day you will leave the schoolroom, and then what is to become of me? No, my dear, my position here is more or less permanent, and I have found stability to be of greater importance in life than almost anything else."

"Stability? That's for ancients who haven't the least imagination or spark of adventure! Do promise you'll at least consider it? The gardens will be magnificent come spring, Great-Grandmama's a darling, and if you're worried about Papa, he's the most generous, understanding, wonderful man in all of England! Why, just look at these watercolors he gave me! Reeves and Woodyar's best, no less. And the mahogany case! And the porcelain palette! Why, it even has little wells so one can mix colors without their running all together and making mud. And real charcoal, and all sorts of brushes. Mr. Turner himself wouldn't spurn them!"

"I imagine he would accept them gratefully, given the traditional remuneration of those who indulge in the arts as a profession," Miss Moore responded wryly.

"Oh, Papa says Mr. Turner's done very well for himself—not like Mr. Constable, who is another artist, and equally talented, but most shy and uncertain of his welcome. Mr. Turner, you see," Lucinda explained with the infinite assurance of the very young who have discovered an infallible oracle, "knows who he is. Papa says it's important for an artist to know that, and that Mr. Constable hasn't discovered his artistic identity yet, or if he has, he hasn't the courage of his convictions. At least that's what Papa says. Since Papa is acquainted with both artists, and has purchased works by each of them, I suspect he must be correct. He does seem to know most everything about everything."

"A highly perspicacious gentleman."

"What has perspicacity to say to anything," declared Sarah, delighted she'd gotten the word out in a single mellifluous whole. "Lord Connardsleigh listens to Lucinda. No one ever listens to us!"

"No, I suppose they don't," Miss Moore agreed, "more's the pity."

"And there's a letter for Miss Broward, too," Lucinda concluded triumphantly. "You may have believed the rest, but this is truly incredible. My father's sent sufficient funds for us to have fires in every classroom, and meat every day, and eggs and fruit and treats and I don't know what all! Papa said it wouldn't be fair for just me to be more comfortable, and that I wouldn't like it, and of course he's absolutely correct. So, until spring we're all to live like princesses. Isn't that wonderful?"

"Positively amazing," Miss Moore murmured. "This letter—you have it safe?"

"Very safe, for I haven't got it at all. Papa's groom from the manor does—his *head* groom, Mr. Stubbs. Mr. Stubbs's been at the manor since before Papa was a boy. Papa says he's a 'fixture.' He came with me all the way to make certain we got the very best job horses at all the posting houses—Papa insisted, though Great-Grandmama said it wasn't in the least necessary. You remember who Stubbs is. He's the one who let me hide in the stables whenever my step-grandmother was on a rampage.

"He has a letter from Great-Grandmama for you as well. He's here somewhere—Stubbs, I mean, not Papa." Lucinda laughed at the look of consternation on Miss Moore's face. "Papa's in London with Uncle Jamie. Can you imagine calling a duke 'Uncle'? But Uncle Jamie insisted I must, and so I do. He's ever so kind, and such fun. Papa's more serious, I think, though Uncle Jamie can be serious, too.

"Stubbs," she called, turning to peer about the entry hall, "Stubbs? Where have you hidden yourself? Oh—there you are! This is my Miss Moore," Lucinda proclaimed proudly, seizing her teacher's hand and pulling her into the gray light of the January afternoon. "You know—the teacher I've told you about. Would you give Miss Moore Papa's letter, please, as Miss Broward doesn't seem to be about, which is just as well. If Miss Moore sees to things, they'll be properly seen to. With Miss Broward, things seem to become 'diverted' somehow. Oh, and please give her Great-grandmama's letter as well."

Stubbs paused on the porch, a sturdy silhouette frozen against a lowering winter sky. Then he came forward, eyeing Miss Moore with considerable interest.

"Ma'am," he said, tugging his forelock, then scowled. "Miss Moore? *My la*—"

"Mr. Stubbs, how do you do," Mary Moore broke in with a note of stern caution as she extended her hand. "I'm pleased to make the acquaintance of one who has been so kind to one of my pupils."

Stubbs stared from her hand to her face, clearly nonplussed. Then, hesitantly, he took her hand and gingerly shook it. *"Miss Moore?"* he repeated.

"Miss Mary Moore," she confirmed. "You have a communication for the school from Miss Connardsleigh's father, the viscount, I believe? And one for me from Lady Connardsleigh as well?"

"I do that, your la—ma'am—miss," he confirmed in some confusion, then glanced about him wildly. "Bein't there some cranny where we can be private-like for a minute or two, miss?" he pleaded. "I—ah—that is, his lordship—"

He glanced miserably from Lucinda to the two other little girls. The youthful trio stared at him in turn with round-eyed amazement as he tortured the cap in his gnarled hands. This was not how servants were supposed to behave—even they knew that.

"There's no need, Mr. Stubbs," Miss Moore returned calmly.

"But you can't be pretendin'—"

"I never pretend."

"Miss Moore! Stubbs!"

The embattled pair turned reluctantly to face Lucinda.

"What is this about," she demanded, essaying her great-grandmother's most imperious tone. "Something is not as it ought to be?"

"Nothing's amiss, my dear," Miss Moore responded with considerable aplomb. "Your papa's Mr. Stubbs is merely a bit befuddled from an overlong journey, and has mistaken me for someone else in this uncertain light."

"Mr. Stubbs is never befuddled!"

"I'd still like a word with ye personal-like, miss," Stubbs persisted.

"No need at all," Miss Moore repeated with the calm of desperation.

"There's every need, an' then a mite more, miss," the groom insisted doggedly. "Changes be happening at t'manor—big changes. You should be knowing his lordship, little missy's father, he's started out on a search, if you catch my drift."

"Lord Connardsleigh's activities are neither your concern nor mine."

"Bein' as how I'm in his lordship's employ, I owe him sartin loyalty, miss. His Grace of Rawdon what's been his lordship's friend since they was lads together? He were with us over t'holidays when his lordship's grandmother was took sick sudden-like, an' he's been advising his lordship on how to look for something particular, an' His Grace be very astuditious."

"Searching and finding are not necessarily the same," Miss Moore countered, "so long as those who are not properly involved do not involve themselves. May I have the letters please, Mr. Stubbs?"

"I dunno," he said, backing away. "There's those as might be given the sack from not informin' his lordship, should they happen on somethin' of use to him," Stubbs protested, his expression as uncompromising as his eyes were compassionate, "an' these be hard times, miss."

"I have never heard the viscount characterized as an unjust man."

"No, miss? Mayhap not, but there were a time he were so unjust, it sat in all our craws, but there weren't nothing we could do. Now, mebbe—"

"The letters, Stubbs," Miss Moore insisted in her most no-nonsense schoolroom voice. "As to his lordship's search, I suggest you seek the counsel of his lordship's grandmother. I understand from Lucinda that the dowager viscountess is currently in command of the household. She will be able to advise you. For myself, I'm certain I neither can nor desire to render assistance to anyone whatsoever."

Stubbs gazed at Miss Moore steadily for several moments. She returned his gaze with defiant self-assurance.

"Ah—so that's the way of it," he finally said, his dour expression lightning. "I'll be doing that, miss, with your permission. The dowager viscountess, now—she be a downy one. To be sure, I'll heed her. An'," he concluded, his eyes suddenly boring into the schoolteacher's, "you might be considering t'do the same, should the day come—an' it will, given his lordship's a mighty stubborn man, though a fair one most times when all's said an' done—if I'm not bein' too froward in givin' ye a piece o' free advice. Your letters, miss, an' pardon if I give you a bad turn."

He handed Miss Moore a pair of missives composed on heavy crested vellum, bowed a bit lower than was the due of a simple schoolteacher, nodded to Lucinda, instructed her to study hard, mind her manners and treat Miss Moore with respect or he'd not be teaching her to ride a pony come spring no matter what his lordship said, and strode through the main door into the frozen, darkening day.

"Hear you," he called, "these nags been standin' overlong, fer all they're nowt but job cattle! All missy's bundles been toted up? Good. Then we're off!"

"Miss Moore, who did he think you were?" Lucinda demanded as her father's carriage pulled into the lane. "I've never seen Stubbs act in such a manner!"

"I haven't the slightest notion, nor need his error concern any of us." Miss Moore smiled, tucking her letters away in a deep pocket and then closing the heavy front door. "I have long acquaintance with your great-grandmama. She'll put him right. As I said, the poor man was befuddled, but it wasn't worth the effort to argue with him. It never is in such cases.

"Now, upstairs with you all. You've quite a bit of unpacking to do before the supper bell, and the dormitory must be swept and dusted, and you've been assigned two classrooms as well."

Spring 1812

Winter's harsh hand lay heavily upon the land that year.

Far to the south, separated from England by league upon league of storm-tossed ocean, Arthur Wellesley's Peninsular forces shivered in winter quarters, held balls and produced plays, uncomplainingly suffering the mud and cold and vermin, the execrable rations and tardy pay of a combat expeditionary force as they braced for the spring campaigns. The allied cause prospered as besieged Ciudad Rodrigo fell in January, Badajoz in April. On the Continent the Corsican Monster prepared for the assault against Mother Russia which, he averred, would make him master of Europe at last.

In the north country, Lucinda and her schoolmates rejoiced in warm fires, sturdy clothes, and nourishing food. If Miss Broward threatened Miss Moore with dismissal for misuse of so many lovely golden guineas, no one knew of the altercation but Miss Moore and Miss Broward. And if Miss Moore in her turn tartly informed her employer that the guineas had been put to the best possible use, that, too, lay between the two women.

Lady Charlotte's days passed with a peaceful sameness as January slid into February, the excitements over and the festivities ended. Rawdon and Connard had returned to London the day of Lucinda's departure, Connard to actively direct the search for his missing wife, Rawdon to resume his mysterious activities on behalf of his dead brother. With Adelle Connardsleigh in Bath, Artie and Lucinda at school, and Lady

Daphne in London, the manor took on a waiting aspect, as if life were for the moment suspended.

The day of his return from Yorkshire, Stubbs sought an interview with Lady Charlotte, braving the main house with grim determination.

"Well?" Lady Charlotte inquired tartly as soon as he set foot in the firelit family parlor, his cap deferentially in hand and his freshly shaved chin outthrust.

"I do be thinkin' it's me as what should be sayin' 'well,' m'lady," he grumbled.

Lady Charlotte sighed. "Of course you recognized her." Old family retainers could be a considerable problem on occasion. Stubbs was merely a stable boy charged with mucking out when she came to Connard Manor as a bride. He had buried two masters. There'd been a time when she feared he'd bury a third. . . . "Well, say your piece."

"Her ladyship bein't the slip of a girl she was," he frowned. "She's changed some, but nothin' could change her that much."

"No, I suppose not. How did she seem? You gave her my letter?"

Stubbs nodded, his face set. "I gave it her right enough, your ladyship. She's come right peaked-looking. No spark like she had a'fore, an' none o' them lights to her eyes."

His scowl would have intimidated legions of Hussars. Lady Charlotte appeared unaffected, watching him and holding her own counsel as she waited for the more that was sure to come.

"Pardon my plain speakin', m'lady," he said at last, "but what game be ye playin' at? Here's his lordship harin' off to Lun'on dead set on findin' her ladyship—we all knows that, though nothin' been said formal-like—an' you not sayin' as how you know exact where she be, an' herself sayin' as how I ain't to be lettin' his lordship know what I know, neither. An' then, there's little missy with no more idea who 'Miss Moore' be than a newborn babe. It don't make sense, beggin' your pardon, but her ladyship said as how I was to bring you my questions if I had any, an' I do got a pouch full!"

"I can well imagine." Lady Charlotte chuckled. For the customarily taciturn Stubbs, it had been a speech of immense length. She could just picture his tenacity and Marianne's consternation when that confrontation had taken place! Then her features sobered. "Shall we merely say I've always had a soft spot for Lucinda and her mother, and I want what's best, both for them and for your master? And for myself, I'll admit. My grandson a reclusive misogynist, Miss Lucinda treated worse than a scullery maid, Marianne hiding in the wilds of Yorkshire, and Adelle Parkins ruling the roost in her stead has never been my idea of a happy household!"

"Ye bein't goin' to inform his lordship of where she be?"

"Not immediately, at least. A little effort on his part is most definitely in order, don't you think? One always places a higher value on that for which one must struggle. Perhaps even a bit of frustrated desperation? No—don't answer that! You've taken his part since he was in leading strings."

"Not always," Stubbs mumbled, examining his cap with apparent fascination.

Lady Charlotte's features softened. "You were fond of Marianne," she said gently. "Everyone was. Well, don't worry, I've been planning this for a long time. Hold your peace until June. If matters don't resolve themselves by then, I'll find some way of communicating the truth to the viscount myself. Not a word to anyone, mind! Not *anyone*—even Parsons. I'm aware you've all tried to shelter Miss Lucinda since I first brought her home. I was glad of your assistance, but leave this to me."

In Yorkshire, Marianne Connardsleigh was thankful her schoolroom duties were absorbing and rigorous. She didn't want time to think, for thinking involved remembering, and her memories of her husband were bittersweet at best.

Nights were the worst. There were no tasks then in which to bury herself, no children demanding her attention. That was invariably when, shivering beneath threadbare blankets in her narrow bed at one end of the younger girls' drafty dormitory, her thoughts ricocheted from the few months of happiness she and Ned had shared to the disastrous afternoon her stepmother-in-law bustled into the family parlor on the pretext of mending the breach between dower house and manor. Ned had been absent that day, gone to a neighbor's to acquire new stock for the home farm and mend social fences shattered by years of Adelle's waspish self-importance.

That Adelle had insisted on pouring out, that the tea had seemed unusually bitter, hadn't struck Marianne until weeks later. By then it was too late by a lifetime.

In the beginning they had giggled together, she and Adelle Connardsleigh. Her stepmother-in-law exuded unaccustomed warmth and practiced charm, rendering Marianne giddy with relief—or so she thought. Ned had proved as loving and tender a husband as he had been courageous and gallant an officer. Only the frozen look on his face when Adelle descended on the manor or was mentioned marred those first rapturous weeks in Kent. With her stepmother-in-law's apparent tendering of an olive branch, the world had become a perfect place.

Dizzy after her third cup of bohea, Marianne had regretfully apologized and begged to be excused. A knowing, almost minxish look suffused her uninvited guest's plump, rather common features.

"Why, my dear, there's no need for apologies!" Adelle had simpered. "I would imagine Ned is no more a laggard in the bedchamber than he was in battle. So—we are to expect an interesting announcement! But your bed is not what you require. Fresh air—that's the thing, trust me! In the meanwhile, have another cup of tea, my dear. I can recommend it most particularly when one is in a delicate condition."

And then Adelle summoned Parsons and demanded the new pony cart be brought around. Exercise, she insisted, and a change of scene, would restore the bloom to Marianne's cheeks. Grateful someone seemed to care about her malaise, unwilling to protest the coldness of the blustery March day, Marianne yielded to her stepmother-in-law's urgings. Once beyond sight of the manor, Adelle wrested the reins from Marianne's numb fingers as the sixteen-year-old bride's world spiraled into an endless black tunnel. Contorted trees thrust out grasping branches to tear at loosened hair and fluttering shawl. Improbable nightmare colors writhed across the landscape, painful to the eyes. Senses whirling, dry-mouthed and disoriented, Marianne pleaded for a quick return to the manor. And Adelle? Adelle laughed, flicked the whip over the pony's back, and trotted down a lane Marianne had never traveled before. Then Ned's face surged up, deformed by rage, his voice roaring words she couldn't decipher. When she was once more herself, she had knelt for what seemed like days at the locked study door, sobbing her soul away in the silent empty corridor. And from there? Cornwall . . . Then rescue, and London. Eventually, Yorkshire—long after Lady Charlotte had taken Lucinda away. It had been months before she regained her health and inveigled her way into her current position by means of a look and manner far older than her years and a willingness to accept lowered wages.

No, the memories were neither gentle nor pleasant nor kind.

Yet, in her rare free moments, Marianne sought the solitude of the moors beyond the glen, where the school huddled beside Broward Tarn at the base of a rugged escarpment, snow-frosted Broward Tor soaring in distant splendor against a sullen sky. There she pondered the unjust past and considered the uncertain future, determination, misery, and longing warring in her heart.

So it was, one day late in March, that she shivered beneath her heavy brown frieze cloak as she sped across the sere landscape, her fingers pinched with cold, her cheeks and nose reddened. Her worn boots crunched on ground crisp with frost. She kept her head down, forcing her way against a wind that seemed a living embodiment of the wild uplands.

She had discovered a tiny cave on one of her rare ramblings, little more than a dimple in an exposed rock face. Now she sought its rude shelter, yet another letter from Connard Manor tucked deep in the interior pocket of her cloak. She knew the crossed and recrossed lines would contain still more importunings from Lady Charlotte. She must reconsider her refusal to so much as see Ned. She must consider Lucinda. She must consider Artie. She must consider her loving grandmother-in-law. She must consider the entire household. . . .

Grateful she might be to Lady Charlotte for having her rescued from that rock-infested farm deep in Cornwall, but gratitude could take one only so far. It would not carry her into Ned's presence, let alone into his home—on that point she was determined. She had forgiven him, yes—but only to an extent that permitted her to repeat the words of the Our Father at the little Anglican church in Winthorp each Sunday. If this meant permanent separation from Lucinda, then that was the price she must pay. It wouldn't do to be greedy. These past five years had been an unexpected gift.

Pride, Lady Charlotte insisted with numbing persistence, was a cold bedfellow. Perhaps, but pride was also all she had. Ned and Adelle between them had robbed her of all else. Lady Charlotte demanded too much. . . .

Now she ducked into the miniature cavern in the rocks, settled herself on the narrow ledge that was her usual seat, dug into her cloak pocket with trembling fingers to retrieve Lady Charlotte's most recent missive, and broke the seal.

"My dearest granddaughter," she read.
  Life here proceeds at its usual pace—which is to say dull and boring now that my dear friend Lady Daphne,

has returned to Town and Lucinda is with you at Broward. But they have not been the only ones to abandon me—though I approve that abandonment most highly.

As I have already written you, Ned was stunned by the revelations of La Parkins, and has expelled the grasping harpy from the manor—for which the dear Lord be praised! Not to be forced to encounter the vicious toad daily and pretend to an equanimity no one could feel is a blessing of the highest order. And he openly accepts Lucinda as his daughter and has forced all and sundry to do the same. This you know. However, now there is more, and that "more" concerns you most closely.

Ned at last believes you innocent of any wrongdoing at the Lame Swan. Indeed, that fool of a Parkins woman as much as confessed to the exact methods she employed first to incapacitate you, then to dupe him. Ned does not stand very high in his own esteem at the moment. . . .

He returned to London immediately following Lucinda's departure for Yorkshire, and has set matters in hand to find you—to the extent that there are now Bow Street runners on your trail—a new development. He is most determined, my dear—a fact you had best take into your calculations, for whenever Ned has decided upon a course of action, he invariably follows that course through to a successful conclusion. One may be polite, and refer to him as tenacious, or one may be a trace less polite and a deal more honest and call him a very stubborn man.

Ned claims he does not care what your whereabouts or condition. He intends to make amends for his youthful folly, and regain your esteem and trust (if not your affections) or expire in the attempt. At the very least, he insists he will see you provided for if you will accept nothing more from him. His dearest wish, however, is to see you reinstalled at the manor as his blameless wife and Lucinda's devoted mother.

Now, before you fly into the boughs, hear me out!

I know what you have said previously on the subject, but Ned's chagrin, his deep mortification, his sense of culpability in the matter, are all you could desire. No— there is no returning to the innocence of your first months together, but something of value may still be salvaged from the shambles which that Parkins cretin made of your marriage—if you are willing. If you will not think of Ned or yourself, think of Lucinda.

I am not currently on my deathbed, but neither am I a chit in her first season. I will do the best by the child that I am able when the time comes if you refuse to resume your rightful place as her mother, but the prospect of shepherding a green young miss through the Season in a few years' time does not appeal—and might well prove impossible. I am not trying to frighten you, my dear, nor to coerce you but if you have the least affection for your daughter, it is a matter you must consider, no matter what your sentiments concerning Ned.

I have not divulged your location to him, nor shall I. A promise made is a promise to be kept, no matter how foolish the promise, or how deeply one regrets making it. However, I am convinced he will find you.

Poor Ned has suffered as grievously through all this as you have—if differently—for he has never ceased to love you, my dear. His fury alone is proof of that. Christian charity demands you forgive him his inability to forgive your apparent betrayal all those years ago, for now he cannot forgive himself—a convoluted expression of a convoluted sentiment regarding a most convoluted situation, and one for which I hold myself at least partly to blame. Had I despised La Parkins one whit less, had my London sojourn been one whit less enjoyable despite my mourning state, had I considered your futures rather than my own comfort and amusement, I should have returned to the manor with you and that creature would never have succeeded in her machinations—had she dared even attempt them in my presence. But, as with you both, I played directly into her hands—for which I have never, and can never forgive myself!

Remember Ned's youth at the time, as well as your own, and the culpability of a third—and even fourth— party. The appearance of wrongdoing was overwhelming, my dear—even I have been forced to concede that. It would have taken a wiser and more sophisticated, not to say jaded and cynical, man than Ned to see through La Parkins's intrigues. Knowing you as I have come to do, you would never have loved that other man as you did and I suspect, do Ned. Did you not care for him even now, you would not be so afraid to return.

You have each had considerable time for reflection. Your lives apart have not been what they would have had you been together—a fatuous statement, but true. Ned, in the interim, has become the mature and capable estate owner we all knew he would. As to his character, that never was at fault—only his experience of the world, and the lengths to which the unscrupulous will go to feather their nests.

If none of this weighs heavily with you, consider the following: Your intransigence plays directly into La Parkins's hands, granting her triumph where Ned would tear it from her. Your best revenge, if revenge is what you truly desire, is to resume your place at Connard Manor, your son and Ned's on your knee—not that I would begrudge Artie the title, but the poor lad is rather a dimwit. The dear Lord knows if he even deserves to bear the name Connardsleigh—though I would never hint at such a thing to him or to Ned—even as I never mentioned the possibility to Ned's poor father, for he

*certainly had enough to bear as it was! Yet I have often
wondered . . .*

    *In closing, my dear, let me say once again how greatly
I miss your bright and shining presence. Letters do not
suffice! Humor an old lady who is not as well as she
might be, avoid unnecessary pain for Lucinda as well
as yourself, forgive Ned—if indeed you have not long
since done so—and come home to us all.*

Your loving grandmother-in-law,
Charlotte Connardsleigh,
Dowager Viscountess Connard

"No!" Marianne muttered, staring at the heavy cream vellum with its unwelcome message. Crumpling the letter in her fist and surging to her feet, she abandoned her retreat, pausing in the little cavern's entrance to stare across the bleak rolling hills, her eyes misting. "No! I shall not!" she shouted defiantly to the silent moors. "No! Not again. Not ever."

But "not again" was less determined than "no," "not ever" barely a whisper, and her lips trembled as she thought of never seeing her daughter again. And yet, how could she completely forgive what Ned had done to her sixteen-year-old self? When she considered the cruel damage wreaked by the Parkins woman, she felt capable of murder, but not even murder would restore the lost years, or give them to Lucinda. Or to Ned . . .

That night, in the free hour granted the children in their schoolrooms between supper and evening prayers, Marianne Connardsleigh paused beside the scarred table her daughter shared with four other students. The child was working intently on yet another watercolor—this time a portrait. Head and facial planes had been roughed in lightly with pencil. As yet, only the background washes had been applied—the barest hints of a pale wintry sky against which indications of barren branches soared, scattered areas of bare paper hinting at their burden of snow in Turner's manner. So far it could have been anyone, and anywhere. Yet Marianne knew and watched, unable to tear herself away.

Lucinda was mixing a generous puddle of yellow with a brush tip of red in one of the porcelain wells, adding water, moistening first one cake of color and then another as she strove to achieve precisely the tone she desired, her lower lip gripped between her teeth. She added the tiniest touch of blue, frowning in concentration, tried the color out on a scrap of paper, added another pinprick of blue, a trace of umber, tested again, nodded, added more water. Then, reversing the handle, she began to wash the face with the larger brush, altering the tone slightly as she worked. Unmistakable features emerged—strong, firm-jawed, hawk-nosed. Dark eyes sank beneath heavy brows. Lines Marianne had never seen before appeared at their corners, plunged from nostrils to generous mouth, furrowed the broad brow, highlighted by more touches of pristine paper.

Her breath caught. He had aged. Well, so had she. And yet he was the same, totally recognizable, totally "Ned." Was she, then, not quite so changed as she thought? Certainly those well-remembered and once-beloved features had the power to make the floor seem to drop from beneath her feet— even such a solid stone floor as this one.

"That's an excellent likeness, Lucinda," she whispered. "Excellent!"

Lucinda glanced up at her wonderful Miss Moore, hand pausing in its delicate work. "Well, *I* think so, but however can *you* tell?" she inquired guilelessly, returning to her painstaking task before the paint could dry. "This is my father, and you've never seen him, have you? Why, even I'd never seen him until just before Christmas."

"One can sense it is a real person," Marianne prevaricated, "and so the likeness must be at least adequate. I am correct, am I not?"

"Oh, yes, Miss Moore—it's as close to perfection as I'll ever come. I've been trying and trying ever since we got back, for I do so want a special gift for Great-Grandmama when I return to the manor, and I thought a portrait of Papa might please her. Papa's very difficult to capture. Mostly he comes out as a beetle-browed gargoyle, or occasionally an ogre," she chuckled, "which is no better, and of course I must work from memory. That isn't easy, but this time I think I'm going to succeed. Great-Grandmama deserves some sort of reward for changing my life so completely, and since she gave me Papa, I thought it appropriate to give him to her in return."

"Most appropriate," Marianne Connardsleigh agreed.

"Of course, I must have gifts for Artie and Papa as well. I haven't quite decided what those shall be as yet. I'm abysmal at horses—they come out all lopsided—but that's what Artie would like best if only I can manage it."

"And for your father?" Marianne inquired hesitantly.

"I'm not quite sure yet." Lucinda dimpled. "It will have to be something very special. . . ."

Three mornings later Lucinda flew to her Miss Moore in tears. During the night the completed portrait of her father had disappeared from the tiny chest she shared with another student. She could find it nowhere.

Jamie Debenham, Duke of Rawdon, leaned back in his chair at White's, gazing across the napery at Ned Connardsleigh. Their meal—adequate if not extraordinary—was over, port and a thick Stilton wedge accompanied by biscuits replacing poached sole, jugged duckling, and truffled lamb collops garnished with young asparagus. With a slight smile Rawdon selected a cheroot from the box proffered by a hovering lackey, rolled it carefully between his fingers, nodded, and waved the man off.

"How proceeds the search?" he asked, delicately trimming the ends, lighting it, then drawing deeply.

"Nowhere, confound it," Connard grumbled, sloshing liberal measures of port in their glasses. "I've a good mind to dismiss Bow Street. They produce nothing but false hints, or traces so old as to be useless. D'you have any notion how many dark-haired women of twenty-eight there are in England?" He drained his glass in disgust, refilled it. "Thousands!

"I've learned my black-hearted witch of a stepmother packed Marianne off to Cornwall, incarcerated her with a tribe of louts so dim they barely remember her. Dear Lord, they hardly know their own names! Then someone appeared on their doorstep—if you care to dignify it by such a term! I don't—and money changed hands. Quite a considerable sum—that they did remember, and more than hinted I should reward them in like manner for what information they managed to give me. This mysterious and well-to-pass stranger whisked her away. Who he was or where he sprang from I have yet to determine. The only certainty is that she disappeared from Cornwall, and then some months later Grandmama appeared with Lucinda. Of Marianne, beyond Cornwall, there's not the slightest trace. By someone's contrivance—Grandmama's, I presume—Lucinda's birth was recorded in our parish register. That's the sum."

"You've inquired of Lady Charlotte? Certainly it stands to reason that if she found the child, she must have found Lady Connardsleigh as well."

"No help there. An anonymous letter guided her to a foundling home near Manchester. I've seen the damned thing. There's no doubt it's genuine."

"So you've been told. Doesn't it all seem the least fortuitous to you?"

"No," Ned sighed, now sipping more temperately at his port. "I've been over that ground with her interminably—and rough ground it has been! No way to get over it lightly. She blames me for Marianne's disappearance, and with every right."

"Still, if I were a betting man, I'd inscribe your grandmother's name in the book as the one who will lead you to your wife."

"No—if she were aware of Marianne's whereabouts, she'd've told me by now. Devoted to her I may be, but she knows it would be worth her life to keep silent at this juncture. Nothing could justify it—though if I believed for a moment she could point the way, I'd crawl to her on my hands and knees!"

The two men stared at each other across the same table they had shared just before Christmas. The light was soft and mellow, the warm air filled with scents of good food and expensive colognes. Around them, spring being well established and the London Season begun, tables were crowded with other elegant diners intent on masculine companionship and conviviality before being forced to do the pretty at assorted balls and routs. General Maitland snored in his customary corner, as portly and sodden and disheveled as ever. Some things never changed—especially at White's.

"I've crossed and recrossed this 'Blessed Isle' these last months," Ned continued as Rawdon pulled on his cheroot. "Nothing! Not a trace beyond Cornwall—not even in Manchester. Grandmama suggests Marianne may have emigrated, or even be deceased. That I refuse to consider. I don't think I could keep going if such were the case."

"Even so, you've made inquiries through proper channels regarding possible emigration? And had the appropriate parish registers examined?"

"What's appropriate—tell me that! I've written so many letters, I should invest in ink and paper manufactories. Lord knows, I'm supporting them well enough single-handed! India. Canada. The Indies—East *and* West. Even the former Colonies. Every place I could think of—letter upon letter. And Bow Street's checked every magdalen, every workhouse, every stew, every prison, every hospital, every parish register within reason. Nothing. Devil take it, Jamie—she's vanished. . . ."

"Possibly that's what she intended."

"Oh, there's no doubt of that," Connard returned bitterly. "It'll be months until I get answers to my inquiries. Even if she did emigrate—which I tend to doubt—she may have vanished once more following her arrival. They don't keep careful records in places like the Antipodes or the American Territories. They've other matters with which to concern themselves, such as mere survival.

"No, my guess is, she's still in England. Scotland, perhaps, but I've been to every major town and city, and many of the smaller places. Nothing. Not a trace. Not even a hint. Ireland? I don't think so, but once I've fetched Lucinda home—at Grandmama's suggestion, by the bye. She claims I need a small reprieve, and I will admit to exhaustion as well as discouragement at the moment. Besides, there's the Moore woman to be dealt with—I intend to try there as well."

Connard sighed, drained the last of his port, then helped himself to a sliver of Stilton and a biscuit. "How fares your own project?"

"Like yours, slowly. So—your searches have concentrated on Scotland. Why?"

"For lack of a better idea. Her father's mother had connections there, I know that much. At least Scotland meant I had the opportunity for occasional forays into Yorkshire to visit Lucinda when things became a bit much."

"Delightful as ever, I presume? And keeping well?"

"Healthy as a Shires filly, in spite of that abominable place. Broward Academy? Broward Gaol, more like! D'you know, the children do most of the heavy work? Old besom who runs the place claims it firms their characters! I say she's too cheese-paring to hire proper servants. As much as told me to keep my nose where it belonged when I protested the sight of a six-year-old wrestling with wet sheets. Infernal woman!

"But"—he smiled fondly—"Lucinda remains my lodestar. Totally uncowed, and insists on staying to the bitter end. She asked to be remembered to 'her Uncle Jamie' the last time I saw her. God, what a fool I was! Bright, sparkling, witty, totally captivating. I dread the day some young buck sees her with clear eyes and whisks her away from me."

"You've a few years yet," Rawdon chuckled. "Don't borrow trouble. I presume you've encountered the redoubtable Miss Moore, then. Is she half the paragon Lucinda claimed, or a mere mortal like the rest of us?"

"Never so much as laid eyes on the woman. Most elusive, Lucinda's blasted Miss Moore. Avoids me like the plague—that, or she's particularly sickly. Always 'indisposed' when I'm there, or 'out.' Wanted to meet her only to please Lucinda, in any case. Dried-out spinsters aren't my choice for companions, even for a brief chat.

"But it wasn't just Scotland and Cornwall. I've been everywhere! Derby. Devon. Lancashire. Even Wales—a godforsaken place if ever there was one. Find a road the length and breadth of this island, and I've traveled it, and can tell you the precise location of each rut and pebble and patch of mud. As to inns serving inedible slop and providing verminous accommodations, I've become an authority!"

"I share both your experience and sentiments," Rawdon drawled with a wry twinkle at the back of his dark gray eyes. "Has Lady Charlotte unearthed a suitable governess for Lucinda yet? One who meets her high standards? I would imagine, with the child's return to the manor so imminent, that must be a priority."

"Dammit, no!" Connard scowled. "Grandmama insists I interview this Moore woman before any others are considered. Claims it's only fair to Lucinda. I've tried," he growled in frustration. "Lord knows, I've tried! I leave for York tomorrow. I'll try once more—but only once, confound it! After that, both Grandmama and Miss Moore can go hang, for all of me. Lucinda will have to content herself with someone a mite less extraordinary."

* * *

Marianne Connardsleigh watched from an open attic window, positioned so she could not be glimpsed from the area lying between the school and the lane leading through the glen. A handsome crested post chaise stood in the small forecourt, its sturdy team snorting as they jostled their harnesses, eager to be off. By the open carriage door stood a rather stocky, muscular figure, his arm encircling the flaxen-haired girl who only minutes before had been sobbing in her arms, despairing of her father's arrival and positive she was once more to be abandoned. Beyond them, footman and groom and abigail toted bundles and trunk from where they had been stacked in the entry, awaiting a departure which it at first seemed would never occur.

Connard was four days late. The weather had been abysmal—fogs, rains, even sleet. To the south, spring flowers might bloom in Hyde Park. Here the season was long delayed, and May had all the appearance of a Kentish March. Roads were mired, she heard Connard say by way of apology, his voice floating to her clearly in the still, damp air. They'd been delayed for a day by a broken axle, an additional two by a bridge swept away in a spring torrent. Detours had become a way of life. If it had not been one thing, it had been another. Connard gestured in excuse at the half-hidden moor lying beyond the gates. Tendrils of mist shrouded the lane, snagged in the still-barren branches of trees contorted by the prevailing winds. The tor was hidden, had been for a week.

Beside him Lucinda's face was upturned in naked adoration, her fair hair flowing from beneath her blue velvet bonnet like liquid sunshine. Under her arm she clutched her precious portfolio. She hadn't let it out of her sight for days, slept with it beneath her pillow. Within resided the recreated portrait of Ned Connardsleigh intended for Lady Charlotte, and several attempts at a roan gelding that looked rather more like a long-legged sow and were intended for Artie. And, there was a study of the bleak moorland for her father, Broward Tor in the distance, the tarn reflecting scudding clouds and wind-tossed trees, a livid Turneresque sun breaking through on the horizon.

"It's all right, Papa," she now assured him blithely, unconscious of her tear-stained cheeks. "I wasn't worried—not really. Well . . . maybe just a little, but nothing to be concerned about. It's enough you're here at last!"

Blast him! Marianne fumed. He should've known the journey from Kent would be plagued with delays. He'd been at Broward enough times to learn that during the preceding months, pestilentially persistent male that he was! But no— he hadn't been willing to start out soon enough, and so caused their daughter needless pain. And there was precisely nothing she could do about it—or at least nothing she was willing to do.

"Lucinda! Propriety, if you please! Such comments are beyond what is acceptable. We train our girls to be profoundly respectful of their betters, my lord," Miss Broward's sharp voice grated in repressive explanation. "It is for them to wait in silent submission, considering only the wishes and needs of others. I disapprove even their little holidays as fostering slothful frivolity, but must have some occasional leisure to recover from my labor on their behalves. Naturally I recommend their days be filled with menial tasks during their absences in preparation for their future positions. I beg you not to encourage sentiments in Miss Connardsleigh which she may not properly entertain, or you will undo all my efforts."

"A silent and submissive daughter is the last thing I want," Connard returned, ignoring the majority of the self-serving homily. "A demanding hoyden would be preferable, though Lucinda is not that either, thank the Lord. I believed you understood me when I informed you I am not my stepmother, and permitted Lucinda to remain here only under severe protest. Her proper position is at my side. Where, by the bye, is your Miss Moore? I have a need to confer with her before our departure, and I wish to be on the road as soon as possible."

"Miss Moore? I haven't the slightest notion, my lord," Miss Broward bristled. "Why this persistent interest in the woman? I do not approve of fraternization between patrons and staff. Any questions you have, you may put to me."

Connard's brows rose as he maintained a disdainful silence.

"I could never permit such an interview in any case," Miss Broward dithered after an uneasy glance at his lordship. "Miss Moore holds a unique position of trust in my establishment, overseeing as she does the molding of young females for lives of service as companions, governesses, and the higher sort of domestics. You would certainly not wish to compromise her situation here?"

"I might not, but my grandmother most definitely would— if it meant the woman would join us at the manor. Lucinda has need of a governess, and it would seem your Miss Moore is the instructress of choice among those who matter."

"Totally unsuitable!" Miss Broward objected, horror narrowing her already small eyes. "Mary Moore? In a noble household? Laughable! The woman has not the slightest accomplishment that would render such a post eligible. Why, she is not even a gentlewoman fallen into distress, which might render her marginally acceptable. What could she possibly teach your daughter? How could she prepare her for a Season? No—it's not to be thought of! I positively forbid it."

Lord Connardsleigh's brows soared in disdain. Miss Broward glanced about her, unease growing. Men—especially those of noble blood—were so unpredictable! Only ladies could be counted upon to understand the niceties of her establishment.

"That is," she amended, "I positively do not recommend it."

"I understand this Moore woman possesses a kind heart and gentle disposition in addition to a superior intellect. I find those qualifications quite sufficient. As to my seeing the woman privately, you may be present if you believe there's a danger she'll cast out lures or I'll ravish her on the spot," Connard returned with scathing contempt.

Marianne retreated quickly from the tiny window.

"My lord!" Miss Broward sputtered. "Have a care! There are young and innocent ears present!"

"Not so innocent that she's never heard the terms, I'll warrant," Connard snapped. "Now—do I have your permission to interview the woman, or don't I? I warn you: When I desire a thing, I can be both persistent and troublesome. Where is she?"

"Well, as to that, my lord, I can hardly say. Tending to her duties, I would presume. I suppose you may speak with her if you must—if she is to be found. We are not in session. Indeed, I must confer with you concerning charges for housing and feeding Miss Connardsleigh four additional days. And for her supervision."

"Walk the horses, Stubbs," Connard called to the groom at their heads. "We may be a while yet." Then he whirled on Miss Broward. "You are, I presume, going to offer my daughter and me the hospitality of your parlor while we await Miss Moore's appearance?" he demanded in haughty—and highly unaccustomed—tones.

With that he stormed the entry, calling for cooks, gardeners, someone to initiate the search as he pulled Lucinda along at his side and ignored the unpleasant cipher who was Miss Broward.

Marianne sighed with relief. The search would be perfunctory. No one would think of coming to the attics, or make the effort if they did. She was safe. Stubborn Ned might be, but he wasn't foolish. Night would fall soon. The track through Winthorp to York was a treacherous fifteen miles. There were other governesses, and from the sound of it he didn't much care for the Miss Moore who had been detailed to him, however much he might defend her against Miss Broward's barbed innuendoes.

It was another half hour before Connard bade Miss

Broward a cold good-bye, giving her a letter with instructions it be delivered to Miss Moore at the earliest opportunity, his disgust at the elusive teacher's continued invisibility manifest.

Fresh warm bricks were quickly bedded in the straw. He handed his daughter into the chaise and leapt in after her. The carriage door was secured. The footman jumped up behind, Tobias Stubbs—with a concerned look about him—before. The coachman cracked his whip. Lucinda's face appeared at the chaise window, slightly woebegone as she peered back anxiously at the stark stone building housing the Broward Academy. She gave a sad little wave in no particular direction. Then curtains were firmly pulled against the thickening mist. Slowly, elegantly, the chaise passed through the gates and into the lane. Tears streaming down her face, Marianne Connardsleigh watched it mount the nearest rise, disappearing into the fog.

"Good-bye, my love," she whispered haltingly. "God go with you," she added, then turned from the window, breaking into helpless despairing sobs.

In the chaise, Connard settled himself comfortably against the squabs and beamed at his daughter. That was over, thank the Lord! How anyone survived in that place he had no notion. Miss Moore, for all she sounded far too much the paragon, had all his sympathies. What a grim and unrewarding life she must lead. . . .

"Well, Lucinda, we're for home at last." He smiled, noting the sadness lurking in her eyes with dismay. "I'm sorry I never met your Miss Moore, but I did my best. You must grant me that. And I did leave a letter for her—if that Broward female ever delivers it. If we don't hear from her in a reasonable time, I may well return myself if that is what you and your great-grandmother want. Or perhaps we might make a family holiday of it, and journey up together. Would that please you?"

"Yes, Papa," Lucinda whispered.

"Well, then," he assured her with forced cheer, "we shall do it! And how have these weeks since I last saw you passed?"

"Very well, Papa."

He shifted uncomfortably, gripping the strap as the chaise jounced through a pothole, then lurched across a series of ruts. Before there had always been others present when he conversed with Lucinda, or else there had been something particular of which to speak. The ground was as rough in the chaise as beneath it.

"How are your special little friends?" he asked, groping for a safe topic. "The twins. Sarah, isn't it? And Emily?"

"They are very well, Papa, and thank you most sincerely for the treats. I've their bread-and-butter notes in here," she replied, indicating the maroon leather portfolio on the seat beside her. "In fact, I've notes from everyone."

"I'll be honored to read them. Perhaps we might have the twins to the manor for a visit, hmm? Do you think they'd like that?"

"Very much, Papa."

"And you? Would you enjoy a visit from Sarah and Emily?"

"Very much indeed, Papa."

Damn! Her chin was quivering. In a moment she'd burst into tears, and what he'd do then he had no idea. "Well, we shall do it!" he exclaimed jovially. "No menial tasks, that I promise—only slothful frivolities. And your Miss Moore, if she'd be willing to come." He'd need someone to keep such a juvenile petticoat-gathering in order!

"Thank you, Papa. You are most kind."

Oh, Lord! There were tears on her lashes now. In another moment there'd be freshets all over the place. He'd never dreamed she was a watering pot! What did one do when a little girl cried? Especially if she were one's daughter? One couldn't simply pull her into one's arms and kiss away the waterfalls as he'd done with Marianne the day her father died. Especially with a round-eyed abigail avidly flapping her ears playing gooseberry next to the child!

"Ahem!" he said. "Ahem! It's rather dark in here. Shall we light the lamps?"

"If you wish, Papa," Lucinda quavered bravely.

Dammit—the child couldn't be sorry to leave that pestilential hellhole. That meant it had to be the confounded Moore female who was causing her tears. Damn, damn, and damn again! Would the pertinacious female never get out of his life, and leave him in peace?

"And once they're lit," he said, busying himself with the task, "perhaps you'll permit me the pleasure of reading Sarah's and Emily's notes. I'd enjoy that! And then perhaps you'll share a small picnic with me. I had a hamper packed at the inn this morning, and I believe there are some of your favorite jam tarts and a flagon of tea remaining. And then perhaps you'll show me your latest paintings? I would truly enjoy that!" There—they had an itinerary for getting through the next minutes. That should help matters somewhat.

"Of course, Papa," Lucinda whispered, working at the portfolio's knotted ties. They stubbornly resisted her fumbling fingers.

"Here—let me try," Connard offered.

Wordlessly she handed him the maroon leather case as he sank back against the squabs beside her and the abigail shifted to the other side. It was open in a trice. He spread it across his knees as a sheaf of notes in childish hands cascaded to the floor of the chaise. Lucinda knelt on the swaying surface to retrieve them as he stared incredulously at the first painting of the stack. Dear God—it was of a young woman still in her prime, dark locks pulled severely back in a tight bun at the nape of her neck. The hazel eyes stared accusingly into his from the paper, the features matured, more definite.

"Dear God," he whispered, "who is this?" already certain of the answer.

Lucinda settled on the seat, peering at the likeness with him. "Why, that's my Miss Moore," she said proudly. "I placed it on top so you'd see it first off. Isn't she beautiful?"

"Very," he managed to say. "It is a good likeness?"

"I think so, though I've not succeeded in getting her hair just right," Lucinda replied critically, suddenly all artist, tears forgotten. "There're coppery lights in it when the sun shines. Of course that's not often in Yorkshire during the winter," she appended, chuckling ruefully. "The eyes aren't quite right either. Hers're much warmer and kinder. Here she just looks rather sad, whereas she's often laughing and smiling. Still, maybe it's right after all," she conceded with a slight frown. "There's always a hint of sadness about her, even on her sunniest days."

Dear God! Now he understood his grandmother's insistence on "Miss Moore" as the perfect governess for Lucinda. Now he understood her suggestion that he begin his painstaking searches in Scotland, visit Lucinda whenever he could. Now he understood the old lady's recommendation that he fetch Lucinda home personally, and interview the elusive Miss Moore for the post of governess while he was at it—a recommendation so strong as to constitute a command.

Lady Charlotte must have promised Marianne she'd not reveal her whereabouts, and she hadn't! Oh, no—she was cleverer than that. She'd told him nothing—precisely nothing! She left him to tear about all of England like a demented dervish, whirling thither and yon to no effect, but always she had persisted: Miss Moore. Miss Moore. Miss Moore. The name had become a despised litany in their often acerbic confrontations. He should have realized! She'd done everything but draw him a map, and Lucinda had provided that. But, blind idiot that he was, he hadn't seen it!

"Is something wrong, Papa?" Lucinda broke in on his roiling thoughts. "I painted this for you because I thought you'd find Miss Moore's face interesting. Of course, she doesn't know about it. Somehow I don't believe she'd've approved, for she tore up the one preliminary sketch she found and forbade me most strictly to make another. I've had to hide this for weeks."

"Oh, I find her face *most* interesting! Did anyone suggest her to you as a subject?" he asked, further suspicions dawning.

"Why, yes—Great-Grandmama. She said you should at least know what my Miss Moore looked like if you never succeeded in meeting her. Great-Grandmama said then you might understand why I love her so dearly. She said it should be a gift, after we departed Broward. I've another for you as well, one of the moors, which you may like better. Here—let me show you."

Lucinda reached for the stack of watercolors and sketches.

"No!" Connard almost snarled. "Leave it!"

"Papa? What's wrong?"

"God bless all mothers everywhere," the viscount whispered in the tone of a prayer, "and most especially, may God bless all grandmothers, most particularly my own!" He sprang to his feet, knocking his head against the low roof, pounded on the trapdoor, paintings and portfolio tumbling to the floor, Miss Moore's likeness clutched in his hand. The trapdoor popped open. "Turn this contraption around!" he ordered. "Spring 'em, John—as much as you can on this pernicious lane! Stop at the bottom of the hill just before you get to that damned school, and remain hidden. I don't want anyone to know we've returned."

"Papa?" Lucinda broke in fearfully as he sank back on the seat next to her. "Papa, are you all right? You're not angry, are you?"

"Angry? No, not that! I've never been better in my life, I hope," Connard reassured his daughter. "Don't worry, sweetheart," he said more gently, pulling her against his side as the abigail gathered up the fallen papers, "I've some rough ground to get over in a few moments, but get over it I will. And then? And then I'll present you with a miracle! I swear it. I've not come this far to be denied. . . ."

Minutes later he was easing from stunted tree to twisted shrub as droplets of condensed mist trickled down his neck. The gray stone school stood silent and forbidding behind its walls, a fortress whose slick roof slates glistened with moisture. There were no lights in the windows. Only the merest thread of smoke twined from the chimney that served the fireplace in Miss Broward's private parlor.

He edged past the leaden tarn, immaculate Hessians sinking in the thick mud at its verge, greatcoat slapping impatiently at his calves, livid green knitted scarf wound high on his neck.

He slipped through the rear gates and past the stables, eyes wary. Not for nothing had he studied methods of infiltrating enemy encampments, discussed them with experienced troopers as well as fellow officers. He eased his way around the grim building, ignoring the main door with its menacing dark porch as he sought some more private way into what he assumed, given a fair knowledge of such places, would be a labyrinth of twisted passageways and tortuous stairs. Nor was he disappointed.

The narrow corridors were dark, the few lamps unlit. The air was dank, foul with odors of must and mildew, the faint effluvia of old cabbage and older mutton. And Lucinda had spent the majority of her days in this godforsaken place! Here Marianne's sparkle had been dimmed to a faint glow. Yes, he could see why his grandmother insisted he view it for himself. Were he not now accidentally seeing more than was permitted the casual visitor, he might have concluded Lucinda unwittingly exaggerated the place's discomforts, given the cozy comfort of the parlor.

He threw cursory glances into room after room, taking care to move swiftly and silently. At last he had his reward: the sight of an overly slender woman packing away books and slates, her graceful figure garbed in bombazine, her glorious chestnut hair skimmed severely back. As she worked, tears streamed unchecked down her face. From time to time she brushed at them impatiently, as if they signaled a weakness she dared not admit, totally unaware she was observed.

Connard waited for her to notice him until he could bear it no longer. Then, diffidently, hat in hand, he softly said his wife's name. She gave an immense shudder, breath catching on a sob. Then she turned in the indifferent light, peering in disbelief at the powerful figure standing framed in the dark doorway.

"Oh, Lord, Marianne—I'm sorry," he said, gesturing to indicate their surroundings, voice breaking.

His wife shrugged. And then they simply stood there, staring at each other across an immense gulf, the years an almost insurmountable barrier, and the pain, and the anguish and the sorrow, their faces stark.

"You've done a wonderful job with her," he offered at last. "She's a total joy."

"Thank you. I'm glad you're pleased. It was, after all, what I was paid to do."

"Marianne!" he protested, taking a tentative step into the dismal room.

"Well, it was," she returned defensively, retreating an equivalent step. "I was paid. Not much, but I was paid. D'you have any idea how demeaning it was—to accept money for caring for my own child?"

"I'm sorry," he repeated.

"Sorry! You're sorry? Is that all you can say?"

He spread his hands helplessly. "How could you bear to see her leave?" he asked.

"I couldn't," her voice came to him in the icy air, "but I had no choice, had I, Ned. You gave me none. She would've been gone in a few years in any case. This way she went to a far brighter future than any I could offer." She paused, then asked, "How did you know."

"She's quite a talented little artist," he replied with the trace of a smile.

Was Connard able to keep his promise to his daughter?

Oh, yes—Lucinda had her miracle, and if the ground was far rougher than he had anticipated, though not half so rough as Marianne Connardsleigh felt he deserved, that was between the two of them. Suffice it to say that an hour after the carriage pulled to a halt at the bottom of the hill, the potboy from the academy kitchens panted up to inform John Coachman he was to proceed forthwith to Broward House, where the viscount and an additional passenger—and a small pile of bundles—awaited him. The dignified Stubbs gave a most undignified (and highly joyful) shout, and the chaise lurched forward with all the speed John Coachman could muster.

Lucinda—after the initial shock wore off—spent her days and nights with a joyful smile gracing her features and a hint of concern lurking in her eyes. There were moments when she reached out to touch her parents—at the table, on a walk, in her father's study—as if to reassure herself of their reality. And, she was—for a time—so perfectly behaved that it was as if she feared the slightest infraction of accepted social norms would cause them to first frown upon her, then vanish. That, with considerable encouragement on both their parts, wore off.

Artie was ecstatic over the return of his well-remembered sister-in-law. Never would there be enough he could do for her, never enough times in the day he could make her feel welcome, the focus of their happiness and peace. The nightmare of the past years was that only, he assured her constantly in his rather bumbling way—a nightmare best forgotten or, at the very least, ignored as meaningless.

Lady Charlotte penned a triumphant—and puckish—letter to her friend Lady Daphne, relating all the details of her success to which she was privy, and inventing those few to which she was not. Being an astute observer of the human condition, her invented details were almost as accurate as those she knew for a fact, even to the exact number of minutes that passed between the time Connard entered the dark and chilly classroom where Marianne was stoically packing books away as tears slid down her face and the instant when she found herself in his arms.

Her second letter—to Adelle in Bath—was entirely different in tone and content, though equally entertaining. As an exercise in the fine art of the cut, it was a masterpiece. As a foray into the realms of slash and parry, it exceeded even that.

Eighteen months after the reunion of father, mother, and daughter, a tiny squalling bundle made its appearance at Connard Manor—to the immense relief of Artie, and the great joy of all concerned. The dreaded and longed-for direct heir had arrived.

Rawdon, by then himself wed and determinedly incommunicado with his spirited bride, yet found time for a brief visit to Connard Manor to inspect both returned wife—whom he found charming when he met her in the winter of '99—and thriving infant: John (after his maternal grandfather) Garvin (after his paternal grandfather) Ulysses (after the Greek hero, in honor of his wife's steadfast virtue at Lucinda's suggestion, and in tribute to her beloved mother and preceptress, "Miss Moore") Connardsleigh. The heir, Rawdon declared, had excellent lungs suitable to the parade ground, though his flailing fists lacked science. Some lessons with the redoubtable Gentleman Jackson would not be amiss when the time came. He would stand the nonsense.

As for the twin portraits, they held pride of place in the manor's family parlor, their legend of reconciliation passed down through the generations. Marianne never relinquished the earlier purloined watercolor of Ned Connardsleigh until, upon her death, she willed it to Lucinda's youngest daughter. Slightly faded now, it hangs in a white clapboard house set deep in the rolling Connecticut farmland of the former Colonies, its chimneys black-banded in mourning for the fateful rebellion of '76.

The likeness of Connard's mother was returned to the manor's small gallery, where it still hangs, beside it Lucinda's crude self-portrait framed in shells, the startling resemblance between the two girls clear to any viewer.

And the miniature Connard carried throughout his despairing search for his lost wife? Artie recieved that—but only upon Connard's death—and, in time, to each eldest son of eldest son of those who followed him. It disappeared at Verdun. Artie always claimed it was the most valuable gift his brother ever gave him.

As Ned Connardsleigh said when he found his heart's desire within reach, God bless all mothers everywhere—and most particularly overly observant, overly astute, determinedly interfering, pestilential aged grandmothers. . . .

And the young buck whose appearance Connard so dreaded? Oh, he came, hair gleaming in the sun, and saw, and was conquered—but that is another tale for another day, as are the fates of Emily and Sarah, who did not become superior domestics.

Gillian's Secret

by
Violet Hamilton

"Just what do you think you are doing, Sybil?" Gillian inquired. Having decided not to accompany some of her classmates on a nature walk, she had returned unexpectedly to her room at Miss Marchison's Academy to catch her cousin rooting through her dresser.

Sybil, having been startled, whirled to face her accuser. If she was discomfited at being discovered in such a shoddy undertaking, she was not prepared to admit it.

"I was looking for letters to you from Sir Richard Willmot," she said defiantly, although her eyes shifted beneath Gillian's scornful gaze. Her only sign of embarrassment was a slight flush that spread over her lightly freckled cheeks, but that might have been due to frustration rather than guilt. Sybil rarely accepted blame for her reprehensible actions.

Sybil Milford might have been an attractive girl, or at least presentable. She had the titian hair and hazel eyes that went with her freckles, but her jealous and spiteful nature was patently evident in her mean, tight mouth and glowering expression. She viewed life with a jaundiced air that spoiled most of her relationships. Both her classmates at Miss Marchison's and the dancing partners presented to her at Bath's assemblies found her unappealing, even repellent.

Unwilling to accept any responsibility for her unpopularity, she blamed her cousin, whom she often accused of being filled with the envy that was her own daily companion. Gillian could easily be the object of envy. She was a lovely girl with gold curls that tumbled artlessly about a pointed face accented by unusual green eyes, and she possessed an elegant figure, dressed today in a smart bottle-green and cream merino redingote.

But it was not just her handsome appearance that attracted both young men and her schoolmates. Despite a determined chin that warned she had a temper and a willfulness that could lead to trouble, she had an infectious optimistic view of life that made her fascinating company. Her unfortunate cousin, who suffered from comparison, blamed her own unpopularity on her cousin and had done so since the two girls were in leading strings.

"If Sir Richard had written to me, I cannot see why that is any concern of yours, Sybil," Gillian reproved with unusual sharpness. Normally she accepted her cousin's mean-spirited ways with a patient tolerance, but this intrusion had roused her temper. Her contempt showed plainly, for Gillian had never learned to dissemble.

Challenged, Sybil was not prepared to admit her mistake and instead rushed into attack, a common ploy when she was discovered. "Oh, don't be so prosy. You always behave with such propriety, but I know you would really like to scratch my eyes out." She spat out the words. "You know I liked Sir Richard. I met him first and he was most attracted. Then, of course, you did your best to annex him, just to spite me."

Gillian sighed. This was an old argument, but this time she was not prepared to ignore Sybil's nastiness. "I did no such thing. In fact, I thought him a dead bore, much too puffed up with his own consequence and a dandified fop besides. You are welcome to him. But that does not justify your sneaking in here when my back was turned to go through my possessions on the off chance he might have written. I doubt if Sir Richard is capable of penning a billet doux anyway. Really, Sybil, you would try anyone's patience with your foolish, spiteful ways," Gillian laughed, the absurdity of the situation overcoming her initial anger.

Sybil, infuriated rather than relieved at her cousin's reaction, was beyond any sensible response or apology. A lifetime of imagined slights rose to exacerbate feelings that, at best, were never far from bitter. She launched into an intemperate tirade.

"You think you are so perfect. You have fooled Miss Marchison, all these silly girls, even Mother and Father into believing you are some sort of paragon. And now when we are about to leave this stupid school you will have a wider field in which to exercise your spells, on Sir Richard and all the other men back home. If any of these besotted fools knew what you really were, what your true background was, they would turn away from you in disgust." Sybil's face was mottled with rage.

Gillian looked at her cousin in stupefaction, her initial irritation fading under Sybil's attack. Was her cousin just wildly hitting out at her because she had been caught spying, or was there some other motive? Gillian sensed that beneath the triumphant spite in Sybil's tone there was an allusion to some mystery that concerned her.

"What do you mean, Sybil? As far as I know, I am not guilty of any grievous behavior. In fact, you appear to be the perpetrator and I the victim," she countered calmly.

"If I told what I really know about you, about your mother, you would be banned from any decent household, expelled from this school, and would receive no proposals from eligible men but the most scandalous ones, all of which you deserve. Why the parents sheltered you I cannot imagine."

"My mother—why, she's been dead for years," Gillian answered, bewildered by this vicious assault prompted by some maggot in Sybil's confused head. She closed the door quietly behind her and crossed the room to confront Sybil, who, arms akimbo, faced her accuser without any sense of shame.

"No, she hasn't. She's very much alive and living under the protection of some nobleman in London. She comes to see you occasionally, posing as our aunt Laura." Sybil blurted out the tale, then retreated before Gillian's stern expression. She was beginning to wish she had held her tongue, but Gillian had roused her never equable temper. She justified her actions by thinking that eventually Gillian must have learned the truth. Any man who proposed to her and was accepted would have to know the truth, and then he would not be so eager to wed her, Sybil decided viciously. Now Gillian would have to abandon that infuriating superior attitude. She was, after all, the daughter of a demimondaine, a member of the muslin company. Sybil faced her cousin, expecting to see mortification, shame, unhappiness, normal reactions when facing such a scandalous tale. But to her bemusement, Gillian only looked thoughtful, not shocked at this disturbing account of her background, which if true would alter her whole life.

"And how did you learn of this interesting information, Sybil?" Gillian asked calmly, watching her cousin with an expression that made that young woman extremely uneasy.

"I just happened to hear Mother and Father discussing it. I think for some time they have been regretting taking you on and raising us together, Mother especially, but Father has always admired your mother and insisted. He reminded Mother that they had not borne the cost. I suspect that noble lord paid for it all, the price of his lust, you might say. Disgusting, I call it. Miss Marchison would have you out in the street in two minutes if she knew the truth," Sybil insisted, a bit tentative now. She was not sure what she had expected, but Gillian's calm reception of this attack on her mother's reputation confused her.

"You really are an odious little toad, Sybil. It's only to be expected that an eavesdropper, a sneak, and a foolish ninny such as you are should be rejected by everyone. If you are so eager to see the last of me, I recommend you run immediately to Miss Marchison with your scurrilous story," Gillian suggested in steely tones. Opening the door of her room, she looked at her cousin with disgust. "Get out, Sybil, before I scratch your eyes out, and you are not worth my dirtying my hands on, you miserable, mean little spy." She did not raise her voice, but some quality in her tone frightened Sybil just the same. She was already regretting what she had done and would have made some cringing attempt to repair the damage if she had thought it would be accepted. But Gillian's whole demeanor rejected any appeal. This time Sybil had gone too far. She scuttled though the door without another word.

Gillian, alone, threw herself down on the window seat and gazed out on the familiar sedate Bath avenue, seeing nothing. Despite her words to Sybil, for some reason she did not doubt the other girl's words. For years, since she had been old enough to notice, she had sensed something unusual in her situation. Her aunt and uncle had explained carefully that her mother had married a Captain Cyril Strange against her parents' wishes, eloped with the officer to Gretna Green, and then had been disowned. She had died giving birth to Gillian after Captain Strange had deserted her once he found her pregnant and without the parental allowance he had relied upon. Sybil's parents had taken in the orphaned baby. Aunt Laura, who made periodic visits to the Milford home, had been accepted as yet another sister, a widow of comfortable means who lived mostly abroad. Now this fiction had been revealed for what it was, a convenient story to protect Gillian. For some reason she was inclined to believe her cousin's mean-spirited tale. Certainly Sybil was not clever enough to invent such an implausible account, and she was certainly capable of eavesdropping on her parents' private conversation. But Sybil's actions and motives were not important. What Gillian must do was contact Aunt Laura, "Mrs. Strange," and learn the truth. Not for a moment did Gillian believe she had heard the real story of her birth and her mother's subsequent life.

She had often wondered, growing up in the Milford household, why Sybil disliked her so. Although both Mr. and Mrs. Milford, Uncle Robert and Aunt Elizabeth, had always treated Gillian kindly and fairly, their first affection had naturally been given to their only child, their own daughter. Gillian had never resented coming second to her cousin. What she found so puzzling was her cousin's jealousy. Of a generous if impulsive nature herself, she made friends easily and until events proved otherwise trusted and liked most people. Sybil, with little cause, viewed life morosely, believing the worst and quite often finding it. Gillian had long ago given up any attempt to change her cousin's attitude or to soften her feelings toward herself. She just accepted that Sybil resented and disliked her. And she could even understand, if she could not condone, her cousin's reasons. Having to share her parents' attention and affection was unacceptable to Sybil. But now Gillian had reached the end of her tolerance toward her cousin. If indeed even half of Sybil's tale was true, Gillian must discover what really lay beyond her accusations.

Looking back on her association with her "Aunt Laura," she could see some basis for Sybil's account. Gillian had memories of a lovely fair-haired lady of quiet manner and the rare ability to treat a child as a person, respecting her views and never acting condescending or impatient. If Mrs. Strange was her mother, Gillian could feel only a certain relief, a gratitude, that certain questions she had sensed about her background would now be answered.

Of course, she could confront the Milfords and demand the truth, but somehow she sensed they would turn off any inquiries and insist that Sybil had mistaken what she had heard. Gillian decided that her task now was to discover for herself if Sybil's angry accusation was based on fact. That "Aunt Laura" was the mistress of a nobleman should have shocked Gillian, but she found she was more intrigued than appalled. She must find Laura Strange and ask her if she was really her mother. Somehow Gillian felt Laura Strange would not lie to her. But how was she to discover the lady's whereabouts? All she knew was that she lived in London. Could she force Sybil to divulge an address? Then she remembered that "Aunt Laura" had sent her a banker's draft for her recent eighteenth birthday. Fortunately, she still had much of her quarter's allowance and with "Aunt Laura's" generous gift she could afford to travel to London and seek out the banker who might tell Gillian "Aunt Laura's" direction. She had been planning to buy some expensive sarsenet and having a modiste design a new dress for her leave-taking ceremonies at school. But she no longer needed the dress, as she would not be present for the final days of school. No time must be lost in reaching London. Turning out the drawers Sybil had left in such disarray, she discovered "Aunt Laura's" birthday letter and the banker's draft. No address was included, but Sybil must be forced to divulge more information. Surely her eavesdropping and spying must have produced some clues as to Mrs. Strange's home. Gillian had no compunction in persuading her cousin to tell her what she needed to know. Setting her chin firmly, and with a fighting gleam in her eye, she set out to do battle.

The jolting movement of the coach, tightly packed with passengers, was proving more of a trial than Gillian had expected. She had never traveled by public stage before and, at first, had found the experience rather exciting. But now the novelty had worn off and impatience was warring with fatigue as the coach rumbled on at what she thought was a slow pace.

On boarding the coach in Bath, she had been eyed with curiosity by the other passengers. They were a mixed group including a timid middle-aged governess journeying to a new post, a buxom farmer's wife and her small daughter returning from a visit to relatives, and a flashy man with a bold glance and his seedy companion. All of them were eager to explain their own reasons for the trip, and she had adroitly turned away their questions by asking about their own plans. She had heard a great deal from the farmer's wife about the perils of a young woman traveling alone, buttressed by quiet agreement from the governess and some innuendo from the flashy man.

They had been closeted together now for four hours and

soon must be nearing the posting inn where they would stop
for the night. Whatever perils awaited her there she would,
at least, have a chance to stretch her legs and satisfy her
hunger. She had not really grasped the difficulties of traveling
without her abigail or protection by relatives. Her only journeys from the Devon village where the Milfords lived and
where she had grown up had been carefully planned and supervised. However, if she felt any apprehension in facing the
dangers of London alone, she refused to surrender to such
cowardice. Surely she was resourceful enough to manage.
She comforted herself with the knowledge of how cleverly
she had eluded both faculty and classmates and wondered if
the note she had left had thrown Miss Marchison into spasms.
Very unlikely. Probably that poised and proper lady had decided to wash her hands of such a disreputable pupil who
had behaved with total disregard of her teachings.

Gillian noticed, with relief, that at last the stage appeared
to be slowing in preparation for the evening stopover. There
were several murmurs of satisfaction from the other passengers, who gathered their possessions and prepared to enjoy
the amenities of the inn after the wearing trip. Stiffly the
governess and farmer's wife descended from the coach, followed by the little girl and Gillian, who decided she would
be wise to cling closely to these two respectable ladies. The
yard of the posting inn, the Blue Heron, was crowded with
hostlers and drivers and several private vehicles demanding
attention. Gillian averted her eyes, not wanting to assume the
aspect of a bold female open to any stray gentleman's attentions, but she was aware of a tall, fashionably dressed man
who glanced at her with insolent assurance as she scurried
into the inn. She should have guessed that traveling alone
might expose her to embarrassing approaches, but she was
determined not to give in to missish fears.

The Blue Heron's host, a jovial, bustling man with a fringe
of grizzled hair ringing his bald, shiny head, and a noticeable
embonpoint, hurried to welcome his guests.

"Good evening, good evening. All is in readiness for you, but I must warn you we are quite crowded this evening, and you might find your meal delayed," he said with self-importance, intent on impressing them with his inn's popularity.

Gillian, who would have liked a private parlor, was hesitant to mention this amenity, always enjoyed on past journeys.

"Can we go to our rooms now, landlord?" the farmer's wife asked, not impressed with the man's jollity or excuses.

"Of course, of course. But you ladies will have to share, as we are fully booked and I can offer only two rooms. A toff arrived and bespoke our best rooms and parlor," he explained with some pride.

Gillian wondered idly if that was the gentleman she had glimpsed in the yard. Well, he was no concern of hers. Having considered the possibility of having to share a room, she chose the governess, thinking this companion would repel any unwanted liberties. If the landlord viewed her with more than passing interest, wondering what a female of her obvious quality was doing traveling unaccompanied on a public stage, and he made no reference to her situation beyond a rather unpleasing leer. She managed to ignore him and trailed after the governess and chambermaid to the assigned room, eager to escape any more scrutiny.

Once inside the bedroom she looked about and to her relief found the appointments clean and neat. She turned to her companion and said pleasantly, "I do hope you will find me an acceptable roommate. We must introduce ourselves. I am afraid I did not catch your name on the coach. I am Gillian Strange."

"Miss Evans," came the brief reply. Obviously Miss Evans had some suspicions about Gillian, but was too polite to voice them.

Miss Evans looked exactly what she was, Gillian thought, a governess who had spent too many years in other people's houses, teaching children not her own, and enduring the slights and condescension such women must suffer for shelter and a certain defined position. Miss Evans's years of endurance showed in her drawn, pale face. She was dressed in a dull brown serviceable merino gown buttoned securely to the neck her scant brown hair drawn into a tight bun that emphasized her plainness. Gillian felt every compassion for her with the passing wonder of the young who could not envisage such a life.

"I do hope this inn will not be filled with rowdy, noisy young men. I am not feeling at all the thing, and I must get some rest. I am already late in taking up my next post with Lord and Lady Ayleston, and must be in good part when I arrive," Miss Evans explained with some pride at the connection with this noble family. But Gillian noticed she looked increasingly pale and could barely stand upright.

"I am sorry. Do lie down and perhaps I can find you a cup of tea," Gillian suggested kindly, touched with compassion for the woman's condition.

"That would be most agreeable." Miss Evans sighed and sat down heavily on the bed. "I really feel most unwell. The jolting of the coach, I suspect."

Gillian, increasingly concerned, decided she must try to help but was not exactly sure of how to summon aid. There was no bell push on the wall, and she shrank from descending to the main salon and facing the company she knew to be assembled there. Looking at Miss Evans's ashen face, she chided herself for her timidity. She must make some effort to alleviate the poor woman's distress.

Gillian began to realize that her impulsive decision to set out in search of her supposed mother might expose her to situations she was not experienced to handle. Well, there was nothing for it. She was committed now and must just plunge ahead, no matter what happened.

"I will see what I can do, Miss Evans," she said with more assurance than she felt but alarmed at the governess's moan of acknowledgment and distress.

Gillian opened the door of their room and peeked out into

the hallway. It appeared deserted, so she slipped forth and walked to the stairs, hoping to find a maid who could supply her with tea, and perhaps some restorative for Miss Evans. But no servant or guest was in sight. Determined, she marched down the stairs. The main salon of the inn seemed crowded with men, all drinking and talking in loud voices, a scene to daunt the most resolute of females. She hesitated, looking in vain for the landlord or a servant. Although she thought her entrance had excited no interest, to her dismay the flashy gentleman who had been her fellow passenger on the coach looked up and ran a bold and assessing gaze over her in a manner she found most insulting.

"Oh, Jakes," he indicated to his companion, "our fair companion has decided to join us. Mustn't disappoint the lady." He leered and crossed the room to put an encroaching hand on her arm. "Come, my dear, let us buy you a dram."

Gillian smiled weakly, not knowing how to refuse the man, and tried vainly to shake off his hand, aware that every eye in the room was now trained upon her with various expressions, none of which she found reassuring.

"No, thank you, sir. I was hoping to order some tea to be served in my room. Miss Evans, who was in the coach with us, seems ill and needs a restorative," she explained as she struggled to escape.

At close quarters she was uneasily conscious of his appraising eyes and an unpleasant aroma of sweat, unwashed linen, and a reek of ale. His close-set, watery blue eyes assessed her in a manner she thought overfamiliar.

"I applaud your good intentions, my dear, but surely the poor lady can wait a few moments while we get acquainted. Come, sit down and tell us all about yourself," he urged smiling in what Gillian thought an oily fashion and not surrendering his tight clasp on her arm.

She looked about wildly but saw no rescue from this intolerable situation. Still, she would not submit to his advances without a struggle. "I am afraid I must insist on completing my errand, sir. If you would release me," she protested, tugging away from him. Turning to escape, she was appalled to find him barring her way.

"Too good for our company, are you. Well, you will not find us ungenerous, my fine lady. Jim Penny and Bill Jakes know how to reward a fancy piece if she pleases us."

Gillian began to feel real fear that he would create a scene. "I do not like either your implication or your manners, sir. Release me at once. You are mistaken if you think I was seeking your company."

But Jim Penny, flown with ale and convinced of his own powers to charm, was not so easily dissuaded. A flush of anger unwisely prompted him to continue his assault.

"Now, see here, my fine madam, if you are such a respectable lady, what are you doing traveling on a stage with us common folk and giving yourself airs when you're no better than you should be?"

"He has a point, you know," drawled a gentleman in a bored, well-bred tone, who had suddenly appeared. "However, my good chap, I think you must abandon any fell desire on this lady's virtue. She finds you not to her taste." And he reached languidly across Gillian and plucked Mr. Penny's hand from her arm without any effort.

Grateful though she was for the stranger's intervention, Gillian did not appreciate his arrogant and patronizing attitude nor his allusion to her unprotected state. Nor did she appreciate his casual assessment of her. His hard, dark eyes ran over her with an expertise as insulting as that of her former accoster.

"Sorry, governor, if I had known a toff like you had an interest, I wouldn't have chanced my luck, but she is a pretty piece, and well worth some trouble." Jim Penny winked and backed away to join his friend at the fireside. He had not liked the look in the toff's eye, and had no intention of challenging him no matter how enticing the goods.

Gillian, both affronted and relieved, faced her rescuer with conflicting emotions. He must be the "toff" the landlord mentioned. This, however, did not reassure her. Obviously a gentleman, he wore a dark superfine riding coat cut by a master, cream Kersey britches, and shining boots. His dark hair cut unfashionably short and his tanned face and well-muscled figure proclaimed him a sportsman, a Corinthian, still some years under thirty. But his most disturbing feature were his eyes, black, knowing, and unwavering. Paying no heed to her unspoken question, he bowed mockingly. "Roderick Trehune, at your service, ma'am. My friends call me Rory." He waited expectantly as if implying that they would soon be on intimate terms. In his way he was equally disturbing as the regrettable Mr. Penny.

"Thank you, sir. You rescued me from an embarrassing situation. I cannot understand why that odious man believed I would welcome his attentions. I would never have ventured into this salon if I could have found a servant to bring some tea to my companion." Gillian did not give her name and offered her gratitude in her most haughty tone, hoping it would relieve her of his company. Feeling the amenities had been satisfied, she turned to leave. But Roderick Trehune was not so easily dismissed. He followed her to a door on the left, and before she could effect her retirement, opened it, ushering her through.

"I am sure that can be arranged more efficiently from this private parlor I have bespoke. Do join me," he urged.

Her protests unavailing, Gillian found herself alone with this dark stranger who seemed to feel he could command her obedience. She raised her chin, determined to take issue with his attitude, but before battle could be joined, he spoke soothingly.

"Now, don't rake me down. That would be cold thanks for my Good Samaritan deed. Sit down and let me get your tea. That will give you time to think up a scathing retort to any other outrageous suggestions I might offer."

Despite herself, Gillian felt a small smile struggling to

overcome her scruples and she subsided into the indicated chair, wondering at his power to compel her.

As if to set her fears at rest, Rory Trehune crossed to a bellpull and yanked it impatiently. Then he turned and in an amused tone said, "Of course, your admirer should have realized you are not one of the muslin company. I suspect you're a schoolgirl eloping to meet an elusive swain. It is obvious to me you have little experience of what a respectable female might encounter on such an adventure. But where is this fortunate man? Pretty shabby behavior toward such a charming girl, I think."

Before Gillian could answer the landlord himself appeared, all bustle and subservience, and received a curt order to provide both tea and Madeira. He bowed with compliance, impressed by Mr. Trehune, as Gillian herself was beginning to be. Belatedly remembering the ailing Miss Evans, she insisted that a tray be sent to the chamber she was sharing with the governess.

When the landlord had hurried away to see to their needs, Roderick Trehune sat down opposite Gillian, waiting for any explanation she might give him. Although she was grateful for his assistance, in some ways she found him more intimidating than Jim Penny. She must tell him some story if only to depress his interest. But before she could launch into any explanations, the tea arrived to delay any further conversation and Gillian busied herself with the pot while accepting the landlord's assurances that a similar tray had been sent to Miss Evans.

Roderick Trehune dismissed the man with a negligent wave of his hand, poured himself a glass of wine, and leaned back in his chair, running a speculative eye over his companion, which she found most annoying. Experienced as he was in assessing female charms, he was not easily deceived. She was certainly no lightskirt but just as certainly a dissembler prepared to spin him some tale. No matter what her reason, and he doubted he would hear the real one, by traveling unaccompanied she had exposed herself to whatever indignities she might encounter. It would be amusing to expose her, but for the moment he would play along with her charade.

"Since I have rescued you from that rather crass man with the execrable taste in cravats who could not possibly appreciate you, and ordered your tea, I do believe you might tell me your name, even if it is an assumed one," he said sardonically.

"Yes, most rude of me. I am Gillian Strange," she replied dulcetly, ignoring his jibe, too busy concentrating on assembling the story she would offer to explain her situation to notice his quickly masked expression of surprise.

"And why is the lovely Miss Strange fleeing from her normal surroundings and natural protectors, exposing herself to insult and worse by her escapade?" he asked.

Gillian knew she must keep her explanation as simple as possible. However, she was a bit piqued that this haughty stranger felt he could demand information. Smiling deceptively, she put on her most demure expression, hoping Roderick Trehune would be gulled by her story.

"I know it looks most peculiar that I should be traveling alone, and normally I would not consider such untoward behavior, but I was really quite desperate," she offered, adopting a wistful guise.

"My uncle and aunt, who are my guardians, are pressing me to accept a quite repulsive friend of theirs as a husband. It has something to do with my inheritance. I thought if I could reach my only other relation, Aunt Laura Strange in London, she might use her influence to dissuade them. Most reckless and rash of me, but I am afraid I had no other recourse." She adopted a pose of innocence and lowered her eyes, not aware that Roderick had heard the name Laura Strange with a frown.

He was convinced that her story was a hum, but for reasons of his own, Roderick Trehune was prepared to pretend he accepted it.

"I quite see your dilemma, and I might be prevailed upon to help you. I am returning to London myself, having had a rather irritating journey to Bath, and am eager to reach town. I am sure that if you consent to complete your journey in my coach, you will be far more comfortable than in the stage, and will be spared Mr. Penny," he said. The mysterious Miss Strange had not told him the truth, but she had roused his interest. How would she deal with his idea which in its way offered as many perils as a ride on the stage?

"That is very kind of you, Mr. Trehune, but perhaps I would only be escaping one unpleasantness to find myself in an equally equivocal position," Gillian protested with a wicked grin.

Not so stupid, the deceptive Miss Strange. Awake on all suits. Well, there was nothing for it but to put on his most disarming manner, for Rory Trehune found himself very eager to pursue this acquaintance.

"You have my promise that you will be as safe in my coach as in church, Miss Strange. But perhaps we might discuss the matter more fully over dinner, if you would be my guest."

Gillian wrinkled her brow as if deciding whether she should commit herself so far. She looked over Rory with a considering air he found most endearing.

Nodding her head as if she had made up her mind, she accepted. "I would be pleased, sir, but first I must see how poor Miss Evans is faring. She really feels ill and I do want to help her." She rose on the words as if the interview was concluded. Rory had no option but to stand and open the door for her politely. He wondered a bit at her secretive smile as she thanked him again and made her way upstairs. Watching her trim figure with approval, he thought, "Now, what maggot does she have in her brain? I don't doubt she has hatched some plan." Returning to the parlor, he picked up his glass and toyed idly with the wine, then threw down the contents of the glass with resolution. Whatever her idea, he ⁝ nded to be more than a match for her. Then he rose to ring again for the landlord and order the best dinner this hostelry could provide.

After ordering the best repast the inn could manage, and conferring with his coachman as to the welfare of his horses, Roderick stretched his long length in an armchair before the fire and turned his thoughts again to the enigmatic Miss Strange.

Surely it was more than coincidence that her "Aunt Laura" answered to the same name as that of a lovely lady who played a role in his own life. If it were indeed the case that Laura Strange was Gillian's mother, not her aunt, that relationship altered several aspects of their relationship. But it did not alter his intention to make Gillian his mistress, he decided. After all, it would be to her benefit. What other fate awaited her? As the daughter of a demimondaine, even one at the top of the trees, she could hardly be hanging out for a respectable husband. Still, he would have to tread carefully. He had no illusions about Miss Strange's obduracy. But she was certainly worth some trouble, for she offered a challenge that would tax his skills.

Experienced in dealing with the muslin set, Roderick knew that Gillian would not respond to the usual lures—a handsome allowance, an elegant establishment, her own horse and carriage, expensive jewelry. No, he suspected he must rely on different attributes, mainly his own charms, and he was confident enough of those to promise himself success. He had accomplished his conquests in the past without lightening his purse too drastically. Since coming on the town some years before, rarely had he suffered a rebuff from the ladies, neither Cyprians, debutantes, nor matrons. That his seduction of Gillian might cause her unhappiness and ruin her chances did not bother him. If she were truly virtuous, and he had his doubts as to that, she would refuse him. He must appeal to her sensibilities, arouse her dormant sensuality that he felt lay beneath her proper exterior. He held no compunction in applying these methods. In the game of love he meant to be the winner.

If Gillian had not read Roderick Trehune's full intentions, she had a good suspicion of what he intended toward her. She would take advantage of his interest while avoiding any commitment, she decided blithely. That young man was much too sure of his appeal. A setdown would improve his character.

On reaching her bedchamber she was relieved to see Miss Evans sitting up and sipping her tea, a little color seeping into her gray face. She looked up and greeted Gillian with a slight smile. "I am most grateful for your thoughtfulness. This tea is just what I needed."

Gillian suspected that Miss Evans had become inured to her occasional discomforts, to being ignored by her various employees unless she behaved badly. Governesses led wretched lives, Gillian thought, barely tolerated by their charges' parents and scorned below stairs with little recourse if they complained about shabby treatment.

"I am happy to see you have recovered from your indisposition, for I am going to prevail on your own kindness," Gillian said in her sweetest tones. "Do let me explain." As she set out her plan that depended on Miss Evans's cooperation, she chose her words carefully. After all, the governess knew little of her. She might be shocked by her boldness and raise several objections. But Gillian believed she could deal with those, and so it proved.

"You are quite correct to take protective measures when it comes to gentlemen, my dear. They are not to be trusted. In my younger years, although you might doubt it to see me now, I was not unpleasing. In my first post, which I took upon my father's death—he was a vicar in a Shropshire parish—I had great difficulty in depressing the attentions of the son of the house. To my dismay, his mother blamed me for attracting him and dismissed me summarily. He made no attempt to come to my defense. It was a bitter lesson but it served me well, and I have been very circumspect in my future dealings, believe me," Miss Evans explained dryly without any attempt to seek comfort.

Rather touched by this confidence, Gillian nodded in sympathy. She could well believe it. And now in middle age Miss Evans could expect only eventual retirement in straightened circumstances after years of coping with other women's children, unless she was fortunate enough to be pensioned off by some grateful parent. If it turned out that Gillian was indeed the daughter of a nobleman's mistress, she might easily face such a future herself. Gillian had few illusions as to how the world would view her situation. In that she had to agree with Sybil.

"I will be happy to serve as your chaperon, Miss Strange, on the trip to London, and applaud your sensibility in making such an arrangement. I think we will both be quite comfortable," Miss Evans agreed with some animation. Gillian, amused, thought Miss Evans enjoyed the prospect of thwarting some young buck's attempt at seduction in retaliation for her own experiences. And so it was agreed. The two friends settled down for a comfortable coze. Not until much later did Gillian marvel at Miss Evans's tact at not asking her why she was making this trip. Was it just natural discretion, or had Miss Evans her own views on Gillian's motives and preferred not to air them?

Whatever Miss Evans's opinions on Gillian's situation she thought it best to refuse an invitation to join Roderick Trehune and Gillian for dinner. Despite the tea and the comforting talk, she admitted she still did not feel quite herself. Gillian promised to have a light repast delivered to the room for her and listened patiently to warnings about what she might expect at the coming tête-à-tête. Miss Evans believed Gillian would be wiser to avoid the dinner, she sensed, but was reluctant to stress the impropriety of the matter.

"Don't worry, Miss Evans. I can handle Mr. Trehune. Unlike our crude traveling companions, he is a more subtle operator. No doubt he has the same intentions, but he will choose his time after he has flattered and cajoled me. However, I am not the gullible little fool he expects. I intend to make use of Mr. Trehune and then go on my way," she informed Miss Evans blithely. If that poor woman wondered if Gillian was possibly being too sanguine, she admired her youthful confidence. And she realized she was both too ill and too tired to mount a proper protest or warning against Gillian's course of action.

Tidying her hair and washing her hands and face, Gillian prepared to join Mr. Trehune in his private parlor. As Miss Evans watched her preparations, she thought wistfully that Gillian Strange in both character and temperament was far more capable of coping with the Roderick Trehunes of the world than she had ever been. And far more appealing, Miss Evans conceded, in her cerulean and cream traveling dress that showed off her trim figure and accented her crop of gold curls. Really a lovely girl, in appearance and in character, Miss Evans thought as she lay back on the bed. A bit impetuous, but kind and intelligent. Not many girls with her assets would have taken so much trouble to aid an ailing middle-aged governess, Miss Evans thought humbly.

Thoughts of Miss Strange were being entertained in another part of the inn. But it was not her character that interested Rory Trehune, although he was prepared to deal with that troubling hindrance to his desires. An only son, indulged by a doting mother and a father proud of his heir, Rory could have developed into a spoiled, self-indulgent fop. That he had not was due to an innate self-discipline and an aptitude for sports—riding, driving, fencing, boxing—and he excelled in not a few of these gentlemanly arts. With the ladies, none of whom he took seriously, he had equal success. His father had been pressing him to marry, but Rory took little interest in respectable females. Finally, under his father's urging he had agreed to inspect a suitable prospect, Lavinia Alderston, and had traveled to Bath for that purpose. He had found her passably attractive but insipid, shallow, and simpering, too eager to please. No, he would have to look further, but perhaps not right away. He was more than intrigued by Gillian Strange. Strange in name and strange in nature, he thought idly. No doubt she had been raised in a respectable home and educated in a proper seminary, as there was nothing common in her manner or speech. But she had proved to be an adventuress, quick to seize an advantage when it was offered and not reluctant to dare behavior no proper young lady would consider. All the better for him. If he had any qualms about seducing a virtuous female, he soon stifled them. Considering her actions, her inclinations, and her undeniable beauty, eventually she would end up in some man's bed. It might as well be his, he decided, and if the relationship was not the legal one, it was not unusual. He was neither ungenerous nor brutal in his conduct with women. And he had rarely been refused when he made them an offer. Surely Gillian Strange would not be an exception. She just needed careful handling.

However, none of these rather cynical conclusions showed in his gallant manner when Gillian appeared for the supper he had ordered.

"You found Miss Evans recovered?" he asked, although he had given little thought to the woman.

"Somewhat. The tea has restored her. I am sure a good night's rest will complete the cure. I thought of asking her to dine with us, as it is really quite improper for me to do so alone, but I suspected you would not welcome her and she would sense your annoyance. I would not want her to suffer any slight," Gillian said demurely but with a wicked glint in her eye.

Rory barely suppressed a chuckle. Really, Miss Strange was quite acute, and not too easily gulled. More intrigued than ever, he set out to entertain and charm her with one view in mind, to get her into his bed, if not tonight, then soon. She would be vulnerable to persuasion when she discovered her mother's true profession, he concluded bitterly.

"What will you do when you reach London, Miss Strange?" he asked casually, implying that her answer was of little moment to him. He had watched her deal enthusiastically with dressed capon, several slices of York ham, creamed celery, and a compote of pears among other delicacies. Now she accepted with equal pleasure the walnuts he cracked for her.

"Well, I have a tentative address for my aunt Laura and will go there. I know she will take me in and answer my questions. She is a most delightful woman," Gillian advised, her attitude one of artless confidence. "I believe she lives in Montpelier Place."

Although knowing full well that was precisely where the mysterious Mrs. Strange resided, Rory was hard put to it to hide his reaction. From the beginning he had accepted that Gillian might be connected to Laura Strange. She had quite a look of her and he had not been at all deceived by Gillian's tale of "Aunt Laura," wicked guardians, and the spurious fiancé in the offing. If he had felt any qualms about luring this delightful girl from the path of virtue, this latest information had settled them.

"You should reach her by tomorrow evening if all goes well," he reassured her blandly with no hint that he had other plans intended for her.

"You are very kind to be so accommodating, Mr. Trehune. I could quite easily finish my journey by stage," Gillian threatened, wondering how he would deal with this suggestion. She had seen the flash of passion in his eyes several times over supper and as the evening wore on. While he did not appear to be drinking heavily, Gillian realized that gentlemen of his stamp were apt to abandon restraint after a generous intake. Somehow this neither frightened her nor disgusted her, although she was convinced this arrogant young man had only the most disreputable motives in offering to escort her to London. Still she could not help but be flattered, and if she were honest, admit she found him attractive.

"Since we are to be . . . er . . . traveling companions, could you not call me Rory. Mr. Trehune sounds so imposing. And might I not call you Gillian, a lovely name?"

"Why, of course, Rory. We must not stand on formality," Gillian agreed, only to realize the deception, the bantering, had gone on long enough. She must return to the safety of her chamber and the irreproachable Miss Evans before any further intimacies were proposed.

She rose and thanked Rory prettily for the supper. Stifling a desire to pull her into his arms and begin her initiation into pleasing a man, Rory accepted her gratitude with appropriate courtesy.

"I do wish you would stay a bit longer. We really seem to have a great deal to talk about," he pleaded. Perhaps he might still manage to satisfy some of his desire if she showed any inclination to linger.

"We will have all those hours on the road, so we must save some conversation for tomorrow," Gillian said, thinking that when Rory Trehune discovered how she had misled him, he would be more apt to rake her down than tamely exchange polite words. Thanking him again, with a saucy smile she bade him good night and tripped quickly up the stairs, aware that he was watching her the whole way.

Once inside her bedroom, she checked to make sure the door had a strong bolt, as it did. Surely Rory Trehune would not be so crude as to enter her chamber and try to seduce her under the eyes of Miss Evans, nor would Jim Penny make such an attempt after being rebuffed, but it never hurt to take precautions. That Gillian might eventually find it more difficult to guard her emotions against Rory's onslaughts was a factor she refused to consider.

After all the adventures of the day, she still managed to sleep well, with all youth's healthy ability to put worries behind her. That Miss Evans had a less happy night was evident the next morning when the two ladies made their preparations for breakfast.

"I wonder if you are really fit to travel," Gillian said, looking with some concern at Miss Evans's pale and drawn face.

"Of course I am. As soon as I have had some tea I will be in fine fig," the governess insisted with a pathetic attempt at lightness.

If Gillian had not been so intent on her own plans, she might have queried Miss Evans's attempt to reassure her, but her whole concentration was on the coming confrontation with Rory Trehune. She must carry off her introduction of Miss Evans on the ride with a combination of firmness and insouciance, a difficult task.

The two ladies breakfasted in their room, gathered their portmanteaus, and descended into the saloon, where they were met immediately by a smiling Rory.

"Good morning, Rory. I don't believe you have met Miss Evans, who has consented to travel with us to London. You must agree it will put matters on a more conformable footing." Gillian introduced her companion with more blitheness than she felt.

However, Rory was too much of a gentleman and too old a campaigner to be caught off balance. Whatever he thought, he welcomed Miss Evans with every courtesy and only inquired if they were both ready to embark.

With a suppressed sigh of relief, Gillian trailed meekly after Rory and the governess to the forecourt of the inn. She had settled her bill the night before, as had Miss Evans. Rory's coach was a comfortable one, and the ill-assorted trio settled back against the squabs as the coachman whipped up the horses. They were on their way.

For the first ten minutes or so there was no conversation. Gillian occupied herself by glancing resolutely out of the window and suppressing any desire to make excuses for including Miss Evans on their trip. She may have thwarted

Rory temporarily, but she was quite sure she had not permanently avoided any recriminations for her ruse.

Rory, both angry and amused, appeared completely at ease. He had to give the girl credit for a clever maneuver, he thought. In fact, her insistence on hiding behind the very proper Miss Evans had only whetted his appetite. Determined to quell any suspicion Gillian might have, he engaged Miss Evans in light conversation, asking her about her post and learning that she was going to join the Aylestons, with whom he had a slight acquaintance. He did not envy the governess her assignment, as Lady A. had a reputation as a Tartar, but of course he did not tell her that.

As they spoke, the coach tooled along at a fast pace, now beyond the town and onto the turnpike. They could not have been on the road more than an hour and a half, when suddenly the coach jolted to a sudden stop and lurched wildly, tipping on its side.

Rory muttered a curse and looked out the window to see his coachman had dismounted and was surveying the damage. A phaeton lay on its side, its wheels turning and its horses rearing while a gentleman hurried to their heads.

With some difficulty Rory climbed out to access the damage. Gillian, on the opposite side of the coach, could see little, but it appeared the phaeton, driven recklessly, had collided with the coach in attempting to pass it. Gillian looked across at Miss Evans and was startled to see that lady slumped on her side in a frightening way, her bonnet askew and her hands flung out helplessly. Had she been injured? Gillian reached across and took one of her hands, appalled at their coldness and Miss Evans's pallor.

The poor woman had fainted, she thought at first, and when her attempts to revive her by chafing her hands and waving a vinaigrette under her nose failed to revive her, she began to worry whether Miss Evans was more seriously hurt. Shocked and confused, she managed to extricate herself from the coach onto the road, where she saw Rory in heated conversation with a tall blond gentleman who was trying to apologize for his lamentable driving.

As she approached them she heard Rory say with some irritation, "Really, Laurie, I might have known it was you. Without doubt you are the most helpless hand on the reins. You have not only wrecked your phaeton beyond repair, but have frightened my passengers with your deviltry."

Seeing Gillian approach, he tried to allay her fears. "This careless fribble is responsible for the accident. I do hope he has not frightened you out of your wits, Gillian. May I introduce Miss Strange, Laurie. Gillian, this is Sir Laurence Runciman, and a more rackety fellow you will never meet." He gave Laurie a searing look, as if to warn him to watch his step.

Sir Laurence, with his merry eyes and cheery smile, showed he normally was of irrepressible spirits but was trying to adapt to the serious plight that his reckless driving had caused, without much success.

"Oh, I say, Rory, I am the one to complain. Your coach is hardly damaged at all while I am completely in the suds with a ruined phaeton and no way to right matters. Please, Miss Strange, accept my apologies. I thought I could pass easily, but I misjudged the space. I am in such a rush to get to London. Can you take me up, Rory?" he asked with little hope.

Gillian nodded at the miscreant, but had a deeper concern. "Rory, I fear Miss Evans has been gravely injured. She did not respond at all just now," Gillian said unhappily, ignoring Sir Laurence.

"Nonsense, she has probably just fainted," Rory reassured her. "I will bring her around." And without more ado he climbed into the coach, leaving Gillian and Laurie facing each other in mute discomfort. Finally, realizing he must put the best face possible on the situation, Sir Laurence turned to Gillian.

"I say, Miss Strange, I am most awfully sorry. I can't think I gave the coach a hard enough jolt to injure anyone. I am sure the lady will be as right as rain in a moment." He put on his most engaging smile, but to no avail. Gillian could not be distracted from her conviction that Miss Evans had suffered a serious injury, and the fault was hers. She had inveigled the poor woman into the coach purely from selfish motives.

She was silent, increasing Sir Laurence's embarrassment, and his confusion. He had several questions of his own, chief among them was what Rory was doing on the road with this charming girl, when he knew Rory had gone to Bath to court that wry-faced Lavinia Alderston. He and Rory were old friends, former classmates at Eton and fellow members of White's. While Rory was a top-of-the-trees sawyer and sportsman of some ability, Laurie could only envy his friend's exploits and try to emulate them with little success. He admired Rory and hated to be in his bad graces. Normally a merry soul whose chief fault was a lack of common sense, he found himself at a loss. What could he say to comfort the charming Miss Strange? For once his mercurial spirits were silenced, and he waited with foreboding for Rory's report.

When Rory emerged from the coach, he looked grave and gave Laurie a disgusted look. "I am sorry, Gillian, Miss Evans seems to have had a heart attack. I am not excusing Laurie, but you did say she had been ailing, and the shock sent her off."

"Oh, my God," Laurie muttered, paling in the face of this disaster. "What have I done?" A veteran of innumerable scrapes from which he had usually managed to escape unscathed, for once it seemed life's nemesis had caught up with him.

Rory, taking pity on him, clasped his shoulder briefly. "Sorry, old chap. But it was not entirely your fault. The shock of the collision probably sent her off, for she appeared frail and Gillian told me she was ailing before we even started. It's just our ill luck it happened this way. Now we must try to sort out the trouble," he insisted, taking charge in a masterful way that Gillian could only applaud.

The next few hours were a nightmare. Laurie was dispatched on one of his horses to find a doctor. The coach, after strenuous efforts by the coachman, footman, and Rory, was righted carefully so as not to further aggravate Miss Evans's condition. Gillian watched and worried, feeling helpless.

They waited some time before Laurie returned with a black-coated, tubby middle-aged man carrying a bag. The doctor entered the coach to examine the patient while the anxious trio waited silently for his verdict. He seemed to have been a long time when he finally stepped down from the coach.

"I have given the poor woman a restorative, but she is in no fit condition to travel. She needs rest, care, and light nourishment. Not a woman of good health generally, I think, but she will pull around."

Rory decided that they had best return to the inn they had left some hours before. Gillian agreed to accompany Miss Evans in the coach, offering what comfort she could, while Rory and Laurie rode alongside.

"I feel so responsible," Gillian said sadly as Rory handed her into the coach.

"You must try to put it from your mind. None of this was your fault. And she will recover, I am sure," Rory consoled her, his compassion for Gillian overriding his concern for Laurie, who looked miserable. His opinion of the lovely Miss Strange had risen considerably. He knew of few young ladies who would not have had a fit of vapors, fainted, or screamed in the face of this accident. But she had coped with great restraint. A girl of character, as he had thought. His own motives in persuading her on this journey now seemed tawdry and made him most uncomfortable, a situation he rarely encountered. He could hardly go ahead with his seduction in the light of recent events. And then there was Laurie, who had attached himself to them and could not be abandoned.

At last they reached the Blue Heron, where Rory supervised the conveyance of the pale-faced and moaning Miss Evans to the best bedroom. The doctor followed his patient while Gillian, Rory, and Laurie waited for his report. Rory volunteered to send a message to Miss Evans's employers. The Aylestons must be persuaded to take some responsibility for the poor soul.

In the meantime, Rory's traveling party would have to spend yet another night at the Blue Heron, for the day was fast lengthening and they could hardly leave until they learned that Miss Evans would recover.

This time Gillian had a room to herself. She at last reached its sanctuary and lay down on the bed, exhausted. Her heedless adventure to find her mother had brought serious consequences. The lighthearted plans she had made to foil Rory Trehune's advances had led to this unfortunate outcome. Should she go on to London, or return to Bath on the next stage? But how could she go back and explain her absence? Sybil would be bound to make a hideous scandal of the affair, and it was doubtful if Miss Marchison would receive her. No, she had to go on, but with much less confidence in her ability to manage her quest in a sensible fashion.

That evening three sober young people met for dinner in the private parlor of the Blue Heron. Each of them felt oppressed by the happenings of the day. Gillian and Laurie carried a heavy burden of responsibility for the condition of Miss Evans, while Rory carried a different kind of guilt. If he had not planned to seduce Gillian, she would not have needed to enlist Miss Evans as a protector, and the poor woman might not now be in such an uncomfortable situation. For all three it was a melancholy occasion and their conversation was subdued.

"I think I must stay here to see how Miss Evans gets on,"

Gillian said with touching gravity as she toyed with her roast pigeon.

"I have made the arrangements with the local doctor for her care. We should try to get in touch with Miss Evans's relatives if possible, but we know so little about her," Rory replied.

"I don't believe she had any, or at least she gave that impression," Gillian responded, her brow furrowed as she thought of that poor woman's lonely state.

"Well, we have done our best for her," Rory remarked wisely.

"Yes, indeed," agreed Laurie, whose normal mercurial spirits had not yet recovered from the tragedy.

"Then we will go on to London," Rory insisted, realizing there was little more to do for the lady.

"May I come with you?" Laurie begged a bit plaintively.

"Of course, old man. And do try to cheer up. You will have us all in the depths if you continue to go about with that grim face," Rory encouraged. His own countenance was not much more sanguine, and Gillian looked on the verge of tears. Remembering his plans for her, Rory could not throw off his disgust with himself. He had behaved like the veriest cad to this lovely girl who had troubles enough if what he feared about her coming confrontation with Mrs. Strange was true. And he had his own stake in that meeting that he had concealed from her, a deception that began to worry him.

"I think I will retire early. I feel exhausted," Gillian said, rising after refusing a restorative sip of brandy.

"The doctor will return in the morning. I think we can leave tomorrow noon and still make London by nightfall," Rory said encouragingly. He wanted to distract Gillian from any more brooding about the governess. After all, there was little more they could do for Miss Evans beyond seeing her decently cared for.

And so it was decided. Once Gillian had bid the men good night, they sat quietly over their drinks, saying little. Finally

Laurie roused himself, determined to discuss another topic that until then he had kept quiet about.

"Rory, how did you meet the delightful Miss Strange? She's a very unusual girl." Laurie broached the subject gently. With Rory it was best to be circumspect.

"Oh, we met in Bath," Rory lied, determined to protect Gillian's reputation as best he might. He knew his friend for a frightful gossip.

"Where you went to consider Miss Alderston as a bride," Laurie reproved.

"Yes, and enough about that. Lavinia is a silly little fool. I don't know why I even thought we might rub along together. I imagine facing her over the dinner table for the rest of my life, and it gives me the shudders," Rory said carelessly.

"Oh, I don't know. She's quite pretty," Laurie protested. He had fancied Lavinia himself until he discovered Rory was in the running.

"And Lady Alderston would be a frightful mother-in-law. No, I had a fortunate escape. Let's not talk about Lavinia." Rory turned off the discussion abruptly. "How about your phaeton. Is it repairable?"

"No, worse luck. I will abandon it and just make some disposition of my horses. I hope my accompanying you to London will not put a rub in your plans, old man," he concluded slyly.

Rory, who had a very good idea of what he meant, dismissed the idea casually. Never do to let Laurie know what he had originally intended toward Gillian. "Not at all. And don't get maggots in your head, Laurie. Miss Strange is a very virtuous female," he warned.

"Of course, of course. I never suggested otherwise," Laurie retreated. Rory could be formidable when challenged, and Laurie was not up to the other's weight.

The gentlemen, too, retired early, and the next morning, in a slightly more equitable frame of mind, the three met to see the doctor. Upon learning that the good Miss Evans would indeed recover, they decided to partake of some luncheon before leaving for London, all feeling a bit relieved that this tragic event could be put behind them. It had been a sorry end to their various adventures.

Upon entering the inn, Gillian went to her chamber to freshen up, and Rory and Laurie waited for her in the salon, having a restorative glass of wine. They were talking quietly when the door opened and in bustled a middle-aged lady, obviously of quality but of a vinegary expression, trailed by an attractive young woman in an overly smart brilliant blue riding dress.

"Oh, Rory, whatever are you doing here? I thought you would be well back in town by now," simpered the girl as she rushed up to him while her mother looked on with a critical eye.

"Lavinia," Rory muttered weakly. It just needed this, the arrival of Lady Alderston and her daughter, to cap the trials of the past days.

"How do you do, Lord Trehune," Lady Alderston said in a quelling manner as she looked over Laurie with a critical eye.

"I believe you know Sir Laurence Runciman, ma'am." Rory introduced them, wondering if he could somehow prevent Gillian from entering the room.

"Yes, of course," Lady Alderston dismissed Laurie as of no account, as indeed he was in the marriage stakes.

"Your servant, Lady Alderston, and Miss Lavinia." Laurie bowed, equally at a loss. He knew enough to realize that Rory was now in the suds, and he wanted to help his friend.

Before any more words could be exchanged, the door opened and Gillian entered, saying brightly, "I am all packed and ready to leave as soon as you are, Rory."

That gentleman suppressed a groan. He had a good idea of what Lady Alderston would think of his apparent intimacy with this lovely girl.

"Lady Alderston, this is Gillian Strange, whom I am escorting to London," he explained in what he hoped was an offhand tone.

Turning to Gillian, he said, "Gillian, this is Lady Alderston, and her daughter, Lavinia, acquaintances of mine in London."

"How do you do, Lady Alderston," Gillian answered quietly. She did not like the look in that harridan's eyes, and had a good idea of what constriction she would put on Gillian's association with Rory.

Lady Alderston made no acknowledgment of the introduction and turned a flushed face to Rory, indignation in every line of her angular figure. "Really, Lord Trehune, this is the outside of enough, to try to introduce me and expose Lavinia to your doxy." She turned her back and walked to the fireplace.

"I must protest, Lady Alderston. You have no call to make these disgusting assumptions," Rory said in his most arctic tone.

"Really, Rory, how could you?" Lavinia said sorrowfully as she joined her mother.

"I think that is quite enough. I must insist that you apologize to Miss Strange for your insulting reference," Rory protested haughtily.

"Never mind, Rory. It's not important," Gillian interrupted, wondering whether Rory could possibly be interested in Lavinia and finding the notion most dampening.

Laurie, determined to come to his friend's aid, rushed into ill-considered speech. "Not at all the thing, Lady Alderston, to make such a shocking judgment about Miss Strange, a most respectable girl."

Lavinia giggled nervously. "Oh, you men always stick together in these affairs. Really, Rory, I am most disappointed in you," she cried.

"That's quite enough, Lavinia. You have no business discussing these matters," her mother objected, vitriol in her voice.

"Come, Gillian. There is no reason for you to stay here

and be insulted," Rory said in a towering rage, and grasping Gillian's arm in a firm hand, almost dragged her from the room into his private parlor, slamming the door in a fury. Laurie, embarrassed, made a slight bow in the Alderston ladies' direction and hurried after them.

"Really, Rory, you were quite rude to your friends," Gillian chided, for some reason immensely cheered by his reaction.

"Nasty old cat. It will be all over London that I had a female in tow on the Bath road," he muttered. What was dreadful was that the Alderstons had correctly surmised the exact role Rory had plotted for Gillian, and he was ashamed.

Surprisingly, Gillian laughed. "I suspect they had their reasons," she said mysteriously. "Now, forget the matter and let us have some luncheon. I am amazingly hungry.

Both Rory and Laurie looked at her in admiration. Really, she seemed not at all irritated or humiliated by that unpleasant encounter. Of the three of them, she had behaved with the most sangfroid. Her spirits appeared to have risen and she had found it stimulating. Rory, however, was not so easily mollified. Both guilt and disgust lowered his mood. Laurie, trying to put as good a face as possible on the situation, temporized. "Lady Alderston is a grasping old cat and no one pays the slightest heed to her evil tongue."

"Oh, don't be so stupid, Laurie. Gillian's name will be bandied all about the town."

"Come, you two. It's not that serious. It is not as if I expected to be welcomed by the *ton,* you know," Gillian soothed them.

Just as well, thought Rory. She has no idea of what lies ahead.

For some reason, as opposed to his usual reaction to women Rory felt an overwhelming desire to protect Gillian from vicious old gossips like Lady Alderston. Immured in that Bath seminary, Gillian could have no idea how petty and vengeful the London haut monde could be. Rory did not like the confused emotions that girl aroused in him. While he had previously plotted somewhat casually to make her his mistress, now he was irate that she could be placed in a position where that very fate would be ascribed to her by the Alderstons. He felt both conscious-stricken and furious, which made him poor company.

Gillian wondered if he felt embarrassed because Lavinia Alderston had seen them together and drawn her own conclusions. Could he possibly care what that vapid little fool thought? Grudgingly, Gillian had to admit Lavinia was quite a pretty girl, and obviously amenable to a fault. Was that the kind of female Rory preferred? If so, Gillian concluded he must find her thoroughly objectionable as well as a nuisance. This conclusion threw her into a depression that she did not want to acknowledge.

While Gillian and Rory were indulging in their separate fits of sullens, poor Laurie was trying without much success to lighten the atmosphere. "At least, Rory, you can now congratulate yourself that you did not offer for Miss Alderston. Not up to your weight, old boy, and I am sure you would find her a dead bore after a few weeks of wedded bliss," he said, hoping to cheer his companion with the realization of his near escape.

"Don't be ridiculous, Laurie, I had no intention of offering for her," he insisted not quite truthfully. Actually he had thought Lavinia fetching until he had met Gillian. Somehow she put Cyprians and respectable debutantes, some of whom he had flirted with quite happily, in the shade. He did not know whether to be angry with her or with himself, but whatever his mood, he did not like it.

Finally, seeing that her companions did not appear interested in acting on the good intentions of that morning, Gillian reminded them, "We should be leaving for London shortly if we are to make it before dark, surely."

Rory glowered, then realized that he was in danger of behaving like a boor. "I hate managing females, but of course, you are right, Gillian. Let us try to make our exit without

encountering the Alderstons again. Another interview with
Lady A. would completely unnerve me," he mocked not entirely in jest.

"Yes, indeed," Laurie agreed. "Poisonous female."

Within a few moments the trio had entered the coach, not
without being noticed by Lady A., who directed some tren-
chant words of warning about Rory to her daughter.

As the coach rolled into the city, Gillian, who had never
been to London before, was disappointed that dusk had fallen
and she could see little of the great metropolis. The journey
had been an uncomfortable one, not because of the conveyance, but because of the mood of the travelers. However, as
they entered London, Rory seemed to throw off his blue devils and make an effort to be congenial.

"It's a shame you can't see some of the great buildings
and avenues because of the twilight. I will have to take you
on a tour once you have settled and rested up from this journey," Rory promised.

Gillian was heartened by the hint that he would not just
abandon her once she had reached Mrs. Strange's home. But
after leaving the Albany in Piccadilly, where they bid farewell
to Laurie, her uneasiness returned.

She suddenly recalled that Lady Alderston had referred to
Rory as Lord Trehune, which must mean he was a member
of the *ton*. Actually, she should have expected him to be a
nobleman. He had all the casual arrogance of that breed.
However, that was not the chief cause of her disquiet. She
had sensed that Rory and Laurie both knew a great deal more
about Mrs. Laura Strange than they had admitted to her. And
Gillian suspected Rory had warned Laurie not to discuss the
lady with her. And why was that? Did he know something to
her discredit? If the tale Sybil had told her was true and Aunt
Laura was under the protection of some mysterious peer,

Rory, and probably Laurie, too, might be acquainted with the man. Gillian could restrain herself no longer.

"You seem to know exactly where we should go to find my aunt Laura," Gillian accused Rory as the coach turned left by Hyde Park and Apsley House, the home of the great Duke of Wellington.

"I have to confess, Gillian, I do know Mrs. Strange," Rory admitted, then hesitated, not sure whether he should tell her of the close association he had with that lady. She would, no doubt, be very angry that he had concealed the truth from her. But he could not in all conscience reveal this business to a stranger, and at the beginning, when Gillian had offered her embroidered tale, that was what she had been. If it seemed as if weeks had passed since their initial meeting in the salon of the Blue Heron, Rory still felt there were several barriers between them that prevented him from a full disclosure of this secret. Although it was hardly a secret to London society, which had chewed over the scandal for more than ten years and now had almost forgotten it, as so many other *on-dits* had replaced it in the public mind. But Rory could not forget, nor relegate it so easily to the past. He dreaded telling Gillian what she would discover all too soon at the Montpelier Place house.

Before she could quiz him further about his strange words, they drew up outside a terrace of new houses built in the classic mode that the Prince Regent and his architect, John Nash, favored. Only recently had this suburb of London come into popularity, and even now few of England's great families were willing to live so far from Piccadilly. It was considered an outré neighborhood by the haut monde.

As their carriage stopped and Rory assisted Gillian to alight, she noticed that a phaeton driven by a groom was just pulling away. There was no sign of its recent driver on the street or before the house, but Gillian hesitated.

"Oh, dear, it seems Aunt Laura has a visitor and I will be intruding," she complained.

"If you intend to spend any time with your aunt Laura, you must get used to seeing a great deal of this visitor," Rory insisted with a wry twist to his mouth. He rapped heavily on the knocker of the trim white house. The door was opened immediately by a neat maid who showed no surprise at seeing him.

"Good evening, my lord. The earl has just arrived and is with Mrs. Strange, but I will announce you," she said, trying to hide her curiosity. Rory was no stranger to her, but never before had he arrived with a female in tow.

"Thank you, Mary. I believe that will be best. This is Miss Strange," he informed her, watching with amusement as she struggled to contain her avid interest.

Gillian, now thoroughly alarmed by Rory's obvious intimacy with her aunt Laura's household, gave him a speaking look, at which he only smiled a bit grimly as they were ushered up the stairs. It appeared Sybil was correct, and this mysterious earl was Aunt Laura's protector. Why else would he be visiting her at this hour? Before she could challenge Rory and demand some answers, at least about his role in the affair, Mary opened the drawing room door and announced, "Lord Trehune and Miss Strange, madam."

Gillian barely had time to notice a charming bow-fronted room decorated in subdued pastels when her aunt Laura, leaving her companion by the fireside, glided across to Gillian and enfolded her in a scented embrace. Gillian recognized the scent she always associated with her aunt, who looked as she always did, amazingly youthful for a lady in her mid-forties. If she was surprised or annoyed by Gillian's sudden arrival, she showed nothing but pleasure.

In the first rush of greeting Gillian did not notice that Rory and the earl, after a more subdued greeting, had drawn apart and were conversing in low tones.

"Gillian, my dear, I am so pleased to see you. I had intended to come to Devon after your seminary broke up for the summer, but this is lovely." Mrs. Strange welcomed Gillian with so much warmth, she could not feel an intruder.

"Come over to the fire. Even if it is May, it is quite chilly still and you must have been traveling for hours." Laura Strange shepherded Gillian toward the fireplace and the two men standing there. Even before her aunt Laura introduced them, Gillian knew what to expect.

"My dear, this is Roderick, the Earl of Southbridge, Rory's father, as I am sure he has mentioned," Mrs. Strange said, not one whit embarrassed by presenting Gillian to her protector.

"No, he did not. But then, Lord Trehune and I have not exchanged confidences. We met just recently," Gillian explained, and shot an icy look at Rory, who grinned back coolly, as if to dare her to say more. She ignored him and turned to smile at the earl, who bowed and smiled with none of his son's falsity.

"I have heard a great deal about you, Gillian, if I may call you that, and I am delighted to meet you at last. I do hope my graceless son has not misbehaved and given you a distaste of the Trehunes," he offered easily.

Gillian could see where Rory had received his handsome looks and stature. Only some gray tinges in his dark hair, and lines in his weather-beaten face testified to the earl's age and experience. He must be in his fifties, but he looked much younger, Gillian decided. He also looked much more engaging than his son, with whom she had a real quarrel. He had known from their first meeting that her aunt Laura was his father's mistress and yet he had let her prattle on and make a fool of herself.

"And just how did you meet Rory, Gillian?" Mrs. Strange asked as she seated herself on a settee next to Gillian and took her hand.

Gillian flushed a bit, then blurted out, "He rescued me from a blackguard in an unfortunate incident en route here, but I am not sure if I would not have been better off with the vulgar Mr. Penny than with him, for he has deceived and lied to me from the beginning." She spoke insistently, then lowered her eyes, feeling the veriest fool. What a way to behave, ranting at Rory. His father would think she had no manners at all.

"Ah, but Miss Strange also lied and deceived me, so I think the honors are even," Rory drawled.

"Stop teasing the girl, Rory. I think it would be prudent if we withdrew and let the ladies have their coze in private. At any rate, I have some quite serious news to discuss with you," the earl said in a commanding fashion. "I will tell him of our plans, Laura, and you may tell Gillian," he said as he turned to Mrs. Strange and gave her what Gillian could think was only the most loving look.

When the door had closed behind the two men, Laura Strange turned to Gillian and asked, "I know you have a good reason for coming here, my dear, and I hope you are not shocked by what appears to be, and is, I must admit, an irregular relationship. But all that has changed now," Laura Strange confided.

What a lovely woman she was, Gillian thought, both in appearance and manner. Laura Strange's blond hair, more silvery now than golden, was drawn back into a simple chignon that showed off her sculptured features to a nicety. Her eyes were an indeterminate shade between blue and hazel, depending upon her mood, and her figure, in the rose silk gown, was as slender as Gillian's.

"I came, Aunt Laura, because Sybil blurted out that she had heard her parents discussing you. They said that you are not my aunt, but in fact you are my mother and are living under the protection of a nobleman in London. That was all she knew and she was quite horrid and spiteful in the telling," Gillian said, hurrying to get the tale behind her.

"I am not surprised she snooped and meddled. She always was a mean-spirited child," Mrs. Strange said, and then faced Gillian calmly, unwilling to lie to her. "It is true, Gillian, you are my daughter. Your father, whom I married against my parents' wishes, turned out to be not the white knight I thought he was. Poor man, he could not stand up to adversity and poverty. He abandoned me when I was pregnant, and, I learned just recently from a fellow officer, died at Waterloo. It seemed in your best interest to let my sister and her husband raise you and for you to think of me as your aunt. A foolish, weak-minded decision I think now, but at the time I thought it best. I had to seek a position and I could not have taken you with me. Don't think too badly of me," she pleaded.

"Of course I don't think badly of you. I am sure you were desperate, and I cannot complain that I suffered in my childhood. Aunt Elizabeth and Uncle Robert were always most kind. Still, I sensed some mystery and am so happy to learn you are my mother and we can be together now," Gillian said innocently.

Mrs. Strange took her daughter in her arms and gave her a loving kiss. "What a dear girl you are not to have any reproaches or questions. I am sure you want to know all about Roderick, the Earl of Southbridge. Well, it is not as shameful as you might suppose," Laura Strange assured Gillian.

"How did you meet and have you been . . . together a long time," Gillian asked tentatively. She was not prepared to insist on confidences her mother did not want to make, but she sensed that Laura was aching to tell her.

"Yes, we have, for more than twelve years. I don't suppose Rory told you that his mother has been ill for years, a victim of some nervous disorder. I met Roderick when he was a guest at a place in Dorset where I was a companion to a dear old lady. After she died and I left Dorset, he prevailed upon me to come here. I make no excuses, Gillian, for my decision. Many would call me a scarlet woman and worse, but I love Roderick and he loves me. It is not as if I lured him away from his wife. They had ceased to be husband and wife years ago, and even Rory does not blame me, I think. And now all has turned out so well, or at least not well, for poor Lady

Southbridge is dead. But that allows Roderick and me to be married very soon," she said with a simple sincerity that completely won over Gillian. How could she judge her mother harshly, or, for that matter, think ill of the earl, who had remained deeply devoted to her mother all these years?

Gillian, speechless at hearing this calm recital of a life that must at times have been lonely, unhappy, and difficult before the final triumph, wished that she had learned of this long before. She had no trouble forgiving her mother, nor in accepting the earl's presence in her life, but she was still angry at Rory. She realized her mother was awaiting her reaction to her tale, and she hurried to reassure her.

"I can only say, Mother"—Gillian uttered the word with some pleasure—"that I can feel only a welcome relief at having what I always sensed was some mystery explained at last. I would much rather have a lovely mother alive than a vague figure who died while giving birth. I only wish I had known all this years ago." She tried to keep any hint of accusation from her voice.

"Thank you, my dear. You are generous. I behaved foolishly. I should never have left you with the Milfords; I thought it was for the best. Roderick urged me to tell you the truth ages ago, but I am such a coward," Laura Strange admitted with a rueful shrug.

"Not a coward, Mother." The word came easier now. "Only beset and frightened, and young," Gillian comforted her in a strangely maternal fashion. She felt great compassion for the young girl who was abandoned by her husband and forced to make her way in the world without support.

"What about my grandparents? Did they ever forgive or support you?"

"Alas, they died soon after you were born. I think perhaps my mother might have relented, but Father was adamant. He was a very stubborn man and disliked being thwarted."

"He sounds horrid. He should have been forgiving or, at

least, understanding." Gillian spoke with all the assurance of youth and inexperience.

"Well, it is all in the past now. And at last Roderick and I are free to seek our happiness with no shadow darkening our future," Mrs. Strange said cheerfully. Then, remembering that Gillian had not extended the charity to Rory that she had to the older lovers, she ventured to plead his case.

"You must not blame Rory for deceiving you, Gillian. He believed he was acting for the best, to protect me and his father."

"I think he behaved atrociously." Gillian hesitated. Should she tell her mother what she sensed Rory had planned for her own future? She found herself strangely protective of this brave woman who had already endured quite enough.

"Well, you must try to forgive him now that you will be related in a fashion."

"That is the only disagreeable outcome of this felicitous business. I suppose he took his mother's part and held you responsible for her miserable existence as a scorned wife."

"No, to be fair, I think he understood his mother was mentally disturbed, and that—I am telling you this in confidence, Gillian—she drank, at times acting quite unmanageable and causing Roderick great embarrassment and pain."

"Poor man, but he had you to comfort and love him. I am so happy you are to be married at last. When will the wedding be?" Gillian asked, determined to guide the conversation away from the irritating Rory. She wondered why she was more angry with him than her mother and the earl, who had also deceived her. Perhaps her anger protected her from some other ill-defined emotion.

"Very soon, and then we are going abroad, to allow the scandal to die down. A member of the aristocracy marrying his mistress will titillate the *ton* for some time, I fear. And until we return from our wedding trip, I think it best if you stay with Elizabeth and Robert. I know that will be a bit awkward, but you cannot stay here unchaperoned. When we come back we will launch you on the town, and society will not frown on the Earl and Countess of Southbridge's daughter," Mrs. Strange insisted with a quaint air of assurance.

"I suppose that is the best plan, but Aunt Elizabeth and Uncle Robert might object."

"Roderick will persuade them," Mrs. Strange insisted. Then, her head cocked to one side, she said a bit impishly, "I wonder what Roderick is saying to Rory."

She might have been surprised. The earl and his son, ensconced in the dining room, were having an equal exchange of confidences without any animosity.

"I know you feel sorrow for your mother, but she was not only sick but unhappy. I will not apologize for my relationship with Mrs. Strange. She has made my life bearable during these years, and I did try with your mother, Rory, I want you to accept that," the earl told his son with a certain diffidence.

"I know, Father. I won't say you never should have married her, because then I would not have been born. But I do hope none of her taint is inherited," Rory said with a worried frown.

"I don't think so, my son. The doctors insist her condition was the result of childbirth. She did not want children and hated the intimacy of the marriage bed. I dislike criticizing her to you, but it was a nasty situation. And then she started to drink, which only exacerbated her condition. I did what I could," the earl said in a tone of despair, not seeking any sympathy, only trying to explain his misery. "She was a lovely girl."

"Well, it's all over now and you will marry Mrs. Strange?" Rory asked, a bit embarrassed by his father's candor.

"Yes, as soon as possible. Then we are going abroad. You will be able to manage the estate," the earl said with a question in his voice. Not that he doubted his son's ability only his interest.

"Of course," Rory answered.

"I hesitate to ask, Rory, but just what is your relationship with Gillian?" The earl was in no position to query his son's motives toward Gillian, but he knew his son's reputation and feared he might have made an unseemly approach to the girl.

Rory grinned, following his father's reasoning without difficulty. "Originally they were what you might expect, but I have since changed my mind."

"You know I want you to marry, Rory, and I take it that Miss Alderston was not to your taste."

If this opinion seemed at first view a non sequitur, Rory knew better. "Quite right, a silly female with a Tartar of a mother. There was no way I would join myself to that family. But I am thinking of marriage," Rory admitted a bit shamefacedly.

"May I inquire as to whom you have selected?" the earl asked, although he had a good idea of the answer.

"Gillian, if she will have me. She thinks me the veriest cad and deceiver now, but I hope to talk her around eventually."

"I won't insist you tell me of your adventures and what caused you to change your mind and decide she would make a better wife than mistress. But I will warn you that for Laura's sake I would not countenance an irregular relationship with Gillian, even if she would consent," his father insisted sternly.

"She wouldn't. She's a most formidable young woman and she took my measure immediately. Of rare quality is Gillian. But I fear I have blotted my copybook with her," Rory admitted.

"Well, when we return from the Continent Laura intends to launch her upon the *ton*. You will have several rivals, I think."

"I have my methods," Rory said with more assurance than he really felt.

His father grinned, clapped him on the shoulder, and suggested they join the ladies.

After a convivial dinner, during which Gillian treated Rory with a certain disdain but congratulated her mother and stepfather-to-be with enthusiasm, Rory rose to take his leave. But he was not going before he had tilted swords with Gillian. He took her off to the morning room, ignoring her suggestion that they should say their farewells in the hall.

Once alone, he lost no time in trying to explain matters.

"I should have told you from the beginning that I knew Mrs. Strange, but you were not completely honest with me either, Gillian, telling me that gothic tale of running away from a disagreeable suitor," he reproached her, thinking that the best defense was to challenge her own story.

"I distrusted you from the beginning, having some idea of your proclivities," Gillian admitted, standing tall against the window and facing him with defiance.

"Proclivities, what a lovely word. What you mean is you thought I was not much better than the unspeakable Mr. Penny," Rory returned wryly. "I suppose you had every right to be suspicious of my intentions. But Miss Evans's accident changed all that."

"Why, because it made you feel ashamed? That does not excuse you. You meant to make disreputable suggestions to me, didn't you," Gillian challenged him, but a pleasurable glow began to lighten her anger at him as she realized what he was about.

"You are an exceptionally lovely girl, enough to tempt any man to make suggestions, you little termagant," Rory said wickedly.

"You are impossible," Gillian retorted, but could barely suppress a smile.

"Well, my intentions have changed and are now thoroughly honorable," Rory insisted, crossing to her side. He had been careful not to make any approach until he had sensed some sign of softening in her manner.

"What does that mean? That you want to be a brother to me," Gillian riposted.

"Be quiet. You know what I want. And in case there is any doubt, I will show you." Before she could utter any disclaimer, Rory took her in his arms and began to kiss her with an expertise and enthusiasm that demanded a response, one which she gave wholeheartedly.

When Gillian emerged from his embrace, rosy and bemused with passion, she opened her mouth to protest, but he only kissed her again. Then, taking her by the shoulders, he looked fixedly at her.

"I intend to court you in the approved style, and when Father and my new mother return from the Continent, we will get married," he said, as if admitting no argument.

"Will we? I am not sure I want a rake for a husband. I could probably do much better," Gillian teased.

"Well, you won't have the chance," Rory concluded masterfully. And he was quite right.

The Oriental Garden

by
Isobel Linton

One

"Send one of the servants after him, Catherine! Why can I not make you understand? It isn't seemly for a noblewoman to go gallivanting about the filthy countryside searching for a youngster!"

Young Lady Sturtevant flushed pink with irritation but made no reply. Heaven alone knew how, she managed once again to hold her tongue in front of her late husband's carping mother. Suppressing even the merest hint of a sigh that longed to emerge, she continued, with steely determination, to re-button her spencer.

"Are you deaf, child?" cried her inquisitor.

"No, Beatrice. I am not deaf. I heard what you said perfectly plainly."

"Then why do you defy me?"

She let loose the sigh at last, replying, "I am not defying you. I am doing what I think is right. I am going out to look for him because Charles is my son."

"I am aware of *that!*" said the dowager Lady Sturtevant sarcastically. "Charles is my grandson, after all, but that is hardly the point. The point, Catherine, is propriety. The staff are perfectly well prepared to go and locate the obstreperous little scoundrel who shouldn't have been out wandering in the woods alone in any case, but should have been back in his rooms studying Latin with Mr. Thymmes! This house is rife with indiscipline, I tell you, rife with it!"

"I wish to go out and look for Charles," she replied, making an attempt to be firm in her resolve and yet inoffensive. "Where is the harm in that?"

"The harm is that it is just not *done*. Why can you not heed me? Let me tell you once again, Catherine Sturtevant, that in our family we place great emphasis on social decorum, and we are proud of it! We Sturtevants know our place in the world, and what consequence is owed us. Leave the work of servants to the servants, I say! Next thing you know you'll be wanting to dress your own hair! Think how *that* news would sweep through the parish by way of the back stairs. I can see it now: 'Lady Sturtevant, the young dowager, dresses her own hair now, did you know? Poor things! They must have lost their whole fortune on 'Change!' No, surely you must see the vulgarity of such goings-on. Search for him yourself! No, it's out of the question. It's ridiculous. I will *not* allow you to disgrace the grand name of our family."

"I'm *not* disgracing the Sturtevant name! I'm just taking a walk in the woods!" replied Catherine, at her wit's end.

"Don't try that tone of voice on me! The behavior of Catherine, Countess of Sturtevant, is *not* a trivial matter. *You* may not mind having your name bandied about the countryside, but I shan't stand for it. You may *not* just do whatever you like, and go wherever you want, in that care-for-nothing way of yours, and so I have told you a hundred thousand times these past ten years. You cannot do so! No more than can I, of course. I, however, am far too gently bred even to be tempted to behave in a manner unsuited to my station in life.

"I tell you very plainly, Catherine, that I won't have you behaving like this. I'll punish you for your insensitive, brazen attitudes and your dreadful, hoydenish tendencies, and just you see if I don't!"

The dowager paused for effect, and then continued her harangue at full tilt.

"I'll send for the solicitors, Catherine, and then you'll see where your hotheadedness and ill breeding have gotten you!

I'll take Charles away from you, Catherine, as one unsuited to raise a noble child! Don't think I can't do it, for I can!"

Catherine felt hot tears rising in her eyes, and she choked them back as best she could. This was what their quarrels always came to, and this unimaginable threat was the sole reason that the old woman always won.

"I know you can take my son away from me, Beatrice. You have told me so in great detail on innumerable occasions."

"Much good it has done."

"P-please forgive me. I was very wrong to seek to join the search in the company of the servants. It is unsuitable. I—I will try to be more conformable, truly I will, and I will do my very best to change my behavior so as to please you, but won't you give me permission, I beg of you, just today, to go out by myself to look for him?"

Catherine hated herself for groveling so abjectly, but what was she to do? She could no more live without her son than she could go without breathing. To think that a grown woman had to beg for permission to search for her own son! It was humiliating in the extreme. It was a crushing defeat. And worse yet, it was emblematic of the way things had been since Frederick's death.

The dowager did not immediately attack again, and, by that hesitation, Catherine surmised that her mother-in-law's mood had been mollified by displayed humility. If Catherine would grovel a little longer, Beatrice would likely relent and let her go. It was the same way the wretched woman had bullied her late husband, and then, later, her own son.

Beatrice just likes to be reassured that one is at her mercy, thought Catherine—she should have been in the army. It's all pretense—she doesn't really believe I behave unsuitably. She just wants me to be aware continuously that the sharp edge of her sword lies placed against my neck at all times.

"Please do forgive my want of conduct, Beatrice. It won't happen again, ever. We can discuss this whole matter at greater length, if you insist, once I return."

"And when might that be?"

"Once Charles is safely found, of course."

"Oh, very well, then. Go out if you must. Of course, I don't approve of your performing the offices of servants, but perhaps we can disguise what your aim is. We will have it put about that you have gone out for some fresh air. Then, if during your walk you should *not* find Charles, no one will be the wiser. If you *do* find him, it will seem to have occurred by chance, and not by design. However, you are not to tell anyone your real reason for going out, and particularly you may not tell that awful gossiping Jenny woman you insist on keeping in your employ at an outrageous salary."

Not rising to the bait, Catherine merely smiled shyly. "I shall take my leave, then."

"And next time have that abigail of yours fasten your clothes properly before you leave your chambers! A lady can't be seen roaming around the corridors until her toilette is perfectly complete!"

"Yes, of course. Thank you, ma'am."

She kissed her mother-in-law's withered cheek, curtsied to the gray-haired old harridan, and made her exit. She would have been ready to say anything, to do anything, just to be able to go after Charles.

She strode out over the West Lawn at a run, as if she were afraid the old woman would change her mind and have her dragged within the house again. Her mind was abuzz with worrisome thoughts. Where was Charles? What had become of him? Had he had an accident? Had he run away on purpose? Had he gone to the wooded place he'd spoken of? How long had he been gone before his absence was noticed?

On impulse, Catherine headed toward the coppice in the far dell. There were so many places he might be—how could she find him? It would be better, far better, if she were the one to find Charles rather than one of the servants, for a servant would bring him to his grandmother, and his grandmother would read him the riot act straightaway. If she found him first, she could absorb some of the blame; she could be the buffer; she could soften the blow. A mother's function, was it not?

Why had he not told her he was going? Why had he gone? Probably to seek out some peace and quiet, and who could fault him for it? However, why had he mistaken the time and failed to return for his lessons? What could have happened to him?

Worrisome, worrisome possibilities presented themselves to her mind. She didn't think he was in any danger, of course, but then again, he might be in danger. What if he had fallen from a tree? What if he had lost his way in the forest? She had to know. Of course she had to know.

The task of being a mother was onerous—one had to give her child independence and at the same time one wanted to protect him. Part of Catherine was confident her son could take care of himself, and part of her felt crazed at not knowing exactly where he was and unable to rest until he was safe from harm.

Ten years old he was now. How the years had flown! Poor Frederick, dying so soon, dying so young, never even being able to dandle his own son on his knee, never able to see the fine, strong young lad he had grown to be. Poor, dear, weak, gentle Frederick, the only time he had ever stood up to his bullying mother was the day he persuaded her that Catherine Moore would make her only son a perfect wife.

And she *had* been a perfect wife for what, how long? Five whole months? It had been a ridiculously short marriage, but it had been long enough for her to turn her warm affection toward Frederick into little more than a resigned and bittersweet tenderness. How could she view him as the conquering hero of her dreams, when every day she was faced with reality? Frederick had been naturally kind and naturally gentle, admirable qualities indeed, and the ones for which she had married him. It was only after her marriage that she realized that Frederick, for all his many gentle virtues, was wholly lacking in strength of character, and had lived his life trapped beneath his domineering mother's thumb.

Like me, she thought grimly. Just like me.

Two

The man walking in the woods was tall, dark, powerful; altogether he presented an imposing figure. His clothes were neat and nicely cut, but were not of the first stare of fashion—even Charles could see that. The man's face wasn't old exactly, but his skin was lined and weathered, and of a color Charles had never seen before, an autumn kind of color, something burnished, olive-tan, like fallen leaves. Charles hesitated, unsure of what to do. The man was a stranger, and an unusual one; all in all, it was hard to approach him, but there was no help for it. He'd have to overcome his damnable tendency toward shyness and come right out and ask.

"Excuse me, sir," said the boy politely, hiding his nervousness as best he could. "Could you please tell me the way back to Apsley?"

"Apsley?" repeated the gentleman.

The boy looked back at the dark man with undisguised wonder. "Apsley Park. Surely you've heard of it?"

The man smiled broadly, revealing a flash of white teeth. "No, I'm afraid not. I've heard of Apsley House though. You mean Apsley House, Wellington's place, in London?"

The boy's jaw dropped to his knees. "Not Apsley House, Apsley Park. It's the largest estate in the area. How can you not have heard of Apsley? Wherever have you been?"

The dark man apparently found his question amusing, and laughed a kind, welcoming laugh that made Charles feel wonderfully at home. It was enlightening not to feel small and stupid in the presence of an adult, the way his grandmama and Mr. Thymmes always made him feel.

"Now, let's see. Just where *have* I been? I've been in India, young man. That's why I've not heard of your Apsley Park."

"You're hoaxing me! People who live there don't live here as well."

"Having spent a good twenty years in India, I have just now retired to England."

"Oh. I see. I beg your pardon; how very stupid of me. How did you find India? I've read about it, and it sounds perfectly smashing. Would you tell me about it? Someday, if you have the time? If it wouldn't bore you too dreadfully?"

"To answer your first question, I found I liked India very well, though it can be a hard place, and due to the climate and the living conditions it can be difficult to survive there. Not all Englishmen adapt well, but I did. I found it a fascinating life and a fascinating country. By all means, you must pay me a visit whenever you like; I'd be happy to recount my adventures, such as they were. I don't know many people in the neighborhood, and I'd be glad of the company."

"This all is *your* place, then, is it?"

"Indeed it is. I bought Simla House, and its grounds, which are extensive, sight unseen while I was abroad, and I've been having it readied for my arrival. Had to have the work done by correspondence, you understand—for some years now. I finally arrived here to take up residence just yesterday, so I've really not had time to become acquainted with anyone just yet. Who might you be? I take it you are a neighbor, and most likely one who comes from Apsley Park. Am I right?"

"Yes, sir. I am Sturtevant, Charles Sturtevant," said the boy in as grown-up a manner as he could manage. He held out his hand politely, and the large man took it in a firm grasp. "Of Apsley Park, just as you guessed."

"I am Robert Mandeville. Of Simla House, which is that way"—and he gestured toward the deeper woods. "It is not very near. I am afraid I have laid out my estate somewhat unconventionally."

He paused, then continued. "Well, young man, look around. Tell me, do you like it?"

"Like what?"

"Do you like my new woods? These woods, I mean."

"Are you telling me you *made* these woods, sir?"

"God *made* them, Charles, I merely assisted Him with the landscaping."

Mandeville smiled at his young listener once more, and stooped down a little to talk to him, putting Charles instantly at ease. "You see, I knew I should feel homesick for the East once I came back here, so I arranged, little by little, over many years, to have part of the East brought back here to Simla House to await my arrival."

"Did you really?" said Charles, rather amazed at the grandeur of this undertaking.

"I did. This section here is of relatively recent vintage, and is my attempt to replicate the forests of the foothills of the Himalayas, near northern villages such as Simla and Pathankot. These particular specimens I brought out with me on my most recent voyage. I think they will look very fine by next spring, though they will take some years to grow to full height."

"I think it's all very fine, sir. If you care for my opinion."

"I do; I do. Why should I not?"

"At my house no one else does. Except for Mummy, they don't listen to me at all."

"Do they not? Then it is they who are missing out on the insight that a young, fresh mind can very often provide. Now, tell me, Charles, did you really lose your way in my woods? You don't mind if I call you Charles, do you? You won't think it too familiar of me?"

"Of course not. I'm just a child, after all. At least, everyone keeps reminding me that I am just a child. My tutor and so many people. They won't let me do what I want."

"It must seem like that, at your age."

"It *is* like that, sir. It's like being in prison. It took me ages this morning to give everyone the slip so I could come out and get a bit of freedom and fresh air before lessons, and now I've made a mull of it. I did get lost in your woods, of all the stupidest things, though I thought I knew all these lands surrounding Apsley perfectly well. Now I think I know why. Your whole place has been done over, hasn't it? All sorts of trees and such that used to be here are missing. It's that great wall over there that really got me muddled up. You've added it in the last year, haven't you? That's what threw me off, for I've not been here for some time. What is there inside the wall? Do you know?"

"I do indeed. It's my most pet project—a walled Oriental garden. Do you like gardens?"

"Not really. Gardening isn't a very manly occupation. Is it?"

Mr. Mandeville laughed again. "I used to think not, but I have since changed my mind. I was very ill in the East for some months, long ago, and was unable to work. While I was recovering, I entered a stage where I was too weak to undertake my normal business but too well to sit in bed and do nothing at all. That's when I started puttering around in my garden, and grew to find it very satisfying. In some circles it's thought to be all the crack, you know. In the end I decided I should like to buy an estate for myself to retire to, and to create at Simla House an arboreal *opus magnus*. Care to have a look?"

"Yes, I would."

As they were about to approach the door to the walled garden, Mr. Mandeville stopped and turned around, having heard a rustling in the bushes. Some yards off he saw a female figure of medium height, slightly built, approaching him at an energetic pace.

Mr. Mandeville began to smile. Who, he wondered, might this be? The auburn-haired woman was lovely; she had fair, regular features, soft, rosy lips matching her rosy cheeks, and gentle hazel eyes framed with dark lashes. Her voice, calling out Charles's name, was musical; her demeanor was shy, almost hesitant, while her eyes held a compelling liveliness.

As she continued to approach, Mandeville felt his breath quicken altogether. By all that was holy in heaven! He suddenly felt that in a lifetime spent appreciating the finer physical points of the fair sex, he had never, till this day, beheld such an exemplary combination of refinement and natural allure.

"Charles, who is that woman coming toward us? The one over there, calling you? Can that be your governess?"

"Governess? I don't have a governess, I have a tutor, Mr. Thymmes, who's beastly and boring. That's Mummy come after me."

"Mummy?"

"Lady Sturtevant, I should say."

It was as if all the air had been suddenly crushed in his chest. He felt how hard it was going to be to keep the disappointment from his face. "I see. Stupid of me, I should have known. Your mother, is she? Well. That's it, then. Splendid. One can only envy your esteemed father. He's a lucky man," said Robert, trying to make the best of it. "She's a very well-looking woman."

"Father? Oh, no, my father's not alive any longer, Mr. Mandeville. In fact, he died before I was born. I—I never even knew him."

"Oh. I see. I'm sorry to hear it, Charles. Then, may I ask, is she—have you a stepfather, then?"

"I? No, no! No, sir. Certainly not."

Well, young man, thought Mandeville, surprised by the swift arising of a new and unusual thought, would you like one?

Three

Catherine, Lady Sturtevant, regarded with some interest and surprise the handsome gentleman who had been speaking so animatedly with her son. When the man had first set eyes on her, his frank glance of masculine admiration had been undisguised and unmistakable. Touched by the raw power of that look, her ladyship had been unable to restrain the spread of a deep blush over her rosy cheeks. Immediately, she felt vulnerable. Dear heaven, she thought to herself, what a long time it has been since any man looked at me in such a way! What a fool I am! I must try to keep my countenance. Beatrice would be so furious with me!

Even before Catherine took note of the man's excellent physique and noble features, she had noticed a marked look of excitement in dear Charles's eyes while the two were conversing. What is this? she wondered. Have they made friends, this man and her son? What could they have been discussing? She felt of pang of guilt when she thought of how long it had been since Charles looked so alive, and so relaxed. It was good to see him without the tense, hunted look that he always had in the presence of Mr. Thymmes and his grandmama.

"Charles, dear! I've been looking for you everywhere!"

"You needn't have worried, Mummy. I'm old enough to find my way back home." The two males exchanged a short, knowing glance. "With a bit of help, that is."

The tall gentleman moved toward her and removed his hat. "Excuse me, madam. Allow me to introduce myself. I am

Robert Mandeville. I have only just recently moved into this neighborhood."

Charles immediately cried out, "Oh, sorry, sir! How rag-mannered of me not to make a proper introduction! This is my mother, Catherine, Lady Sturtevant. Mummy, Mr. Mandeville has been kind enough to invite me to his home."

"Has he?" she inquired, extending her small, perfectly shaped hand. "How do you do, Mr. Mandeville. I hope Charles hasn't been talking your ear off. He's terribly curious by nature and a most enthusiastic inquisitor."

"I am pleased to make your acquaintance, Lady Sturtevant. Your son and I have been discussing enlightening topics of mutual interest, such as landscape architecture and the various wonders of the Orient."

"Is that what we were doing, sir?"

Mandeville laughed, and said, "Shouldn't I put the best face on it?"

Catherine hastened to add, "Whatever you were discussing, Mr. Mandeville, I am sure it was both fascinating and educational. Charles, you should be going, for you must know that the whole household is in an uproar at your abrupt disappearance."

"Oh, no! I know what *that* will mean."

"You are quite right. You are in for a horrid scold from your grandmama and your tutor, but at least you needn't worry that I will give you a scold, for I never do, Charles, do I?"

"No. You are the very best of parents," said the boy, hugging his mother impulsively.

"Spoiled child!" said her ladyship fondly. "However, young man, I do think you should have told someone where you were going; it is a miracle that I happened to choose to come in this direction and was able to find you at all."

"Mother, if I had told someone where I was going, they wouldn't have permitted me to go."

Catherine's lips pressed together. "I suppose that's so. Your grandmother has very strong ideas about what one may and may not do. She's very—decided in her opinions. But she means no harm, really."

"I don't think that's so, Mama. Grandmama's stuffy and stubborn. And she bullies you. She *likes* to bully you."

"That will do," said Catherine warningly.

"But it's the truth."

"Charles please."

Lady Sturtevant shook her head and turned around away from her son. Smiling sweetly, she held out her hand to Mandeville. "I'm afraid we are expected back. Thank you so much for taking the time to talk with Charles. It is very kind of you. We have few families in the vicinity just at present, and it means a great deal to Charles to meet new persons from whom he can learn a little of the world."

Robert Mandeville did not immediately release the small white hand that had been, for the second time, willingly extended to him. Lady Sturtevant felt herself tremble for just an instant at his touch.

"I am your neighbor now, you know, Lady Sturtevant— now that I am settled permanently at Simla House. I have already invited Charles to come calling on me, for he wishes to learn about life in the East, and he has accepted my invitation. I should like to extend an invitation to you as well. As soon as the house is put in better order, I'd like to invite you—and some others from the neighborhood, of course," he said, improvising furiously, "for a dinner. Would you be able to come, do you think, Lady Sturtevant?"

"Why, yes, I would. We are so thin of company these days. Yes, I would like that very much."

"I'll send a card, then." Robert Mandeville made a slight bow and backed away. "Better yet, I'll deliver it."

"Fine. Good day, Mr. Mandeville."

"Good day, ma'am. And, Charles, remember your word. You have promised to visit me. I can show you a splendid collection of knives and swords, including some from Japan, and some from China, and even a curved sword called the khukhuri, from Nepal."

A wide smile lit up Charles's face. "Yes, sir! Thank you, sir."

"You are very kind, Mr. Mandeville."

"Believe me, Lady Sturtevant, any act of kindness I may be able to perform on behalf of your family or yourself can be only a source to me of the most intense pleasure."

At this bold piece of flattery, Catherine, Lady Sturtevant, like a green girl in her first Season, felt another great blush spreading over her cheeks. What is wrong with me? she wondered. Unnerving fellow! Really, I must be going mad!

Four

It was already early afternoon when she pulled the bell to summon her butler to her, and the summons boded ill. Beatrice, Lady Sturtevant, had not slept well, and the pall cast by her irritation had fallen like the gloom of dusk upon the entire household. It was just a matter of time before her furies receded once more, but until that time everyone would be quite naturally on edge, cringing just a little when they heard the hard whine of her ladyship's voice. The butler was no exception.

"Hawkings!" shouted the elderly woman.

"Yes, your ladyship?" asked the butler, bowing to her deferentially when he appeared and showing none of the apprehension or irritation that he felt at her peremptory command.

"Look out the window, Hawkings! Isn't it incredible? There is a person riding up the avenue! Who can he think he is, coming up here on that enormous prancing creature without any sort of invitation, for I know I certainly did not issue one, and furthermore, I do not recognize the man. I do not know him. Do you?"

Hawkings studied the features of the handsome gentleman most carefully, noting that whoever he might be, he would, as they say, strip to advantage. Hawkings wished he were able to have a few days to himself and be able to attend a good mill for once.

"No, your ladyship," replied Hawkings imperturbably. "I

do not know him. I do not believe I have ever seen him before."

"That's what I meant! An unknown person coming to Apsley Park uninvited! Such impertinence! Send him away at once!"

"Certainly, your ladyship," said Hawkings, bowing himself out. Just as he was to close the door behind himself, he added with what he hoped was the utmost delicacy, "Although, perhaps the gentleman is intending to call upon the younger Lady Sturtevant?"

"Nonsense! Catherine? Who would call on her? She has no admirers, and if there were any fellows hanging about her, I should have been informed of it long since. No, it is some error. He has taken the wrong turning. See to it now and send him away!"

"At once, your ladyship."

Hawkings withdrew in order to carry out her ladyship's commands. On many days at Apsley Park, such as this one, the thought arose in the butler's mind that he wished he had remained with his father in service at Brinton—even if he had had to remain a mere footman. It was difficult, highly difficult working for the dowager, who in Hawkings's humble opinion sadly lacked the good character that her daughter-in-law possessed in great measure. Even among the quality, he thought to himself, their own quality comes in many and varying degrees.

Five

"Mummy, look!" cried Charles excitedly, pulling aside the hanging to get a better view of the front lawn. "He's come!"

"Who's come, darling?"

"It's the gentleman from yesterday, from Simla House, he's come to call. Look at that prime piece of blood he's riding! I'd give anything to have a horse like that. I'm so glad he's here!"

"Why, dear?"

"I've never had a grown-up as a real friend. Mr. Mandeville's so knowledgeable! This morning I went into the library and found some books about the Orient. I've been reading all about our trade in India, and the East India Company, and about Sikhs and Pathans and princely states, and tremendous fortunes and precious jewels and Malabar spices, and I've a thousand questions to ask him about it all. Shall you come down too?"

"Yes, of course I shall, Charles," replied his mother, checking her appearance in a mirror and giving a swift pinch to her cheeks. "I think he has come not only to see you, dear, but to pay a formal visit to the household. It would be very rude of me not to receive him. I would not dream of such a thing. Besides," she added ingenuously, "I quite like him."

Charles gave his mother an odd look. "Do you?" he said.

"It is always good to make new friends. Change your clothes, Charles, and meet us in the drawing room."

"But, Mother . . ."

"You look like a ragamuffin. Do as I say."

Catherine straightened out the folds of her morning dress, glad Jenny had chosen the new apple-green one and not the apricot, which always made her look a little old and drab. She pulled a few loose tendrils down from her lace cap and went quickly to the landing. She had just reached the last step of the main staircase when she heard Thomas inform the caller that "Lady Sturtevant was not at home." At this Catherine cried out, "Thomas! What are you saying? I am acquainted with Mr. Mandeville, and I have not asked to be denied. I am so sorry, Mr. Mandeville. Do come in."

Mandeville handed his hat to an embarrassed first footman and entered the large, tiled hallway. Even amid the grandeur of the Apsley entrance, he loomed large over his surroundings. He was taller than she had remembered, and more broad of shoulder. Mr. Mandeville was, clearly, a gentleman to be reckoned with.

"Good day, Lady Sturtevant. I am happy to at last find you in. I was about to leave, having been informed by your man here that Lady Sturtevant was not at home."

"Not at home? Thomas, how could you say such a thing?"

"I was beginning to fear you did not wish to receive my call," Mandeville said with a raise of an eyebrow.

"On the contrary," Catherine said, directing an inquiring glance at the red-faced footman who stammered something about the dowager Lady Sturtevant having asked to be denied to all callers.

"Thomas refers to my mother-in-law, Beatrice," Catherine explained as she preceded Mandeville into the drawing room. "She sees relatively few visitors. It would have been Beatrice who gave orders that Hawkings deny her. I most certainly did not."

"I am relieved to hear that, Lady Sturtevant."

"Are you, Mr. Mandeville?" she asked, suddenly teasing.

"Very much so."

The unmistakable warmth of his tone led Catherine near

to the blushing point once more; she tried to suppress her feelings, but what could one do? They came of themselves. It was only lucky that Beatrice was not present to witness her questionable deportment.

Catherine sat down in her usual place, a chair by the pianoforte near the long windows. She indicated a gilded chair for her visitor, and the two sat in silence for a moment.

Receiving a gentleman to whom one felt attracted but whom one did not know well was really very awkward, Catherine thought. It was almost like the awkwardness one felt at Almack's during one's first Season—desperate to make a good impression and not at all knowing how. The tension was almost unnerving; the pressure to say just the right thing was omnipresent and crushing.

"The weather has been very fine this week," Catherine ventured finally, if only to break that awful lingering silence.

"It has indeed," her visitor agreed with equal insipidity. Inwardly, he was kicking himself. What in heaven's name was the matter? He found himself frozen—he was self-conscious and tongue-tied, like any young puppy first come down to town.

Moments passed. No word was said. The ticking of the clock on the mantel grated on the nerves as two normally keen minds groped about wildly, searching for a comment, any comment, that would serve to continue the conversation.

"It has not rained for some time," her ladyship observed at last.

"No," said her visitor. "No, that is quite true. It has not rained for a week at least."

The awkward silence between them surfaced again like a rising fog.

"A whole week?"

"That *is* rather a long time," said Mandeville. "For it to go without raining."

"True."

"Very true."

The silence returned. The mantel clock ticked inexorably on, punctuating their mutual discomfort

"Well, then, Mr. Mandeville," said Catherine, casting about for a remark in utter desperation. "Do you suppose that it may rain tomorrow?"

"I do not know," replied Mr. Mandeville.

Most unhelpfully, he added, "What do *you* think, Lady Sturtevant?"

This was the outside of enough for Catherine.

"I think, Mr. Mandeville," said her ladyship, putting her hands firmly in her lap, "that we really *must* stop talking about the weather."

"What a splendid idea!" said Mandeville, almost laughing with relief."

"It is, isn't it?"

"I can't recall ever having spent so very many minutes pondering precipitation."

"That is all to the good, surely?" commented Catherine wryly, and Mandeville smiled.

The ice having been broken at last, the couple leaned back on their silk-upholstered chairs and relaxed just a little. Mandeville suddenly leaned forward toward her ladyship, declaring, "You know, ma'am, it is very hard to think of you as having been a widow for many years. You must be in your twenties still, are you not?"

"I am twenty-seven, and have been widowed these ten years."

"Forgive me, Lady Sturtevant—if this subject is at all painful to you, we can talk of something else."

"Is that so? Of what shall we speak? The climate?" she asked with an air of assumed innocence. "Heaven defend me! I pray we shall not attempt it! We clearly have no talent whatsoever for meteorological discussion."

Mr. Mandeville cast her an appreciative glance and smiled again. He waited for her to continue.

"Really, Mr. Mandeville, I don't mind talking about my

marriage or my late husband," said Catherine. "It all seems as if it happened a lifetime ago. I was wed when I had just turned seventeen. M-my husband, Frederick, died only a few months after we were married. Of the influenza."

"That must have been difficult for you."

"It came as a great shock. He took ill quite suddenly, and the end was swift; one week he was fine, and the next he was gone."

"And you and your son have lived here at Apsley Park ever since? With your mother-in-law?"

"Yes. Charles, of course, succeeded to Apsley upon Frederick's death. I often wished we could have settled in London, where there is a bit more society, but my mother-in-law wouldn't hear of it."

"Couldn't you settle there anyway?"

"According to the terms of Frederick's will, I must have Beatrice's consent to any changes in Charles's living arrangements."

Mr. Mandeville raised an eyebrow in disbelief. "That is not a normal disposition of things, Lady Sturtevant. Generally the wife becomes legal guardian to any children."

"Just so. You can imagine how very disappointed I was when I learned how things had been left, particularly since Beatrice and I have strongly opposed opinions on many topics. I have no doubt that Beatrice brought pressure on Frederick in order to obtain his consent to it, but there's no use crying about it now. I have become inured to the way things are. That's why we are out here at Apsley when everyone else in the county is in London having a lovely time. Since Charles is the Earl of Sturtevant, Beatrice believes it is important that he be brought up on his ancestral lands, as were his father and his father before him. Myself, I disagree. I think he needs the stimulation of company. Charles is, I think, really rather lonely out here."

"Are you as well?" asked Mandeville, pushing his chair much closer to hers.

Catherine raised an eyebrow at this bold question and allowed the most attractive hint of a smile to play upon her rosy lips.

"You are very frank, sir!"

"One must profit from the example of Wellington: Turbulent times call for swift and direct action. After all, I have nothing to lose but my pride."

Catherine laughed, and then her face changed as she carefully considered his question. She lowered her lashes for just a moment, then raised her soft hazel eyes to look directly into those of Mr. Robert Mandeville. Her heart in her hand, she replied in a whisper that made the gentleman lean so close to her that he could smell the warmth of rosewater perfume, "Yes. Yes, I am, Mr. Mandeville. Very much so."

The conversation of the lady and the gentleman would doubtless have taken a different and yet more personal turn, save that young Charles at that very moment rushed into the drawing room and plopped down on a chair next to Mr. Mandeville.

"Sir! I'm so glad you came! I have so much to ask you. Oh, look!" he said, gesturing toward a maid who had just entered bearing a heavy silver tray. "Minnie's brought lemon cakes. You must try some, sir, they're delicious."

"Yes, Mr. Mandeville," said Catherine, rising, "do have some, won't you? They're Cook's *specialité de maison.*"

"I have a particular weakness for English cakes after so many years abroad."

"Haven't they cakes in India, sir?" asked young Lord Sturtevant.

"Some native cooks have learned to make facsimiles of our cakes which look like the originals but somehow never taste quite the same, I think, because they haven't precisely the same ingredients. Indigenous Indian sweets and desserts are quite delicious, but are an entirely different affair. *Gulab jamun* became my particular favorite, but it would seem very odd, I think, to most English palates. It is made, you see, using rosewater."

"They put *perfume* in it?"

"How extraordinary!" interjected Catherine, amazed.

"Once one becomes accustomed to the unusual blending of fragrance and taste, one grows quite addicted to it. It is a celestial experience, I assure you."

"You certainly have led a fascinating life, Mr. Mandeville. So different from ours, I am quite envious of you. I'll pour out the tea, shall I?"

Lady Sturtevant busied herself with the tea, and Charles took the opportunity to have a special word with Mr. Mandeville. "Sir, I've been thinking about the things you told me ever since yesterday. Now, here's my first question: Is it true that the heads of princely states in India wear jewels and necklaces like women do in England?"

"Not only is it true, Charles, but they wear them on a much more lavish scale than women do here. Indian princes wear ropes and ropes of the most magnificent pearls. Many of them also wear turbans, which are also ornamented with priceless jewels."

"Such wealth is unimaginable," said Catherine.

"The wealth of India *is* unimaginable, as is the poverty. I have never, in England or on the Continent, seen such lavish displays of riches as I saw there, nor have I ever seen, in England or on the Continent, human beings living in such squalor."

"Do they have poor people there too, then?" asked Charles.

"Even poorer than in the worst slums of London."

"I have never seen a slum. And I have never been to London—my grandmama won't let me go. But I have read about such things, and I am interested to learn about them. When I am grown, I hope to look after my lands and my tenants very well. Tell me, Mr. Mandeville, in India, do these wealthy rulers do nothing to relieve the suffering of their people?"

"Ordinary people, even people who are not well off, consider it to be virtuous to give what they can afford to the poor. The poor are part of the cultural landscape. The rulers make little real effort to make improvements. Of course, it is hard to imagine what could be done, everything being on such a vast scale."

"I don't think I'd like to see that," said Charles. "I don't even like it sometimes when we pass the poor villagers here."

"No, of course not, Charles."

"You must miss it," said Catherine.

"I do, just a bit, but India is both very magnificent and very hard."

"How long did you live there, Mr. Mandeville?"

"Nearly twenty years."

"That's a lifetime! Did you find you got more used to the state of things over the years?" asked Catherine.

"By no means. How can one ever become used to human suffering?" said he softly.

Catherine felt her heart touched and opened by his simple statement of compassion. For so long there had been little enough of warmth of human kindness around her, and now she had before her a gentleman who was moved by empathy for others. Warmth flooded through her, and a strange joy with it. Mr. Mandeville was, obviously, a fine human being, a good man, a man with a sense of virtue. Instinctively, she moved closer to him, and was about to ask another question when the main doors to the drawing room were suddenly thrown open by a footman.

Beatrice, the dowager Countess of Sturtevant, swept into the room dressed in an odd mauve creation with a peculiar matching turban that did nothing for her looks. She strode over to Catherine's chair and stood there, towering over her in a menacing fashion. Catherine rose immediately, concerned at the scene she might create in front of Mr. Mandeville.

"What does this mean, Catherine?" she demanded. "Who is this man you have let into this house?"

"Beatrice! How can you speak so? Mr. Mandeville is our guest."

"I am not acquainted with the person to whom you refer. Further, I will thank you to keep your behavioral strictures to yourself, who is in need of them."

Catherine declined to respond to this directly, but stated with a calmness she did not feel, "Beatrice, may I present to you Mr. Robert Mandeville of Simla House, our new neighbor. Mr. Mandeville, this is my mother-in-law, Beatrice, dowager Countess of Sturtevant."

Mr. Robert Mandeville rose and bowed deeply. Her ladyship's mood failed to improve.

"Mandeville?" she sneered. "Never heard of any Mandevilles, not in this neighborhood. Who is your family? Who are your relations? What is this Simla House?"

It soon became apparent that Robert Mandeville was the sort of man unafraid to take up the gauntlet for a good cause; the irrepressible twinkle in his eye presaged his encountering the dowager's challenge with the swift, direct action he had but recently recommended."

"Simla House! Hah!" barked the dowager. "A preposterous name! It sounds like something one of those filthy rich, sunburnt, trading nabobs would call his home. Why have you come here, sir? Who are you *really?*"

"I have the honor to be *really,*" he replied, his eyes dancing, "a nabob."

"What?"

"I am a nabob. I am a nabob come into Hampshire to take a wife."

The younger Lady Sturtevant made an odd, gasping sort of sound while her mother-in-law reeled back, shocked.

"A nabob? In *my* house? Infamous!" she puffed, her face reddening awfully. "Take a *wife?* Who, *Catherine?* No, you shall not, you encroaching mushroom! I will thank you to leave my house and leave my daughter-in-law alone, for I have no doubt it is she to whom, in your presumption, you refer. How can you dare to say such things in my drawing room?"

"I dare to say such things in this drawing room because, Lady Sturtevant, they are true—regardless of the venue in which voiced. And, by the bye, Lady Sturtevant, isn't Apsley Charles's house, *really?* Thus it follows that I am saying such things in *his* drawing room. Really."

Catherine was choking in an admixture of delight and sheer, utter horror. She began making signs with her eyes, trying to attract Mr. Mandeville's attention, desperate to convey to him that no matter how great the provocation, the elder lady occupied such a position of power in the family that she was not to be provoked or offended, not for any reason, not for any whim, and certainly not merely from a surfeit of high spirits.

"What signal impertinence! Mr. Mandeville, I take leave to tell you that this acquaintance will not do for us, it simply will not do."

"Won't it?" he asked pitifully, his dark, boyish eyes all innocence.

Catherine had to suppress a loud laugh while, simultaneously, her heart was sinking through the floor. Mr. Mandeville mustn't quiz Beatrice so! Granted, it was deeply satisfying and, to be sure, terribly amusing to watch Beatrice being baited for once, and baited so shamelessly; however, Catherine had no doubt that in the end the high-spirited Mr. Mandeville's joke would be had at her own—and her son's—expense.

"No, it won't do at all. I never heard of such a thing!" said the elder woman ruthlessly. "Charles, you will come with me this minute. Your tutor is calling you."

"But, Grandmama, Mr. Mandeville—"

"You will leave the room at once. Do as you're told!"

"Good-bye, Mr. Mandeville." Charles shook his hand and managed to whisper to him that he'd come to Simla House just as soon as he could get away. "Don't mind Grandmama. She's just high in the instep."

"I shan't regard it. Besides, I have a godmother who is very like her. It is my own fault, you know: I did provoke your grandmother in a most shameless and ungentlemanly fashion. Do come by soon, Charles."

"Good-bye, sir."

"Charles! Don't speak with him!" said the dowager Lady Sturtevant, turning on her daughter-in-law ruthlessly and gesturing toward the door. "You, Catherine, will come to me in my chamber this evening. I have some things I particularly wish to make clear to you, but I am in too great a state of shock to convey these things to you now."

Catherine paled at the thought of another such an interview with her mother-in-law, for she knew well what it would mean.

Mr. Mandeville rose, picking up his whip.

"Lady Sturtevant," said he, addressing Beatrice directly, "before I go, I must apologize for speaking as I did just now. In India, manners are more free than are apparently acceptable here. I deeply regret my levity; if I was impertinent, I do beg your pardon. It will not happen again."

"It will not happen despite your pretty speech, because there will be no such opportunity," said the dowager, directing a black look at both Mandeville and Catherine.

"I think there will be one, at least. I look forward to Thursday week, and I do thank *you*," he continued, addressing himself this time to Catherine, "for the honor of having accepted my invitation to dinner at Simla House."

"Dinner?" said Catherine blankly. "On Thursday week?"

"Dinner?" cried Beatrice hideously.

"Dinner. Supper. Repast. Refection," supplied Mr. Mandeville helpfully. "On Thursday week. Had you forgotten? You accepted my verbal invitation when we met at the garden just yesterday. That's why I came; I thought to deliver the card in person. I'm sure I mentioned my intention. Here is the card." He reached into his pocket. "Of all the awful luck! I came all this way and have forgotten it. No matter, I will send it, but let me explain that I am holding a dinner in which I welcome my new neighbors to Simla House. The company will be very gay. I have the honor to hope that the Duchess of Underhill, with whom you are perhaps acquainted, will come."

"Are you mad? Lydia Underhill?" asked Lady Sturtevant, staring at him, horrified yet enthralled. "Dining at *your* house?"

"The rest of the invitation cards will be inscribed today. I do hope," Mandeville said, turning to the elder lady, "that *both* of you ladies will do me the honor of attending?"

Seeing with no small satisfaction that this claim of acquaintance with an extremely fashionable noblewoman had left Beatrice dumbstruck, Mr. Mandeville bowed politely and withdrew.

Lady Sturtevant staggered to the sofa and sank down upon it, shuddering in a most well-bred way.

"Lydia Underhill going to dine at the home of a person involved in *trade?* An avowed *nabob?* How could she do such a thing? Good God, what is the world coming to? Vinaigrette, Catherine! Ring for my vinaigrette!"

Six

The threatened interview between the dowager and the young widow did not take place until a full day had passed, due to Beatrice's having contracted a stubborn headache. When the discussion finally occurred, the circumstances that caused it were of the most unfortunate kind: Charles had once again disappeared from under the eagle eye of his long-suffering tutor, Mr. Thymmes, and was supposed by the disapproving household to have run off to visit the nabob next door.

Catherine, wishing to avoid the sort of scene with Beatrice that had preceded her last search for her wayward son, had Jenny fetch her shawl and bonnet in the privacy of her chambers; thus she was able to slip outdoors by way of the back stairs and the servants' entrance. She made her way through the path in the woods, and within twenty minutes of fast walking arrived outside the walled garden where she had first seen Charles with Mr. Mandeville.

The wooden door of the walled garden was ajar. Admiring the exotic carvings that adorned it, she knocked tentatively twice, and then went on within.

It was as if a new universe had opened up before her, one that was alien and yet somehow perfect in itself. To her left there were beds of unusual red and purple flowers planted in patterns, and terraced so as to form miniature mountainsides. To the right was a section done entirely in rhododendrons and azaleas, making a shadowy place that sheltered a small, beautifully carved wooden pagoda.

At the end of the central path was a great glass greenhouse that housed a jungle of tropical plants: enormous palms of different kinds, lacy ferns, elephant ear, and other plants that provided a home for a collection of brightly feathered tropical birds: ring-necked parrots, egrets, and, on the ground, a peahen and peacock. Behind that, looming up twenty feet into the air, was a carved stone temple, clearly ancient, that must have been brought stone by stone from abroad and reassembled.

She gasped aloud, overcome with wonder. It was an extraordinary creation, and was clearly the work of an extraordinary mind.

"Lady Sturtevant," a deep voice called out from behind her.

"Oh! Mr. Mandeville!" said Catherine, surprised. "I had thought you were within the garden. How do you do?"

"I've just come back from the house; I was missing some drawings I needed. How very nice it is to see you again, Lady Sturtevant. I hope you will forgive my shocking want of conduct yesterday. I could not help myself. I'm afraid it is a character flaw of long standing."

Catherine felt a warm shiver go through her at the sound of his voice. She tried to keep her mind on her business, not on the gentleman speaking with her, but it was difficult.

"I cannot blame you for something I have longed to do myself were I only in a position to do so. I am looking for my son, who has slipped away again. I am eager to bring him back before he is missed," she said "Have you seen him?"

"Yes, I put him to work categorizing seedlings. I was about to send him off home. I don't approve of his missing his lessons, and have informed him that his future visits here mustn't occur at the expense of his education."

"That is most kind. Now that I have seen your garden, I

must tell you, Mr. Mandeville, how very much I admire this place. How did you come to create it?"

"I designed this garden when I was living in the East, and sent the plans here to England over the years, along with seeds and seedlings, and so on. When I visited the Shalimar Gardens, I sent back roses—they're in bloom now. I'd think you'd enjoy seeing them. I copied some of the planting patterns the Mughals used at the gardens, though I was, of course, unable to provide the extraordinary view of the snow mountains in the background that makes Shalimar so particularly exquisite."

"Is it all done, or are you still working on it?"

"Now that I've come back, I notice that there are places where either the plans I sent were not followed correctly or where I am dissatisfied with the effect. I will be amusing myself in the next few years by fine-tuning my little Oriental garden."

"Your 'little Oriental garden?' What a hum! It is immense. From outside you cannot tell at all what extraordinary things are within. You must have done that on purpose."

"I did. I thought it prudent. Sometimes the English can be very narrow-minded. I built these high walls for privacy, not wishing to provide food for gossip or to end up being known as 'Mandeville the idolater' simply because I've placed a statue of Shiva in my garden."

"Shiva? What is that?"

"Shiva is one of the three main Hindu deities. He is frequently depicted in a dancing pose with one leg raised, very graceful. I was lucky enough to obtain a rare old stone statue of him from a ruined temple near Khajuraho. I've put it in the section just over there." Mr. Mandeville hesitated for a moment, and then said, "May I show you my garden, Lady Sturtevant? I should like to very much."

"I would love to see it."

"Would you like to do so now?"

"Yes. Let me just send Charles back to Apsley."

Charles appeared at his mother's call. He expressed great delight with all he had seen and learned under the informal tutelage of Mr. Mandeville, so much so that he did not balk at her command to return home, merely saying how much he would look forward to his next visit.

Mr. Mandeville and Catherine spent the next hour touring the grounds of the immense Oriental garden. Mandeville pointed out to her ladyship the most important pieces, artistically and arboreally, and she paid him rapt attention. Then, having completed their circuit of the garden, they began to walk back toward the coppice door in silence, until Mr. Mandeville asked Catherine what, if anything, she had liked best.

"It was the roses you brought back from Kashmir. I don't think I've ever smelled a fragrance so complex and so intense. English roses just aren't like that—they're flat, and rather simple—just a pretty scent. But those roses, each of them in its own way, were just—exquisite. And so *passionate.* There's no other word to describe them."

At this, Catherine looked directly at Mr. Mandeville, and, as he returned her gaze, something extraordinary passed between them.

Mandeville stopped, turned toward her, and drew Catherine into his arms. She did not resist, but, on the contrary, welcomed his embrace as she had never welcomed those of Charles's father. She felt as if she were on the brink of discovering lasting bliss.

Neither one noticed how much time had passed until the two heard a knocking at the gate, and sprung apart, surprised and embarrassed. Mr. Mandeville unlocked the door and admitted Baxter, the groom from Apsley, bearing an urgent missive for Catherine.

Baxter handed her the envelope. She broke it open and scanned its contents quickly. Her face had turned scarlet by the time she put the envelope in her reticule.

"I am afraid I must return home at once."

"Is there anything wrong? Didn't Charles arrive home safely?"

"Charles is fine. This note concerns my mother-in-law."

"Is she ill?"

"I suppose so, if one counts as infirmity a predilection for strong hysterics. Forgive me; that was unkind. I should be more compassionate to Beatrice. I am beholden to her."

"Beholden? Perhaps in the future you need not be," he said, taking her hand and giving her a speaking glance. "Lady Sturtevant, there are some important matters between us I wish to discuss with you at the very earliest opportunity."

Looking back worriedly at the groom, blushing slightly, and smiling in her shy way, she withdrew her hand. "I cannot do so at this time, sir, though I wish I might. I must go back to Apsley at once."

"Till we meet again, then." He bowed. "Please be assured, Lady Sturtevant, that I am always your most obedient servant."

"Thank you so much. I must go. Good-bye, Mr. Mandeville," she said, once again loosing that lovely smile that had first endeared her to him.

In a moment she was gone, and he was once again alone in the Oriental garden. It seemed to him at that time not a place of solitude any longer, but merely a place of emptiness and vacancy. He knew at that moment that he could not, would not, live without her.

Seven

Beatrice, Lady Sturtevant, was laid out full-length on the gold damask sofa in her chambers. When Catherine arrived, she did not at once acknowledge her entrance directly, but called out miserably to her dresser, "Smithers—bring hartshorn! More hartshorn! Heaven help me, this headache has destroyed me utterly!" Giving Catherine a dark, withering look, she added, *"Some* persons have, besides no conduct to speak of, no compassion for the sufferings of the infirm."

Catherine shifted on her feet from side to side, impatient to get this interview over with; it was an inevitable event, of course, and she wished only to have Beatrice's wrath fall on her and be done with. Beatrice, however, preferred to lengthen the experience and spice it with a long list of complaints, beginning with her deficiencies of character, her miserable taste in clothes, her failings as a mother, and assorted errors tallied up over many years. This extensive summary completed, she turned to her daughter-in-law to deliver the coup de grâce.

"Wicked, wicked child! Have I not provided you a home these long ten years since my darling Frederick died? Have I not generously permitted you to stay on at Apsley, when others might have sent you away forever? Your conduct is a torment to me, I tell you! Why? Why do you persist in misbehaving, Catherine? Why? I have prayed to God to send me an answer this long hour, since I discovered, from your young son of all people, that you were disgracing yourself in the company of that unmarried person of the male sex"—and here her ladyship grimaced awfully—"Mandeville! That nabob! That bachelor who, who—*made his fortune from trade!* Why did you go?"

"Why did I go there? You know perfectly well: I went there to find Charles."

"I told you *last* time it was unsuitable for you to do that! Not only did you contravene my explicit desires, but you sent Charles home and proceeded to remain in the company of that man for over an hour!"

"He was merely showing me around his garden."

" 'Showing you around his garden'! Rubbish! That garden is *walled,* and locks with *a key.* I know so because Charles, under questioning, admitted as much to me. I know also there were no servants present in his garden—neither his nor yours. You may as well have visited his bedchamber! That Mandeville person means to ruin you, and I can see now that you mean to be a willing participant in your own ruination. How is it possible that your own dear mother, may she rest in peace, and your late excellent father did not manage to impress upon you the proper conduct expected of a lady of quality?

"It is incredible to me, all of it. All the man wants is to worm his way into Apsley. He will compromise you and force marriage on you, and try to force Charles's properties and fortune out of me. But it won't work. I'll see to that even if you can't.

"I tell you plainly, Catherine, while you may not care for your reputation, your reputation concerns this family and my grandson. You will not be allowed to make a mockery of the name of Sturtevant. Further, you will make no imprudent *mésalliance.*

"You may go to your room. I will see to it that this situation is resolved. When I have made my decisions as to your future, I will inform you."

Catherine left her mother-in-law's room, fairly reeling from the impact of such unmitigated aggression. She went to her own room and was greeted by her abigail, Jenny, who tried to soothe her mistress with lavender water on a handkerchief.

"There, there, your ladyship. The dowager will calm down again, and the storm will blow over. You know what she's like: It's always the same, the storm breaks and the calm comes after. Her bark is worse than her bite. She won't do nothing."

The countess's hazel eyes reflected deep misgivings. "I think she will this time, Jenny. This time I think she will."

Eight

It rained most dreadfully for the next two days, accurately reflecting Catherine's increasingly despondent mood. Both the dowager Countess of Sturtevant and Catherine, Countess of Sturtevant, received the invitations to dinner at Simla House. The dowager destroyed hers on receipt, and sent the pieces to her daughter-in-law on a silver salver with a curt note bidding Catherine to respond at once with a letter sending her regrets.

Catherine did so reluctantly, her spirits already depressed by the news penned in a strong fist on the reverse of her card of invitation that Mr. Mandeville would be gone to London for some days on business. He did say that he would call upon her as soon as he returned, but she found his sudden, unexpected departure from her life most oppressive. She missed him.

One more soggy day later, Catherine, at work upstairs on some embroidery, was surprised to hear the sound of a carriage and four pulling up at the front entranceway; by the time she went to the window, the visitor had already disappeared inside.

A few minutes later Thomas knocked and informed her that she was wanted in the drawing room. Her heart leapt, hoping that it was Mr. Robert Mandeville returned from London, and she hurried to put her hair in better order before going down. Did she look as old as she was? She hoped not.

A gentleman caller come at last. Dear Mr. Mandeville, she

believed with a happiness heretofore unknown to her, had been on the point of offering for her when she was called back by Beatrice to Apsley. Another five minutes in that extraordinary garden, she thought, and my future might have been settled as well as any woman could wish. Please, she prayed from the depths of her heart, let it be Mr. Mandeville calling. Let him take Charles and me away from Apsley Park at long last.

When Thomas opened the doors so she might enter the drawing room, Catherine was immediately repelled by the sight of a tall, thin, mincing man with straw-colored hair whose shirt points were so ridiculously high that they pinched his cheeks. His smile to her was closer to a leer. Catherine looked at her mother-in-law with consternation. Who was this fellow? What was Beatrice up to now?

"Catherine, dear," said Beatrice, rising and coming toward her with a thin smile, "do allow me to make the Earl of St. Auburne known to you."

"How do you do, Lady Sturtevant?" said the earl, taking Catherine's hand to his lips and kissing it wetly. Catherine removed her hand at once, appalled, and wiped it unobtrusively on her apricot muslin gown, of which, thankfully, she was not fond in any case.

"St. Auburne is so kind!" said the dowager with animation. "You see, I wrote him that we were down here all alone in Hampshire, simply pining with boredom and loneliness, and Lord St. Auburne was kind enough to leave the gaiety of the best part of the London Season and come down to entertain us. Wasn't that friendly of him? His kindness and compassion are legendary in London, and thus you must have heard of them—and him. I am sure you will like St. Auburne excessively. I'll leave you two alone, then, shall I? I believe someone is calling me."

"You will not leave us here, Beatrice," Catherine whispered through gritted teeth.

"Certainly I will, Catherine. Don't be missish," hissed her

mother-in-law. "St. Auburne is an old friend of the family; he has particularly asked to have speech with you, and he shall have it. I am a very busy woman, and am needed elsewhere! Don't be such a goose!"

The dowager extended her thin hand to her guest. "I'll see you at dinner, St. Auburne. Thank you again for coming all this way to see us. Too kind."

Catherine tried to maintain her composure for an interview she was sure would be a dead bore. Why did Beatrice use her so? Why did she have to endure Beatrice's little whims, entertaining persons with whom she had nothing in common? She had little doubt that Lord St. Auburne had decided to rusticate himself at Apsley as a result of having fallen short of funds toward the end of the London Season; why was she needed to exchange small talk with a person who had come to the country no doubt to escape his creditors and leech off his friends and family for a while.

She was quite surprised when, instead of sitting on one of the gilt chairs intended for visitors, St. Auburne chose to seat himself directly next to her on the silk brocade sofa; his positioning made her feel very ill at ease. The presumption of the man was truly annoying, especially considering that they had not been introduced more than two minutes. When would Beatrice return?

"What is it that you wish to discuss with me, Lord St. Auburne?" Catherine asked more sharply than she had intended.

"We will come to that in a moment, Lady Sturtevant, if you please. Your mother-in-law has been telling me that it has been very trying for you living in the country, far from London society, and attempting bravely to raise the young Earl of Sturtevant all by yourself."

Immediately, Catherine became suspicious. London? Was Beatrice intent on sending her to London at last? What did this Lord St. Auburne have to do with her and her son's living arrangements?

Her eyes narrowed, and she asked with little attempt at civility, "Perhaps you would do me the honor of telling me what business that is of yours, sir?"

"Perhaps you would do me the honor of becoming my wife?" he riposted smoothly, not missing a beat.

"Your *wife?*" cried Catherine. "I've just this moment met you!"

"That is hardly an impediment. Many of the most fashionable couples rarely meet even *after* they are wed. We might follow their example."

"How dare you, sir! Your presumption, your encroaching manner—this is all entirely unforgivable!"

"Unforgivable? Why, then, dear lady, I beg you must forgive me! Of course, I admit, it is all a little rushed, this marital business, and I am sure its suddenness has overawed your delicate female constitution. I can easily see why you might have been taken by surprise at my offer, but nevertheless I have strong reason to believe that you will, in the end, accept my hand in marriage, and I feel sure that we will suit."

"If Beatrice gave you to understand that she could talk me into marriage, she must be mad. I can tell you frankly that it is not so."

"With all due respect, I have been given to believe that it *is* so, Catherine. I may call you Catherine, may I not? You are a very well-looking woman, Catherine. I am so glad that Beatrice wrote to me. I think I am going to enjoy losing my bachelor status finally after these many long years."

"I assure you again, sir, that your suit has no chance of success."

"Speak with your mother-in-law, my dear, and we will talk again," said Lord St. Auburne, patting her hand with infuriating solicitude.

"I shall, sir. This interview is at an end!"

Nine

It was really rather fortunate that the middle of the Apsley dining table was home to an enormous ornate silver epergne, for Lord St. Auburne might have expired of basilisk glances that Catherine, Lady Sturtevant, threw at him from her side of the table. She had flatly refused to sit next to him, so he had been seated in the place of honor next to Beatrice, who naturally occupied the head of the table. Beatrice and St. Auburne chatted raucously through course after course, giggling and joking about London life, downing excessive quantities of vintage intoxicants, and generally having such a fine time for themselves that Catherine was ready to murder them, serially or simultaneously, whichever was fastest.

Catherine had not yet had the opportunity to discuss with Beatrice this latest outrageous piece of interference; and the only thing that kept her from leaving the table in a rage was her intense desire to confront Beatrice when they withdrew after dinner so she could inform her mother-in-law of the utter defeat of her bizarre plan to marry her off to St. Auburne.

The door to the withdrawing room had barely closed behind the last exiting servant when Catherine launched into a spirited attack, the very first one she had ever made upon her mother-in-law during ten long years of oppression.

"This is the outside of enough, Beatrice! How can you have set that, that *creature* upon me?"

"I will not have you use that tone of voice with me, Catherine. I am doing this for your own good as well as for the good of the family, and for dear Charles's good. He ought really to be raised by a nobleman. A nobleman can teach him about consequence and propriety, particularly since those things are apparently so unimportant to you. It is the perfect solution to all our problems. I'm only sorry I didn't think to arrange for your remarriage long ago—I must beg your pardon! Thank God your meeting with that horrid Mandeville made my duty clear and the solution evident. As the Countess of St. Auburne, you will occupy a position of the first respectability; St. Auburne can oversee your conduct and your moneys and Charles's conduct and Charles's estate, and for yourself, you will be able to spend several months in London, as you have always wished to do. A happy ending for everyone, and a crushing load finally lifted off these aging shoulders."

"Listen to me, Beatrice, and listen well: I will not marry that man! You cannot force me to do so!"

Beatrice's eyes narrowed, glittering with malice.

"I hold your reins, child, and you know it."

"Don't you dare hold Charles as a sword over my head. Not in this!"

The dowager's lips turned up in a triumphantly malicious smile.

"Whyever not?"

"Because it simply isn't done! You can't force me into a marriage against my will."

"No, my dear, of course I may not," said Beatrice with sudden buttery smoothness. "You are of age, and you may marry whomever you like. I can only present St. Auburne to you as a very desirable life partner. If you wish to do otherwise, it is entirely your affair."

"Thank you."

"Save that, should you elect to continue your friendship with this Mandeville, or should you elect to remain a widow living here without the supervision of a husband, I shall use my legal authority outlined under the terms of Frederick's will to have Charles removed from Apsley and sent away. To Eton, I think. They'll make a man of him."

"No!" cried Catherine.

"Yes, my dear, that is how it will be," replied the dowager countess. "After all, I have Charles to think of—he has his whole life before him. He will be deeply affected by the circumstances of his upbringing, by the examples of propriety set by those around him, by the tenor of the household in which he is raised to manhood. You can't raise him in the sloppy, care-for-nothing manner I have suffered you to do these many years—he's too old now. The situation is critical, absolutely critical. I can't allow you to go on as you have done here—it would be wrong for Charles. He requires a noble education, and he requires it from a nobleman.

"So suit yourself, my dear: it's entirely your decision. Marry St. Auburne at once. Or lose your child."

Ten

Jenny found her mistress huddled on her bed, her cap so deeply buried in the lace-covered pillow that it was hard to make out just why the figure was trembling so. It was not easily evident that her ladyship had been crying until she raised her head toward her abigail, and held out her hand. Jenny took it and chafed it, saying, "It'll come right, your ladyship," though she knew well that never before had she seen her mistress in such a desolate state.

"It won't come right, Jenny. It's just as I thought. I'll never escape from her clutches, just like Frederick. Beatrice always wins."

"What's that old weasel wanting you to do for her this time?"

Catherine wiped the tears from her face and blew her reddened nose into the linen handkerchief Jenny proffered her. She shook her head in dismay and disbelief.

"This time, Jenny, the dowager would have me marry."

"That's all to the good, your ladyship!" cried her abigail hopefully.

"It might be, save for the fact that she wants me to marry the wrong man."

"No! You don't say so! She don't want you to be shackled to that odd frippery fellow who came down here from London?"

"Yes. Beatrice wants me to become Mrs. Fashionable Fribble—or, rather, the Countess of Fribble, I should say. Heaven knows how I can joke about it—she's got me where she wants me, all right, and the Countess of Fribble I shall soon be."

"How can she *do* that?"

"She's brought out the long cannon once again."

"Not going on about Charles again, is she? The woman has no conscience. She's no Christian, if you ask me."

"Beatrice says she'll send Charles off to Eton unless I wed St. Auburne. I couldn't let that happen, no matter what it costs me. I'd die rather than be parted from my son."

"You'll accept his lordship's offer, then?" cried Jenny, shocked.

"I've thought about it and thought about it. It seems that I have no choice. I can't be separated from my son!"

"No, of course not, your ladyship."

"Beatrice planned this all very well, and is in a terrible hurry to be rid of me. St. Auburne brought down with him a special license from London, if you please, with our two names conveniently filled in. I could become his countess in the blinking of an eye. I have nothing to do but say yes. It's like waking to a nightmare."

"It ain't human."

"It is inhuman, and it's terribly ironic. What a thing to happen to me now, just when I thought that my life was finally taking a sudden turn for the better, just when I thought there would be an end to this prisoner's life I've led for so long."

"Can't that nice Mr. Mandeville help you?"

"What can he do? Beatrice says that I may marry where I like, but that only marriage to St. Auburne will prevent her from taking away my son. Choose between my son and Mr. Mandeville? If I must, I choose Charles. I am his mother."

Jenny hugged her mistress, but she had no idea how to avoid any further damage, or how to help her. Seemed like what her ladyship said was so—she'd have to marry that dandy. Hard choices were the way of the world, and even Jenny knew it. Jenny was a practical young woman—she hadn't been able to marry the man she loved either, for there just wasn't money enough to be able to do it. Sometimes things you wanted just didn't work out.

Jenny held her ladyship tight for a long while as Catherine cried and cried for her lost happiness. Neither woman was in a position to see the young boy, dressed in nankeen trousers, creeping out of his mother's room in deep distress.

Eleven

In the morning, after a long and sleepless night, Catherine sent for pen and paper. After many attempts and much crossing-out, and a certain amount of tears and wretchedness, she finally succeeded in composing a note to his lordship. She had Thomas deliver it to his lordship's room with his breakfast tray, saying it was urgent. As far as Catherine was concerned, the sooner it was all over with and settled, the better it would be.

The Earl of St. Auburne tore open the envelope with triumphant anticipation. He had no doubt of what it contained: The girl would surely give in to him! He read the letter, laughed out loud, and slapped his valet on the back.

"It's done and over with, Bedloe! I've found gold at the rainbow's end at last. Listen to this note of surrender she's sent up to me."

He read out the following to his fascinated valet:

Sir:

I have thought deeply upon the proposal you most kindly made to me yesterday. After further reflection, I see that it is in my best interest and the best interests of my dear child Charles to do as you suggested. I thank you for suggesting I reconsider: It was an act of kindness I will long remember.

I therefore by this letter formally accept your proposal

of marriage. I will try my utmost to make you a con-
formable wife.

> *Yours most sincerely,*
> *Catherine, Countess of Sturtevant.*

"That's it, Bedloe! We're out of the woods at last!"

Bedloe simpered. "We are very thankful that your lordship has found a solution to your financial difficulties. We have been worried for you, as your lordship is well aware."

"I owe Beatrice Sturtevant for this one, Bedloe. Didn't think it would ever come to this, but now that it's happened, it's just as well. Catherine's a pretty thing with no head for finances, and she'll make me a sweet and gentle wife. I can't believe my luck in happening upon this treasure trove: I felt sure that after that last game I played with Danbury, it would be bellows to mend with me. I'm sure you feel as I do, that an early retirement to the Continent, in the manner of poor Brummell, would not do for either one of us."

"Indeed not, your lordship. May I offer you my most sincere congratulations? And of course, I wish you joy."

"Thanks, Bedloe."

"Will your lordship be requiring my services any further? Does your lordship wish to dress at this time?"

"No, no, Bedloe. Now that I've got her consent, the hard part's over. I was up late last night, and I drank too much of that French brandy. My head aches like the very devil. Draw the drapes again, Bedloe. I wish to go back to sleep."

"Certainly, your lordship."

"Wait a minute. Bring me a pen and paper first. I must write a note to Beatrice to let her know her plan has paid off in full. I know she'll want to make the arrangements and tie this business down. It's best that we get married before the chit thinks to change her mind."

"Yes, your lordship. Perhaps, under the circumstances, later we might discuss an increase in my salary?"

"Bedloe!" cried the earl, aghast.

"Yes, your lordship?"

"How *can* you be so mercenary?"

Twelve

Beatrice, the dowager Countess of Sturtevant, was extremely pleased to receive the note from the Earl of St. Auburne. She had thought it would take longer to convince her daughter-in-law, and was pleasantly surprised to learn that the girl had caved in so quickly.

St. Auburne was, of course, quite right about the need for swiftness. Catherine could be so very temperamental—if they were wed at once, the trouble would be all over and she could sleep in peace again.

"Smithers!"

"Yes, your ladyship?"

"Have someone sent to that new vicar, Ashecroft, is it? Tell him we'll be needing his services; I must meet with him this afternoon at the very latest."

"Yes, your ladyship."

"And, Smithers, send my grandson to me at once."

"His lordship, is, I believe, gone out."

"Gone out? At this hour? It's not possible. He's not gone out wandering again, has he?"

"I believe so, your ladyship."

"This whole household is run like Bedlam. Send Thymmes to me, then, and send the staff out after Charles. I must see him this morning, and I must keep him away from that awful Indian man."

"Yes, your ladyship."

When Smithers had gone, the dowager settled down in her

bed to sip contemplatively on her chocolate. All in all, everything was going very well. Catherine would be under control in a matter of hours, or some days at worst, a connection with an old and noble family would be made, Charles would have a respectable stepfather at last, and things at home would once again be made to take their proper course.

Thirteen

Catherine, who had immured herself in her room, not at all in the mood for company, was dutifully trying to remind herself that some benefits would accrue from this marriage no matter how distasteful she found her future husband. Chief among these benefits would be the final removal of herself and her son from Apsley, and from the baneful influence of her interfering, domineering mother-in-law. That move could only do herself and Charles great good. A life in London, as well, would probably be much more satisfying than life at Apsley had ever been since Frederick's death.

It was beyond doubt that she and the earl would come to an arrangement that suited them both: He had joked that some London couples hardly ever met, and it was often true. They could lead separate lives under the same roof, and things would still be far better than they were with Beatrice breathing down one's neck. As for Mandeville? It was a sad and a horrid thing—but then, life was often filled with unsatisfactoriness. Only in fairy tales could one be assured of a happy ending.

She was working on selecting silks of subtle colors and planning how the embroidery pattern would be achieved, when Jenny knocked at the door, carrying a note. Catherine tore it open and read its contents quickly.

"It's from Charles!" she said to her abigail, white-faced. "It seems he rose early to pay Mr. Mandeville a visit, and there was some sort of accident. He's injured."

"Injured, your ladyship?"

"It's his leg. Tell Thomas to have Bellefleur saddled for me at once, Jenny, and then come help me into my riding costume."

It took but a few minutes to fling on her boots, her skirt, blouse, and jacket, and throw a hat on her head. She was halfway down the corridor when she had the misfortune to run into her mother-in-law, who demanded to know where she was going and why. When Beatrice was given that information, she erupted with characteristic wrath.

"Catherine, you are not to go to Simla House, do you hear? No matter what has become of Charles, I absolutely forbid you to go to that man's home!"

It was the last straw, and the edifice crumbled. Something deep within Catherine shattered forever.

"Do shut up, Beatrice! I've had quite enough from you already, and I won't stand for any more, I tell you. It's still the beginning of the morning. Do you actually suppose that Mr. Mandeville might ravish me over sausages and coffee? I said that I'll wed that odious featherbrained dandy of yours, and I will do so, but I'm dashed if I'll put up with the rest of your idiotish precepts a single moment longer!"

"Catherine!" cried the dowager, horrified.

"Quiet, Beatrice!"

"Listen to me! At least take a groom along with you, for propriety's sake! You must not be alone with that man in that garden of his!"

"Out of my way, Beatrice, or I vow, I'll strike you down!"

Catherine swept away toward the stables, brandishing her whip and leaving an astonished dowager Lady Sturtevant behind in her wake, her mouth opening and closing in astonishment like a gasping fish.

She watched until Catherine had finally disappeared, and somehow managed to regain her senses. Beatrice shrieked, "The girl's gone mad at last!" and stumbled back to her rooms, intent on discovering how this latest misstep could be put right.

The dowager yanked savagely at the bellpull, continuing unabated until the footman entered; Thomas was once again amazed at the vast amount of noise and commotion the quality could produce when out of temper.

"There you are, Thomas, finally! Find his lordship's man! Find his groom! Have him saddle a horse for his lordship! See that St. Auburne is awakened at once! At once, do you hear me? It is urgent! His lordship must go after her and fetch her back!"

Fourteen

It was some hours later, and not far past noon by the time the Earl of St. Auburne, with dazzling manicured hands, and sporting another wretchedly high necktie, finally finished his toilette and galloped off to the rescue of young Lady Sturtevant at her mother-in-law's anxious request. His lordship demanded to be admitted to Simla House, and was in fact admitted there, only to discover that Mandeville was not at home. Learning that Mr. Mandeville and Lady Sturtevant were out in the Oriental garden, St. Auburne's next demand was that he be taken there immediately; his lordship's wishes were obliged in full by the staff.

He and, perforce, Mandeville's groom set off again at a blistering pace and arrived at the gate of the garden with both animals blown, just as if they had been racing at Newmarket for a thousand-pound purse. The earl, apparently in a fit of temper, pounded on the garden door with the silver head of his whip. This went on until Robert Mandeville, looking none too pleased, appeared at the door and demanded, "What's all this racket? Who are you, sir?"

"I am," the earl replied most terribly, "St. Auburne!"

Mr. Mandeville's lips began to twitch with amusement.

"And *that,*" the earl continued in the same sneering, threatening voice, pointing within the garden with his whip, "is the woman to whom I am, sir, *betrothed!*"

"What a coincidence!" replied Mr. Mandeville affably. "That is the woman to whom I am, sir, *wed!*"

"What?" cried St. Auburne, visions of Marshalsea Prison and unpaid debts arising awfully before him. "It cannot be! I have a special license in my pocket!"

"What a coincidence! I have a special license in my pocket as well. But I'm afraid that mine predates yours, St. Auburne. Furthermore, mine has been used."

"You dare to tell me that you are now married to Lady Sturtevant?"

"Why, no," replied the nabob.

"Aha!" cried the earl.

"Indeed, I do not dare to tell you that I am now married to Lady Sturtevant, for in fact I am now married—to Mrs. Mandeville! Logically enough."

At this, the Earl of St. Auburne began sputtering like a cheap candle. He turned red and then white and then red again. Catherine, watching from behind, could almost feel sorry for the foolish creature.

"My very deepest regrets, sir, I'm sure," said Mandeville smoothly. "But pray, don't just stand there. I'm glad you thought to come, for I feel sure that now that you know how things stand, you will want to wish us joy and help us celebrate this excellent day. Do come inside the garden, won't you? We are just about to enjoy some refreshments."

A stunned St. Auburne allowed himself to be drawn inside by the madman who had first greeted him.

"St. Auburne—you did say that was your name, didn't you? Lord St. Auburne, please meet our local vicar, Mr. Ashecroft, who performed the wedding ceremony here on short notice, a favor for which I will be ever grateful."

"How do you do?" said St. Auburne stiffly, wishing he were anywhere else on earth.

"And here we have the new Mrs. Mandeville, with whom, as you have said, you are already acquainted. Here is her son, Charles."

St. Auburne took out his quizzing glass and peered at Catherine with a cold fury.

"You cannot do this to me, madam."

"I'm afraid I have done this, Lord St. Auburne," said Mrs. Mandeville, smiling prettily back at him.

"I will not permit you to make a fool of me in this way. I will not let this humiliation go unnoticed. Your mother-in-law will make you pay dearly for having the audacity to trifle with my affections."

Robert Mandeville, offended by St. Auburne's words, stepped close enough that he loomed over the earl, and dwarfed him.

"You will not speak that way to my wife, sir, at my home. I have the honor to inform you, sir, that the dowager will not make my wife pay for what you term her 'audacity' at all. Lady Sturtevant has no power to do so."

"She has!"

"She avers that she has, but in law she has not," he corrected the earl patiently. "I went to London just recently particularly to discover how things were left by Catherine's first husband. I arrived back in Hampshire only this morning, having had it confirmed by the solicitors of my godmother, the Duchess of Underhill, that the late Frederick, Earl of Sturtevant, very properly left his wife Catherine, Countess of Sturtevant, as sole legal guardian of their son, Charles."

"How should *you* ever find out such a thing?"

"I thought from the first time I heard of it that the supposed disposition of Frederick's estate was very odd. I went to London to see the duchess, who has always had a distinct talent for uncovering intimate information, and has personal ties all throughout the London world. It took her little time at all to discover that the duke and the Earl of Sturtevant used the same firm of solicitors, and to learn that it was widely believed among the *ton* that the dowager countess had misrepresented her position, vis-à-vis her son's estate. The solicitors were able to confirm that the dowager Lady Sturtevant has been misleading her daughter-in-law all these years. I'm afraid Lady Sturtevant has misled you, Lord St. Auburne, as well, into thinking that your marriage to Catherine was within her power to accomplish. Alas for you, that is not so."

"Well!" Lord St. Auburne pouted. "I have been deeply deceived! It is unforgivable. Madam, I am deeply shocked by your conduct. You accepted my suit and were pledged to me. I cannot pretend to understand why you would prefer to connect the young Earl of Sturtevant with a family involved in trade, but I begin to realize that you are just as unstable as your mother-in-law told me you were."

"You insult my wife, sir," said Mr. Mandevill in an icy tone.

St. Auburne, realizing that he had crossed the line, began to beg pardon, when his speech was interrupted by the arrival of the dowager Lady Sturtevant, who had been shown into the garden through the northeast gate.

"Catherine! Go home, you baggage!"

"I'll thank you not to speak to my wife in that fashion, Lady Sturtevant."

"Your wife?"

"We were married just an hour ago," said Catherine, enjoying herself thoroughly. "I know you will want to wish us joy."

"I shall do nothing of the kind. You always were a stubborn girl, and never could see what was good for you. Very well, child. You've made your choice, have you? You have your tradesman now, for all the good it will bring you. You have your low-born husband, and I'll have your son in return."

"You lack the power to do so, Lady Sturtevant," interjected Mr. Mandeville. "Catherine now knows the truth."

"Impudent puppy! I'll have you horsewhipped!"

"I'll thank you not to speak to my godson in that vulgar way, Beatrice," rang out a silvery voice approaching from the rear. "Though you always did have a sad tendency toward vulgarity."

"How dare you! Who—?"

As Lady Sturtevant turned to see who had the effrontery to contradict her, she became instantly aware of the identity of the silver-haired lady. It was her grace, the Duchess of Underhill, whose carriage had also deposited her at the northeast gate of the garden. She went directly to Mr. Mandeville, kissed him warmly, and begged to be presented to his new bride.

"I am sorry I could not be present at the ceremony, but I understand that the need for swift action was paramount, due to Beatrice's meddling," she said, directing that lady a withering glance.

Lady Sturtevant had turned white, and was trying to stagger away from the scene, wishing that the very ground beneath her would cleave asunder and swallow her up.

"And don't you think that I shan't make all the details of this sordid affair known throughout the *ton,* Beatrice, for I shall. Everyone will know how badly you've treated this girl, lying to her all these years and threatening her. You will be ruined socially, and well you deserve it."

"Don't, Lydia. Please don't—I shall die of shame!" said the dowager in a small, whining voice.

"Be gone, Beatrice," said the duchess, dismissing her with a wave of one hand. "Begone, St. Auburne. We've all had enough of you."

The Earl of St. Auburne, and Beatrice, dowager Countess of Sturtevant, wandered off to hide themselves, each one lost in fearful thoughts of what the future would bring: there would be *on-dits,* scandal, gossip. To be publicly exposed to the whole of the London *ton* by the Duchess of Underhill—it did not bear thinking of. Even escape to the Continent would be insufficient to obscure such profound humiliation.

The atmosphere within the Oriental garden quickly resumed a festive tone. Servants busied themselves serving refreshments for the tiny wedding party, and the afternoon passed gaily. It was near five o'clock when Charles went back to Simla House with the duchess, the weather having grown too cool for her. The servants were clearing away the refreshment table as the bridal couple strolled slowly toward the greenhouse arm in arm.

"I must say, Mr. Mandeville, that I think it dreadfully clever of you to have arranged this on so little notice," said Catherine. "Getting the special license from London, and contacting Mr. Ashecroft—you must have been very sure of my consent. I begin to feel quite fast."

"I *was* sure of you," said Robert Mandeville, taking his wife into the obscuring shade of the largest bougainvillea in the greenhouse. "I knew what I wanted almost as soon as I laid eyes on you, and soon I was pleased to believe you had some warm feelings toward me as well. Charles in particular assured me you have held me in the highest regard for all these six long days. Charles's arrival this morning informing me that you needed to be swiftly extricated from an unhappy predicament merely speeded up my marital plans considerably, for I picked up the license in London once I knew for certain, through my godmother, that Charles's future legally lay in your hands, and not your mother-in-law's."

"It was a wonderful, timely rescue, and I do thank you for it, as does Charles. He admires you so and is very happy about our marriage."

"No more than I am, I assure you," he said, his lips twitching with good humor.

Mandeville thought for a moment, and asked, "Catherine, had you actually accepted that wretched fellow's offer of marriage?"

Catherine sighed. "I don't know what you must think of me. I'm afraid I did accept him, under great duress, just this morning."

"Now I can at least better understand St. Auburne's outrage. Imagine! A woman accepts one man, and hardly a few hours later is discovered married to another! Outrageous! I think I must pronounce you a shameless jilt of the first degree."

"A shameless jilt, am I?" she inquired, looking up tenderly at him, "When I think what would have become of me had I kept the word I gave him, I am glad to be a jilt. In fact, I thank heaven for it!"

"I thank heaven as well, my dear Mrs. Mandeville," he replied, his eyes savoring his wife. "I shall explain to you what I mean later, in much greater detail, once we leave the Oriental garden."

"Mightn't you explain to me right here *in* the garden, dearest? I am particularly fond of that little pavilion, the one with a glassed-in room and the lotus pond. You have really made it very comfortable."

"Once we are alone, I might."

"What about our guest, the duchess?"

"I think it safe to say that Her Grace understands all about wedding nights."

"What about Charles?"

"I've sent him to spend the evening with Mr. Ashecroft."

"How foresightful of you," she murmured tenderly.

"Foresight, my love," replied her husband, "is a necessity in a nabob."

"To be sure, it is an extremely useful attribute!"

"Of course, I *do* possess others."

"Indeed?"

At which, Mr. Mandeville thought it necessary to take his new bride in his arms, and to embark upon a long and extremely pleasing kiss in order to more clearly demonstrate the truth of his proposition.

Motherly Advice

by
Sheila Rabe

Rebecca Winter watched her daughter catch her trembling lower lip between her teeth and felt a nearly irresistible urge to box Matthew Overton's ears. Never mind the fact that the honorable Mr. Overton was only twenty years old, a very foolish and ignorant age for a male. At the moment, the future Earl of Stilton deserved a strong kick in the seat of his elegant evening breeches. Rebecca sighed. Such was the curse of manners that one could not always give young men what they deserved.

She frowned as the love of her daughter's life happily twirled Miss Helena Swan across the ballroom floor while poor Letty sat partnerless on a gilt-edged chair. Rebecca supposed she couldn't, in all fairness, blame the boy for being besotted with Miss Swan. The young lady was the toast of the Season, and far more skilled at flirtation than poor Letty. And the fact that Matthew and Letty had practically grown up together didn't help. What young man could be expected to show interest in an old playfellow when someone new and fascinating demanded his attention?

The musicians ended with a flourish, the dancers bowed and curtsied, then the crowd eddied to the edges of the ballroom to switch partners.

"Never mind, dearest," said Rebecca, patting her daughter's arm. "You have missed only one dance. And here comes that nice Mr. Throckmorton. I am sure you will enjoy dancing with him."

Instead of serving as consolation, these words brought horror to her daughter's face. "But, Mama, what if Matthew wishes to have this dance with me?"

"Mr. Overton may partner you for the next one," Rebecca assured her. Accurately interpreting the expression on her daughter's face, she admonished, "Now, don't be difficult, Letitia. You have already missed one dance on his account. It won't do for you to be sitting about while all the other young ladies dance. And besides, there will be many opportunities for your friend to find you before the ball ends. Good evening, Mr. Throckmorton," she said to the nervous-looking young man approaching them. "How very good to see you."

"Good evening, Mr. Throckmorton," parroted Letty dully.

Mr. Throckmorton swallowed and his Adam's apple danced nervously over his cravat. He cleared his throat. "Miss Winters, do I find you free for the quadrille?"

"You do," Rebecca answered for her daughter, "and I know she will be most delighted to dance it with you."

Letty produced a smile and allowed Mr. Throckmorton to lead her onto the ballroom floor while Rebecca sat back in her chair and heaved a sigh of relief. A child as pretty as Letty didn't deserve to be labeled a wallflower, and Rebecca had no intention of letting her daughter's foolishness put her in such a position.

She watched Letty take her place in the set and bow to her partner. The child was a dainty little thing. Her papa would have been proud to see her now. She had Charles's brown eyes and his dab of a nose. She had her mother's glossy chestnut curls. Rebecca idly twirled a curl and wondered what the gentlemen saw in yellow-haired females. They always seemed so washed of color.

Matthew Overton had now procured Miss Swan a glass of punch and was keeping her company while she drank it. Really, thought Rebecca, frowning at the spectacle, if she weren't so fond of Matthew's mama, and if he weren't in line for an earldom, she would discourage Letty from even considering him as a husband. Oh, he was a nice enough boy, typical of young men his age—fond of sport and gambling. And she could see why Letty was so enraptured with him, for he was quite pleasing to the eye with that finely muscled body, the square chin, and those brown eyes. Rebecca watched him snatch Miss Swan's punch cup and hold it high, making her jump for it and laugh and pout, and hoped Letty wasn't observing any of that.

She looked in her daughter's direction in time to see her face fall, and it plunged Rebecca into gloom. Odious boy! Really, men were the most exasperating creatures.

As if drawn out of the card room by this last thought, the Earl of Briarvale appeared on the edge of the ballroom, giving the cuff of his evening jacket a tug, then adjusting his signet ring. At forty, he still had a body men ten years his junior envied, and the dark hair so generously salted with gray was a thick mane Rebecca knew for a fact half the females present longed to run their fingers through. Including, she had to admit, herself.

The corners of Rebecca's mouth turned down. After six years of mere friendship, she should have been accustomed to the idea that the elusive Lord Briarvale would not be offering her marriage in spite of the fact that he seemed to enjoy her company. Evan Milton Hart, the Fourth Earl of Briarvale, had been a widower for eight years, and Rebecca was beginning to suspect he planned on spending the rest of his life alone. There were those—men, of course—who would argue that partaking of every entertainment the London Season had to offer and keeping one of the Wilson sisters as mistress was hardly living alone. But Rebecca knew what a man needed most was a wife by his side to run his household and sit with him in front of the fire on a cold winter's night. Friends grew old, mistresses grew tiresome, but wives were a boon a man could count on for a lifetime.

And what better woman to wed than herself? She knew she was still accounted a fine-looking woman. The chestnut curls of which she was so proud held only the smallest hint of gray. And the lines around her eyes were tiny. Of course, her waist had thickened a little, but she still had a nicely turned ankle. Other men had sought her hand. How tiresome of Briarvale not to be one of them!

The earl sauntered along the side of the ballroom, stopping to talk to first this person, then that. Rebecca watched his progress out of the corner of her eye and realized he was coming to speak to her. "How very attentive," she muttered. "After spending most of the evening in the card room, he at last seeks my company."

The dance ended and Letty's partner returned her to her mother's side. "Thank you, Mr. Throckmorton," said Letty politely.

"It was my pleasure," said Mr. Throckmorton earnestly. "Miss Winters, are you perhaps free to take a drive in Hyde Park tomorrow afternoon?"

Letty looked across the ballroom to where the honorable Matthew Overton stood. "I am not sure. I believe I have plans."

Mr. Throckmorton looked downcast. But he recovered, and said with hope, "Perhaps day after tomorrow?"

"Perhaps," replied Letty noncommittally.

"Splendid!" he exclaimed. "I shall call at half past four. Just to see if you are free, that is," he amended.

Letty was too busy trying to keep track of Matthew's movements to answer, so her mother said all that was proper. "That young man seems quite smitten with you, dear," Rebecca observed after he'd left them.

"Oh, Mr. Throckmorton. He is nice enough, I suppose," Letty remarked absentmindedly. "Perhaps I should go over and say hello to Miss Swan."

Rebecca followed her daughter's gaze to where Miss Swan stood, now busily flirting not only with Matthew, but with two other ardent suitors. She sighed. "By all means. Go tell her how lovely she looks. And *don't* remind Matthew that you are saving a dance for him.

"But, Mama. If I don't remind him, how will he know?"

"Gentlemen have a way of remembering what they really wish to remember," said Rebecca. Letty looked unconvinced. "Go say hello to Miss Swan," said Rebecca wearily.

Letty rushed off, bobbing a quick curtsy to Lord Briarvale on the way. "Your daughter is looking lovely tonight," he said to Rebecca as he took a seat next to her.

"I am afraid that chestnut curls, no matter how finely styled cannot compete with golden ones," said Rebecca.

"Ah, Miss Swan."

Rebecca nodded.

"Well, she is a lovely thing," admitted Briarvale. "But not all men are so captivated by yellow hair. I myself feel a darker shade is more interesting."

Rebecca lazily fanned herself and surveyed the crowd. "Do you? How very interesting, my lord."

By the time Letty reached her rival, the circle of admirers had grown. "Good evening, Miss Swan," she said timidly.

The girl looked tolerantly down at her. "Miss Whimper, is it not? How good to see you."

"Winters," corrected Letty, but Miss Swan didn't hear her. She had already returned her attention to the gentlemen around her. "Really, you are all so gallant. How can I possibly choose one of you? You must decide among yourselves who is to take me driving."

Letty frowned and angled for a spot next to Overton. "Matthew, I am still saving a dance for you," she said.

"That's nice, Letty," he replied absently, then called over the rumble of voices, "I have the newest and best-sprung curricle of all. I think I should be the one to take Miss Swan driving tomorrow."

Letty kept the smile on her face as she backed away from the group. There was only a trace of it left when she rejoined her mother and the earl.

"Are you not feeling well, dearest?" asked Rebecca, aching afresh for her daughter.

"My head is beginning to hurt a bit. Would you mind very much if we returned home?"

"Of course not," said Rebecca.

"I shall have your carriage sent 'round," offered Briarvale, and he set off in search of a footman.

"Oh, Mama."

"Not here, Letitia," Rebecca cautioned, and laid a hand on her daughter's arm to give her courage. "You must wait until we are inside the carriage."

Letty bit her lip, blinked hard and nodded.

"Good girl. Now, we will just bid our hostess good night. Can you do that, darling?"

Letty nodded again and followed her mother. She managed a smile for her hostess, and she was able to blink back the tears as they waited with Lord Briarvale for the footman to return and tell them their carriage was ready. She even found one last smile and polite good-bye for her mother's friend as he bid them good night. But once the door of the carriage was shut and they'd rumbled off down Upper Grosvenor Street, the tears burst noisily through the dam she'd kept against them.

"There now, darling," cooed her mama, taking her in her arms. "Everything will be all right. You'll see."

"Nothing will ever be all right," wailed Letty.

"Of course it will," said Rebecca.

"I hate Miss Swan," Letty stormed. "I wish she would hurry up and become engaged. And move far away—to Ireland, or France . . . or America!" Letty pulled out of her mother's embrace and turned pleading eyes to her. "What can he see in her, Mama? Oh, I know she has that golden hair and that pouty little mouth. But really, her behavior is quite silly." Letty trilled out a giggle in a good imitation of Miss Swan. "You are all so gallant. How can I choose one of you?"

What a pity it was that ladies could not tread the boards,

thought Rebecca, for fame surely would embrace such talent as Letty's.

"She is a shocking flirt," continued Letty. "Why, one moment she is listening to Mr. Bailey as if he is the most interesting man in London although everyone knows he is a total bore, and the next she is begging Lord Tarleton to tell her all about his new curricle."

"And what was the result of that conversation?" asked Rebecca.

Letty shrugged and muttered, "They all fought to see who would take her driving."

"Um-hmm," said Rebecca thoughtfully.

"I don't know what the gentlemen see in her," said Letty, harping back to her earlier theme. "Oh, of course she is beautiful. But really, Mama, one moment she is flattering a man, the next she is saying something perfectly odious to him."

"It does seem rather false," agreed Rebecca. "But it was ever thus. Gentlemen prefer—"

"Golden hair," interrupted Letty sourly.

Rebecca tried again. "Gentlemen prefer ladies who are not easily won. For men, courtship is another form of sport, rather like fox hunting. If the fox is clever and hard to catch, the huntsman is much the happier. They like the challenge. Do you see, dearest?"

Letty's brow furrowed. "I'm not sure."

"Matthew Overton has known you since you were both children. You are as familiar to him as his own skin, and I am afraid that makes him take you very much for granted. If you wish to gain his affections, you must not sit in his pocket. When he reaches for you, you must be just out of reach. Then he will reach again."

"And I suppose you will next say I should flutter my eyelashes and swat him with my fan," grumped Letty.

"I think you should behave like your own sweet self," said Rebecca. "Only remember the fox."

Letty said nothing, but her thoughtful expression told her mother that her sage advice was being taken to heart.

The following week Rebecca saw first-hand how well her daughter had learned her lesson. She watched Matthew Overton recover his memory and present himself to claim the dance Letty had saved him the week before. Letty peeped at him over her fan and said, "I am so sorry, Mr. Overton, but I am going to dance this next dance with Mr. Throckmorton."

"Throckmorton?" echoed Matthew.

Letty ignored this. "As I remember, you are wont to trod on ladies' toes, so I suppose it is all for the best. Mr. Throckmorton is an excellent dancer," she added.

"Excellent dancer? He looks like a dancing stick," protested Matthew.

As if on cue, Mr. Throckmorton presented himself.

"Hello, Mr. Throckmorton," warbled Letty. "I have been saving this dance for you."

"Really?" Mr. Throckmorton looked surprised, then pleased, and offered Letty his arm.

"Now, wait a moment!" protested Matthew.

Letty patted his arm. "Never mind. We cannot all be skillful on the dance floor. And you do have rather big feet, don't you?"

Matthew's face reddened and his eyebrows lowered.

"I am afraid if you stepped on me you would quite crush me," Letty continued. "Because the rest of you is so very big also. And strong. Rather like Samson in the Bible, I suppose," Letty added, then bid Matthew farewell with a wave of the fingers. She could be heard to say as they walked off, "How very handsome you look tonight, Mr. Throckmorton!"

"Why, thank you," Mr. Throckmorton said, wonder evident in his voice.

"Handsome? Bah!" spat Matthew, and stalked off.

Rebecca grinned.

"Good evening, Lady Winter," she heard and turned to see Lord Briarvale at her elbow. "May I have this dance?"

"Certainly," she murmured.

Once on the floor, the earl wasted no time. "I meant to let you know sooner," he said casually. "But I am afraid I'll be unable to attend your dinner party next week."

Her face had fallen, she was sure. "Naturally, things come up," she managed.

"Yes, I am afraid they do," he replied. "But I am sure you'll have no trouble replacing me. The gentlemen wait in line for invitations to dinner parties at the home of Lady Winter."

"I would hardly say that."

"No? Come now. Don't be so modest."

Rebecca smiled. "It will be most difficult, but I shall try hard to find a replacement for you."

They had barely finished their dance, when a mutual acquaintance strolled by and hailed the earl. "Looking forward to seeing you at Halston's card party next Thursday," he said.

"Thursday?" repeated Rebecca.

The earl's face took on a ruddy hue. "I am sure he has mistaken the day," he said, then hurried to change the topic.

Rebecca allowed him to think he had distracted her, but while her mouth said all that was appropriate, her mind clung to the damning words like a terrier to a rat. Next Thursday. The same evening as her dinner party.

She stewed about the earl's inconsiderate behavior all night, and only half heard her daughter's happy prattle as their carriage finally made its way home through the streets of Mayfair. One sentence did manage to seep through the wall of dark thought that surrounded her mind.

"I took your advice, Mama."

Rebecca smiled. "Good for you, my darling. And you see how very much more eager our dear Matthew was to dance with you when you were not dying to do so with him."

Letty nodded. "You were right. From now until the day

Matthew offers for me I am going to say to myself, " 'Remember the fox.' "

"Good girl," approved Rebecca.

It wasn't until her abigail was pinning up her hair that Rebecca experienced her flash of insight. It came upon her like lightning on a midnight sky. Letty wasn't the only one who needed to remember the fox! "Of course!" she declared. "How could I have been so blind?"

"Beg pardon, my lady?" said Minnivers.

"Never mind," said Rebecca. "I was merely thinking aloud. I am afraid I have been very stupid. I need to listen to my own advice."

"I am sure that is a good idea," Minnivers agreed loyally.

"Yes, indeed. I have been a tame little fox," mused Rebecca. "But no more. I am going to lead a certain man on a very merry chase."

Rebecca did manage to find a gentleman to take Lord Briarvale's place at her dinner party. Sir James Blessing, a middle-aged widower just out of mourning, was only too happy to step into Briarvale's boots. And when Lord Briarvale called two days later and inquired how her dinner party went, Rebecca airily informed him that it had been perfectly splendid. "Sir James made up my twelfth and we all had a delightful evening. I had not realized how very witty he is."

Briarvale raised an eyebrow. "Pray, what did that pompous windbag say to earn such undeserved flattery?"

"Several things, really," replied Rebecca evasively. "I found him a most pleasant addition to my table. And he is a handsome man."

"He has a neck like an ox," observed Briarvale. "And little more intelligence."

"Your lordship!" declared Rebecca, shocked. "Why, such a thing to say."

Briarvale shrugged. "I have nothing against Blessing. I am

merely surprised you should fuss over the man so. He is thick and dull, and I had thought you admired more liveliness of wit."

"Ah, well," said Rebecca. "I am sure you would have rivaled Sir James in wit had you been present. But let's talk no more of him. Tell me, what brings you to us today?"

"I thought, perhaps, you and Letitia might enjoy accompanying me to see Kean as Richard III this Friday night."

Rebecca would have dearly loved to join the earl in his box at the Theatre Royal to see the little man whose acting kept audiences transfixed, but remembering her advice to her daughter she replied, "Why, that would be delightful. But I am afraid I shall have to decline."

The earl's smile shrank.

"I am afraid I am not feeling quite the thing, and I am sure that by Friday I still won't feel up to an outing."

"Perhaps another time," said Briarvale gallantly.

"Perhaps," replied Rebecca.

When Sir James called later that same day to pay a thank-you call and asked her to the very same performance, she accepted.

"Excellent," said Sir James.

He regarded her with big brown eyes that drooped at the corners, and, looking at those eyes and the thick, jowly chin, she couldn't help thinking he rather resembled a large dog. No matter. He would serve her purposes admirably.

Friday evening, as she and Letty sat in Sir James's box, she caught sight of Lord Briavale scowling at them.

Sir James leaned forward to say, "Rather a good actor, isn't he?"

She smiled at him as if he had just said something profound, then, still smiling, turned her face to the earl and nodded. Briarvale's eyes narrowed and he gave a terse nod in return. Rebecca directed her attention back to the stage, well pleased with her performance.

"We had a most enjoyable evening," she told Sir James

when he returned them home. To herself, she added, *and most profitable.*

The following afternoon she suggested to her daughter they take a drive around Hyde Park. "Oh, yes," agreed Letty. "Perhaps we will see Matthew."

And Lord Briarvale thought Rebecca. The look on her daughter's face recalled her to the most pressing need of the season—to find a husband for Letty. "I hope you don't intend to wear your heart on your sleeve, my darling," she cautioned.

"Oh, no, Mama. I have learned my lesson," said Letty. "You were quite right. Did you notice how eager Matthew was to see me at the theater last night? He was the first visitor to our box."

Rebecca smiled, remembering how a perturbed Lord Briarvale had stayed away from them. "Yes, my dear. You are being a clever little fox, and I am sure if you continue to evade him, we will have brought young Matthew up to scratch long before the season is over." *And I will have Lord Briarvale down on one knee offering matrimony as well!*

Hyde Park swarmed with fashionable ladies and gentlemen. They strolled the paths and crowded the drives with park phaetons and curricles. Gentlemen on expensive horseflesh navigated what space was left. Ladies twirled parasols and peeped up at the gentlemen from under the brim of poke bonnets or straw Gypsy hats. In short, Hyde Park at five o'clock was a veritable crush, a party outdoors.

"Oh, look, Mama! There is Miss Barnstable," said Letty. "And she's wearing the new bonnet she told me about. I can see why it was so dear. It is positively adorable." Letty stole a look at her mother. "I might not object to owning such a bonnet."

Rebecca smiled. Just seeing Letty happy and in high spirits

made her own soar. "I think we might be able to manage a new bonnet," she said.

Letty grinned and returned to scanning the crowd. "There is Matthew's friend Lord Winfield. Do you think we will see Matthew here? Mama! Look at those ladies," continued Letty, indicating a park phaeton with two women lounging in it.

Rebecca looked and scowled. The notorious Harriette Wilson had curls as auburn as Rebecca's and a more voluptuous bosom. Her sister, Amy, Lord Briarvale's current lightskirt, was just as eye-catching. Yes, eye-catching, thought Rebecca sourly, watching the creature wink at a passing gentleman. Like brass. "Those aren't ladies," she informed her daughter.

Letty's eyes widened. "Oh," she breathed. "You mean they are . . . ?"

Rebecca nodded. "And you mustn't acknowledge their existence by so much as a look in their direction," she replied, not taking her own advice. As if feeling Rebecca's gaze, her impure rival looked at her and gave her a smile that could only be described as superior. "Well!" huffed Rebecca. "Of all the nerve."

Letty giggled and returned to searching the crowd. The giggle was quickly replaced by a frown.

"You have seen Miss Swan?" her mama guessed.

"And Matthew," Letty replied, and sighed.

Rebecca patted her shoulder. "Never fear, darling. Things have a way of working out."

"But what if they don't work out so that Matthew offers for me?"

It was Rebecca's turn to sigh. This was, of course, a possibility, and she felt it would be unfair to her daughter to pretend it wasn't. "A lady can do only so much," she said, "then she must hope that Cupid's arrow will strike."

Letty was still looking in Matthew's direction. Suddenly she grabbed her mother's arm. "He's coming this way!"

"Calm yourself, child. You mustn't appear overeager."

Letty squirmed into a position of nonchalance, and when the honorable Mr. Overton hailed them, she was able to nod and smile and lower her eyes as if seeing him sitting his horse beside their phaeton were a matter of complete indifference.

Matthew said all that was proper to Rebecca, then turned his attention to Letty. "Do you attend the Stanhopes' ball next week?"

Letty nodded.

"Then save me a waltz," Matthew instructed. "I intend to prove to you that I won't tread on your feet," he added with a smile.

"Had Miss Swan already promised every dance?" replied Letty.

"Well, I suppose she might have," stumbled Matthew.

"Just as I thought," said Letty.

"What has Miss Swan to do with anything?" said Matthew crossly.

Letty raised her chin. "I am sorry, Mr. Overton, but I had rather not take Miss Swan's leavings."

"Leavings!" Matthew exploded.

"Now, I am sure Letty did not mean . . ." began Rebecca.

"That is what I said," interrupted Letty, "and I most certainly did mean it."

"I suppose you think Miss Swan isn't interested in me," said Matthew haughtily.

"I suppose you think she is," retorted Letty, ignoring her mother's poke in the ribs.

"Well, we'll just see, won't we?" snapped Matthew. "Good day! Your servant, Lady Winter."

"Oh, Letty, what have you done?" fretted Rebecca as they watched Matthew melt into the throng of carriages and riders.

"You told me to stay out of reach," said Letty stubbornly.

"I did not tell you to drive him away."

Letty bit her lip. "It was a stupid thing to do," she admitted. "But really, Mama, I don't care anymore about Matthew Overton. If he is so fickle as to want a silly woman like Miss Swan for a wife, then he may have her with my blessing. And I hope she makes him as thoroughly miserable as he deserves to be!" she added with a wobbly voice and a furious nod.

They had barely finished their discussion when they encountered Lord Briarvale, looking splendid in buff riding breeches and a bottle-green coat, and sitting a huge bay. He swept off his hat to them and came alongside the carriage. "Good afternoon, ladies. I am glad to see you in better health, Lady Winter."

"Thank you," said Rebecca sweetly.

"In fact," the earl continued, "I couldn't help but notice that you found your health in time to attend the very performance to which I'd invited you."

Rebecca nodded. "Yes. I was feeling so much better by the following day that when Sir James asked me to the play I thought perhaps I might go after all."

"You had only to send word to me that you were better and I should have been happy to take you," said Briarvale.

"Ah, but I thought that something might have . . . come up," Rebecca replied, remembering the damning words with which the earl had slithered out of his social obligation. "And I would have hated to obligate you to give up any plans you might have made since asking me."

The earl said nothing to this, merely bowing his head. "I trust you enjoyed yourself."

"Oh, yes," replied Rebecca.

"Well," he said stiffly, "I am glad you and Sir James are finding each other's company so enjoyable. I'll bid you good day now."

Rebecca watched him ride off, and frowned.

Her daughter laid a comforting hand on her arm. "Never mind, Mama. He'll come around."

Rebecca smiled at her daughter and patted her hand. "It is of no consequence, dearest, I assure you."

"But you like Lord Briarvale, don't you?"

"Of course I like Lord Briarvale, dear. We have been friends for a long time."

"Yes, but would you not like to be something other than friends with him?" persisted Letty.

"I must admit that if Briarvale offered me marriage I should not be loath to accept. I think once you have a husband and a home of your own, I will be rather lonely."

"If I ever get a husband," said Letty glumly.

Rebecca sighed. "I am afraid we have neither of us been very good foxes today."

Letty's chin set stubbornly. "The hunt is not yet over, Mama. Let us not give up hope."

Lord Briarvale was present at the Stanhopes' ball, and from the way he smiled across the room at Rebecca, she was sure she had been forgiven her mistake of attending the play with another man. She gave him a beckoning smile in return and he began to thread his way through the crowd to her.

But someone else had also seen her smile and was effectively using his broad shoulders to swim to her through the crowd. "Oh, dear," she muttered. "Sir James."

Sir James was the first to reach her. "My dear Lady Winter," he said, taking the chair she had intended for Briarvale. "How good to see you."

His gaze had fallen to her low décolletage.

Rebecca raised an eyebrow. "All of me, or simply part?"

Sir James looked confused. "I beg your pardon?"

"Never mind," she said. "Are you enjoying yourself?"

Sir James pulled out his handkerchief and mopped his brow. "In this crush? How can anyone enjoy himself when he can barely move. And it's devilish hot in here."

Rebecca saw her chance. "It is terribly close. I am afraid my throat is so dry, I can barely speak."

"Well, then," said Sir James. "I shall find you a cup of arrack."

"That would be wonderful," cooed Rebecca. As soon as he was gone she searched the crowd for the earl. When she finally caught sight of him, she saw his progress toward her had been arrested by a middle-aged female with brassy curls and a gown as low cut as her own. Rebecca scowled. Lady Anne Bradford was another admirer of the Earl of Briarvale's. Rebecca's scowl deepened as she watched Lady Anne rap Briarvale playfully with her fan. Shameless flirt!

At last Briarvale freed himself from the woman and resumed his slow progress in her direction. Unfortunately, Sir James was once more before him, and Rebecca's spirits plunged when, on seeing Sir James sink his crushing bulk onto the chair next to hers and hand her a punch cup, the earl frowned and turned back into the crowd.

Rebecca sighed inwardly and forced a smile to her lips.

Her daughter wasn't faring much better on the dance floor. Letty waltzed with the skinny Mr. Throckmorton, craning her neck to look up to his face and trying to pretend she was enjoying herself. This task was no easy one, as Mr. Throckmorton was a very poor dancer, but seeing Matthew waltz by earlier with the golden-haired Miss Swan had made it herculean.

"Are you enjoying the ball?" Mr. Throckmorton asked as he tried to navigate them safely through the swooping, twirling couples.

"Er, yes. Oh, my! Do be careful, Mr. Throckmorton."

Just in time, her partner gave a jump and scooted her past a teetering gray-haired couple. "Beg pardon," he mumbled, and, blushing, moved them away.

"It is a terrible crush," said Letty, trying to ease his embarrassment. "It must be very difficult trying to lead someone through this crowd."

"It is," agreed Throckmorton. His face turned red afresh. "That is, it's not at all difficult to lead you, Miss Winter. It is only a difficult thing to do in general. One must keep time to the music and watch one's feet and . . ."

Mr. Throckmorton's sentence went unfinished, for at that moment he glided backward into another man. Even before all four people had come to a halt, Letty knew with whom they had collided, and felt a sudden desire to be traveling on the Continent, back at her home in Devon, in the schoolroom even—anywhere but Lady Stanhope's ballroom.

"I say! Do watch what you are about!" began Matthew, turning around. On seeing the twin red faces of Letty and Mr. Throckmorton, a wicked smile spread across his face. "Why, Miss Winter. How do you do?"

Letty was aware of Miss Swan looking as if she were about to burst into giggles, of her partner apologizing earnestly, and worst of all, of that wicked, superior smile on Matthew's face. "Come, Mr. Throckmorton," she said grandly. "The floor is much too crowded, and all manner of poor dancers are making enjoyment impossible. Let us sit out the rest of the dance." With that she turned her shoulder on the odious Matthew Overton, took Mr. Throckmorton's arm, and steered him from the dance floor.

"Really, it is quite crowded," blustered Mr. Throckmorton. "Old Overton should watch where he is going."

"Of course he should," agreed Letty, and felt as if everyone at the ball were staring at her.

She and her partner found two vacant seats along the wall and, once seated, Letty had the dubious pleasure of watching Matthew and Miss Swan waltz gracefully by several times before the musicians stopped playing.

"Rather a crush, isn't it?" ventured Mr. Throckmorton.

"Yes, it is," agreed Letty in a tight voice.

"I am really not so fond of balls myself," he confided.

Letty looked sadly to where Matthew stood smiling down at Miss Swan. "Neither am I," she said, and tried to swallow the painful lump in her throat.

Rebecca bit her lip and regarded her daughter, who sat huddled against a corner of the carriage, her face to the window. How she wished she had some great words of comfort, some fresh pearls of wisdom to hand to her daughter. But at the moment she could think of none. At last she said, "My dear, I am so sorry."

The words caused Letty's wall of silence to tumble into tears. "He danced with Miss Swan and never once asked me," she sobbed.

"Well, dearest, one can hardly blame him, for you did goad him into acting the way he did." This had not been the right thing to say, for it brought forth a fresh wail from Letty.

"He will never offer for me now," she lamented.

"The hunt is not over yet," said Rebecca with determination. "Now, I want you to promise me that the next time you see your old friend you will offer him the olive branch."

"Very well," Letty sighed.

Rebecca tapped her chin thoughtfully. "I do believe Mr. Throckmorton has a good fifty thousand pounds per annum," she said at last.

Letty's eyes widened in horror. "Oh, Mama! You cannot mean to force me to accept Mr. Throckmorton. I wouldn't wish to marry him even for one hundred thousand pounds."

"Why, Letty!" scolded Rebecca. "Mr. Throckmorton is a nice young man."

"I am sorry," said Letty. "He is, indeed, nice. But Matthew is so very handsome. And so funny. And . . . oh . . ."

Again the tears began to flow, and Rebecca hugged her daughter. "I know, dearest. When one is so terribly fond of a gentleman, no one else can quite compare, no matter how nice he may be."

Letty looked up to study her mother's face. "Are you thinking of Lord Briarvale, Mama?"

Rebecca shook the thought of Lord Briarvale from her brain. "I am thinking of your future, darling, and I have just had an idea which, I think, will ensure a happy one."

The following day the ladies set out to pay morning calls. "Whom shall we visit first?" asked Letty, who was now sufficiently recovered from the previous night's grief to be looking forward to the outing.

"I think, perhaps, we shall call on Lady Swan," replied Rebecca casually.

"Lady Swan!" gasped Letty. "Mama, how could you even consider such a thing!" She scowled and crossed her arms over her chest. "I shan't go."

"Letitia."

The arms uncrossed. "Don't make me go visit that horrid creature, Mama. Please."

"I am afraid we must pay a call," said Rebecca. "Else I cannot put my plan into action. For, unfortunately, the girl is never free of suitors long enough to have any sort of conversation with her."

"She may have callers," Letty pointed out.

"We shall manage," said Rebecca firmly. Letty frowned and Rebecca patted her hand. "We will make it a short visit. I promise."

Letty sighed. "I am sure you know best," she said in a martyred voice.

"I do," said her mother. "Just remember, should the subject come up, that you are no longer interested in Mr. Overton."

"But," began Letty. Suddenly, her eyes widened and she matched her mother's smile with one of her own and nodded. "Oh, Mama, you are too clever by half."

* * *

Miss Swan greeted Letty with the mild interest due a lesser rival. Rebecca noticed this and meted out the same treatment to the conceited young lady as she lowered herself onto Lady Swan's sofa. She let the conversation drift for several minutes, discussing the problem of servants, offering to share with Lady Swan the Prince Regent's punch recipe, listening to Lady Swan gloat over her daughter's success. At last she deemed it time to take control. "I congratulate you on a most successful come-out," she said to Miss Swan.

The girl lowered her eyes and murmured, "Thank you."

"One of your admirers, the future Earl of Stilton, is an old playfellow of Letitia's," continued Rebecca.

"Really?" said Lady Swan, leaning forward in her seat. "He seems a nice young man."

"Oh, yes," agreed Rebecca. She smiled at Letty. "Were you not good friends with Mr. Overton, my dear?"

"Yes, Mama," said Letty. "Perhaps that is why I was not so interested in him after I met other gentlemen."

"Mr. Overton is absolutely wonderful," raved Rebecca. "But you know how it is with old playfellows. One becomes too familiar with them. They wear. And, of course, a lady must look to the future."

"Oh, yes," agreed Lady Swan. "I quite agree."

"And Mr. Overton will be an earl," put in Miss Swan.

Rebecca nodded. "A title is a good thing."

"Mr. Throckmorton will be only a baron," added Miss Swan in a silky voice, and Letty's face reddened.

"Ah, yes," agreed Rebecca. "But we all know titles cannot purchase ball gowns or park phaetons. And one must be practical. Now, I could be wrong," she continued in a conspiratorial voice, "but I believe poor Mr. Overton's family might have had a bit of a setback."

"No!" exclaimed Lady Swan incredulously.

Rebecca shrugged. "As I said, I could very well be wrong. You know how quickly rumors can circulate. At any rate, it is no matter with us, for Mr. Throckmorton we know to be in fine financial health."

"He is worth sixty thousand pounds per annum," purred Letty.

"Sixty thousand?" echoed Lady Swan and looked consideringly at her daughter.

Letty smiled. "It is why I lost interest in Mr. Overton. But I see you have found him," she said to Miss Swan, "and so now everyone is happy," she finished sweetly.

Miss Swan smiled too, and Rebecca was pleased to note it wasn't a particularly happy smile.

"Sixty thousand pounds," mused Lady Swan.

Rebecca smiled.

"Mother, you are the most brilliant woman in all of London," gushed Letty as their carriage moved off down Albemarle Street. She turned serious. "But poor Matthew. I hope his family is not in serious difficulty."

"I know of none."

Letty stared at her mother "But you said . . ."

Rebecca shrugged. "I never said for certain that the earl was in difficulty. I said I believed it. One may, after all, believe anything one wishes, whether it is true or not. And besides," she added righteously, "I said I might be wrong."

Letty giggled. "I hope someday I may learn to be as clever as you."

Rebecca patted her daughter's arm and sent up a silent prayer that her plan would work.

That night the ladies attended a rout and saw not only Miss Swan but Mr. Throckmorton as well. Mother and daughter watched while Miss Swan waylaid him en route to them and smiled coyly up at him from behind her fan. "I wish I might know what she is saying," said Letty.

"Well," said Rebecca, "she is telling the young man that she is sorry she's had so little opportunity to speak with him since coming to London. Perhaps they can become better acquainted this evening?"

"How can you know that, Mama?"

At that moment Mr. Throckmorton nodded enthusiastically and offered Miss Swan his arm. "That," said Rebecca, watching them with satisfaction, "is how I know."

"Well," huffed Letty. "He certainly proved to be fickle!"

"Never mind, dearest," said Rebecca. "He is serving his purpose. Now we have but to hope that Miss Swan is at our friends' ball tomorrow night."

Miss Swan was obliging enough to be present at Lady Stilton's ball the following night, along with her papa and mama.

"I am certainly glad Clarissa has another year to go before her debut," confided Lady Stilton to her old friend. Miss Swan seems to have garnered all the attention this Season."

"She is lovely," admitted Rebecca.

Lady Stilton nodded, watching Miss Swan take her place for the quadrille with Mr. Throckmorton. "She is, and although I was prepared to take her as a daughter-in-law, I am relieved to see she has found someone else to tease other than Matthew. For we both know there is nothing more tiring than a spoilt beauty."

"Has Matthew lost interest, then?" asked Rebecca innocently.

Lady Stilton frowned. "More like she has lost interest in him. You know, my dear, for a time I truly thought she meant to have him, the way she was encouraging him. But tonight she has given him a cold shoulder in favor of the baron's scrawny son." Her ladyship shook her head. "There certainly is no accounting for taste. Ah, if only arranged marriages were in vogue. I would still love to see Matthew and Letitia make a match of it. She is such a sweet child."

"A mother really has so little control in matters of the heart," agreed Rebecca.

On another side of the ballroom, Matthew had joined Letty. Noting the glum expression on his face, she asked, "Matthew, what is wrong?"

He slumped in his chair and stretched his legs out in front of him, glaring at his silver buckled slippers. "How can females be so fickle?" he demanded. "One moment they are hanging on your every word, the next they are telling you to go away."

"Go away?" repeated Letty. "Why, who would say such a thing to you?"

"The Swan," grumped Matthew. "I came to ask her for a dance when she was with old Throckmorton, and she told me to do go away and quit bothering them. Can you believe it? I warn you, Letty, you'd better bring Throckmorton up to scratch in a hurry, for it would seem she means to have him."

"She can have him with my blessing," said Letty fervently.

Matthew cocked his head and studied her. "Sour grapes?"

"No. Not in the least," replied Letty amiably.

"He was your suitor," pointed out Matthew. "I should think you'd be a little peeved that she stole him away."

"No. I am grateful actually, for I quickly found that Mr. Throckmorton really didn't suit me."

"Well, I wish I could feel grateful to Miss Swan," said Matthew. "But—" He clamped his lips together a moment, obviously in the grip of strong emotion. "It's curst rude to behave like such a flirt and lead a man on."

"You're right, Matthew," said Letty gently. "I'm sure I would never wish to do such a thing to a gentleman."

Matthew regarded her. "No," he said thoughtfully. "I am sure you would not."

"I think Miss Swan must have very poor sight indeed,"

Letty continued. "For anyone with eyes can see you are the handsomest man here."

"Do you really think so?"

Letty smiled and nodded, then lowered her gaze. Matthew grinned.

"Say," he said, "would you care to dance?"

"I should love to dance with you, Matthew," she replied.

Rebecca saw her daughter's success and felt like dancing herself—until she noticed Lord Briarvale flirting shamelessly with Lady Anne. Drat the man! He was not behaving the least bit jealous. In fact, from the way he was smiling at Lady Anne, it would appear he was going to accept defeat and let Sir James have her. Well, she had best do something now, before he took up with some other female. She would follow the advice she'd given her daughter and offer Briarvale the olive branch before Lady Anne got her claws into him any further.

Pinning a smile on her face, she strolled to where he stood with Lady Anne. "Good evening, Anne," she said. "Briarvale."

The other woman looked decidedly unenthusiastic to see Rebecca, but she smiled politely and inclined her head.

The earl grinned and bowed.

Rebecca smiled sweetly at him, then glanced at the back of Lady Anne's gown. "Oh, dear," she said. "Just as I thought." Screening her face with her fan, she whispered, "I believe you have a tear at the back of your gown, dear."

Lady Anne looked over her shoulder. "Where?"

"It would appear," continue Rebecca, "that a seam has split. Oh, nothing overly noticeable. Yet. But if you let it go, I am afraid you will be most embarrassed by the end of the evening."

"Oh, my," said Lady Anne in consternation.

"I suggest you repair to the red room and mend it," finished Anne. She took Briarvale's arm. "I shall be happy to keep Lord Briarvale company in your absence."

Lady Anne frowned, but left.

"Neatly done," he said. "And just where did you invent the tear in poor Lady Anne's gown?"

"Invent?" protested Rebecca, taking his arm amiably. "I did no such thing. I was sure I saw the beginning of a split in the seam of her skirt. I did her a favor."

The earl made no answer, only smiled. "And where is your faithful cicisbeo tonight?"

"Why, Lord Briarvale. I always thought you were my faithful cicisbeo."

"So did I," said Briarvale.

"You are put out with me?"

"I am only wondering if you have developed a preference for large men."

Rebecca hesitated. She had no more desire to sit in Lord Briarvale's pocket than she had to see her daughter sitting in young Matthew's. "I have a preference for men who don't intend to remain in a solitary state forever," she said, observing the crowd.

"Having once been caught in the state of matrimony, my dear Rebecca, I'd have thought you immune to the disease," said the earl.

"And I'd have thought you ready to catch it long before this," retorted Rebecca.

Briarvale looked genuinely puzzled. "Why on earth should I?"

"Well," stuttered Rebecca, "most men wish to have a family, sons to carry on the name."

"You may have noticed that my brother has two fine sons," pointed out Briarvale.

"Yes, but they are not yours."

"Thank God."

"Really," said Rebecca in disgust.

"Actually, I am being most considerate," said the earl. "At

this point in my life none of my family expects me to marry. My poor eldest nephew, in fact, would feel quite cheated were I to take a bride, since for the last ten years he has been waiting for me to stick my spoon in the wall so he can step into my shoes."

"I am sure your nephew is thinking no such thing," Rebecca scolded.

"Oh, I am sure he is," said Briarvale amiably. "They are playing a waltz. Shall we?"

"You know I adore to waltz," said Rebecca, and let him lead her out onto the floor.

The earl put his hand on her waist and pulled her into the steps. She felt his strength as he guided her through the throng. She was aware of his hand resting intimately on her waist, of her hand on his shoulder, of the strong contrast his hard body made to hers.

"We dance well together," he observed.

"We have had much practice these last six years."

"That we have." The earl smiled. "When was the last time I told you, Rebecca, what a handsome woman you are?"

"I cannot remember," replied Rebecca lightly, wondering if, perhaps, now that she'd planted the matrimonial seed it might bear fruit in a proposal this very moment.

The look on the earl's face spoke of kisses and caresses. "A lovely woman such as yourself need only say the word and she could enjoy all the benefits of marriage . . . without the shackles."

What was this? "I am not sure I understand you, my lord," said Rebecca.

Briarvale's smile turned cynical. "Oh, I think you do."

Rebecca felt her face reddening as if she were sixteen and not thirty-six. "Are you offering me such benefits, Lord Briarvale?"

For an answer, he brought her hand to his lips.

"You pick an odd time to make your proposal, my lord," Rebecca observed, her voice level.

"I do," he agreed. "Forgive me. Perhaps you will allow me to call on you tomorrow."

"Perhaps I will."

Again the earl kissed her hand. "May I call at, shall we say, three o'clock?"

"You may," said Rebecca sweetly.

During their conversation they had been marking time. Now the earl moved them back into the dance with gusto, pulling Rebecca into a dizzying turn. He began to hum.

Rebecca forced her lips into a smile, and many a bystander watching the two friends glide by could be heard to observe that the Earl of Briarvale and Lady Winter were certainly smelling of April and May tonight.

The dance ended, and Lord Briarvale showed no inclination to leave Rebecca's side. He remained there until Matthew arrived with Letty.

"Oh, Mama!" cried Letty. "Matthew, er, Mr. Overton has asked me to go driving in Hyde Park tomorrow in his curricle. May I?"

"I suppose that might be possible," said Rebecca, noting her daughter's shining eyes.

"If you take her at three, I shall be on hand to bear her mother company in her absence," Briarvale said.

"Yes," agreed Rebecca, a glint in her eye. "That is an excellent idea."

Letty's high spirits alone could have carried her home from the ball. She danced in the front door past the butler. "What a lovely, lovely evening," she declared. "I am going driving with Matthew Overton tomorrow." She danced back to her mother and hugged her. "And I owe it all to you, Mama! I vow, I have the smartest mother in all of England. No, the whole world!" She spun in a circle, hugging her shoulders. "Do you know, Mama? He said he really prefers reddish hair to yellow."

"I am happy to see young Matthew has finally come to his senses," said Rebecca. "Now, darling, let us find our beds. I vow I am exhausted."

But once in her room, Rebecca found tremendous energy for a fatigued woman. She hurled a bed pillow across the room and kicked over the stool in front of her dressing table. "That, Rebecca, was a very immature display," she lectured the reflection in her looking-glass.

Again the image of Lord Briarvale's smirking face came to mind, and with fresh energy she sent another bed pillow flying. Craven man! So this was how he rewarded the woman who gave him so many years of friendship and easy camaraderie. Well, tomorrow he would learn what she thought of his offer.

Letty spent the entire morning choosing her ensemble for the all-important drive with Matthew. At last she settled on her pamona green gown, and her new pelisse and bonnet.

When he arrived at ten minutes before three, Matthew rewarded her efforts with an admiring look. "I say, Letty, er, Miss Winter, that's a smashing get-up," he observed.

Letty flushed and thanked him, and Rebecca beamed, reminding herself that no matter what other disappointments life might hand her, she would bask in the warmth of knowing she'd secured a happy future for her daughter.

She saw the young people safely out the door, then settled herself on the drawing room sofa to await Lord Briarvale's arrival.

As the ormolu clock on the mantel was chiming three, the butler appeared to announce Lord Briarvale. "Thank you, Jemson," said Rebecca. "Please bring sherry for his lordship. And the other refreshments I ordered as well." The butler bowed and departed. Rebecca smiled and gestured for the earl to join her on the sofa.

He leaned back against the cushions and surveyed her with

an odious, self-satisfied grin. "I've thought of nothing but you since our conversation last night," he said, his voice a caress.

"How very flattering," answered Rebecca. "I too have thought much. Who would imagine that after these six years of friendship, feelings of a deeper sort would spring up between us."

Briarvale took her hand and raised it to his lips, and she fought the urge to yank it free and slap his face. "I have always thought you a beautiful woman, Rebecca, and I have long wished for a more . . . intimate friendship."

The gentle clink of dishes from outside the drawing room door heralded Jemson's return, and Rebecca slid her hand out of the earl's grasp. "Thank you, Jemson," she said, as the butler set the heavily laden silver tray on the small table before the sofa. You may leave us now." She poured a glass of sherry for the earl from the crystal decanter and handed it to him, saying, "I too thought we would deal well together. We have so much in common—a love of nature, music. We seem to see humor in the same situations."

The earl chuckled. "I'll never forget our first meeting."

"Ah, yes. At Lady Thornton's musicale. Miss Warble."

" 'What Miss Warble needs most,' you said, 'is to return to her nest and stay there.' " Briarvale raised his goblet to her in salute.

"Yes," said Rebecca, her voice deceptively amiable, "I knew then we were forging not a mere friendship but a true meeting of minds." She took a plate from the tray. "I had Cook prepare a special treat in honor of this occasion. Would you care for a . . . tart?"

Briarvale looked from the serving plate of tartlets to Rebecca's delicately raised eyebrow, and his easy smile turned wary.

"Oh, but perhaps you are anxious to repair to my bedroom," she continued calmly. "Or we may forge our new relationship right here on the sofa. After all, Letty is conveniently away, and the servants shan't disturb us."

"Rebecca," began Briarvale, his voice coaxing.

"No, of course you will wish something first." Rebecca set a tartlet on the plate. "Oh, let us make that two. Rather symbolic, don't you agree? One to represent Miss Wilson and the other . . . myself," she finished, her voice chilled.

Now the earl was truly shocked. "Rebecca!"

"I do hope you don't intend me to dress in the same fashion as your other mistress," she continued.

"My God, Rebecca. Have you taken leave of your senses?"

"One might ask the same thing of you, Evan. After six years of friendship, of meeting at nearly every social event London society has to offer, of countless dinner parties, and even a house party or two, you know so little of me that you offer me a casual affair! You should count yourself fortunate that I don't throw this tart in your face."

"I meant no insult," protested Briarvale. "I truly thought that being a woman of good sense, and having already experienced marriage, you would rather not sacrifice both fortune and freedom to a man a second time."

"What is love but sacrifice? I don't wish to spend the next thirty years of my life alone."

"Nor do I," said Briarvale. "I had thought you would see the sense in my proposal. Last night . . ."

"Did you think me so lacking in social graces that I would have made a public scene last night?" demanded Rebecca.

"There is nothing over which to make a scene," insisted Briarvale. "I am merely proposing we do what over half the *ton* does!"

Rebecca's chin went up. "I don't wish to be part of that half. I want the sort of commitment that comes only with marriage. And I want a man who values me highly enough to make such a commitment. I am sorry you are not up to it." Her speech finished, she handed the plate of tartlets to the astonished earl, rose from the sofa, and headed out the door.

As she sped down the hallway to her room, she told herself that the loss of Lord Briarvale didn't matter a whit. He was an odious, selfish man, and she'd give no more thought to him. She would see her daughter happily married and take up with Sir James. *He* would offer matrimony.

Once the bedroom door was closed, the prickling at the back of her eyes evolved into tears and she plopped onto her bed, buried her face in her hands, and sobbed.

She was still so absorbed in her misery that she didn't hear the gentle tapping at her door an hour later.

The door opened and Letty peeped around it. "Mama, there you are!"

Letty entered the room, the picture of youth and hope and happiness, and Rebecca took a quick swipe at a tear and smiled for her daughter.

"I have had the most wonderful drive with Matthew," said Letty. "We talked of everything imaginable. And you'll never guess what he said. He said he wondered what he'd ever seen in Miss Swan. That, really, she was a most conceited creature and a shocking flirt and—Mama, you've been crying!"

"Of course I haven't," said Rebecca. "I did not sleep well last night and my eyes are red."

"And swollen," added her daughter in concern. "Lord Briarvale. He did not come?"

"Oh, he came," said Rebecca.

"Oh," said her daughter, her voice full of pity. "Oh, Mama. What can have happened? You and Lord Briarvale are such good friends."

"I am sure we will always be friends," said Rebecca. "Now," she continued with false heartiness, "never mind about myself and Lord Briarvale, tell me more of your drive with Matthew."

Letty obliged, and soon Rebecca had managed to push aside all thoughts of the troublesome earl.

* * *

Lord Briarvale had no daughter to put balm on his troubled mind. And as he tooled his curricle back to his town house, it was, indeed, troubled. Although she was being utterly ridiculous and impractical, he hated to think of losing Rebecca's friendship. She was one of the few females in the Upper Ten Thousand with whom he felt comfortable. Of course, he was disappointed she was being so ridiculously prim. He'd thought of little else the night before but what pleasure it would give him to become as well acquainted with her soft curves as he was with her sense of humor.

Tarts, indeed! He chuckled in spite of his irritation. Well, a man could make an honest mistake. She would forgive him with time and they'd continue comfortably on as they had for the past six years. Someday they'd both look back on this incident and laugh.

Of course he'd need to make a peace offering. He'd have flowers sent to her tomorrow. And perhaps he'd pop round to Gunther's to pick up a treat of some sort. The surest way to show repentance, short of taking his life, would be to give the Lady Winter something for her sweet tooth.

The earl smiled, well pleased with himself. That took care of that. Now he could look forward to an evening of unalloyed enjoyment at his club.

Briarvale slept late after a night of heavy gambling at Brooks's. He took his time over breakfast, reading the *Gazette* as he ate. After that he dealt with correspondence. Finally, by midafternoon, he embarked on his mission to purchase a present for Rebecca. The sun was shining, the birds were singing, and all was well with the world of the Earl of Briarvale. He had just gotten down from his curricle and handed the reins to his tiger, when he spied Rebecca herself across the street, walking on the arm of Sir James Blessing.

Well! He saw she'd wasted little enough time getting a new fish on the line. Whale, to be precise, thought Briarvale sourly, eyeing his rival.

Rebecca chose that moment to look the earl's way. At the sight of him her smile froze.

The earl gritted his teeth and stretched his lips, politely tipping his hat and making a half bow in her direction.

She gave him the barest of nods and returned her attention to Sir James, who had talked through the entire interchange, oblivious to what was happening.

For the first time in years, unfamiliar feelings of shame mixed with anger flushed a dark red stain onto Briarvale's cheeks. She'd as good as cut him, the harpy! Even now he could hardly credit it. The earl snatched the reins from his tiger and got back into his curricle. Lady Winter would get no gift from Gunther's this day. Let her collect her presents from Sir James Blowhard!

Rebecca turned before entering her town house and gave Sir James her hand. "I had a most enjoyable afternoon," she lied.

"As did I," he said. "I always enjoy your company, Lady Winter."

"Thank you," replied Rebecca, slipping her hand from his. She turned to go inside.

"Lady Winter."

Rebecca stopped and looked over her shoulder.

"I would very much like an opportunity to enjoy more of your company."

"I am sure we will be seeing much of each other in the weeks to come, Sir James," said Rebecca.

"With a crowd of giddy people around." Sir James shook his great head. "I was thinking of doing something, just the two of us. Would you allow me to drive you out into the country this Saturday?"

"This Saturday?"

"I thought, perhaps, a drive to Sadler's Wells. We could enjoy a bite at *The Angel,* take in a farce. There is nothing like a drive down a peaceful country road for inspiring two people to open their minds . . . and hearts."

The thought of Sir James opening his heart to her made Rebecca's sink to her toes. "I hope you will allow me a day to consult my calendar," she prevaricated.

He bowed. "I am at your disposal."

"And how I should like to dispose of you," she muttered after she'd shut the door on Sir James.

She had just taken off her bonnet and checked her reflection in the hall mirror when her daughter came out of the drawing room. "Oh, Mama! Where have you been all this time? Matthew has called twice hoping to catch you home."

"He has? Might these urgent calls mean what I suspect?"

Letty nodded excitedly and took her mother's arm, strolling her into the drawing room. "It was so very romantic. He called the first time and said he must speak to you. I told him you had gone out with Sir James. Really, Mama, what can you see in that man? He is such a boring old prose. At any rate, Matthew asked when you would be back and I said I didn't know, and what on earth was so urgent that he must see you immediately. He said, 'I have come to realize that I wish to marry you, and once I make up my mind to something, I like to have it settled straightaway.' Is that not the most romantic proposal, Mama?"

"It leaves me quite breathless," said Rebecca. "I assume he waits to confess his undying love after he has obtained my permission to pay his addresses." Letty's face turned pink, and Rebecca smiled. "Would I be correct in guessing he has already done that?"

Letty nodded. He said if I didn't consent to marry him, he would have no choice but to go home and instantly put a dueling pistol to his head." She hugged her mother. "Mama, I vow I am the happiest woman alive."

"And I am the second happiest," said Rebecca. "The glow on your young face warms my heart."

"I owe my happiness to you, for without your advice I am sure I'd never have brought Matthew up to scratch."

"Oh, I think perhaps you would have," said Rebecca, then added wistfully, "Some things are meant to be."

Her daughter's smile faded, and she looked at Rebecca with concern. "Mama?"

Rebecca forced a fresh smile to her face. "Well, now," she said briskly. "Let me go and change my gown, and you ring for Jemson and tell him to fetch ratafia and biscuits. We shall have a celebration."

The ladies were still celebrating when Matthew returned for the third time, and after showing him into the drawing room, Jemson was dispatched to fetch another goblet and some sherry. "Well, Matthew," said Rebecca, "I understand I shall soon call you son."

Matthew looked at Letty and grinned. "If we have your approval, Lady Winter."

"I suppose I had best give it," said Rebecca. "Else I shall be responsible for your early demise."

Matthew's cheeks reddened and Letty giggled, and Rebecca smiled even as she cursed herself for a fool to let wistful longing for Lord Briarvale shadow this moment.

Granted, it tinged only a corner with its black despondency, but even that was more than he deserved. She wouldn't think of him, the selfish beast. She wouldn't! And to prove it to herself, she went to her room as soon as Matthew had taken his leave, sat herself at her secretary, and penned a note of acceptance to Sir James.

The following night, at Lady Hestor's ball, it became quickly apparent to the guests that young Overton and Lady Winter's child had made a match of it. Matthew was with Letty at nearly every opportunity, and the look on her face could only mean love. Expressions of congratulation began to flutter on the perfumed air.

"I say," said Sir James to Rebecca toward the end of the evening, "do I imagine it, or is Stilton's cub beginning to develop an interest in your daughter?"

"Yes, he wishes to marry her," said Rebecca patiently, and shooed away the little thought that Briarvale would have already understood and offered congratulations.

"He does seem to be showing a preference," continued Sir James.

"Yes, he does," agreed Rebecca, and sighed inwardly.

The couple returned to them from the dance floor, laughing, and Sir James smiled on them. "Well, now, Mr. Overton," he said heartily, "we are certainly seeing a great deal of you this evening, aren't we? Suppose you and I go in search of punch for the ladies."

"An excellent idea," approved Matthew. "Be back in a trice, Letty."

Letty watched them go, frowning slightly. "What can you see in that man, Mama? He is so stuffy and . . . pompous."

"He is a good man," said Rebecca mildly.

"He is dull as dust."

Rebecca sighed.

"I don't understand why you are encouraging him," continued Letty. "He isn't at all your sort." She turned from watching Sir James in time to catch her mother looking wistfully across the ballroom at Lord Briarvale.

"I suppose he will offer marriage when we drive to Sadler's Wells this Saturday," said Rebecca dully.

"Mama! You wouldn't accept him, would you?"

Rebecca sighed again, and shook her head. "No. It would be most unkind. At my age, a lady is better off doing without than settling for less than what she wants."

Letty studied Lord Briarvale, who was standing on the opposite side of the ballroom. She was sure she saw the earl cast a furtive glance in her mother's direction. "Yes, Mama.

I believe you are right." She bit her lip, contemplating, then said, "I think, perhaps, you might not have to do without, however."

"Letty, I haven't the foggiest notion of what you are speaking."

"Never mind, Mama," said Letty, her eyes dancing. "Tell Matthew I shall be right back."

"But where are you going?"

"I must use the water closet."

Letty followed a circuitous path around the ballroom, then, when she was sure her mother was no longer watching, headed for Lord Briarvale. She waited patiently for the earl to finish his conversation, then curtsied and said a meek "Good evening, your lordship."

"Good evening," he replied. "Would I be premature in wishing you happy?"

Letty flushed and shook her head. "The announcement will be in the *Gazette* next week."

"You make a fine couple," said Briarvale.

"Thank you, your lordship. I will enjoy being a bride the same time as my mama."

"I beg your pardon?"

Making good use of the acting skill her mother so admired, Letty looked at the earl with wide-eyed innocence. "Why, did you not know? Mama, too, will be marrying soon."

Lord Briarvale frowned. "Do you mean to tell me your mother has accepted a proposal of marriage?"

"I believe she and Sir James will be off to Sadler's Wells this Saturday. Mama says they are going there to see a farce, but I am sure I heard Sir James say something to her about a special license when he thought I wasn't listening. Of course, I don't believe Mama cares for Sir James the way a wife should care for a husband, but I think she is afraid of being lonely after I am gone, and I suppose a lady must take what offers she can get."

"Umm," grunted the earl, looking across the room at Rebecca.

"Oh, there is Matthew looking for me," said Letty. "Will you excuse me, your lordship?"

"What? Oh, certainly."

Letty left the earl, and her smile was as big as the one her mother had worn after they paid their life-changing morning call on Lady Swan.

Friday night Rebecca prayed for gray skies and a spring rain on Saturday. She got blue skies and sunshine. For the hundredth time she told herself she should have never accepted Sir James's invitation. An entire day spent in his company—she would be bored before they were halfway to Islington! She pulled on her lemon kid gloves with a jerk and went down to Sir James, Letty trailing behind.

"I hope you have a wonderful time," said Letty as the butler opened the door for her mama. She hugged Rebecca and whispered in her ear. "And here is some advice from your daughter. Remember, there comes a time when the fox must get caught."

Rebecca looked questioningly at her, but Letty merely smiled and stepped back.

"I am sure we will have a wonderful day," predicted Sir James, a complacent smile on his face.

"I hope it will be memorable," said Letty, and she bit back a giggle.

This was not lost on Rebecca, and she tried to search her daughter's now-innocent face for further signs of mischief, but Sir James, like a mighty wave, moved her out the door and down the front steps.

He settled her in his landau, then fell in beside her. "Let

us be off," he said grandly to his driver, and turned to Rebecca. "Lovely day for a drive, isn't it?"

"Yes," she agreed, and resigned herself to an eternity of conversation that would rise to no loftier heights than a discussion of weather and crop-rotation.

Sir James did not disappoint her. As they rolled out of town, he treated her to a weather prediction, the observation that London seemed more crowded this year than it had last year, and the hope that soon he would be able to return to his country seat in Berkshire.

Now will come crop-rotation, thought Rebecca morosely.

But instead, Sir James began to extol the virtues of Berkshire in general, and his country seat in particular. "The only thing lacking is the companionship of a good woman," he finished. He smiled at Rebecca. "But I hope soon to rectify that."

She smiled back weakly. "I am sure you miss your wife greatly," she said. "She was a lovely woman. So gracious."

Sir James nodded. "It is not good for a man to be alone."

"I certainly miss Charles," said Rebecca quickly, even though it had been a good two years since she had actually remembered to miss her dear departed.

"But one cannot live forever in the past," pointed out Sir James.

"Oh, no," agreed Rebecca. "However, one shouldn't rush into anything. Marry at haste and repent at leisure."

"Which is why," said Sir James, taking her hand, I have given much thought to what I am about to ask you." He lowered his voice. "Actually, I was going to ask you later, when we were more private, but this seems such an opportune time."

The carriage came to a halt and Sir James looked up. "What are you about, Harris?" he called. "Why have we stopped?"

"I am afraid there is a carriage blocking us," the coachman called back.

Sir James craned his neck to look down the road. "What on earth? Well, go tell the fool to move his equipage!"

"No need," called a cheerful voice. The Earl of Briarvale sauntered into view. He opened the carriage door, let down the steps, and held out his hand to Rebecca. "Come down from there, Rebecca, before you do something we will both greatly regret."

"Here now!" protested Sir James.

Rebecca stared at the earl as if he had taken leave of his senses. "Briarvale! What *are* you talking about? And what are you doing here?"

"Saving you from folly disguised as practicality. Your daughter told me all."

"Told you what?" demanded Rebecca.

"This is most irregular!" protested Sir James.

"I know where you are bound, old fellow," said Briarvale, "and I must tell you, it would be a great mistake."

"Mistake?" spluttered Sir James.

"What *can* you mean?" put in Rebecca. "We are simply on our way to Sadler's Wells to see a farce."

The earl grinned. "It would certainly be that. Now, are you going to get down, my dear, or must I carry you out?" Rebecca was still staring at him. The expression on his face changed from amusement to desire, and his voice became a caress. "Not that I wouldn't mind doing that."

"Evan," she said softly.

"Come," he said, his palm stretched to her.

"Briarvale, this is not only rude, it is ridiculous! To waylay a man on the road like this is unthinkable. Bad *ton*. I cannot imagine what Lady Winter thinks about such behavior, but . . . Lady Winter! What are you doing?"

Rebecca stepped daintily over Sir James's thick legs and took Briarvale's hand. "I do hope you'll forgive me, Sir James, but it would appear you were right." She stepped down from the carriage and turned back to the astonished occupant. "There is nothing like a drive in the country to inspire two people to open their minds"—she smiled up at the earl—"and hearts." She took his arm and allowed him to lead her to his carriage, oblivious of Sir James's protests.

Once inside the closed carriage, the earl wasted no time in taking Rebecca in his arms. "When I think of what a selfish fool I was, and what I almost lost, I could kick myself."

"And I could help you," murmured Rebecca. "And please don't think that I wasn't charmed by your dramatic rescue, but you could have waited."

"And how long would you have had me wait?" retorted Briarvale.

"Well, I must admit, I'd have died of boredom before the day was over, but I'd have made it through somehow."

The earl looked at her blankly.

"Never mind," she said, laying a hand on his cheek. "Tell me instead what changed your feelings on the subject of matrimony."

"When I heard from your daughter of your impending nuptials," said the earl. "I confess, the thought of some other man possessing you was more than I could bear."

Rebecca blinked at him. "Nuptials?" she repeated.

"Yes. Your daughter told me you and Sir Bag of Wind were bound for Sadler's Wells to marry by special license."

"We were bound for Sadler's Wells to spend the afternoon and see a farce."

"Farce?" repeated Briarvale.

"Oh, my," said Rebecca. Her mouth twitched.

Like a mirror image, the earl's did the same, then both burst into laughter. "Oh, that is rich," he said at last. "Well, you got your farce after all."

"And I did not have to endure a day of Sir James's company to get it."

"Would you have married him?"

Rebecca stopped herself just in time before the truth escaped her lips. Instead, she merely smiled. "Did you have something particular to ask me, Evan?"

He took her hand and kissed it. "Rebecca. Only when faced with the loss of you did I realize how very much I value you. How essential your companionship is to my well-being."

"Ah, but what of those shackles?" teased Rebecca.

"They shall feel like velvet."

"And your poor nephew?"

Briarvale grinned. "Let him find his own bride. Rebecca," he said, suddenly serious, "would you do me the great honor of consenting to become my wife?"

Rebecca felt her eyes fill with tears. "I would," she replied, and just before the earl kissed her, she made a mental note to remember when next she saw her, to tell Letty that she was the cleverest child in all of London.

The Mother and the Marquess

by
Jeanne Savery

"Gothic, my dear Miles. Quite, quite Gothic."

Madeline, Lady Sitwell, shook her head at her tall, dark, and, at that instant, scowling brother. Ten minutes previously, the Marquess had taken up his characteristic stance before her grate, his left arm lying along the mantel and the tips of the fingers of his other hand stuffed in the waistband of his unmentionables. Miles, she thought, despite his nearly forty years, was still a well-looking man.

But "well-looking" hid a stubborn and, at times, misguided insistence on his own way! He'd been bad enough when merely Miles Amesbury. Since inheriting his title, he'd become impossible. At least sometimes.

When he didn't respond, she decided this was one of those times. "You cannot justify such a measure," she prompted.

"But you'll have them?" asked Miles abruptly.

Madeline hesitated. "Do you know if they are even presentable?"

Miles, Lord Herrington, rubbed his chin, the frown deepening. "I found the boy surprisingly well grounded in those things a mother is capable of teaching her brats. He is polite, yet determined. He does not grovel. And his school reports have been excellent. But then, Tim's boy"—even after all the years Miles's friend had been dead, one could still detect a certain sadness when he mentioned Sir Timothy Lawrence—"one would expect that, you know."

"Ah—I forgot you'd been left the children's guardian. That explains how you can order them to London, does it not? Of course, you've met them!"

Mile's chin rose. His exceedingly square chin fairly screamed that here was a man who would not be crossed. The arrogance was also evident in his voice: "I've met the boy, as I said. Once and only recently. He came through London on his way home for the short vacation."

Lady Sitwell's brows climbed her alabaster brow. "Might one ask—without danger of losing one's head—*why* this determined, although polite, lad came to London?" When Miles's jaw tightened, his sister grimaced. "I mean, if he has not made it a habit to come running to you for every skinned knee and bloody nose, then there must be a reason, must there not?"

Again her brows arched. This time queryingly. A bark of laughter answered her and Madeline smiled, pleased to have turned Miles's ready temper toward his equally easily tickled sense of humor.

"You have, my overly astute sister, guessed there was a problem. Sir Kenelm did not docilely accept my newest decision for his future. He told me he'd reluctantly accepted my first, which was to send him to Eton, but now he has notions of his own—and this time will have his way."

Madeline digested that. "You don't think his sister, Miss Euphemia Lawrence, might also have notions? Or, if not she, then surely her mother?"

"Bah." Herrington's frown returned, doubled in its intensity. "I never approved Tim's choice of wife. Never. From the moment I first heard he'd married I've been certain he was caught on the rebound from that widow—that *harpy*—who got her claws into him just before I left with my regiment."

"Ah. You've met her, then?"

"An older woman who thought she'd found a young fool who would marry her and set her up for life. A harpy, I say!"

Madeline's shoulders lifted and fell on a sigh. *"Not* the harpy with claws, Miles, but the wife?"

"Why would I have met *her?"* he asked. "Was it not

enough I found myself—at a time when I had far too many problems of my own—guardian of my friend's children? At least it was never put upon me to take on *her* affairs as well, whatever they may be," he added, his tone dismissive, and then seemed to think again, the scowl much in evidence. "And there's another thing, is there not? I must see she isn't a trial to the boy! His father did reasonably well by him, and I've done better, but Sir Kenelm hasn't so much he may squander the ready on a flighty widget's impetuous demands. Women," Miles said grandly, if insultingly, "have no sense of economy—and," he added portentously, "they know nothing of financial management."

Madeline debated the wisdom of arguing but decided it was irrelevant. "Well, Miles, your Lady Diana Lawrence may have allowed you your way with the boy, but if she is *not* the widget you expect, and has any backbone at all, I doubt she'll be so sanguine about her daughter!"

"Nonsense." Miles prepared to leave, satisfied his sister would take the unknown and unwanted Lawrence females in hand. "Lady Lawrence will jump at the opportunity to sit in your pocket, my dear. After all, who else is there to give countenance to her chit?"

The "who else" was Lady Ellen Bushnell, who sat at her breakfast table a week later chortling over the blistering tirade her dear friend Diana had written. As Diana admitted, she found it necessary to relieve her temper with a letter to her understanding Ellen before settling down to write a letter to her solicitor and, after that was finished, an excessively polite and proper letter of thank you-but-no-thank-you to Lady Sitwell.

Lady Ellen nudged her husband with her toe. "Do listen, Bushy dear. Diana is furious and, to say truth, I cannot blame her. Bushnell? Do you listen?" Lady Ellen glanced up from her letter and met her husband's gaze, which peered patiently over the top of his paper. She grinned. "Oh, very well, my dear," she said. "Do drink your coffee. I may wait to relate to you this tale of domineering guardians and ignorant menfolk and insensitive brutes, to say nothing of demanding bores and . . . !" Ellen saw her husband's lips twitch and was content.

She sorted through the rest of her mail, pausing at an invitation. Lady Sitwell, it seemed, planned a ball. Lady Sitwell was mentioned in Diana's letter along with the ranting about her daughter's guardian. Assuming Ellen had correctly deciphered the crossed lines, dear Diana couldn't decide whether to commiserate with her ladyship for having such an overbearing brother, or blame her ladyship that she'd not modified his grossly unfair behavior while still in the nursery and, somehow, made of him a gentleman!

Lady Ellen, her own daughter safely married, had expected the Season this year might be unbearably dull. Now, after all, there was something to which she might look forward! Because, thought Ellen, if Lady Sitwell is the sister of the unknown gentleman whom Diana has taken in such dislike, then *he* must be none other than Lord Miles Herrington!

Lord Herrington, the bane of matchmaking mothers ever since he unexpectedly inherited the title some years before and resigned his commission in the army to take his place in the *ton. Lord Herrington,* the handsomest man still unwed in all England—even if his hair was graying at the temples. *Lord Herrington*—who, it suddenly occurred to Ellen, would be perfect for dear Diana—who had complained, in a separate paragraph in her overly long letter, of one or two gray hairs of her own!

"Bushy dear, are you acquainted with Lord Herrington?" asked Lady Ellen in the innocent tone that immediately informed his lordship his wife was up to something.

He rattled his newspaper.

She pulled down the corner. "Dear?"

"Of course I know Herrington." Which meant he also

knew the temper that was his lordship's byword. "I take leave to warn you, my love, do not attempt one of your little games with Herrington."

"I haven't a notion what you might mean!" Ellen let go of the newspaper and settled into her chair, plans weaving through her fertile mind—none of which would have the approval of her friend. Or, for that matter, of his lordship. *Wouldn't Diana throw a tizzy!* thought Ellen, using a vulgarism she'd learned from her maid.

But that was for the future. The first step was to go, per dear Diana's request, and see what must be done to Diana's house on Duke Street. It must be refurbished and made ready for the Lawrences' occupancy by the end of the month! *What fun,* thought Ellen. Luckily, Diana could easily afford whatever blunt must be laid out to see her long-empty town house comfortable.

Lady Diana Lawrence laid her knitting in her lap and looked from her daughter beside her to her son opposite her in the well-sprung traveling carriage. She smiled a trifle mistily. "I wonder what I did to deserve such wonderful children. *Whatever* would I have done without you?"

"You might have had all the time you wished to make your gardens the very best in all of England," suggested her daughter, smiling.

"No she wouldn't," contradicted her sixteen-year-old son. "If the portrait done by Reynolds is anything near a true likeness, she'd very likely have been hauled off to the altar just as soon as she was out of widow's weeds!"

"Now, Kenelm," said Lady Lawrence, blushing slightly. "Even then, at the very last of his life, Reynolds's paintings were magnificent. It had nothing to do with the sitter, but everything to do with the artist," she scolded, looking closely at her knitting to hide still more blushes.

"Mother is still beautiful," said seventeen-year-old

Phemie, who preferred they praise and compliment and fluster their mother rather than return to the previous discussion which had included conjectures about her own marriage prospects. "Mama could still take London by storm if she wished."

Diana shook her head. "I am nearly thirty-five and quite ancient, so enough of your teasing," she said, looking out the window. "Why, we've finally arrived in London," she added to divert them.

Then, discovering her son had a penchant for hanging out the side of the coach to stare at passing sights, Lady Diana searched her reticule and pulled out the letter that had been the start of this journey.

"Kenelm dearest," she said. "You've met the . . . the *gentleman* who ordered us away from our comfortable home. Do, please, tell us," said Lady Diana in a coaxing tone her children knew well, "that you believe the tone of this letter to have been in jest?"

Kenelm, pulling in his head and sitting into his seat with his back to the horses, looked from his mother to his sister and back again. He compressed his lips and huffed. "You *do* wish the truth, do you not?"

"But of course." Diana's needles clicked steadily.

"Then, Mama," said her son, his large, well-lashed brown eyes that looked so much like her own taking on a sad note, "I fear the, hmm, terms he sent you are *not* in jest." Immediately, he moved back to his window.

"But surely," said his sister, "my guardian cannot order us to London in this abrupt fashion . . . well, yes, I understand he *can* do that . . . but to insist that I be married by the end of the Season? It is *Gothic!* Surely what he has said there"—Phemie pointed with her knitting needle at the letter lying in her mother's lap—"cannot truly mean that if I do not find a man with whom I may be happy, the . . . the *monster* will simply choose me a husband?"

"Phemie," said her brother, once again turned from absorbing and exciting sights, "Lord Herrington is not a monster. Somewhat abrupt, perhaps, in his manner, but when I went to him, insisting I wished to study to become a surgeon rather than waste my time at university gambling and wenching and playing the fool, he accepted my arguments, did he not? He agreed that I might go to Edinburgh rather than to Cambridge, which had been his decision."

"That is all very well, Kenelm," said his mother, "but it may not be a help in this particular case. Dear Phemie is a mere female, you see," said Lady Diana a trifle testily. She turned her needles, untwisting her yarn as she did so. Diana frowned at an overly loose stitch and debated with herself whether she should take it out. She decided she must. "What I do not see," she added after fixing it, "is why, when he has ignored our Euphemia's existence all these many years, he should now take it into his head to upset all my careful plans in this particularly irritating way."

"What plans, Mama?" asked Phemie.

"Lady Ellen Bushnell and I put our heads together—you remember Ellen, do you not? She invited us to their country home near Bath once the London Season ended and, while there, you were to meet any number of young people, including females with whom you might form friendships and a few gentlemen with whom you might practice flirtations." Diana smiled at her blushing daughter. "We felt it would ease your introduction, *next* year, into tonnish circles—of which Ellen is very much an ornament." Diana's lips compressed. "I still feel it a good plan. You would have had friends when we went to London and, too, you would have known how to go on, thanks to Ellen."

"What a lovely notion, Mama," said Phemie wistfully. She did not feel ready to face the *ton* and felt especially unready to be paraded before marriage-minded males. "Can you not discuss it with Lord Herrington? Perhaps we may still do it that way?"

"It is, I think, too late, my dear," said her mother, her eyes sparkling with anger. "We were ordered to London and to London we have come." Lady Diana let go her knitting with one hand, lifted the letter, and shook it. "The man is impossible, telling us, if you please, that we will be the guests of his lordship's sister who, poor dear, is in no way responsible for us and cannot have liked to have totally unknown guests thrust upon her in this odd fashion." She dropped the letter as if it were something not quite nice.

Diana took a deep breath, and her nicely rounded but exceedingly firm chin lifted. "At least I've taken care of *that* problem," she continued. "We've obeyed your dratted guardian in that we have come, a whole year before it is necessary, to London. But you, Phemie," she finished, a militant light in her eye, "will not be forced into a marriage of convenience by that cold-hearted man merely because he has become tired of looking after your affairs!"

"Do you think that is it?" asked Kenelm, curious. He reached for the strap when the coach lurched over a gutter.

"I haven't a notion," said his mother, checking to see if she'd lost a stitch when the coach bounced in that odd way. She had—a whole string of stitches—which only added to her irritation. "I've never interfered in that . . . *gentleman's* decisions, because, up to now, I've not felt a need to do so. But this! As you said, Phemie, quite quite *Gothic!* You may believe that I'll not allow you to be married off where you do not will it."

Early the next morning—in tonnish terms—Lady Ellen hugged Lady Diana and turned to Kenelm and Phemie. "Oh, my dear, I see why you tell me there are no better children in all of England! Your Kenelm is the image of his father, is he not? Except for those eyes which are very like your own? And although she takes her coloring from her father, I believe Euphemia is as well looking as you were at that age, Diana— and *you* were acclaimed a diamond!"

"Nonsense," said Diana, watching the color rise in her daughter's cheeks and feeling her own warming as well. "We are, as a family, not to be ashamed of ourselves, but one's beauty or lack of it is not so important as those things one cannot see. Character, for instance."

"However that may be," said Ellen with a chuckle, "it is the beauty that first draws attention. All too often character is discovered only *after* marriage."

Phemie, whitening, looked to her mother. "Surely not!"

Her mother pulled her close, a comforting arm around the girl's waist. "We'll not allow you to marry someone who has even the slightest taint upon his reputation. Do not fear it, my love."

"But my guardian . . ."

"Your guardian will have me to deal with if he so much as hints at an unacceptable match!"

"And me," said Lady Ellen, realizing Euphemia, who appeared poised and confident at first glance, hid those fears any young woman of sense felt when contemplating marriage. She waved a hand as if to dismiss serious thoughts. "You recall I asked that you send your measurements? If you are not overly tired from yesterday's traveling—or even if you are—we must instantly take ourselves off to Valentine. She has gowns for you that need only a fitting to see that they're ready for tonight's soiree."

Phemie looked at her mother, and Lady Diana shrugged. They both turned to look at Lady Bushnell.

Ellen laughed. "Have I been such a featherhead that I've not told you that I've obtained cards of invitation for you to the Lievens'? Princess Lieven is a patroness of Almack's, you know, and Lady Jersey and perhaps others will attend as well. Vouchers to Almack's are not always easily come by, but I think our little beauty here will have no difficulty achieving them."

"This evening? Is it proper?" asked Diana slowly. "We've

yet to meet the children's guardian and Phemie has not been presented. I don't know . . ."

"Lud, Diana, don't worry about Herrington. I'm sure merely the fact you've obeyed his order and come to London for dear Euphemia's presentation will satisfy him. He'll want nothing to do with the details. And so simple a party as this is acceptable. Now, do call for your pelisses and bonnets and we'll begin our raids on the shops." Ellen grinned like a young girl. "Diana, you can have no notion how much I'm in charity with Herrington!"

"You are?" asked Diana, a wary look in her eye.

"But *yes.*" Ellen grinned. "If it were not for him, you'd not have come to London. And if you'd not come to London, I would have died of boredom! So you see, Herrington is very much in my good book at the moment!"

"Only at the moment?"

Ellen's grin broadened. "Well. Herrington, you know. Or perhaps you do not? By next week he'll likely have done something to put himself in my bad book again."

She said this in such a droll manner, both the Lawrence women chuckled, but Diana suspected there might be more to her old friend's comment than appeared on the surface.

By the time she was ready for the evening's entertainment, Diana wished Herrington to the devil. They'd been in town a mere twenty-four hours and already she wished for their lovely Cotswold manor with the protected gardens in which she loved to dirty her hands, however unladylike that might be. She wished for their friends with whom they might visit without all this nonsense of fashion and formality. In fact, she had, it occurred to her, forgotten just how very much she disliked London.

At least, during their visit to the Lievens' tonight, no real attention would be called to Phemie. She wouldn't be truly out until her presentation at the Queen's next drawing room which would be followed, immediately, by the ball dear Ellen planned for Phemie's formal introduction to the *ton*. Thank her stars for dear Ellen, who loved to entertain as much as Diana hated it!

Diana hid a yawn and glanced at the clock on the mantel. Ellen was due any moment now. She yawned again. How utterly ridiculous. She was ready for bed when it was just time to begin a London evening! At not quite thirty-five she was acting like the most decrepit of dowagers! Perhaps Ellen was correct? Perhaps she had rusticated for far too long? Perhaps it was time she made the effort to insert herself back into society? But why should one? It was always all so boringly the same.

The butler announced the Bushnells' arrival. Diana took one last glance at her excited daughter, pronounced the girl perfection itself, and, accepting their cloaks, the two women, mother and daughter, took their places in the Bushnell carriage.

The Lawrence ladies' days proceeded in much the same way—shopping in the daytime and one or two parties in the evenings—up until the day Euphemia was to be presented to the Queen. Now, the moment nearly upon her, the Bushnell carriage was again momentarily expected. Lady Diana attempted to calm the constant shivers of apprehension that coursed one after another down her daughter's back and arms.

"My dear, you will do perfectly."

"But, Mother, you won't be there."

"You like Lady Ellen. She'll see all goes comfortably for you."

"But what if I can't stand up? What if I curtsy and my legs collapse!"

"Then one of the equerries will come lift you. You must apologize quietly and efface yourself immediately. And later you must laugh about it."

"Oh, Mama!"

"You won't fall," said her brother scornfully. "How could you?"

"I'm so nervous!"

"The Queen is, as I remember, a very nice lady," said Diana placidly. "You've no reason to be nervous."

"But the *Queen!*"

Diana chuckled. "Yes, poor lady, the Queen."

"Poor lady?" Phemie dared not sit down for fear she'd crush her gown, so she leaned on the back of her mother's chair. "How can you say so?"

"Think, Phemie. You will go before her and make your bow, perhaps say a word or two, and it is over. *She* must remain pleasant to one young and nervous girl after another for far too many hours. Do you think she enjoys these drawing rooms?" Diana look doubtful. "I cannot believe it. But she must go through with them again and again and again and . . ."

Phemie's light laugh floated into the air. "I must feel sorry for her. Is that what you mean?" Her mother nodded. "Then I will," she decided.

The visit to the palace went off with only one hitch: When the presentation to Her Majesty was over, Lady Ellen was required to supervise a far more difficult one. Lord Herrington was among the gentlemen invited to attend, and he approached her and his ward. He took out his quizzing glass once he'd been introduced and looked the girl up and down. "Presentable," he said.

"Uncharitable," chided Ellen.

He met her eyes for a moment. "True, but one must not turn one's ward's head. You'll do well, Miss Lawrence. I'll be very surprised if you don't capture an earl at least and you might look still higher for a husband."

Phemie blushed, but her chin rose much as her mother's would have done. "I wish only for a man whom I may love and respect and who may love me."

Herrington's brows arched in the Amesbury way, and the warmth left his face. "Love? Nonsense. Love has no place in marriage. Whoever has taught you such nonsense"—his tone implied he knew but would refrain from insulting his ward's mother—"should be shot. You listen to me, child, and don't throw your cap over the windmill for the nonsense called *love.*"

Phemie blenched. "No one taught me love is important. I *saw* that it was by watching my parents. I hope I may be half so happy in my own choice." She closed her mouth firmly and curtsied, fearing she'd been impertinent.

"Another Lawrence with convictions, hmm?" The quizzing glass came out again. "We'll see," he said, his voice cold.

Herrington watched the child follow Lady Ellen from the long room where the audience was being held. He was surprised to find he approved the girl. She *would* do—and not merely because she was quite the most beautiful young woman he'd seen so far this spring.

But that bit about her parents. Bah. That was nonsense. It *must* be nonsense: Poor Tim had been deeply enamored of the harpy. He could not have turned around and, so quickly, fallen in love with Miss Lawrence's mother. It didn't happen that way.

But the mother must not be quite so bad as he'd thought. No fortune-hunting flitter-wit could have raised two children to be such paragons! Ah, well. He'd meet her ladyship at the come-out ball at the Bushnells'.

The Bushnells. That was a surprise too: Who'd have thought a woman who lived retired all the years since poor Tim died could have a friend such as Lady Ellen Bushnell. He'd believed the reason that Lady Diana had not come to London was that she wasn't entirely presentable, but it must have been choice, if she were so well acquainted with one of the *ton*'s foremost hostesses!

Herrington felt a trifle confused. He didn't like the emotion. His temper rose to swamp the confusion and he managed to forget it by indulging in a rather intemperate argument, given they were in a royal presence, concerning the progress of the war!

The Bushnell ball was well under way when Lady Diana slipped behind the secret door that hid the stairs up to a balcony overlooking the ballroom. Ellen had Phemie in hand and was reintroducing her to a plethora of young people Diana could not keep straight although she, too, had met them in the receiving line. Besides, she was tired. Or, perhaps, merely bored? In any case, she'd leave Phemie to Ellen and take a rest before rejoining those crowding the Bushnell rooms that evening.

The balcony was well shadowed. Diana had no fear someone might look up and see her staring down into the crush, occasionally smiling at something she saw. Certainly the gentleman, who had arrived a short time before and had also escaped the crowd—as soon as he thought he could do so without being seen—was surprised to discover his hiding place occupied. He made a slight noise and the woman turned sharply, concern evident.

"Excuse me," he said, exasperated. "I'd no notion of disturbing a tryst."

Diana chuckled, an enticing throaty sound of pure amusement. She relaxed. "You do nothing of the sort. Can you really see someone my age arranging a tryst? My children would laugh at such an odd notion."

Lord Herrington strolled nearer and could see the woman more clearly. "You don't look ancient to me, but perhaps children would think me on my last legs?"

Diana nodded. "I fear it is likely." She sighed. "What it is to be so young and . . . and ready for all life hands one."

Herrington felt a sudden interest. The woman's beauty had captured his immediate attention, of course, but would not have held it long. Her words, however, he found intriguing. "You feel, perhaps, that you are no longer prepared to face the vicissitudes life hands us? You are what? All of thirty perhaps? You cannot have suffered so much so soon."

Startled, Diana admitted what she normally would not have done: "I am nearly thirty-five and have suffered . . . enough," she finished. Sadness filled her eyes. She turned away from him.

"I apologize," he said softly.

"Accepted."

"Then speak to me, to prove you do not find me an utter bore and uncivilized as well!"

Diana turned and leaned back against the railing. "A bore? Now, how could a man so handsome"—she inspected him much as he'd studied her—"and presumably wealthy, be considered a bore? No, no. It could not be."

Startled, not certain he really wished to know, he asked, "Why not?"

She gestured toward the crowd below. "It is a rule. Wealthy men are handsome—and not boring—and beauties are forgiven anything. It is only those less well endowed who must always be engaging and, perhaps, pretend to wealth they do not have."

"You mean you and I are privileged and should not take advantage of that privilege?"

She nodded, giving him an approving look. "The man has sense as well as a handsome face and, if he is not pretending, wealth!"

He laughed softly. "I will take that for a compliment. May I return the favor and suggest you are indeed a beauty to whom all must be forgiven?"

The approval faded from her eyes. "I am what God made me. I hope it is more than a pretty face." She again turned away.

He had, perhaps, truly done the unforgivable and bored her! Herrington, more intrigued than ever, decided to ignore her hint that he was not wanted. "I was surprised to discover another knew of this balcony."

"Hmm? Oh. I used to play with Lord Bushnell's sisters."

"Hmm," he said in turn. With just a hint of suggestion in his tone, he added, "I, on the other hand, was once shown it by a woman who always knows of a place where one may be quite alone, whatever house she is in."

"Always? I wonder how she can always lead one to such a place."

He laughed again. The woman would not be put to the blush, but perhaps—if her tone meant anything—she wouldn't be led into a flirtation either! Herrington decided she *would* flirt with him. "Have you never found a quiet place where you might be quite alone with . . . someone?"

"Only with my husband . . ."

"You are married."

"I mentioned children, did I not? Where would I have gotten them had I not married?"

He smiled. "Do you truly wish me to answer that?"

She chuckled. "You are impossible."

"So I've been told. Perhaps you could reform me?" Again that sly note.

She turned. For a silent moment she met and held his eyes. When a faint red brushed his cheeks, she turned back, shaking her head. "I think the task would not be impossible, but only if you were to love the woman who took it on. You do not love me—therefore I'll not attempt a thankless task."

"Love," he growled. Still another woman who mentioned love casually—the *emotion* love and not the physical pleasures too many called love.

"Ah," she said, as if enlightened. "You do not believe in it."

"You do?"

"Of course."

"You say that as if it were obvious."

"Which, to you, it is not." Diana sighed. "When one has known love, then one must believe, must one not? I have."

"Known it?"

"Of course."

Another silence fell between them. Herrington was surprised to find it comfortable rather than the usual sort that was filled with a tension as each strained to think of something with which to fill it.

"You are a strange woman," he said at last.

"Am I? Perhaps you have associated with the wrong people. I am quite ordinary, actually."

"That you are *not."*

She chuckled. "Do you say so? Is it a fault? Dear me, should I apologize for not fitting the mold into which you would place me?" She turned again to smile up at him. "Tell me what it is and I will attempt to do so. Merely to be polite, of course."

He too turned, looked down at her wide, friendly gaze. He frowned. Those eyes . . . But no. He could not think where he had seen their like. "You wish to fit the expected mold?" Surprising himself, he took her roughly into his arms, his mouth finding her soft lips with—still more surprising—the result that he didn't wish to punish her, wished only to drink from them, to feel them respond and, for an instant, he thought they did.

Then, carefully, she extracted herself from his embrace. "I have," she said, a touch of a scold in her voice, "been from society far too long if *that* is what is expected of one! Or"— she tipped her head and looked thoughtful—"rather, I should immediately retire, again, to my much-loved home, where a lady is still treated as a lady!"

"I won't apologize. You said you wished to fit the mold into which I would put you."

"And the mold includes your bed."

"Of course."

"How strange." She studied him much as she might an outlandish and exotic animal that had strolled into her path. "How can you wish to bed someone you do not know?" His brows climbed his brow in the Amesbury way. "You see," she explained gently, "I believe a couple should be friends before they become lovers."

The concept of friendship between lovers was alien to Herrington's thinking, and he came close to gaping at her. *Any* friendship between a man and a woman was very nearly beyond his understanding. Realizing he must look like a landed fish, he closed his mouth.

"Friends?" he asked cautiously.

"Hmm."

"I presume you mean yes by that murmur?"

She smiled. "Yes," she said distinctly, enunciating carefully.

He laughed. "I don't believe I've ever laughed so much—with a woman, that is. You are amusing."

"For a woman." Her eyes twinkled merrily.

His smile froze. She was laughing *at* him! For a moment Herrington's temper struggled toward the surface. Then he recalled that he'd laughed at her. Was it fair to become angry if she returned the favor? "You *are* odd."

"Careful! I believe you repeat yourself."

"Yes, but I mean something different this time. You don't take offense when I insult you. You make me laugh when I do not wish to. You tell me politely you'll not indulge in an affair—which is exceedingly unusual."

"It is?" Again she studied him. "I suppose . . ." She shook her head. "No, I do not understand it."

"Am I so unattractive?" he asked politely.

She chuckled, a velvety sound that wrapped him in warmth. "How absurd. You know you are not. But how can what you say be true? I, you see, can *make* love only where I already *love* . . . if you see the difference?"

"Then why do you believe friendship should come first?"

She stared at him. "But surely you understand *that.*" When he merely bowed and waited, she added, "But, my dear sir, it is obvious. Friendship is an important aspect of love! Without it there is no love."

His features lost all tension, relaxing and going utterly blank. This woman could not possibly believe the nonsense she'd just uttered. It was insane, and, since she was mad, it would not do to bandy words with her. "I would continue to argue with you, but I have been hidden away for quite long enough now. Having come, having stayed a reasonable length of time, I may find my hostess and depart. If you'll excuse me?"

"Of course. But I think you mad, you know."

"Mad?" he asked politely, thinking a lunatic must believe the rest of the world the oddity.

"That you can have so little understanding of the concepts of love and friendship. You are, I must assume, older than I. Surely you have, at some time in your life, known love and friendship."

"Friendship, yes. The sort of fairy-tale love of which you speak, of course *not*. And I lost my friend, so I haven't even that now."

Her great eyes widened and she stared at him as if she felt sorry for him. Surely not . . . Why would anyone feel sorry for him? He was fêted. He was chased by marriage-minded women. He was . . .

"Poor, poor man," she said softly. "How very lonely you must be."

". . . lonely!" For a moment he stared blankly. Then he shook his head to clear it, bowed politely, and left the woman standing looking after him, pity in her eyes.

Pity! How dare she pity him! He wasn't lonely. . . .

Was he?

"You!" Lady Diana stilled, stared across her drawing room at the guest who had just been allowed entry for a morning call.

Lord Herrington felt as if he'd been punched by Jackson— or by one of Jackson's young instructors—far too low in the bread basket. Standing, scowling at him, was the woman from the night before, the woman on the balcony. *She* was his ward's mother? No. It couldn't be.

"You," he asked cautiously, "are Lady Diana Lawrence?"

"Of course."

"Was your initial and exceedingly impolite reaction because you did not recognize me?"

"On the contrary. It is because I do recognize you. From last night, my lord."

He glowered. "But that's what I meant," he persisted. "I am to believe that you did not, then, know to whom you spoke?"

"If I had known, I certainly would *not* have spoken in such a way—but then," she added thoughtfully, "perhaps it was for the best. We know a great deal about each other that we could not otherwise have guessed."

His glare changed to one of bemusement. "What is it? From the look in your eye you appear to have grave reservations about something."

She paused, then admitted, "Only that I wonder at Tim's choice. I cannot feel you were the best possible recourse for a guardian to our children. But," she added, "it is done and we neither have a choice in the matter. Do, please, come in and sit down."

Instead, Herrington strode to his favorite position on the hearth. He stood there in his usual casual pose with his arm along the mantel and the tips of the fingers of his other hand stuffed into his waistband. "Not the best possible guardian," he repeated, polite ice coating his words.

"No, of course not. Tim cannot have guessed you would grow so cold and unfeeling. Certainly *not* the friend he remembered, the friend about whom he told so many tales . . ."

"Unfeeling . . ." he said, ignoring the rest. How dare this . . . this intruder say Tim had been wrong to trust him! "If it is unfeeling to concern myself with your son's inheritance and see that it is not wasted on a frivolous Season for his sister, then yes, I am very likely unfeeling." Once begun, he couldn't stop. The ensuing tirade followed predictable channels, upbraiding Lady Lawrence for her extravagance in renting a house instead of coming to his sister as he'd arranged and telling his ward's mother, in far more detail than he'd intended, that *it would not do.* When he'd finished he glowered at the unruffled woman sitting silent before him who should, by rights, be cowering and pleading with him for mercy.

Instead, she simply looked bright-eyed and interested. "Have you finished, my lord?" she asked when the silence stretched.

"No, I have not," he decided, although he'd thought himself done. "Do not expect me to dip into your son's funded monies to pay for this nonsense." He removed his fingers from the waistband and gestured around the obviously recently refurbished salon. "If you outrun the carpenter—"

"I have everything well in hand," she interrupted. "You need have no concerns about the expenses of my daughter's Season."

"Nonsense." He stared rudely down his nose. "You cannot have a notion of what all this costs. If you did, you would not sit there so placidly—so *stupidly,* one might say."

Diana's eyes flashed. "You are insulting, my lord. I have listened to your ignorant ranting for far too long—"

"Ignorant!"

"—and, since we've an appointment with Valentine which we must not miss, I must ask you to leave."

His eyes widened. "Valentine! You and your daughter cannot afford to be dressed by Valentine. I haven't a notion who has given you such ill advice that you intend such ridiculous extravagance, but—"

"Lady Ellen Bushnell," announced the butler, and closed the double doors behind Ellen, who entered the room with her usual exuberance, already talking as she came.

"Diana! Was not our ball absolutely wonderful? Didn't everything go off perfectly?"

Lady Lawrence rose to her feet, her hands extended, her face glowing. "My dear Ellen. What a wonderful job of work you have made of us! And the house, which I think I did not thank you for—everything is right up to the knocker, as dear Kenelm would say!" Suddenly and obviously remembering his existence, Diana turned to include Lord Herrington in their conversation. "You, Ellen dear, are, of course, acquainted with Lord Herrington?"

"Of course." Lady Bushnell grinned at him, forced a pretend frown. "I hear you have been acting the tyrant, my lord," said Lady Ellen, her lips compressed against a wide smile.

"Tyrant? I haven't a notion what has come over tonnish women. First I am ignorant and now I'm a tyrant." He raised his quizzing glass and looked from one to the other. Now, he thought, hiding a rueful response, he had *two* women staring back at him as cheeky as perky sparrows! "Perhaps someone would care to elucidate this mystery?" he added, pretending boredom while feeling more alive than he'd done in a very long time.

"I'd think you'd have come down out of the boughs now, my lord," said Diana, a mischievousness she'd almost forgotten she owned coming to the fore. "After all, you've now discovered who led me into such terrible and unwarranted extravagance, have you not?"

"So it is you I have to thank for this foolishness?" Herrington asked, his frown returning in earnest. The boy's inheritance was something about which he could not and *should* not feel amused. "First this house—which I did not approve and for which I will not disburse funds, and then to suggest the Lawrence women go to Valentine when you must know how ruinously expensive she is? I'd not previously thought you such a goosecap, Lady Bushnell, as to lead a friend into debt!"

Lady Bushnell goggled. Then she burst into laughter. "Oh,

dear," she said, wiping her eyes. *"Did* my dear Diana call you ignorant? How very true. How very very true." She turned a shoulder on Herrington, looking back to Diana. "Is dear Phemie ready to go?"

"I'm not certain. I was about to see to her when my— er"—she looked Lord Herrington up and down, a scathing look which she'd have been happy to know he found exceedingly unsettling—*"guest* arrived without the least warning."

"My dear Herrington," said Ellen, her eyes wide with pretended shock, "did you indeed make such an early morning call without determining if it was convenient?" She shook her head, chiding him. "Tut-tut, Herrington! Such a lack of manners! I'd not have thought it of you!"

Since Miles could not argue the truth of that and could hardly say he'd thought his hostess of such small consequence she'd have no plans, he merely bowed—and as he straightened, looked toward the doorway that opened just then. His ward stood there. He'd met Euphemia at the Queen's drawing room, but obviously paid too little attention to her. The child—a natural beauty—was already gaining assurance and blossoming into special loveliness.

"Euphemia?" asked Lady Bushnell softly. "You improve with each day, my dear child. Diana, you should have warned me before you came to London that she is perfection itself! We'll have no trouble turning this one off! No trouble at all," said Ellen. "How wrong I was," she added, a glint in her eye, "when I worried that this Season might be dull!"

"Lady Lawrence," said Herrington, still studying the slim girl whose faint blush enhanced her ivory complexion, "I congratulate you. She is indeed a beauty." A glint of humor was finally roused in his icy gray eyes. He turned slightly, bowing toward Ellen. "Lady Bushnell, I beg to differ with you. We—or, at least, *I*—will have no end of trouble this Season. The chit will cause such a stir, I, at least, will have no peace from her many suitors until she is safely leg shackled!"

With a few polite words Lord Herrington took his leave, the child's beautiful face immediately slipping from his mind. It was a trifle confusing to him, therefore, that, off and on throughout the day, he found himself contemplating the mature and perhaps still *more* lovely version of that beautiful face which was his ward's mother's!

Lord Herrington was gone and silence reigned for several minutes. Then, a spot of angry color in each cheek, Diana exclaimed, "That ridiculous excuse for a gentleman said not two words to my Phemie! He is her guardian and didn't say boo to her!"

"He *was* a trifle out of countenance, was he not?" responded Ellen, her tinkling laughter floating on the air. "You don't suppose, do you, that he was so struck by her, he'll court her himself?"

Phemie, nearly as insulted as her mother was for her, threw a startled glance toward Lady Bushnell. "Oh, I *hope* not!" Her pale skin paled to an ashy gray. "Do say not!"

"He is far too old for her," said Diana in the same instant. Then she wondered why it was not disgust she felt, but a touch of something that could only be called distress at the notion Lord Herrington might court her Phemie.

Diana drew in a deep breath and pushed thoughts of tall, broad-shouldered, and overly handsome men from her mind. She had far too much to do as mother to her children to be thinking extremely silly thoughts about an inordinately attractive man. Especially a man who knew his assets and traded on them—as he'd done at the Bushnell ball when he'd casually suggested an affair!

"I was not serious, my friends," said Lady Bushnell in a conciliatory way. "Lord Herrington is known for excellent manners if a trifle of height toward his acquaintances, so today must have been an aberration on his part for which you must forgive him." She gave neither Lawrence woman time to respond, adding, "Are we ready? My horses are waiting, which is something my coachman abhors and, come to that, it does not do to keep Valentine standing around either. She's been known to inform a client who has been delayed that she cannot be fit in and the client must make a new appointment!

"Do let us go," she finished coaxingly, her busy mind wondering just how she was to bring about a match between her friend and Herrington if they continued to rub each other up the wrong way.

Ah, but arranging such a match would be a challenge—and Lady Ellen did like a challenge! She'd find a way.

"You do like to find a pocket of quiet and creep into it, do you not?" what was becoming a familiar voice asked several evenings later.

Lady Diana turned from the row of her host's books which she'd been scanning in the hope she'd find something of interest. Lady Ellen had, as usual, taken Euphemia in hand, which allowed Diana to escape the crush in the public rooms in which this particular ball was held.

"Lord Herrington," she said politely.

He bowed.

"If I am accused of looking for peace, then one must suppose you, too, find the crush out there"—she waved toward the door—"equally unwelcome."

There was no way he'd admit he'd looked for her among the guests, decided she must have found herself a room apart as she'd done at her daughter's come-out and one or two events since, and gone looking for her, interrupting at least one pair of illicit lovers while in the process of opening doors his hostess had vainly hoped would remain closed that night.

Instead of admitting his interest in her, Miles looked at his sleeve and carefully picked away an almost invisible piece of lint before glancing up to meet her questioning look. "I find I can tolerate only the minimum of time pretending polite interest in the polite nothings that are the correct way of speaking at polite parties such as this," he admitted. It was, after all, no more than the truth—if not the whole truth.

"We are alike in that. Do you spend all Season in London, my lord?" she asked, utilizing a polite nothing such as he'd just said he despised.

"I spend most of the year at my estate in Wiltshire. But when Parliament is in session I cannot escape to the country, of course."

"Then I must assume Parliament has adjourned for the evening? The last few nights you've sat very late, have you not?"

He was surprised she knew anything of such a subject—and then recalled her friendship with Lady Bushnell. "So your friend has complained that her husband is unavailable to escort her of an evening, has she?"

Diana blinked, wondering what Ellen had to do with it, finally guessed at his meaning, and scowled. "Why do you always come to the worst possible conclusion about everything?"

"Do I?"

"If I understand your last comment, you've assumed I know nothing about politics and, moreover, that I'm not interested. Am I supposed to have a completely empty head which is incapable of understanding even the least little thing?"

"Are you then a bluestocking?" he asked politely.

She gritted her teeth. "Must one be the one thing or the other? Is there no medium ground?"

"The one or the other?"

"An empty-headed featherbrain or a bluestocking. May I not simply have a reasonably good mind which I prefer to use than not and, as well, a trifle of common sense?"

"Common sense?" Miles, finding himself on shaky ground, did his usual turnabout and attacked on a different front. "But how can that be? According to my informants,

you continue to spend money as if it were water you might
dip from the Thames! How can I believe you've the least bit
of common sense?"

Diana turned away. The last was an accusation she couldn't
refute. She *was* spending money extravagantly, but mostly
because he'd made her so angry, telling her he'd not pay the
bills—as if she need ask him to do so!

But he didn't know that.

"No sharp response, my dear?" he asked, an edge of triumph in his tone.

She turned back. "My lord, you will refrain from your
easy—and insulting—endearments. And," she added in a
voice of doom, "I suppose it is time I stopped the lovely
game of baiting you."

Baiting me? he thought. *What could she mean by that?*
"Well?" he asked when she didn't go on.

"It is your own fault," she warned.

"What," he asked with pretended patience, "is my fault?"

"That I did not explain immediately."

"And what," he asked, a glimmering of a notion in his
head, "did you not explain?"

"That I have a more than adequate fortune to pay for my
daughter's come-out and that you must not concern yourself
with it. I've always assumed I would pay for it. It never occurred to me that you'd expect it to come from dear Kenelm's
estate! And the house . . ."

"The house."

"The house on Duke Street?" she elaborated.

"What about the house on Duke Street?"

She glowered at him. "You won't help me, will you?"

"You mean I'm to tell you that the house is yours?" The
polite tone was gaining more than a touch of ice.

"Thank you."

After a moment, during which he stared at that simple
thank-you, he laughed. "That's all?"

"All my confession?" Diana tipped her head, considering. "I think so."

"You are certain you can cover your expenses for the Season?" Suddenly he felt concern that she might put *herself* into difficulties rather than her son. "It takes a great deal to spend as freely as you are spending, you know."

Diana glowered. "There you go again."

"What have I done this time?"

"You become condescending and unbearably rude the moment you take up the notion a woman has no understanding of . . . whatever."

"And you do?"

"I have, I'm told, an unladylike interest in finance, my lord. My father was first to inform me of it. Dear Tim teased me about it. Now my solicitor is quick to accuse me of it. But you! You suggest the reverse is the case, which is just as bad, by assuming I cannot possibly know whether I may afford a new pair of silk stockings . . . or whatever." She felt her teeth gritting and forcibly relaxed her jaw. "I am so tired of it!"

"Then perhaps you should leave such things to those who are competent to deal with them."

There was a moment's silence in which Diana grappled, again, with her temper. "Lord Herrington," she asked sweetly but in the tone of one who truly wished to know, "to what degree have you increased my son's inheritance since Tim died?"

His very expressive Amesbury brows climbed. "I believe," said Miles in a modest tone, "that I've done rather well by the boy. His inheritance has nearly doubled what it was when it came into my hands," he added with some pride.

"Merely doubled?" Diana scowled, then sighed. "I *knew* I should have taken a hand in things!"

It was Miles's turn to scowl. His brow blackened far more than hers had done. "What do you mean, *merely doubled?*"

"My own fortune, which was not so little to begin with,

has more than tripled in the same period of time *and at my personal direction!* If it is unladylike to admit to it, I apologize, but my father—finally—saw that I was serious in my interest and, by the end, knew I could be trusted with handling my own affairs. My monies are, as a result, in my hands. Thank goodness!"

Herrington thought about that for a moment. "I do not see how that is legally possible," he said a trifle accusingly.

"Never mind *how* it was done, just accept that I am neither brainless nor ignorant. Do not, again, condescend to me."

He bowed, scrambling to assimilate all she'd said. It was nearly impossible, given his experience with the women in his family and later those, of a different sort, whom he'd taken under his protection. *All* of them had given him a predisposition to find women—except for a certain purpose—more a nuisance than not. "I'll try to remember to treat you as you'd wish, but if I do not, you must remind me," he said politely if a trifle absently.

"Do not fear that I will not!"

Her tone brought his eyes back to hers. Hers were sparkling with laughter and, in spite of himself, he smiled. "Very well. I will expect a setdown whenever I forget no matter what the circumstances." He gestured at a comfortable-looking couch. "May we be seated? It would be far more comfortable while we debate current investment opportunities, would it not?"

Diana eyed him. "Are you laughing at me?"

"No." He discovered, to his surprise, that that was true. "No," he said more firmly. "I'd like your opinion of a canal proposal. I've an opportunity to invest in it, but admit I know nothing of such things, so I've been dragging my feet."

"Is that Riddle's project?"

Herrington had suggested that topic in a spirit of devilment, never believing she'd actually have an opinion. That she knew of it and the man who conceived it was a shock. "It is," he managed to respond.

"Hmm. He's successful more often than not, but I dislike

his treatment of his workers. I have nothing to do with him. I've quite a bit of money in the Worcester and Birmingham Canal, however."

Herrington searched his mind. "Isn't that the one with the flight of locks at Tardebigge?"

"Thirty of them. They lift the canal boats two hundred and seventeen feet," she responded absently. "But I'll not invest in a project where no care is taken of its workers, which is why I do not invest in most mines—have you ever been down a coal mine, my lord? It is unbelievable the horrible conditions under which our miners, both the men and the children, are forced to work!"

He blinked, turned, and brought one knee up on the cushion between them, laying one arm along the back of the couch as he stared at her. "Have *you* been down a mine?"

"Yes. Years ago with my father and some other men who wished to write a proposal to the government requiring certain measures be taken for the safety of the workers. Nothing was accomplished, of course."

"So you do not approve of mines as investments. Where, besides the W and B Canal, do you invest your funds?"

"There are several manufactories which I helped develop—two foundries and several cotton mills. Because I own enough of the stock, I may insist on certain innovations that cost very little but result in better and safer work conditions. A percentage of my fortune is invested in the East India Company—my grandfather saw to that. Let me see," she added thoughtfully, "I am also involved, in a relatively small way, in a shipping company, which is my only gamble! And, of course, my safe investments in government Consols!"

"I see you've a balanced notion of investing. I also sense merchant blood," he said dryly.

"You think I come from the merchant stock?" she asked, knowing he'd believe it another insult.

"Do you not?" he challenged.

"I think you may discover that for yourself, my lord." She

rose to her feet. "My daughter has been a burden on poor Ellen for nearly an hour now. I had better take myself back out into that madness and relieve her." She curtsied and turned away.

"Why do I feel I've just been given one of those setdowns of which we spoke?" he asked softly.

"Perhaps, my lord, because it is true?"

Diana closed the door without looking back, but paused in the hallway. She wasn't particularly surprised to hear laughter coming faintly through the door. Rude, overbearing, and condescending he certainly was—but he was also willing to laugh at himself, and that could cover a multitude of sins, or so Diana believed.

She strolled back into the ballroom, a small smile playing around her lips, and immediately attracted several men to her side who, previously, had not taken much notice of her.

A week later Ellen arrived even earlier than was her wont. "Dear me," she said, coming into Diana's bedroom and pulling open the curtains. "Such a sleepyhead! Do get up, Diana. We've so much to do if we are to have your ball properly organized."

Diana, who had groaned and buried her head at Ellen's entrance, popped up. *"My what!"*

"I doubt very much you've gone deaf. You heard me."

The door opened and a maid entered, the tray she held wobbling slightly.

"There you are, my dear," said Ellen cheerfully. "Do, please, set that on the table before you drop it!"

"Is that breakfast?" asked Diana from the nest she'd made of her covers.

"My dear Diana, breakfast was hours ago."

"It can't be that late."

"It is going on for twelve and"—Ellen again adopted her

scolding tone—"we must bestir ourselves. Where is your robe?" She looked around.

"I don't have one." Diana eyed her friend. "Is it your normal practice to go into other people's homes and order things as you please?"

Ellen sighed. "But, my dear, it was necessary to get you up. You cannot have a notion how much work is involved in planning a ball!"

"Can I *not?*" asked Diana mildly, deciding that here was another who thought she didn't know her head from her toe. "How is it that I have managed my life for years now, but the moment I come to London I am thought, by everyone, to be as ignorant as a newborn babe?"

"Everyone?" pounced Ellen.

"I am sick of it," said Diana, hugging her knees. "It is insulting. In fact, it is not to be borne."

"You're saying I've insulted you?"

"Hmm. For instance, just when did I decide to give a ball?"

Ellen's skin turned bright red. Her ears, where they peeked through her deliberately mussed-looking coiffure, were shiny! "Well . . . as to that . . . er . . ."

"Actually," interrupted Diana, "what I *have* planned is a breakfast. I've gone so far as to discuss the catering with Gunther's and have been so forward as to have ordered my cards. I do apologize, Ellen, if I have done wrong," she finished, the demurely apologetic note in her voice not fooling her friend for a moment.

Ellen plopped onto one of the chairs beside the round table in the window. She absently reached for a sandwich and bit into it. When she'd swallowed, she looked at Diana, who stared steadily back at her.

"I don't suppose," Ellen asked in a small voice, "you'd like to give a ball as well?"

"Give me a reason why I should."

"Well. Hmm. Er . . ." She eyed Diana. "Well, you see," she said in a confiding tone, "I've always thought it *such* a lovely occasion on which to announce an engagement . . ." Ellen smiled brightly. "Do you not agree, Diana?"

Diana straightened, lifted the covers, and slid over the side of the high bed to land with a thump, having once again forgotten how far it was to the floor. She stalked toward her friend, and hands on hips, stared at her.

"What do you mean, an engagement? Whose engagement? What has been going on that you've not told me? That *Phemie's* not told me?"

Ellen laughed and raised her hands in pretend defense. "Got your attention, did I not?"

"You did indeed." Since she was up—much to her disgust—Diana wrapped a shawl around her shoulders and seated herself. She poured a cup of steaming hot coffee and sipped it.

"I know you, Ellen," she said after a moment. "What have you seen that makes you believe an engagement is imminent? Phemie is too young to marry. We agreed on that when I first arrived in London."

"We may think her too young, but I suspect *she* has—or, at least, will—change her mind."

Diana compressed her lips, forced herself to relax, and said, "I have been remiss, have I not? Hiding away as I do, and leaving my child to your tender mercies? Do tell me, Ellen, who is this paragon who has dared to attach my daughter's affections? *And why has Phemie not told me?"*

"The gentleman is Lord Aftondale's second son. The earl has done well by his younger sons, and William has a very nice estate in Dorsetshire very near the Wiltshire border. Not far, in fact, from Herrington's lands. The lad is not so wealthy as you are, my love, but capable of giving his wife the elegancies of life. As Tim did you," she finished on a significant note.

"And you think my Phemie truly smitten?"

"I believe they are falling deeply in love."

"Hmm."

"You are wondering," said Ellen, "why dear Euphemia has said nothing to you?"

"I must admit I feel a trifle hurt."

"I can explain that. The poor dears have not yet admitted to themselves the case they are in. How, then, might they discuss it with anyone else?"

Diana sighed, sipped her coffee, sighed again, and said, "So. You think a ball the proper milieu for announcing this engagement that does not exist?"

"I feel it in my bones, dear. There will be an announcement and our dear Euphemia will be very happy in her choice. You know I'm always right about such things," she finished in a smug voice, hiding an uneasy suspicion she might actually be *wrong* that Diana and Herrington would make a match.

"I see I must not leave her to you tonight, but must see for myself whatever it is that has you in such a mood."

"And the ball?"

"I had hoped, I admit, to avoid opening up the ballroom until next year, but if you are certain . . . ?"

"I'm certain."

Diana sighed, but obediently set her mind to planning a gala evening at which her daughter's so-far-nonexistent betrothal would be announced.

Miles Herrington strolled into the Jerseys' salon and glanced around. The glance was perfunctory since he assumed Diana would have already made her escape. He was actually entering the hallway that led to Lord Jersey's library before he realized Diana was still in the salon and surrounded by several men. He turned back and found they were all laughing at something she'd just said. On her face was that secret little smile he'd begun to think only he could bring to existence, and an inexplicable emotion rose in his chest, sending him hotfoot to the library, where he'd find the solitude he needed in which to examine exactly what it was he felt. It took no more than five minutes.

He was jealous! He, who never thought highly enough of a woman to do more than shrug and move on when he found her paying attention to another, was racked by an emotion he'd believed a sign of immaturity, and unnecessary. But why? Why would he feel such a thing?

Miles found Lord Jersey's private stock of brandy, poured himself a goodly dollop, and took himself to a high-backed chair facing a window overlooking the garden which had a small table conveniently to hand. He settled himself to analyze what exactly had happened to him. He'd gotten to where he smiled at something Diana once said to him, when the door opened.

"No one is here," said a young male voice.

"I think we should go back," said an equally young and faintly worried female voice.

"Just a minute, Phemie. Please? We are never alone so that I may tell you . . . what I feel . . ."

"But I know what you feel, William. Truly I do. Because I fear I feel it as well."

"But that's incredible. That's wonderful. That's—"

"Shush," said Phemie. "You don't know. You can't understand. My guardian . . ."

"Well?" asked William impatiently.

"He's said . . . he told me . . . oh, just believe me. He won't approve," said Phemie on an anguished whisper.

"Why the devil should he not?" There was an indrawn breath, and the young man apologized for using language inappropriate in a lady's presence. "But, Phemie, I don't think it immodest to think myself something of a catch. Not a great catch, but not to be despised. Surely it is incredible that he could find a reason to turn down my suit."

Euphemia drew in a deep breath. "He said I must catch an earl . . . at the least. That I could do better if I put my mind to it. William, I do not *want* to do better," she wailed softly.

"You're quite certain you understood him?"

"He said it plain as anything. I thought I'd sink."

William's footsteps could be heard treading back and forth. "Who is he, this perfectly Gothic example of the genus guardian?"

"Lord Herrington."

Lord Herrington, eavesdropping from behind his chair, proceeded to hear nothing good about himself—as it is purported such sinners do. A muscle twitched in his jaw. Was he really thought so cold and unfeeling? Did he have such a temper, the whelp feared to face him—although the lad promised Phemia he *would* do so, that he'd *do* anything . . .

And, wondered Herrington when Phemie took up the tirade, had he been so very domineering and aristocratic when he'd decided it time his female ward was to be presented—ah. So Diana already had plans for that, until his orders countermanded them. . . .

"But *that* I can forgive him," said Phemie, "because I might not have met you and we might not have"—she paused, and Herrington thought it likely she blushed—"have discovered how well we suit."

"It's a coil, Phemie. I admit I wish it were anyone but Herrington, but"—William drew in a deep breath, expelled it—"it is not. I'll see him tomorrow."

"Not too early!" warned Phemie. "He's a Corinthian, is he not? He'll lie abed until all hours after drinking too much and spending too much time *wasting the ready* at the gaming tables."

Herrington had trouble repressing a snort. He never spent hours at the gaming tables. Wasting the ready, indeed! The minx should know better than to use such cant language! However that might be, if William was to arrive on his doorstep at some suitable hour of the day, he'd have to arrive, himself, on the Lawrence doorstep at an earlier—and very likely unforgivably *unsuitable*—hour!

How, he wondered, did one go about discovering a very young female's true feelings? How did one distinguish between an infatuation and an emotion that would lead to a decent marriage—because, despite what Euphemia believed, having misinterpreted what was merely a compliment concerning her marriage prospects, he'd no desire to push the chit into a fashionable marriage in which the parties involved went their separate ways as soon as the nursery held an heir. Similar values, similar interests, similar ambitions—those were things that led to a good marriage.

And, he recalled, friendship. Friendship . . . had Diana Lawrence been Tim's friend? She'd implied it was so, but why, if that were the case, had Tim never spoken of her?

It occurred to Miles the couple behind him had been silent for an overly long period, and if that meant what it would mean if *he* were the man involved, then the pup was kissing his ward! What should he do? Ah . . . the door was opening.

"Oh, dear," he heard—and how familiar and welcome that voice sounded. "Phemie, love, I believe it more than time you returned to the salon. No. Let me look at you. Hmm. Your hair, my dear . . . yes. That will do. Now. William, is it?"

"Yes, my lady," said the young man, his voice sounding as if the words might strangle him.

"I'd like a word with you, I believe. No, Phemie," said Diana when her daughter attempted to interrupt, "your explanation for this hoydenish scene must wait until later. Now, child," she chided, "I expect you to show a good face to the public. No megrims and no vapors. Pride, child."

"Yes, Mama," said the young voice on a sigh.

When the door closed again, William spoke. "I proposed even though I should not have done so before speaking to her guardian. Miss Euphemia has done me the honor of accepting my suit—contingent upon Lord Herrington's approval, of course," he added with a faint touch of despair and a long sigh.

Diana chuckled. "Yes. There is that, is there not? It is also the case that Phemie is very young, William."

"Yes. I know. I'm six years older and I've tried to restrain my feelings for her—but tonight . . ." He stalked from one end of the room and back again. "She's so very beautiful tonight. That lovely dress and her hair just so and . . . and then she looked at me with those wonderful eyes and I could bear it no longer. I have feared from day to day to hear an announcement or to read it in the newspapers. Too many men crowd around her and some"—he scowled—"not so young and perhaps more eligible than I!"

"But she appears to have chosen you."

"Yes."

Herrington could imagine the young man straightening, his features clearing, his pleased grin. Miles shifted slightly in his seat.

"Hmm," said Diana. "You didn't notice that I say she *appears* to have chosen you."

"What do you mean?" asked a suddenly wary William.

"I mean, as I said, that she is very young."

"You would forbid the banns?" he asked after a moment.

"The banns, yes. The engagement? Perhaps not. What I wish to know is how firm your feelings are for each other. It is never a good thing to break an engagement, but it is far better than to break up a marriage! What I would ask, assuming, of course, that Herrington gives you his blessing, is that you and she wait at least until Christmastime—and perhaps into the spring—to wed. During that time you may visit us in our home and perhaps we could all be guests together at some house party—"

Herrington guessed Diana meant one organized by Lady Bushnell and immediately began planning one of his own as well as questioning how he might connive to get himself included in the hypothetical Bushnell party.

"—where you may learn more about each other. William, it is not that I dislike you or that I think you would not suit. It is that I love my daughter and," she finished softly, warmly, "I would have her as happy in her marriage as I was in mine."

"I too wish her happy," said the young man with quiet dignity. "It will be as you say."

"So," said Diana, laughing lightly. "You and I have come to a reasonable agreement, but, remember, you must next face his lordship."

"I promised Phemie—Miss Euphemia, that is—that I would visit Lord Herrington tomorrow."

"Very well. Whatever his decision, I suggest you not despair. I doubt my daughter will agree to wed another during this Season at least!"

"Thank you. I will take my leave now. Will you tell Miss Euphemia that I will come to her after I've seen her guardian? Perhaps you will permit her to drive with me in the park?"

"An excellent thought," approved Diana, and again Miles heard the laughter in her tone. "In an open carriage you may have a modicum of privacy and upset no shibboleths. We will expect you tomorrow."

The young man must have bowed, because there was the smallest of pauses before steps moving toward the hall door were heard. Then the door closed.

"You may come out now," said Diana, a chuckle accompanying her words.

"How did you know I was here?" Miles rose to his feet and faced her.

"The glass on the table. The foot on the window ledge!"

"You recognized me from my evening pump? I do not believe it."

"I knew someone was there because of it. But I know *you*, do I not? I freely admit I'd have been much embarrassed if someone else had risen from that chair!" She chuckled. "I'm rather amazed you did not interfere long before I arrived! You must have known they were embracing."

"I guessed it, but only the moment before you came in. I was musing over some of the things I overheard, you see."

"Hmm?"

"Why did you not tell me you already had plans for Euphemia's introduction to the *ton?*"

"Did Phemie tell William that?"

"She did. Also what a tyrant I am, and that I expect her to make a grand marriage and several other things I'd as soon forget!"

"So?"

He chewed for a moment on his lip. "I think your plan is probably the best. Let them be engaged, but postpone the wedding until we may be certain it's the right decision." *And*—the thought crossed his mind—*until I return you from our honeymoon.* Herrington fought a brief vertigo. What had he just told himself? *Our honeymoon?* But that would mean— Miles stared at Diana, studying her as if it were for the first time.

"What is it, my lord. Are you ill?"

"Ill?" he asked absently. So that was why he'd been jealous of those men earlier! He wanted her for himself. And not just for a day. Or a month. But forever!

"Lord Herrington! What is it?"

"What . . ."

Diana said sharply, "My lord, tell me what's wrong."

"Wrong?" Suddenly he chuckled. His chuckle turned to a laugh. "Wrong! I'll tell you what is wrong"—he grinned a trifle sardonically—"in a day or two—or perhaps three." *Or at whatever date I gain the courage to propose to you.* He stared at Diana with a warmth that startled her. With effort, Herrington regained his usual sardonic manner. "If I am to talk to that puppy tomorrow," he said, "then I'll make an early night of it tonight. I had thought to take that chit of yours driving in the morning to discuss the thing with her—to try to get a sense of how strong her feelings are, but your notion of a long engagement is better. With *your* permission,

I'll give Aftondale's *son* permission to address my ward— upon that condition."

Diana chuckled that warm laugh he looked for. Her eyes twinkling, she said, "You will very likely shock the children with your condescension!"

"So I will," he said affably. "Do you think they'll ever recover?" He looked down at her. "Shall I ask my sister to give a ball at which we may announce their engagement?" He guessed Diana would not be enamored of the notion of giving one herself.

"No." Diana puffed air out between her lips. "Dear Ellen saw what was in the air some time ago. She insisted I plan a ball for just that purpose. The invitations will go out later this week."

His brows arched in that characteristic manner of his family. "I believe I've already received an invitation to a breakfast?"

"Yes. I'm not fond of entertaining. I'd hoped that would be sufficient for this year. I'd thought that next year I'd force myself to plan more elaborately. But Ellen assured me the children would reach an agreement, and she is nearly always correct in guessing who will suit."

"It's good to meet someone who is not happy with the constant round of crushes that makes up the Season—as I've learned you are not. I much prefer small dinners and conversable evenings."

"Exactly. That's one reason I prefer the country. There it is impossible to fill one's rooms to the degree one must do when in town!"

He wished he could pull her close and hug her. Just hold her. It was an odd feeling. He'd never thought to just *hold* a woman. If he'd a woman in his arms, it was for a perfectly normal reason and *involved* holding . . . but far more as well. Not that he didn't wish that intimate behavior with Diana. It was just that the idea he might gain a great deal of pleasure *simply* holding her, hugging her, laughing with her, and talking with her was a very strange idea indeed. He feared it would take some time before he managed to figure it all out.

"I'd better go now," he said.

"I've been gone overly long as well, given I'd decided that tonight I'd not leave Phemie to Ellen's care, but would see for myself what was what."

"You found out, did you not?"

"So I did." She frowned. "I really must have a word with Phemie about allowing such familiarities . . ."

He gently pulled her close, putting his arm around her waist, his other hand lifting her chin.

"Familiarities such as this?" he asked softly.

"That too," she said equally softly.

She didn't move, didn't push against him, but only looked up frankly and openly, perhaps a trifle questioningly, into his face.

"And this?" he asked, giving in to further temptation.

This kiss was gentle in a way his first, on the balcony at the Bushnells', was not. It tempted and teased and warmed and asked rather than demanded more. But more was not forthcoming.

Very gently Diana released herself from his embrace. Again she stared at him, that questioning, wondering look again in her candid gaze. He gazed back, very likely more confused than she—something she appeared, finally, to recognize.

She shook her head. "We're a pair, are we not? Neither of us knowing what we're doing—when all we *should* concern ourselves with at the moment are the children."

"If you mean William and Euphemia, then you are out. They'll come about. Frankly," he said, that confused look more evident than ever, "I'm not certain that I will! Good night, my dear. I'll very likely drop by tomorrow after I've seen the young chub who will *not* come at too early an hour—per your perspicacious daughter's instructions!"

Miles strode from the room, leaving Diana staring after

him. He wondered rather desperately how she'd reacted to his kiss. If she'd been affected even half so much as he, then the proposal he'd begun to make in his mind, his daydream supplying her answer as well, might actually occur. And then, once she'd said yes, how soon would she agree to wed . . . and then, if she demanded they wait until Euphemia wed, would she also insist on waiting for . . . other things . . . or would she allow him into her bed. . . .

Damn, he thought, *only minutes ago I was thinking how nice it would be if I had the right to merely hold her close . . . so now already I'm back to thinking of bedding her?* His thoughts roiling, Lord Herrington actually forgot to find his hostess and make polite good-byes before leaving the house.

Lady Ellen stared moodily across the breakfast table. She'd eaten her usual piece of toast and drunk more than her usual two cups of coffee. Twice her husband had looked over his newspaper, the first time wondering if she was actually there—since she'd not said a word—and the second time to see if he could discern *why* she'd not spoken. He studied her for a moment and decided he couldn't.

"Something the matter, my dear?" asked Lord Bushnell.

Ellen blinked, focused. "Did you say something, Bushy?"

"I wished to know what has you in a dither, my love."

Ellen sighed. "It is very difficult to arrange a match when one cannot get the principals together even for a moment—and then, when one does, they do nothing but argue."

"Then perhaps the, hmm, principals are not a match."

"I am never wrong."

"I seem to remember—"

"Oh, yes, of course," interrupted Ellen, "but I was very young at the time, was I not? I haven't been wrong in *years*. Well? Have I, Bushy dear?" she demanded.

"No, I cannot say that you have. Just who are these uncooperative souls who appear to be ruining your record?"

"But you know! It is Lord Herrington and my Diana, of course. Do not tease so. It is serious, I tell you. I wonder if I should hold a small intimate dinner . . ."

She didn't continue, and her lord, alarmed, asked, *"How* intimate?"

"Oh, perhaps just Lord Herrington and Diana?"

It was as he'd feared. "I feel in my bones that that would be unwise."

Ellen sighed. "Unfortunately, so do I. It is most distressing. I cannot understand why they've not seen how perfect they are for each other."

"I think I told you at the beginning not to meddle."

"But how else am I to make them see—"

"Perhaps," he interrupted, "you should *not* attempt to make them see anything at all!"

"Bushy," she said, glaring, "you are becoming *stuffy*."

"Am I, my dear? I see it is a fault and must conquer it immediately." He folded his neatly ironed paper, rose to his feet, and came around the table. When he reached his wife's side, he raised her to her feet, pulled her into his embrace, and kissed her soundly.

She kissed him back enthusiastically and then looked at him. "Bushy?"

"Mustn't be stuffy, must I?" His eyes smiling, he mused, "I wonder what the footman would say if I were to carry you up the stairs . . . ?"

"Bushy!"

"I'll try the experiment," he decided, and Lady Bushnell, while rediscovering that her husband was not so very stuffy after all, quite forgot, for *quite* some time, that she'd been fretting herself to flinders trying to find a plan to bring her friend together with England's most eligible bachelor!

Lord Miles Herrington, on the other hand, was feeling exceedingly stuffy. He couldn't bring himself to court his lady in the usual fashion. He feared that if he appeared on her doorstep, bouquet in hand, or with some trifle wrapped in silver paper, she'd laugh and laugh and laugh. The problem was far too serious for his behavior to be taken for a jest. He'd thought and thought before he remembered Lady Diana's comment that friendship came before loving. But that raised its own problems: It had been a very long time since Miles had considered himself more than an acquaintance to anyone.

And friendship with a woman? How did one go about that? He recalled what he knew of Diana's friend Ellen and her husband. The two were a byword among the *ton* for their unusual behavior. Not only did they live in each other's pockets, but they obviously enjoyed each other's company! It was no longer a scandal since it had been going on for so long, but when they'd first married, their behavior was so astounding an *on-dit,* even Herrington had heard it, and that while occupied with his duties with the army in the Peninsula!

So what was it that made the Bushnells different? That they talked to each other even in public was one thing— something Diana and he did whenever they found themselves together. What else? That they appeared interested in each other's doings. Well, he found himself surprisingly interested in Diana's doings—and wondered if she ever thought about his. . . . There was the fact the Bushnells traveled together and never accepted invitations to separate house parties. . . .

Which reminded Herrington that he must arrange his party for his ward and her fiancé. It occurred to him that such a party was also a time during which he and Diana might get to know each other better. Which was all very well, but it was at least a month yet before anything could come of it. What could he do in the meantime . . .

Once again he thought over things Diana had told him, and remembered a chance remark that gardening, especially her rose garden, was important to her. Would she have visited the botanical gardens? Would she accept an invitation to go there with himself?

Lord Herrington, who had never in his life found it necessary to woo a woman, dithered. When the day of Diana's breakfast arrived, he had still to do anything at all—fearing that whatever he did would be wrong. He approached Diana's London home with trepidation, totally ignoring the fact that only the evening before he had again found her in one of her hiding places and again had a long and interesting discussion with her—this time about the progress of the war—during which neither had felt the least bit of strain.

No strain, that is, if one discounted the constant and growing awareness each was secretly feeling of the other.

Transport of all types and styles crowded the street leading to the Lawrence home. It occurred to Miles that there would be no opportunity today to forward his interests. He sighed, inched his matched pair another yard nearer the door, and wondered what his acquaintances would think if he turned the rig over to his groom and got down and *walked.* But it wasn't done. It was another fifteen minutes before he could join the crush mounting the stairs to where those in the reception line greeted guests.

Miles laughed softly at the wry look Diana gave him, which ended in a smile and a nod that he'd understood her boredom with doing the polite. He complimented Euphemia on her beauty, told Sir Kenelm they should have a chat concerning the boy's financial situation before the Season ended, and, expecting boredom himself, strolled on into the already crowded rooms.

Later he watched Diana carefully suppress a yawn and moved to stand beside her. "Good day to you, my lord," he said politely to the balding man who, his hand on Diana's arm, was holding forth on his favorite subject of the Regent's extravagance. "Lady Lawrence, I've been sent," he lied, "to say Miss Euphemia would appreciate your presence in the music room. She cannot find a certain piece of music which she is certain she saw only yesterday."

"Oh, dear. I wonder where it can be. Please excuse me, my lord," she said to the bore and, accepting Miles's arm, walked away. "Euphemia couldn't have chosen a better time to need me," she said when they were well away, "although I don't understand how music can have anything to do with it."

"Why not?"

"Because, although my daughter is talented in a number of ways, music is not one of them. I believe the expression which fits is that she has a tin ear?"

"You have caught me out, my dear: I told a bouncer. She was the only one not visible in the salon who might have wished your attention, and I thought it likely you'd so appreciate escaping Lord Tripmore, you'd forgive a taradiddle."

"Now, there," she said, smiling up at him, "was real friendship. Didn't you hesitate even a trifle at your danger, my lord?"

"My danger?"

"You might have been trapped as well. I don't think Lord Tripmore the sort to give in easily, and if we'd allowed him to open his mouth, we'd still be there attempting to get away, would we not?"

"Which means you think quickly when the occasion demands it."

"Demands it! Removing myself from that man's presence was a dire necessity! I'd have fallen on any excuse to leave before I made a cake of myself by yawning in his face."

They laughed together at that, and Lady Bushnell, observing them from across the room, swore fluently, if softly.

When, she wondered, had Lord Herrington and Diana become so comfortable together? So far as she'd been aware, they barely knew each other. And yet there they were, talking like old friends, chuckling over something that was obviously between only the two of them, and strolling together from the room, as little rattled by such proximity—and what the *ton* would say about it—as if they had been doing so for years.

She swore a bit more.

"Well, my dear?" said Bushnell in Ellen's ear, coming up to her just then. "How did you manage *that?* I thought I told you not to meddle."

"But, Bushy dear, I have *not* and if *I* have not, then who has?" Ellen had a sudden notion. "Do you suppose his sister . . ."

"I think," said Bushnell, "if you look over there by the doorway, you'll find Lady Sitwell is as astounded as you yourself."

"I cannot understand it, then."

"Are you excessively outraged?"

"Why, I think I am," she said softly, her eyes widening as she recognized the emotion in herself. "Here I've planned and conspired and schemed and connived and been unable to maneuver them into spending even five minutes together. It is insulting that they appear to have managed the thing all by themselves!" She turned a wide-eyed gaze upon her husband and, tongue in cheek, asked, "Bushy dear, what will become of my reputation as a matchmaker if people dare go making matches all by themselves?"

Ellen looked so like a ruffled kitten that her husband decided it was time to go home so he could spend an hour or two unruffling her. "You are a complete hand, my dear. If anyone asks, I'll tell them you knew it all along, shall I? Will that help?"

"It might—oh, dear. I fear Lord Tripmore is headed this way."

"Lord Tripmore," said Lord Bushnell, "how good to see you. Too bad we were just leaving and have no time for a discussion, but I'm sure we'll see you again soon. Good-bye," he added, and grasping his wife's arm, he led her away.

"You shouldn't have said that," she scolded.

"Why not?"

"But, Bushy, it is perfectly obvious. Having told Lord Trip-more we're leaving, we must go or make you out a liar!"

"Now, why," said her husband a trifle sardonically but with a twinkle in his eye, "didn't I think of that myself. . . . There's your friend. Shall we make our adieus?"

"Bushy!" she said, recognizing a falsehood when she heard one. "You wanted to leave!"

"Hmm," he said, and surreptitiously patted her hip.

"Bushy!"

"Yes, my dear?" he asked innocently.

Ellen blushed delightfully. "Well . . . yes." They left.

On still another night in still another private library behind closed doors, Miles found the courage to ask Diana if she would join him on a visit to the botanical gardens. He was delighted with how promptly she agreed.

"I've been wishing to go. I'm told there are any number of foreign plants. I'm planning an addition to our gardens and will be very glad of an opportunity to decide if there is something new which I might use in my borders."

"Then borders it shall be. I myself am interested in the succession houses. Perhaps I've more interest in my table than in the view out my windows?" he suggested only half jokingly.

"I believe it is not unusual for gentlemen to be practical and for women to delight in the whimsical. One's stomach is far more practical than mixing floral colors in new and dif-ferent patterns, which is my favorite occupation."

"I believe I must visit this Cotswold garden of yours. You make it sound intriguing." *Would she take him up on that?* he wondered. *Would she invite him to visit . . . ?*

She would and she did, hesitantly it was true, and he wasn't certain of the reason for wariness, but nevertheless promptly accepted. "Then, perhaps, later, you'll come view my Wiltshire estate?" he added. "I've planned my own house party where my ward and her fiancé might have unexceptional time together." He watched her closely and saw nothing but approval in her eyes when she agreed it was an excellent notion.

"I'll ask the Bushnells to come to the Cotswolds at the time you visit, my lord, and perhaps one or two other people . . ."

"Keep it a small party, my dear." When she looked at him questioningly, he added, "If too large, it'll become overly organized and the whole idea is to give the children a relaxed time in which to become better acquainted, is it not?"

"So it is. I fear Ellen's party will be just that over-organized sort." She sighed. "I love Ellen dearly, but she is so very much the social creature that I am not!"

"But you will attend her party?" Miles plotted ways of getting himself invited when he was assured she would. "That's good," he said. "The more they are in proximity with each other, the more likely it is they'll discover they either are, or *are not,* suited. At the moment, I admit, I am agreeably surprised at how well they get along."

"The important thing, I think, is that they discover interests in common. Dear Tim and I had so much that interested us both, it was impossible for us to become bored with each other."

She spoke so calmly, Miles despaired of her ever being interested in another man. But then he remembered how sweetly she'd responded to his kiss, and relaxed.

"We'd known each other forever and were friends from childhood." Her eyes twinkled. Her tone was such, it drew Miles's eyes. He was surprised to discover a surprisingly mischievous expression. "Often he'd come home from London in *such* a state and needing a friend. He had, as you, who knew him then, must remember, always fallen in love with the most *unsuitable* women"—her brows arched—"What is it? Why do you look that way?"

"You didn't mind?"

"Oh, no. He would come home to me and I would commiserate and soothe and get him over it. The last time it happened, he told me," she continued, tongue obviously in cheek, "that he'd been *forcibly* separated from his most recent infatuation." She pressed her lips tightly together, her eyes sparkling. "We were so in love," she said, remembering.

"You mean when he came home from London after I left England with my regiment?"

"After . . . ?" She looked startled. "Oh, no. I assumed you knew. We fell in love *before* he went to London that time just before you left for Portugal. You see, our parents, neither his nor mine, thought ours a suitable match. *We* didn't agree, so we made a plan." She chuckled.

"A plan . . ." But he was getting a glimmer. Damn Tim. How could he have had the audacity to trick his best friend along with everyone else!

"Yes. You see, our plot was that this time his *infatuation* would not only appear serious, but would be less suitable than ever." Her chuckle warmed the air around them. "It worked too. His father heard the, er, *lady's* name and hotfooted it up to town, brought Tim home, and came *begging* my father to agree to my marrying his son!" She glanced at Herrington. "He once said he sometimes thought he'd fooled you as well as everyone else?"

"He did." Miles looked grim, studying the woman before him with a rather harsh look. "I thought you'd caught him on the rebound. . . . You sound," he said carefully, "as if you still miss him."

"I do. I always shall. He was my friend as well as my love." She must have noticed he found that a trifle upsetting. "I've memories that will always be with me, Miles, but they do not interfere with my getting on with my life. They can only enrich what will come to me."

"You are willing to get on with life . . ."

"Oh, yes. I think so." She eyed his grim look. "At least,"

she said, and hesitated before adding, "I was beginning to think so."

"I thought you'd trapped him. I thought . . . all sorts of things."

"Of course you did if he never explained. Silly clunch," she added lovingly, and Miles didn't know if she meant Tim or himself. "He should have told you the truth in one of those long letters he was always sending you."

"Those letters occasionally saved my sanity but rarely mentioned you."

"He often read them to me before sealing them up. Perhaps he'd have found it embarrassing to read *about* me *to* me?"

"But you still love him."

"Do not you?"

A tinge of red colored Miles's cheeks. "That's different."

"I don't think so. I don't think one ceases to feel for those we lose. We simply put it away as one does an old diary."

"And begin a new one?"

"One might think of it that way."

The door opened while Miles still wore a frown and Diana swore under her breath. Something was wrong, and she hadn't a notion what Miles had gotten into his head. She turned. "Yes, Ellen?"

"Don't you think it time you returned to the world?"

"Oh. Oh, well, I suppose I must. Come along, my lord."

"I don't think I care to join that crush again. I'll take my leave now, Lady Lawrence, and go."

"No, no. Now, do be sensible," said Ellen chidingly, looking from one to the other. "Of course you'll stay. Come along now."

They came.

Two weeks later Phemie's ball opened gloriously. It was rumored that even the Regent might have a look-in and, if he were to do so, it was thought he'd not be disappointed. It was, perhaps, the most sparkling ball of the Season. Those who had come expecting to find much to disparage—such a country mouse as Lady Lawrence was—were surprised.

Her friends were not the least astonished. They'd expected Diana to titillate without shocking the more rigid sensibilities, and she *had*. She'd turned her house into a country fair! There were stalls with the traditional games. There was a painted scene of the sale of horses, cattle, and sheep in front of which musicians played for the dancing. There were strolling piemen giving away their wares—it was all quite the greatest imaginable fun.

There was even a tented corner in which one could have one's palm read by a real Gypsy and the music was actually a group of Romany men playing their fiddles. Sometimes they strolled around the room as they played and some of the more timid guests worried they'd not reach home with all their jewels! After all, the Gypsy was always a thief, was he not? But even that fear added rather than distracted from one's enjoyment.

But, as usual, Diana soon had more than enough of being polite to people she barely knew. Asking Ellen to watch Phemie, she promised she'd be gone no more than twenty minutes, but that she had to go. "I wonder that it doesn't surprise me to find you here," she said a few moments later when she closed the library door and Miles stood to face her.

"You don't wonder at all. You might, however, have been surprised if I'd *not* been here," he said on a dry note. She chuckled, that lovely warm sound that was becoming more and more necessary to him. "I'll freely admit, however, that I'm surprised to see you," he added.

"I simply cannot understand how Ellen does it. Hour after hour. Day after day. Year after year . . . although I remember her saying she'd wondered what would keep her from boredom this year, and then we came to town, so she isn't . . . but why not? I mean, we are here, but how does that change anything?"

"Lady Bushnell is," said Miles after a moment, "deeply interested in people. I suspect she has a touch of the manipulator in her makeup and that she needs someone to organize and take over. Hasn't she done that for you?"

"Only a little." Diana sat down, sighed a long relieved sigh, and looked up at him. "Shortly it will be time to announce the engagement. You'll do that, will you not? As Phemie's guardian? I think Tim would have liked you to do it."

"I'd rather announce my own," he said abruptly. Seizing the opportunity, he dropped to one knee before her. "I know you'll never love me, Diana, but if you could find some small bit of affection in your heart for me and accept my love for you, I'd be exceedingly grateful."

Diana looked bewildered. "Grateful! You say you love me and then you say you'll feel *grateful*. You make no sense."

He captured her hands and tried again. "My dearest Diana, you cannot forget Tim and I cannot ask that you do so, but you have said you wish to live again. I am asking that you live again with me at your side."

"Let me see if I understand you. That I'll never forget Tim means to you that I can never love you?"

"Of course. I've accepted that."

"Nonsense."

Miles rose to his feet and stared down at her. "Nonsense?"

"Of course. Absolute unmitigated nonsense."

Once again the door opened at an inopportune moment in their conversation, and Ellen stepped into the room. "It's time for the announcement."

Miles said something under his breath about what they could do with the announcement that had both Ellen and Diana blushing hot and giggling like schoolgirls.

"Come along, my lord," scolded Ellen. "What you suggest is impossible, so do be sensible and make the announcement."

"It's a conspiracy."

"What is?"

"This forcing me to make the announcement. First Lady Lawrence suggested it, and now you do so. I don't think I care to do it."

"But you must. As Phemie's guardian, it is proper for you to do it," she explained as if to a child. "Now. *Do* come," coaxed Ellen.

They came.

Several days later, on a warm, sunny day surprising everyone who expected still more rain, Miles sent around a note reminding Diana that she'd agreed to go with him to Kew Botanical Gardens. Today, he said, seemed ideal for their purpose. Diana returned a cautious answer saying she and Euphemia would await his pleasure. He promptly responded via the rapidly tiring footman with the message that he'd not invited Euphemia, only Diana. The footman, hoping this would be his last trip between the Lawrence house and Herrington House, returned with capitulation: She'd not understood, she claimed. She alone awaited his pleasure.

"If only she did," said Miles fervently when he read those words, and startled the footman who'd not yet been dismissed.

Miles drove his phaeton with a groom up behind, and while they proceeded to their destination, they talked of commonplace things that would not shock the poor lad. But soon after paying the fee and entering the gardens, Miles found a bower with a bench in it and seated Diana.

"The other night we were interrupted, again, by your friend. If we've any luck in this world, she'll not take it into her head to visit here today, and we may actually finish a conversation to our satisfaction. Why," he went on to ask before Diana could respond, "were you upset with me?"

Diana didn't pretend to misunderstand him. "I cannot believe you've such a lack of understanding of what love is, what it involves, what it can do, and how it behaves."

"Instruct me."

She blinked. "I don't know that it is something one can teach. It is something one feels."

"I know I've come to feel a great deal for you, my dear," he said softly, and she smiled quickly, but sobered again. "Tell me?" He allowed her time to think, only picking up the hand closest to his and gently playing with her fingers.

"My lord, when you were young, did you love your mother?"

"Of course."

"And your father?"

He hesitated, his hands stilling on hers. "I respected my father. He did not seem to require love."

"And your sister? Your nurse? Your friends?"

"I've never thought of it. Nurse—" He smiled, a remembering sort of smile. "Well. Yes. I guess I actually loved Nurse best."

"But you loved your mother as well?"

"Until she died, yes, I loved her as well."

"Do you still feel love for her memory?"

Again he paused. "I . . . guess I do. As you feel it for Tim's memory?"

"Perhaps this won't be impossible. What I can't understand, Miles, is that you seem to feel there is only so much love in a person, that once it is given, it is used up and gone and not to be replaced with more."

"It is not true?"

"Love is the one emotion that grows to fill the need. Fear kills other emotions, as does hate or a need for revenge. Love gathers in more and more, and it grows, the more you give it." She looked sideways and discovered he was frowning. "Fiddle. I knew I'd not have the words to explain." Diana scowled, trying to find another way. "Miles, I love my children. That doesn't take away from my love for Tim. Nor do I love them *less* because I love Tim. I suspect I love them the *more*. And there is Ellen. I feel love for her. My uncle still lives. I feel love for him. I feel love for my governess, who was also my friend."

Miles lifted her hand to his lips, interrupting her thoughts. "The important thing is that you're telling me you can love Tim—and the children, and your uncle and Ellen and, perhaps, the whole world—and love me as well?"

"If you can accept that it does not mean I love you *less,* then perhaps you've come to understand."

"I love you."

"Are you certain? Are you sure it is not an infatuation and that you'll soon recover?"

"I know that when we are apart I will suddenly think, *That will interest Diana. I must remember to tell her.* Or I will see something and think, *I must remember to describe that to Diana,* or I will go someplace of interest and I will make a note to take you there or I will meet someone new and wonder if it is someone you will like too. I do not believe I will recover, Diana," he finished with that dry humor she was coming to appreciate very much.

"We've become friends, I think," she said hesitantly.

"Is that why I find myself thinking of you that way so often?"

"I believe so."

"You once said friendship was necessary for love."

"Yes."

"But you do not feel it enough and you fear that is all I feel?"

"I have," she said slowly, "more than once been surprised that you do not simply *know* about friendship and love and affection and all those emotions that have always been important in my life."

A muscle rippled across the edge of Miles's jaw. Diana saw it and wondered if she had, perhaps, insulted him. She looked up and met his eyes, a hard look in them that had her glancing away and back.

"Diana, I have had, as you say, little experience of love.

At least the sort you mean, but there is another sort I do understand, and it is also a part of marriage." He looked down at her, but she remained silent. "Will you say you feel nothing of it?"

"Friendship and a desire to get me into your bed . . ." She shook her head. "Miles, it is *not* enough."

"But how am I to know if I feel this special emotion which I am to understand will decide my fate?"

Diana sighed. How did one know? She had come to believe she felt it again . . . but what if it were no more than that he was an attractive man and she so long without one!

"You do not know either," he said, interrupting her thoughts.

"I believe we've become friends. That's a beginning."

"I want more, Diana. I want to wake up with your hair spread across my pillow. I want to look up from my morning paper and see you pouring your coffee. I want to take you places. I want to tell you things. I want . . ." He eyed her. "It is not important what I want, is it? What do *you* want, Diana?"

"I don't know that that is important either. Miles, do you think we might do as the children are doing and spend the next few months getting to know each other? We'll be attending the same house parties. We'll have time. . . ."

"I don't want time, but that is another thing that is not important, I suppose. It will be as you say, Diana. We'll be friends and, with any luck at all, you'll soon agree we've become much much more."

Euphemia and her William were married just after Christmas. Once the wedding was over and the newly wedded pair gone, Diana reluctantly asked Miles to depart as well from her Cotswold home. Reluctantly, he obeyed.

Once a week Miles wrote Diana a long letter, telling her of those thoughts and experiences he wished to share with her.

Once a week Diana wrote Miles a long letter, telling him of those thoughts and experiences *she* wished to share with *him*.

The winter ended and a day came when Miles's letter did *not*. Diana assumed it would arrive the next day. Still it did not. Nor the next.

Diana fretted. Had Miles discovered he did not love her? That would be terrible since she'd become more and more certain of her feelings for him!

Another day passed with no letter.

And another.

And then, when she was working almost frantically in one of her new borders, she looked up at the sound of someone driving toward her . . . and dropped her trowel, her hands going to her hair. Then she realized her dirty gloves would do her straggly coiffure no good! Miles! He was here! Regaining the use of her limbs, Diana raced at a furious and exceedingly unladylike pace toward the side door to the manor. She would *not* meet him for the first time in months looking as she did!

Miles watched her run toward the house and smiled. She'd looked wonderful to him, but he suspected her feminine pride would not agree. He'd allow her time to primp if it would help her when they met. But this time there would be no arguments, no hesitation, no denial. This time he knew very well what he felt, and he'd not allow her fears or her uncertainty to dissuade him from what he knew.

He was shown into a pleasant salon, the windows wide to the mild spring breeze and flower-scented air. He gazed out on the wild mix of color that was Diana's precious borders and identified flags and crocuses. He was wondering if a pink flower was something called sweet William, when he heard the rustle of silk behind him and turned.

He drew in a quick breath. "Diana . . ."

She smiled. "I wondered if something was wrong when your letter did not arrive."

"No letter?" His brows arched. "But I sent word I'd arrive today."

"It did not come." They stared at each other. "It doesn't matter," she said. Feeling shy, knowing it was absurd, she motioned toward a seat. "Will you be seated?"

Miles glanced toward the open door to the hall, where he could hear servants moving around. He looked out the windows toward where a gardener worked a roller over the lawn. He'd no desire to sit down. All he wanted was to take Diana into his embrace and never let her go, but one could not do so under these circumstances!

"Perhaps you'd prefer a walk, my lord," she suggested when he didn't move. "When I've been overly long on the road, I prefer exercise at the end of it."

"An excellent notion. Why do you not show me that walled rose garden about which you told me? Your favorite garden?" *Perhaps,* he thought, *with any luck at all, there'd be no one there to spy on them.*

"You remembered?"

"I remember everything you've ever told me." Miles approached and gave her his arm.

Some minutes later he sent a satisfied glance around the enclosed garden, took a last check to assure himself they were truly alone and that the house windows did not overlook them, and shut the high gate behind him. Then he reached for Diana, pulled her into his embrace, and kissed her. Thoroughly.

After the first moment's surprise, Diana's arms crept up around his neck. She felt his hand at her back pressing her closer and relaxed against him, allowing all those fears and worries that had plagued her the last few days to flow from her.

"Marry me," he said, and immediately made it impossible for her to respond, kissing her again.

When he came up for air, he stared into her eyes, wondering what he'd see—and was pleased to find a smile. "Marry me?" he asked.

"Yes."

He stilled, his whole body tense. "That's it? Just yes?"

"Some time ago I realized we felt for each other exactly as we should."

"You might have given me a hint," he said, faintly irritated.

"No. You had to realize it yourself."

"But I did. I never thought otherwise."

She shook her head, the smile growing. "Nonsense. It is only recently you've displayed any understanding of it all."

"Here we go again," he muttered. "I suppose you'd best explain that."

"In your recent letters. The extra things you've done for your tenants. And agreeing to finance a Sunday School as your vicar has wished you to do forever. And the neighbor's boy who wished to learn to shoot—would you, before, have offered to teach him? You yourself expressed surprise that you'd done so."

"I still don't understand."

"Miles, it is perfectly simple. When one loves, one loves the whole world! You've begun doing whatever possible to make others happy, all because of the depth of the emotion involved in your feelings for me! Now do you see?"

He thought over the preceding months and decided that was reasonable. "Marry me?" he asked a third time, forgetting she'd said yes.

"There'll be time for everyone to get here if we post the banns this Sunday"— a faint blush appeared across her cheekbones as it occurred to her she was ordering everything without consulting him—"assuming, that is, that that would be all right with you?"

"You've been too long making all the decisions for everyone, have you not? I'll have to watch that you do not make mine! Actually, my dear, I *do* object to posting the banns."

She blinked. "You do?"

"I've an alternate notion." He seated her on a bench and pulled a folded paper from a hidden pocket. "This, my love," he said, waving it under her nose, "is a license that permits us to be married within the hour."

"Hmm. Within the hour, is it?"

"Why may we not?"

"I think Kenelm and Phemie would wish to be present when I remarry."

He sighed. "Are you suggesting you wish a big, elaborate wedding?"

"Certainly not! I merely suggest we wait for Kenelm who is due home from Edinburgh and that, if waiting for banns is too long for you, the three of us then travel to William's estate which, I think, is not far from yours?"

"That is so."

"We may marry there, leave Kenelm there, and—" She blushed.

"I like *that* the best of all," he said, teasing her.

"However much I love you, I'm still a mother, Miles. Do you mind very much that we may not be married within the hour?"

"I mind . . . but it is as you say, and we mustn't disappoint the children."

"It would, you know," she said, still worried.

He smoothed away the small frown. "I've agreed to the delay, my love. But, *now,* since we needn't seek out the vicar . . ." The end of the sentence disappeared as his lips and tongue became far better occupied in other ways.

The spring sun rose high over the garden, warming the two who, somewhat later, sat talking quietly about their future. ". . . And one thing more," Miles said, the scent of roses rich in his nostrils. "Will you take an interest in the gardens at home? I find I'm not so completely practical after all. I would, for instance, like a rose garden very much like this one."

With the addition, he silently added as he changed position on the marble bench, of a small summerhouse in which there would be placed some other small comforts such as a chaise longue. That decided to his satisfaction Miles returned to the far more interesting occupation of kissing his betrothed.

Lost Love, New Love

by
Lois Stewart

The Earl of Linwood circled the picturesque little duck pond, surrounded by graceful weeping willows, in the center of the village of Millbridge and drove to the end of the short high street. There he slowed his curricle as he neared the gate of an unassuming house set back in a well-tended garden. Instead of stopping in front of the house, however, he abruptly urged his team forward and drove out of the village.

Coward, he savagely reproached himself. He was a grown man of thirty-seven, the possessor of an ancient title and extensive estates in Leicestershire, a man of consequence and respect, and yet he couldn't steel himself to confront the wife he hadn't seen in seventeen years. Candace, the woman who had long ago robbed him of his honor and now seemed prepared to rob him of his daughter.

As he guided his team along the narrow road, he was hardly conscious of the beauty of the undulating wooded countryside of the North Downs. Rather, his thoughts drifted back to a day in the high summer of 1796, when, as nineteen-year-old Jack Brereton, not yet Earl of Linwood, fresh out of Easter term at Oxford, he had been riding along a very similar road among the chalk downs of Surrey. . . .

Jack took deep breaths of the bright, sunny air redolent of the pink honeysuckle blossoms in the hedges. It had been miserably cold and rainy during his last week at the university. Here in Reigate, only a day's journey from Oxford, it felt like summer at last.

He frowned as he thought of Oxford. What would Papa say when he learned Jack had decided not to return to the university for a third year? But surely Papa must know by now that his son and heir was no scholar. Putting his father out of his mind and resolving happily not to open another book for at least a year, he urged his mount into a gallop, only to rein in sharply around a bend in the road when he spotted a woman's body sprawled on the verge.

As he was hurriedly dismounting, the woman stirred and sat up, exclaiming in a disgusted voice, "Drat the mare! Now Papa will say 'I told you so.' " She was a young woman, hardly more than a girl, with delicately pretty features and wisps of red-gold hair escaping untidily from a cluster of curls on the crown of her head. A jaunty riding hat lay forlornly nearby.

"Are you hurt, ma'am?" Jack inquired as he walked up to her.

Long-lashed green eyes widened at the sight of him. "No. To tell you the truth, I'm simply embarrassed. Well, humiliated is a better word. My horse threw me."

"So I gathered." Grinning, Jack reached down his hand to help the girl to her feet.

Close up, she was even prettier. A perfect creamy complexion set off the green eyes and reddish hair, and her figure in the well-tailored riding habit was slender, but rounded in just the right places.

"How may I be of help?" Jack asked. "Can I take you to your home?"

"Yes, thank you." The girl flashed Jack a dazzling smile that momentarily took his breath away. "I live a short distance down the road, at Ashdown Farm. I'm Candace Frazier, by the way."

Jack bowed. "At your service, Miss Frazier. My name is Drayton."

"How do you do, Mr. Drayton."

"Er—actually, it's Viscount Drayton."

The green eyes widened again. "So you're a lord?"

"No, no, not really," Jack replied, feeling a little foolish.

"That is to say, it's my father who's the lord. Drayton is only a courtesy title. Come along, Miss Frazier. I'll help you mount. I hope riding astride won't be too awkward for you. You're accustomed to a sidesaddle."

"Only since I became a young lady," she replied cheerfully. "When I was small I always rode astride, although Mama could not like it. She said folk might consider me unladylike." She arranged her skirts around her legs after Jack lifted her into the saddle, in the process unselfconsciously displaying a generous amount of trim ankle.

"Are you visiting in these parts, Lord Drayton?" she asked as Jack began walking along the road, leading the horse.

"Yes, I'm the guest of Lord Colton at Moresby Abbey. His son Tom and I are fellow students at Oxford. We arrived yesterday after the close of Easter term. I'll be staying with the Coltons for several weeks before I return home to Leicestershire for the summer. Doubtless you know the Coltons, Miss Frazier?"

"Oh, I know who they are, of course, but I'm not really acquainted with them, you know. My family isn't on visiting terms with the Coltons." As Jack turned his head toward her with an inquiring look, she added, "You see, Papa is the local squire."

Jack did see, and felt a pang of disappointment. He had already been making plans to see more of Miss Candace Frazier. Unfortunately, he was perfectly familiar with county society. The aristocracy might mingle with the higher reaches of the gentry—the baronets and the knights and the occasional substantial but untitled landowner—but socially they had very little to do with the prosperous farmers, the squires who conducted most of the actual business of the counties as justices of the peace and in other capacities.

"Take the first turning to the right, Lord Drayton," Candace ordered. "That's the driveway to Ashdown Farm."

A quarter mile of winding road brought them to a courtyard surrounding a large house and extensive outbuildings. As

Jack led his horse through the gateway, a large gentleman in breeches and gaiters bustled up to them, his ruddy face drawn with concern. "Candy, my love, are ye all right?" he inquired anxiously. "When the mare came back to the stables wi'out ye, I didn't know what to think. . . ."

Candace slid down from the saddle. "No, Papa, I'm not hurt." Her face assumed a contrite expression. "I'm sorry I took the mare out when you told me she was too strong for me."

Obviously torn between relief and anger, the man growled, "And so she was too strong for ye. P'raps ye'll listen to me the next time I tell ye something." He looked at Jack. "I gather I must thank ye, sir, for rescuing my daughter from the consequences of her folly."

"I was happy to be able to offer Miss Frazier a ride to her home, sir."

"Well, I thank ye, sir, I'm sure." The man extended his hand. "I'm Matthew Frazier."

"Drayton, sir."

"Papa, it's *Lord* Drayton," Candace broke in. "His lordship is staying with the Coltons at Moresby Abbey."

Matthew Frazier's expression changed subtly. "I'm pleased to meet ye, I'm sure, my lord." To Candace he said, "Be off wi' ye, my girl. Ye're a sad sight, wi' your hair every which way."

"Yes, Papa." Candace cast a dimpled smile at Jack. "Thank you, Lord Drayton, for the ride."

"My pleasure, Miss Frazier."

Watching his daughter scamper off, Squire Frazier said fondly, "I fear she's a sad romp, my lord. Always taking the bit in her teeth, and I don't mean just with horses she's no business to be riding. She did ought to have been a boy by rights. Her mother can never find her when it's a question of doing her embroidery or practicing the pianoforte, or learning how to manage the dairy. No, our Candy's usually off wandering the countryside, talking to the tenants, watching some farmer deliver a calf." He shook his head. "My wife swears Candy will never make a proper lady." The squire squared his shoulders. "Well, that's as may be." He extended his hand. "Again, my thanks to ye, my lord. I hope ye enjoys your visit to Moresby Abbey."

It was definitely a dismissal. No invitation to take tea or drink a glass of wine. No suggestion that he call again.

Later that day Jack's adventure met with an interested reception from his friend Tom Colton.

"So you rescued old Squire Frazier's girl, did you, Jack? I hear she's become quite a beauty. Haven't seen her for some time myself, not since she was a hoyden of a schoolgirl. She can't be more than seventeen or so now, come to think of it." A smile that could only be called a leer lit up Tom's face. "Well, well, old boy, planning to have a bit of fun with the Frazier chit while you're staying with us?"

"I'd like to know Miss Frazier better, if that's what you mean," Jack said so stiffly that Tom's eyes shifted and he began talking of something else.

On the following day, when Jack returned to Ashdown Farm, he encountered a polite stone wall in the burly form of Squire Frazier.

"Good day, sir," said Jack when he met the squire in the courtyard. "I came to inquire about Miss Frazier's recovery from her accident. She's well, I trust?"

"Indeed, my lord. Merry as a grig is my Candy. It's kind of ye to ask."

"Er — might I see her?"

"Begging your pardon, my lord, she's not to home." The squire stood foursquare, polite, noncommittal, definitely not welcoming.

"Pray tell Miss Frazier I called," said Jack, and took a regretful leave. He mounted his horse and rode out of the courtyard. He knew better than to argue or entreat. The squire had made up his mind that Jack was to see nothing of Candace. End of a romantic daydream.

Jack cantered down the driveway and turned into the winding lane leading away from the farm. He might as well return to Moresby Abbey. Tom had mentioned fishing in the little stream that ran through the estate.

"Lord Drayton! Hello!"

Jack turned his head to see Candace trotting up behind him. She was riding a spirited mare. He reined in.

"I hope that's not the horse that threw you yesterday," he said, grinning, as she came up to him.

"Oh, no. I've learned my lesson," she replied, returning his smile. "I'll not ride Lilibet until Papa has schooled her a bit more. Were you visiting the farm, Lord Drayton?"

"Actually, I came to see you. Your father said you weren't at home, and I thought—" He stopped short, reddening in embarrassment.

"You thought Papa was telling you a bouncer," Candace finished. "You thought I was really at home, and Papa didn't want us to meet."

"Well . . . yes. I don't think the squire wishes me to know you better."

"Quite right," she said, cocking her head. "Last night I told him I hoped you would call again, and he said he wouldn't allow it. And then he gave me a long lecture about the importance of staying within one's class, and—and other things." A sudden warm color filled her cheeks.

He said quickly, to relieve her embarrassment, "I don't much care to talk about class, Miss Frazier. All I know is that I'd like to be your friend. Is that wrong?"

Recovering herself, Candace said demurely, "Friendship is a virtue, so I've been told. And I *like* having friends."

"Well, then . . . it seems we have a problem. What are we to do about it?"

Seemingly at a tangent, Candace remarked, "I ride every day about this time. Mama was used to insist I take a groom with me now that I'm a grown-up lady, but I've managed to convince her that the grooms would be much more useful working in the stables."

Raising his eyebrows, Jack said, "So if I were to take a ride in this vicinity every morning, I might very well encounter you?"

She shot him a roguish glance. "So you might, Lord Drayton."

"My name is Jack."

"Everybody calls me Candy."

For the next two weeks his hosts saw nothing of Jack in the morning hours. Every day he rode to the crossroads near the turnoff to Ashdown Farm, where Candace was waiting for him. From there they roamed the length and breadth of the lovely Holmedale Valley, nestled in the circle of the chalk downs. Candace guided Jack to all the local beauty spots, including the little streams where they stopped to sample the wariness of the trout population. Several times she provided an ample picnic lunch, laughing as she told Jack, "Cook keeps wanting to know why my appetite is so much bigger these days!"

They carefully avoided the vicinity of Ashdown Farm, because, as Candace said forthrightly early on, "If Papa's tenants should see us riding about together, they'd doubtless mention it to him."

Occasionally Jack felt a pang of guilt. He knew perfectly well why Squire Frazier didn't want him to associate with Candace. Romantic encounters between amorous scions of the aristocracy and pretty farmers' daughters had no future. They rarely ended in marriage, and all too often they ended in disgrace. The squire wanted no part of such a fate for Candace. And the man was probably unusually protective of his daughter, Jack reflected, because Candace was an only child.

Jack soothed his conscience with the reflection that he had no intention of trying to seduce Candace. But what was the harm of a casual, friendly relationship for a few weeks between two young people who happened to like each other? He and Candace would part at the end of his visit to the Coltons with no more than pleasant memories. After all, he told himself more than once during the succeeding lazy summer days, he more often thought of Candace as an amusing, vivacious companion than as a female toward whom he might wish to make romantic advances.

Just how fatuous his view of the situation really was came home to Jack several days before he was due to return home to Leicestershire. He and Candace had ridden to Reigate to explore the ruins of the medieval castle outside the town.

Little remained of the castle now except several acres of neglected grounds, an entrance archway, remnants of the old walls, and the mound on which the keep had stood. But from the center of the mound a flight of steps and a tunnel had been constructed to lead down to a series of vaults making up the "Barons' Cave," popularly believed to be the secret conference hall of the rebellious barons before they went on to confront King John at Runnymede.

Jack and Candace borrowed a key from the caretaker of the castle grounds and bought some candles from him, and then scrambled down the stairs and the tunnel into the dark, damp vaults.

"Why, there's really nothing to see," Candace remarked in disappointment as she flashed her candle around the cavernous empty spaces. "Do you think the barons really did meet down here before they forced the king to sign the Magna Carta?"

"Probably not," Jack said as he grinned, "but it makes a good story, don't you think?"

"Well, good story or not, I don't wish to stay down here another minute. I'm perishing with the cold even if it is July."

Halfway up the dank steps Candace slipped, losing her balance and dropping her candle.

"Candy! Are you hurt?" Jack inquired anxiously as he bent down to pull her to her feet, in the process losing his own candle. However, enough light came from the staircase entrance above to make up for the loss of the candles.

Catching her breath, Candace leaned against him. "I think I twisted my ankle."

Jack tightened his arms around her to give her more support. "Can you walk? Shall I carry you up the stairs?"

Candace smiled. "No, silly. I just turned my ankle a bit. . .,." Her smile faded as he looked deeply into her eyes, as if he were seeing her for the first time.

"You're so lovely, Candy," he murmured, and bent his head to kiss her. For a long, blissful moment she responded eagerly, her lips warm and clinging. Then, abruptly, she wrenched her mouth away from his.

"Candy, what is it?"

"Jack, you know we shouldn't be kissing each other."

"Why not? I like kissing you."

She shook her head, pushing herself free. Favoring her tender ankle, she hobbled up the remaining steps and began walking across the castle yard. He caught up with her as she neared the entrance arch.

"Candy, wait. We must talk."

She paused, turning to face him. Her expressive features looked somber. "Yes, we should talk. Jack, I thought I knew better than Papa, but now I see I was wrong. Remember I told you that he didn't want me to be friends with you? I didn't tell you everything he said. He was afraid that sooner or later you would want more than friendship, and then I might be very unhappy."

Taking her hands, Jack said quietly, "Your papa was right about one thing. I do want more than your friendship, Candy. I want your love. I want you to marry me."

She tried to pull her hands away. "Oh, no . . . you can't mean that. Papa says that men from your—your station in life don't marry girls like me."

"This man does, if the girl is you, and you love me as

much as I love you." He paused, suddenly feeling an immense doubt. "That is—*do* you care for me, Candy?"

A tremulous smile curved her lips. "Oh, Jack, you ninny-hammer, of course I do, but what's that to say to anything? Papa says —"

His face lighting up, Jack exclaimed, "I don't care a rap what your papa says. All I know is that I love you and you love me and we're going to be married."

"But —"

"No buts." Catching Candace in his arms, he gave her an exuberant kiss, and then, grabbing her hand, he pulled her through the castle arch and out to the area where they had left the horses. "I'll just return the key to the caretaker, and then, Candy, we're going to Ashdown Farm to tell your papa and your mama to start preparing for a wedding!"

Obviously torn between joy and apprehension, Candace said, "Jack, maybe we should think about this a little more carefully before we talk to Papa. . . ."

"There's nothing to think about," said Jack firmly, but he was reckoning without Squire Frazier.

On the ride to the farm from Reigate, Candace gradually lost her air of excited happiness and became more and more subdued as the miles passed. When they reached the cross-roads, she said quickly, "Don't come with me. Let me talk to Papa first."

"No, Candy. We'll go together."

She opened her mouth to protest and closed it again. Her hands clutching her reins showed white at the knuckles.

As they entered the courtyard of the farm, the squire was just emerging from the stables. Quickly dismounting, Candace said, "Papa, Jack and I have something to say to you. . . ."

"Go inside the house, my girl."

"But, Papa . . ."

"Do as I say, Candace."

Hesitating only long enough to give Jack a troubled glance, Candace walked to the house.

Crossing his arms across his burly chest, the squire fixed Jack with a black scowl. "Well, now, my lord, I reckon as how ye owes me an explanation. How is it ye were out riding wi' my girl wi'out my permission? And don't ye be telling me ye met her by accident and politely escorted her home, for I wouldn't believe ye. What's more, I'll warrant this isn't the first time ye've ridden out with Candace."

Jack gulped. The squire was a formidable presence. Jack suddenly felt like a grubby schoolboy. Clearing his throat, he said, "You're quite right, sir, and I owe you an apology. Candy and I have been riding every morning for several weeks. I know I should have asked your permission."

"And why didn't ye?"

"Because I thought you wouldn't give it."

"Too right, my lord, I wouldn't have given permission," the squire snapped. "I won't have my girl gadding about with the likes o' ye, and ye persuading her to deceive me, like as not. I must ask ye to leave my property and not come back."

Jack held his ground. "I'll go, sir, but not before I've put my case to you. Mr. Frazier, pray allow me to request the favor of your daughter's hand in marriage."

For an instant the squire was too surprised to speak. Then his face reddened with fury, and he growled, "So that's how ye schemed to inveigle my girl into giving ye what ye want from her—tell her ye love her and promise to marry her. Ye're lower than I thought, my lord."

Trying to hold his own temper in rein, Jack said evenly, "I haven't promised Candy anything I'm not prepared to give. I love her. I want to marry her."

Something in Jack's tone must have carried conviction. The squire's eyes narrowed, and he stared at Jack for a long, thoughtful moment. "Very well, my lord. I believe ye, or at least I believe in your good intentions. The fact remains, however, that any marriage between ye and Candy is out o' the question."

"I don't accept that, sir. Why shouldn't we marry? We love each other. . . ."

"Love!" the squire snorted, throwing up his hands. "There's far more to marriage than love. Have ye thought how my Candy would fit into your world if ye marry? Ye're a lord's son, someday ye'll be a lord yerself. Candy's a farmer's daughter."

Suppressing a vague feeling of disquiet, Jack retorted, "Candy's beautiful and intelligent. She could easily learn any social graces she might need to 'fit into my world,' as you put it."

"Is that so? Do ye reckon your family would agree wi' ye? For that matter, have ye spoken to yer family about marrying Candy?"

"No, of course not. There's been no time. I return to Leicestershire next week. I'll speak to my father then."

The squire nodded. "Ye do that, my lord. I think ye'll find that your father believes as I do, that when it comes to marriage, young folk should stick to their own class."

"And when I come back to Surrey with my father's consent, sir, will you then allow me to marry Candy?"

"We'll cross that bridge when we come to it. Go home and talk to your father. Until then, I don't wish ye and Candy to meet."

Several days later Jack arrived at his family estate, Brereton Court, beset by mixed feelings. In the past he had always been happy to return, from school or from visits, to his home near Melton Mowbray. He had never found another corner of England to equal this area in the heart of the shires in the rolling upland grasslands of East Leicestershire. On this occasion, however, he mounted the steps of the stately Georgian mansion with a certain amount of trepidation.

"So, my boy, you're back from your visit to the Coltons," the Earl of Linwood greeted his heir as Jack entered the library. "I trust you enjoyed yourself. Now you'll have a good two months at home before it's time to return to Oxford."

"Well, as to that, Father, and with your permission, naturally, I've decided not to finish at Oxford. I'm no scholar, as you well know. I think it's time I started learning about estate duties."

The earl leaned back in his chair behind his desk, giving Jack a long, thoughtful look. In appearance he and Jack were much alike, tall and slender, dark-haired and gray-eyed, with strong, regular features. There the resemblance ended. In personality Jack was more like his dead mother, warm and outgoing. The earl was a cool and distant man with a pronounced, almost exaggerated pride in his lineage and the position of his family.

"I daresay there's no need to return for a third year at Oxford," the earl agreed now. "What I would have preferred for you, in any event, was a grand tour, but of course the war has made that impossible. By all means start making the rounds with our estate agent. And now I expect you'll want to greet your aunt. She's been looking forward to your arrival." He nodded a pleasant dismissal.

The interview had been characteristic, thought Jack. He and his father rarely did more than brush the surface in a conversation.

"Er—Father, could I have a word with you?"

The earl lifted an inquiring eyebrow.

Clearing his throat, Jack said, "The fact is, I'd like to get married."

The eyebrow went higher. "This is rather sudden, is it not? You're young to be thinking of marriage. Eighteen, as I recall."

"Nineteen, Father."

"Still very young. I was thirty-five when I married. It's Sarah Marston, I presume. You know her father and I had agreed that she should have her come-out before there was any discussion of marriage." The earl smiled indulgently.

"Ah, well, you young people will be impulsive. Now that Sarah has enjoyed a most successful Season . . ."

Jack gritted his teeth. A match between him and Sarah Marston, the daughter of a neighboring estate owner, had always been a fond dream of the two fathers, but he and Sarah had never been more than rather tepid friends.

"Father, it's not Sarah."

"Not Sarah? Who is the young lady, then? Do I know her?"

"No. I met Candace—Miss Frazier—while I was visiting the Coltons."

"I see. Who are the Fraziers? Friends of the Coltons?"

"No. Candace's father—Squire Frazier—owns a prosperous farm near Reigate. He's also the local justice of the peace."

The earl's eyes were like chips of ice. "If you're serious, Jack—which I find hard to credit—you must know I would never consent to your marriage to a young woman from—I was about to say a young woman from the dregs of society, but I won't exaggerate. No doubt Miss Frazier is accounted perfectly respectable within her own circle. To me, however, and to all our friends and acquaintances, such a marriage would be a gross mésalliance."

"I'm sorry you feel that way, Father. The fact remains, I've already proposed to Candace."

"Oh? I suppose she snapped you up before you could change your mind, did she? No doubt her father the farmer was even more enthusiastic."

"Actually, Squire Frazier is as much opposed to the marriage as you are. He believes people should marry within their own class."

"Wise man," sneered the earl. "That settles the matter, then. We'll talk no more about it."

"I'm afraid we must. I came here to tell you that I intend to marry Candy with or without your consent, or her father's."

The earl's expression hardened. "Don't attempt to defy

me, Jack. The law is on my side. You may not marry until you're twenty-one except with my consent."

"Aren't you forgetting several options that are open to me? Candy and I could elope to Gretna Green. A trifle scandalous, perhaps, but the marriage would be perfectly legal."

"In Scotland. There's some doubt about the validity of Scottish marriages in England."

"Unless you were willing to court even more scandal, however, I doubt you would contest the marriage in court. And there's another possibility, you know. I could marry Candy by special license, at a place and time of my own choosing. You could contest such a ceremony, of course, but again, only at the price of scandal."

Obviously controlling himself by the greatest of efforts, the earl grated, "If I were to cut off your allowance and forbid you to bring your new bride to Brereton Court, how would you live?"

"Uncle Harry's bequest comes to me when I'm twenty-one, remember? Until then, perhaps Squire Frazier would allow me to work on his farm."

The earl stared at Jack fixedly, but he said nothing. As well as Jack, he knew it was checkmate.

Candy looked up from her book as the maid entered the parlor to say, "The poor child is still asleep, Mrs. Bennett. She must have been powerful tired."

Candy smiled. "Yes, she had a very long journey yesterday. Tell Cook to delay lunch for a while."

After the maid left the room, Candy didn't resume her reading. She sat looking into space, her lips curved in a tender smile as she thought about the sleeping girl upstairs. Amanda. The daughter she had never expected to see again. Amanda, grown-up and beautiful and, miraculously, happy to know the mother who had abandoned her so many years before.

Candy came out of her reverie at the sound of a carriage

approaching from the direction of the village center. She rose from her chair and walked to the window of the parlor, which looked out on the high street. A smart curricle slowed almost to a stop in front of her gate and moved on again.

Candace drew a sharp breath. She'd caught only a glimpse of the driver of the curricle, but even after seventeen years she couldn't be mistaken in the confident set of the head and the graceful carriage of those broad shoulders.

She wasn't really surprised to see him. She'd been certain he would come sometime. Not this soon, she'd hoped, but sooner or later after he discovered Amanda had run away he would suspect their daughter had gone to her mother. And of course he would know where to go. Candy had long suspected that Jack or his father was keeping tabs on her whereabouts. But why had Jack driven on without stopping? Would he return?

She returned to her chair and picked up her book again, but in her agitated state the words were meaningless symbols on the page. Suddenly her mind was flooded with memories of her brief year of married life, memories she'd kept at bay since the night she'd fled from Brereton Court, never to return. Memories she hadn't allowed herself to dwell upon because they hurt too much, and because they had no place in the new life she'd built for herself in Austria. . . .

After Jack had returned to Leicestershire to obtain his father's consent to their marriage, time had passed in slow torture for Candy. *Her* father kept warning her, "Candy girl, he won't be coming back. He wants to come back, I'll give him that, he means to come back, but in the end his father the lord will persuade him he should take a wife from his own kind."

Much as Candy longed to prove her father wrong, as the days passed, and Jack didn't return, the dull ache in her heart grew stronger. Then one day, walking from the house to the stables, she saw Jack riding into the courtyard. She stopped, still as a statue, as he dismounted and came toward her. She couldn't read his expression. He looked sternly serious. "You've come to say good-bye, Jack, haven't you?" she said in a low voice that was almost a whisper.

He took her hands, grasping them tightly. His face relaxing in a radiant smile, he said, "Say good-bye? Don't talk fustian. My darling, I've come to ask you to set a date for our wedding. Please make it soon."

He caught her up in his arms and kissed her until she was lost to any reality except the urgent pressure of his lips and the taut hardness of his body against hers.

"Well, my lord?"

Abruptly releasing Candy, Jack turned to face her father, who confronted them like an avenging angel, his eyes like flint, his mouth a grim slit.

"Mr. Frazier, I've come to marry Candy. I'd like to do so as soon as possible. Will you have your priest call the banns, or would you prefer that I obtain a special license?"

The squire's expression changed subtly, became uncertain. After a moment of obvious indecision, he said, "Banns or special license, my lord, either would do, provided you have your father's consent."

"Here's my father's written permission, sir." Jack handed the squire a note from the earl, which stated tersely: "To whom it may concern: I hereby consent to my son's marriage to Miss Candace Frazier. Linwood."

After he had quickly scanned the note, the squire tucked it into his pocket. "The Reverend Jordan will be wishful to see this, seeing as how ye're underage, my lord."

He paused, staring hard at his daughter, his brows drawn together. At last he said, "Candy, love, I reckon as how yer mother and me will give our consent to this marriage, since his lordship the Earl of Linwood has done the same, but I want ye to think long and hard on't. Ye're sure now that love is the most important thing in the world, and that ye and Lord Drayton will live happily forever after, as the fairy tales put it. But ye'll discover life ain't a fairy tale. I don't believe ye've thought ahead enough as to how it will be to leave your home and kin and go to live wi' folk who're as different from ye as night is from the day."

Clutching Jack's hand, Candy exclaimed, "Thank you for caring about me, Papa. I *have* thought about leaving home, and I know I'll be lonesome for you and Mama and the farm, and life will be different in Leicestershire, but in the end all that's important is that I want to marry Jack as much as he wants to marry me."

Her father shrugged. "Very well, my girl, if that's what ye really want."

Candy floated through the days preceding her wedding in a kind of deliriously happy daze from which she emerged only long enough to try to calm her mother's nerves about the prospect of marrying her daughter to a lord.

"We can't have Lord Drayton's family thinking we don't know how to do things properly," Mrs. Frazier fretted. "And we don't want them to think ye're a frump, neither. We'll go to Tunbridge Wells for your gown and your wedding clothes, Candy. They tell me there's a real French modiste in town. She'll dress ye in the latest fashion."

"Mama, a French modiste will charge the earth. And Jack doesn't care what I wear!"

"No, perhaps not, but I'm sure his family will notice your clothes," Mrs. Frazier replied grimly. She had her way with the trousseau, but her husband had to put his foot down when she started making plans to replace the furniture in the parlor and the dining room.

"I'm not ashamed of my home, wife, and there's no call for Lord Drayton's family to be ashamed, neither, so leave us hear no more about buying new furniture."

For Candy the wedding was dreamlike, exquisitely perfect. The gown concocted by the French modiste made her feel like a fairy princess. The little church was packed with friends and relatives and neighbors, and Candy was too happy to take much notice that the Earl of Linwood and his sister Charlotte,

Lady Willoughby, together with a handful of other Brereton relations, seemed distinctly out of place among the local guests.

Candy came down to earth on the last morning of their honeymoon in the secluded villa near Brighton, loaned to them by one of Jack's cousins. She awoke early, propping herself up on her elbow as she looked down at Jack's sleeping face. Her heart swelled with love for him. These two weeks at the villa had been sheer bliss, in which for the first time in her life she had shared the closest of intimacy with another person. Jack was a perfect lover, gentle and considerate, even as he brought her to the heights of ecstasy.

Jack's eyes opened. His lips curved in a smile, and he pulled her down against him, saying with a little laugh, "Darling, I can't think of anything more wonderful than to wake up with you every morning for the rest of my life."

Snuggling into his embrace, Candy murmured, "Jack, must we really leave here today? Can't we stay a little longer? I've been so happy here."

Jack sat up, cradling Candy in his arms. "So have I been happy here, darling, happier than I've ever been in my life, but honeymoons don't last forever, worse luck. Have you forgotten that my father and Aunt Charlotte are hosting a dinner in our honor on the evening after we arrive at Brereton Court? And I should think you'd be eager to see your new home."

She smiled at him. "Well, of course I'm eager to see Brereton Court, Jack. But you mustn't mind if I'm a little sentimental about leaving the villa. After all, it was our *first* home!"

However, as the miles slipped away on their journey to Leicestershire, Candy found it more and more difficult to keep up a carefree façade. Unbidden, her father's early misgivings about her ability to fit into her new life crept into her thoughts. She remembered how stiff and distant Jack's father and his aunt had seemed at the wedding and at the breakfast that followed it. She quailed at the thought of living in the same house with people who didn't like her.

"Jack," she said suddenly as they left the post stop at Bedford halfway into their journey, "did your father really approve of our marriage?"

He reddened. "Well, no, not at first. He acted like *your* father, always talking about the wisdom of young people marrying within their respective social classes. A pack of nonsense."

"How did you persuade him to change his mind?"

Jack bit his lip, remaining stubbornly silent. After a moment he said reluctantly, "If you must know, I threatened to elope to Scotland. That, or get a special license that would allow me to marry at a time and place of my choosing." He added hastily, "Father soon came to his senses, just as Squire Frazier did. If Father needed any last-minute convincing, all he had to do was look at your beautiful face, darling. Father knows now that I made a perfect choice in my bride."

Candy wasn't so sure. She was appalled and humiliated to learn that Jack had had to resort to a form of blackmail to force his father to consent to their marriage. She wasn't at all convinced that the Earl of Linwood was reconciled to acquiring a farmer's daughter as his new daughter-in-law. But she hid her growing apprehensions from Jack.

They made a final post stop in Melton Mowbray and drove north.

"We're almost there," said Jack, gazing out of the windows of the carriage, a smile of anticipation on his lips.

Candy sat in a tense silence as the carriage passed between the pillars of elaborate wrought iron gates and proceeded along a winding driveway through an extensive wooded parkland. As the carriage emerged from the park and entered a circular courtyard, Candy stared at the stately mansion in front of her and gasped, "Oh, Jack, it's enormous. You never told me you lived in a castle."

"It's not a castle, you goose," Jack said with a laugh. "It's only a good-size Georgian house."

But Candy knew that Ashdown Farm, reckoned locally to be a substantial establishment, would have fitted comfortably into a tiny corner of Brereton Court.

As the carriage rolled to a stop, a crowd of people poured out of the great double portal of the house. "Oh, Lord," Jack muttered. "What a bore. Here's the butler and the house-keeper and the whole indoor staff to welcome us home. Well, there's nothing for it but to do the pretty. It will soon be over."

Pasting a pleasant smile on her face, Candy stood beside Jack as the dignified butler delivered a solemn welcoming speech to the newlyweds on behalf of himself and the house-keeper and what appeared to be an army of servants. Candy felt acutely uncomfortable. It seemed to her that every eye was boring into her with a barely concealed curiosity.

She was grateful to escape with Jack to their own quarters, consisting of two large, well-furnished rooms connected by a dressing room. Even here, however, there was little respite. Within minutes the housekeeper tapped at the door.

"With your permission, my lady, since you did not bring an abigail with you, I will assign one of the maids to help you temporarily. Clarice is a neat, well-behaved girl. I think you will like her."

"Why—thank you, Mrs. Shaw."

"Perhaps, my lady, you would wish me to engage a permanent abigail for you?"

"Thank you," Candy said again. "That would be most kind."

Hardly had the door closed behind the housekeeper, however, when Candy wailed, "Jack, I've never had a servant whose only duty was to help me dress, or wait on me hand and foot. I won't know what to do with this Clarice, or whatever her name is."

"Nonsense," Jack said with a hint of impatience. "You must have an abigail. Every lady of quality has an abigail.

Aunt Charlotte, for example, wouldn't dream of appearing in public without the assistance of *her* abigail! And the other servants will think it very strange of you if you don't employ a personal maid. I daresay you'll soon wonder how you ever managed without one."

Candy smiled weakly. "I expect you're right. After all," she added daringly, "You won't be around every time I need to have my stays laced, the way you were on our honeymoon!"

Jack whooped with laughter, and the awkward little moment passed. Later Candy was agreeably surprised to find that the maid, Clarice, performed her duties unobtrusively, without making her new mistress feel gauche, and that the girl even had a deft hand with hair.

Before they went down to dinner that evening, Candace asked Jack nervously, "How do I look?"

"Beautiful, of course," he said promptly. He gazed admiringly at the gown of gossamer-thin muslin in a shade that matched her eyes. "That's a lovely dress. I don't believe you wore it at the villa. And I like those little yellow rosebuds in your hair."

"The rosebuds were Clarice's idea." Candy flushed with pleasure at Jack's compliment. She felt a sudden rush of gratitude to her mother for insisting on employing the French modiste in Tunbridge Wells to make her trousseau.

Still, as she and Jack went down the stairs, Candy remained mildly apprehensive about this first family gathering at Brereton Court. True, she wasn't really a stranger to Jack's father and his widowed Aunt Charlotte, Lady Willoughby, who had been in charge of the household since the death of Jack's mother many years before. Both of them had attended the wedding, but her encounters with them had been brief and formal.

Her heart sank during the first few moments in the vast drawing room. Jack's father and his aunt were every bit as stiff as she remembered them from the wedding. The earl, with a smile that could at best be described as wintry, confined his remarks to Candy to a terse few words of welcome, and then began a conversation with Jack about estate matters.

Aunt Charlotte, a handsome woman who strongly resembled both her brother and her nephew, was a majestic figure in a towering turban trimmed with feathers that matched her gown of puce satin. Though her manner was as formal and unsmiling as the earl's, she was considerably more talkative. After a perfunctory inquiry about the Brighton villa, she proceeded to describe all the families in the neighborhood who would be calling on Candy, and on whom she would be expected to call. After the first four or five names Candy couldn't remember one from the other.

Charlotte then turned her attention to Candy herself. "You have a pretty speaking voice, my dear. Not a trace of an—er—accent. Did you have a governess?"

"Why, no. I attended Miss Wainwright's Academy in Tunbridge Wells for several years."

"Ah. That explains it. Then no doubt you play the pianoforte, speak some French and Italian, paint in watercolors?"

"Very indifferently, I fear," Candy replied with a laugh. "I wasn't a prize pupil."

Charlotte raised an eyebrow. "You're being modest, I trust. I'm sure I needn't tell you how important it is for a young female to have certain accomplishments. Perhaps it's even more important for someone in your—er—position."

Suddenly nettled by Charlotte's patronizing tone, Candy blurted out, "No, I really don't play the pianoforte very well, but I do have other accomplishments. I know how to shear a sheep, for instance, and I'm told I make very good cheese."

Stiffening with disapproval, Charlotte said, "My dear, I realize you were funning, but I would be remiss if I didn't tell you that you really must learn not to make such ill-advised remarks. I shudder to think what our friends might think if you were to announce, at a dinner table, say, that you used to shear sheep! I'm sure you wouldn't wish to be considered coarse."

Biting back a retort, Candy murmured, "No, indeed, Aunt Charlotte. Please excuse me."

Charlotte inclined her head a fraction, but obviously her sensibilities were still ruffled. She said very little to Candy during dinner, addressing most of her remarks to Jack, as did the earl.

Later, when Candy and Jack had retired for the evening, Jack said uneasily, "I hope you didn't consider Father and Aunt Charlotte a trifle high in the instep because they didn't talk to you very much. They don't mean to be unfriendly. Both of them are very formal people, you see, and they're not much given to small talk."

Candy was now convinced that the earl and Charlotte had received her into the family very unwillingly, and the realization left her feeling hurt and resentful. She also suspected that if she allowed her emotions to show, Jack would be very uncomfortable, caught between his family and his new bride, obliged to take some kind of stand. She gave him a quick hug. "Of course I don't think your papa and Aunt Charlotte are unfriendly," she said, smiling brightly. "It will take a while for us all to know each other better, that's all."

With a faint look of relief, Jack replied, "When they know you better, they'll love you as much as I do, you'll see." And Candy knew she had made the right decision, to make a niche for herself at Brereton Court without entangling Jack in any difficulties she might encounter.

In the days that followed, Jack settled into a relaxed routine that he appeared to find very satisfying. He made daily rounds with the Brereton estate agent, making good on the resolve he had made to his father to begin learning the fine points of estate management. He renewed his friendships with the young men of the neighborhood, enjoying the cubbing and the shooting and the fishing in their company, and making plans for the fall hunting season. His nights he spent in Candy's arms, plumbing the depths of a passion that was seemingly inexhaustible. And when, a scant month after their return from their honeymoon, he learned that Candy was pregnant, he was exultant.

"I hope he—or she, of course—will be the first of many," he told Candy, grinning broadly. "It was dashed lonely growing up here at Brereton Court as an only child."

But if Jack was supremely content with the start of his married life, from the beginning Candy had problems adjusting to her existence at Brereton Court. For one thing, she soon became resentfully aware that Charlotte was keeping a close eye on her behavior, primarily by having the servants report on her activities.

Candy first became aware of the surveillance when, after she had spent a satisfying afternoon in the kennels, assisting the kennelmaster to deliver a promising litter of hound pups, the episode was promptly reported to Charlotte, who said, "Really, you know, we employ servants to manage our kennels. They don't require your help at whelping time."

On another occasion Candy visited the kitchens, where she happily whipped up for Cook a sample of a special cake that her mother had always prepared for Michaelmas. Charlotte's comment was, "You'll be mistress of Brereton Court one day, Candace, and you'll do well to remember that the head of an establishment gives orders by way of the housekeeper to the kitchen staff. She certainly doesn't prepare food with her own hands!"

Although Candy in her more despondent moments felt that she was surrounded by spies who reported on her every movement to Charlotte, she tried to keep her resentment from showing. She told herself that Charlotte meant well, that she was doing only what she considered her duty, to ensure that Candy learned how to conduct herself as the future Countess of Linwood. Doubtless, as time passed and Candy committed fewer mistakes or indiscretions, or what Charlotte considered mistakes or indiscretions, Jack's aunt would become less critical.

A more irritating thorn in Candy's side was the problem of boredom. She didn't have enough to do at Brereton Court. At Ashdown Farm her days had been busy, helping her mother in the management of a large farm household. Here in Leicestershire, time hung heavy on her hands. After she had received bride visits from the ladies of the neighboring gentry and had dutifully returned the calls, she had very little to do. She was no needlewoman, she had no taste for sketching, and, though she liked to read, she was too full of energy to occupy her entire day with a book.

Riding had always been her favorite recreation, but early in her stay at Brereton Court Charlotte objected to Candy's custom of riding about the countryside unaccompanied by a groom.

"I never had to take a groom with me when I went riding back home in Surrey," Candy protested.

"That's as may be, my dear. Here in Leicestershire the custom is different. Ladies of quality are always escorted by a groom. And there are other factors to be considered. What if you should fall from your horse, for example? In your present—er—delicate condition, you might need immediate help."

"I'm a very good horsewoman, Aunt Charlotte."

"I don't doubt it. Pray indulge me, however, if only because of my concern for the future heir to Linwood!"

"Yes, Aunt Charlotte," Candy said resignedly. She considered it was worthwhile to give up her cherished solitary rides in order to avoid unpleasant friction with Jack's aunt, even though she soon discovered, to her annoyance, that her groom was simply another of the servants who kept Charlotte informed about her activities. During one of her initial morning rides Candy stopped off at the home farm to chat with the farmer and his wife, and accepted an invitation to partake of tea and freshly baked scones. That same day Charlotte told her reprovingly, "I understand you took tea with Mrs. Carrington at the home farm. Really, Candace, it's all very well to express an interest in our tenants, but one doesn't sit down to a meal with them!"

Despite her vexation with the spying groom, Candy's rides continued to be the most pleasurable part of her day. She roamed far and wide across the countryside, just as she had been used to doing in Surrey.

Sometimes she stopped in the nearby village of Linwood, which reminded her of her home village near Ashdown Farm, where she knew the names and life histories of everyone living there. To date, at least, Aunt Charlotte had expressed no objection to the visits, which she undoubtedly knew about, thanks to Candy's groom. The housewives of Linwood had gradually lost their awe of the earl's daughter-in-law and chatted easily with her, and she was a prime favorite of the children, to whom she often took sweetmeats.

On one of her visits to the village the children challenged her to a game of hide and seek, and during a particularly spirited chase she slid into a puddle of mud, the result of a recent shower, and fell headlong.

"Oh, the devil," Candy exclaimed as she sat up, gazing ruefully at the muddy splotches on her riding habit.

An amused voice said, "Allow me to help you, ma'am."

Startled, Candy looked up to see a tall gentleman bending over her, hand outstretched. She took the proffered hand and stood up. The gentleman extended a large white handkerchief to her, saying, "Perhaps this will help to get rid of some of the mud, ma'am."

Candy brushed vigorously at the mud stains for a few moments before giving it up as a bad job. She handed the soiled handkerchief back to its owner, saying, "I thank you, sir, for your good intentions, but I fear my riding habit will never look the same again."

"I wish I had been able to emulate Sir Walter Raleigh and throw my cloak across the puddle before you stepped in it," replied the stranger with a whimsical smile. He was a tall, slender man in his late thirties or early forties, with a thin, pleasant face and friendly gray eyes. "Please allow me to introduce myself. My name is Gareth Mason. And you, I suspect, are Lady Drayton."

At Candy's startled look he laughed, saying, "I just returned to the neighborhood after a long visit to friends in Bath, and on catching up on the local news I discovered that young Jack Brereton had taken unto himself a bride. There can't be *two* beautiful ladies in the area with whom I'm unacquainted, so I assumed you must be Jack's wife. As a matter of fact, I'd been looking forward to meeting the new Lady Drayton at the dinner party to which I've been invited at Brereton Court on Saturday."

Candy smiled. "I'll be very pleased to welcome you on Saturday, Mr. Mason."

"Actually, it's Sir Gareth," Mason said apologetically.

"Sir Gareth, I beg you not to tell everyone that the first time we met I was sitting in a mud puddle," Candy said with a mock shudder.

"My lips are sealed," he assured her.

I wish I could be sure that my groom's lips will be sealed, Candy reflected resignedly as she rode home.

It was a vain hope. Aunt Charlotte found out about the mud puddle. She was only mildly reproving, however, saying, "I think you're a bit old for children's games, Candace. Do try for more presence."

Jack laughed when Candy told him about her tumble in the mud and his aunt's disapproval. "Don't pay any attention to Aunt Charlotte," he said indulgently. "She's forgotten what it's like to be young. It's been too many years since she was a child and played hide-and-seek!"

He seemed interested in her meeting with Sir Gareth. "Mason's a good chap. Older than I am, of course, so we're not close friends, but very agreeable. He's by way of being a very

fine amateur painter, you know. Some people have urged him
to exhibit publicly."

"Is there a Lady Mason?"

"Not anymore. His wife died some years ago, and Mason
shows no interest in marrying again."

During the next several weeks Candy frequently encountered Sir Gareth on her morning rides. The meetings were no
accident, as he confessed at one point, "I hope you don't
mind my joining you. I dislike riding alone. I'm not really a
horse person, you know, like Jack and the other young bucks
in the neighborhood, throwing their hearts over any fence
their horses can clear. I ride for the exercise, and I prefer
riding with a companion."

There was never a hint of gallantry in his manner, and
Candy simply accepted him as an interesting new friend, a
pleasant addition to her life, which had seemed to be pro-
gressing more smoothly—it had been some time since she'd
run afoul of Aunt Charlotte's displeasure—until the fatal day
when Betsy, one of the housemaids, came down with a toothache.

Returning from the stables after her ride, Candy heard a
faint whimpering sound as she passed the drawing room, and
peered inside to discover a housemaid wielding a feather
duster halfheartedly with one hand while with the other she
mopped the tears streaming down her face.

"Good heavens—Betsy, is it? What's the matter? Are you
ill?"

"It's my tooth, my lady," stammered the girl, a slight, timid-
looking creature only a few years out of her childhood. "It
hurts something awful. My cheek's all swelled up."

"Yes, I can see that. You shouldn't be working if you're in
pain. Go to the housekeeper. Tell Mrs. Shaw she's to send
you to the nearest dentist at once."

"Yes, my lady. Thank ye." Nursing her swollen cheek, the
housemaid trailed out of the drawing room.

Shortly afterward, in her bedchamber, changing out of her

riding habit, Candy heard a peremptory knock on her door, followed immediately by Charlotte's entry into the room.

"Really, Candace, this is too much," said Charlotte angrily.

"Why—what is it?"

"Mrs. Shaw informs me that you sent her orders—*orders!*—to dispatch one of our housemaids immediately to a dentist."

Candy stared in Charlotte in some confusion. "I did that, yes. The housemaid, Betsy, was in agony from a toothache."

"Agony? Oh, come now. Betsy was probably preying on your sympathy. In any case, you exceeded your authority. I do not coddle my servants. I certainly don't allow them to neglect their work because of some trifling personal ailment. Do you realize that Mrs. Shaw had to detach a stablehand from his duties for the better part of a day in order to drive this Betsy to the nearest dentist, who happens to live ten miles from here in Melton Mowbray? You should have referred the girl to me. If she had still been in discomfort at the end of the day, I would have sent her to Dr. Emerson in the village, who doubtless could have helped her."

"Dr. Emerson isn't a dentist. And Betsy wasn't in 'discomfort.' She was in great pain. There was no question of coddling her. It would have been inhuman to oblige her to work all day in her condition."

Charlotte said coldly, "May I remind you that I am the best judge of what my servants should do?"

Candy lost her temper. "Betsy may be a servant, but she's also a human being who feels pain just as we do, and I think you're being rather cruel and insensitive to overlook that fact, Aunt Charlotte!"

Charlotte exploded in her turn. "And you, my dear Candace, are the rudest person I have ever met! But I daresay I shouldn't be surprised at your behavior, considering your origins."

Jack strode into the bedchamber just then, pausing to stare

in surprise from one angry face to the other. "What on earth is going on here? Are you two quarreling?"

"You may well ask," retorted Charlotte, and gave him a detailed account of Betsy's toothache and its aftermath.

Drawing a deep breath, Jack said, "Aren't you making too much of this, Aunt Charlotte? Perhaps Candy should have consulted you before sending off the wretched housemaid to the dentist, but she was only trying to help the girl, after all. You forget, I think, that she's not accustomed to living in a large establishment like Brereton Court. On the farm where she grew up she was used to thinking of the servants almost as family."

He looked startled when his aunt, a sudden spot of color appearing on either cheek, snapped, "I doubt your wife will ever become accustomed to living in a superior establishment."

"What do you mean?"

"I mean that Candace seems unable to conduct herself with the decorum required of the future Countess of Linwood."

Jack's normally good-natured face turned chilly. "I think you must explain yourself, Aunt Charlotte."

"Certainly. Since her arrival here, in my opinion Candace has been entirely too free and easy in her ways. I had to put my foot down to make her take a groom with her when she rides. She pays surprise visits on our tenants and sits in farmers' kitchens, having tea with their wives. She consistently fails to keep a proper distance between herself and the servants. The other day, for example, I found her in the kitchens, showing Cook how to make a special kind of cake that's apparently locally famous in Surrey. Not long ago she was actually seen playing hide-and-seek with the village children."

Jack said coldly, "None of these things sounds like a particularly heinous offense to me. Candy happens to be a very warm and friendly person, and I think she should be praised rather than criticized for those qualities. In fact, in *my* opinion, you owe her an apology."

Charlotte drew herself up to her full impressive height. "I assure you, I was only trying to be helpful." Tossing her head, she swept majestically out of the room.

"Jack!" exclaimed Candy when the door had closed behind Charlotte. "You shouldn't have spoken to your aunt that way. *I* shouldn't have spoken to her as I did. I called her cruel and insensitive. Papa says I always speak before I think, and he's right."

Jack gave her a direct, sober look. "I won't have you blaming yourself. Aunt Charlotte has been making your life difficult, hasn't she? Why didn't you tell me?"

Candy said slowly, "Well, perhaps she did hurt my feelings a bit, but I always knew she meant well, just as she said. She wanted me to act like a future Countess of Linwood, and I needed her advice. Jack, I grew up on a farm. Brereton Court is like a different world to me."

Smiling at her tenderly, Jack said, "It won't seem like a different world to you for long. I know that someday you'll be a ravishing Countess of Linwood. And I'm glad you understand that Aunt Charlotte was truly trying to be helpful."

Candy threw herself into his arms, holding him closely. "Darling, I love you so much," she murmured. She had never loved him quite as much as she did then, she thought. She felt so intensely happy and grateful for his support and understanding, and yes, even a little surprised. It would have been only natural for him to have taken his aunt's part. She vowed silently to avoid any possible source of friction with Charlotte in the future.

As it turned out, Charlotte had also apparently had second thoughts. She never referred again to Betsy and her toothache, and in the following days and weeks she obviously tried to refrain from overt criticism of Candy. At one point, in fact, she told Candy with a mild approval, "When Lady Ellison called today, she remarked about what a pretty, well-behaved female you are."

As autumn faded into Christmastide and the New Year,

Candy's worries about fitting into her new life at Brereton Court gradually subsided.

Touching her heart, Jack invited her parents to spend the holidays with them. Her father politely refused, citing prior engagements that Candy considered purely imaginary. She knew her father. He had long since decided that a vast gulf existed between him and the aristocracy and the gentry, including his own daughter's relatives by marriage. But even though he refused the hospitality of Brereton Court, Candy was sure he was pleased and relieved to receive her assurances that she was blissfully happy in her new life.

To her surprise and satisfaction, as the year drew to a close, Candy arrived at a more amiable relationship with her father-in-law. Doubtless the earl would always regret that his son had married a nobody, but the news that Candy was increasing, bringing with it hopes of another heir to the estate, had apparently softened his attitude toward her. He ceased virtually ignoring her presence, or, at best, treating her with a chilly courtesy. He actually seemed to be inching toward a grudging cordiality, until the dinner party one evening when an incautious remark by Candy precipitated another family crisis.

The conversation at the dinner table that evening had begun innocuously enough. Mr. Walter Dillingham, the Member for the Melton division, was speaking about the coming session of Parliament. "The opposition will be tremendous, no doubt—I foresee petitions in the thousands—but I see nothing for it but to pass a bill limiting the importation of foreign grain priced at less than eighty shillings the quarter."

As the other male guests, all of them landowners, nodded their assent, Candy said impulsively, "But, Mr. Dillingham, won't such a law raise the cost of bread?"

Dillingham raised an eyebrow. "Doubtless there will be some increase in the cost of bread. Better that, wouldn't you agree, than to risk the prosperity, nay, the very existence of our English landowners? Because, if we allow the importation of unlimited cheap grain into this country, many farmers will be unable to grow crops except at a loss."

"That would be very bad, of course, but shouldn't we also give some thought to the poor? Only this week I was talking to several of the village women, who told me how difficult it was for them to make ends meet, and, if the cost of bread goes up, it will be even more difficult for them. I believe bread is the chief staple in their diet."

"My dear Lady Drayton, even though the war with Napoleon has ended, we must all be prepared to make sacrifices for the country."

Curbing her annoyance at Dillingham's faintly patronizing tone, Candy said, "But should we ask the poorest among us to make most of the sacrifices? Raise the price of a loaf of bread, and many people in this country would go hungry, or even starve."

The earl intervened, saying repressively, "My dear Candace, surely we should leave these matters to those who know best. Your own father, for example, is a landowner. I daresay he, like myself and our guests at this table tonight, will support Mr. Dillingham's proposal to protect domestic corn."

Candy said hotly, "Oh, yes, Papa is a landowner, but he also has a heart and a conscience. He would never agree to feather his own nest over the bodies of starving women and children!"

The words were hardly out of her mouth before Candy realized she had made a serious gaffe. For a moment a dead silence fell over the table. Then, as if at a signal, all the guests began chatting animatedly to each other, carefully avoiding looking at Candy. She glanced across at Jack, who averted his eyes and turned with a remark to his dinner partner. The earl's face was a grim mask. Only Gareth Mason, the neighbor who had been her companion on so many early morning rides, looked her straight in the eye with an almost imperceptible nod.

For the rest of the meal Candy sat with her eyes cast down,

pushing food from one side of her plate to the other, waiting miserably for the dinner to end. After the ladies withdrew to the drawing room, leaving the gentlemen to their port, Candy found herself isolated on a sofa. The other ladies, including Aunt Charlotte, sat together in pairs and groups, speaking to each other in low tones. Candy might as well have been invisible.

When the gentlemen returned to the drawing room, Candy glanced eagerly at Jack, willing him to join her. He hesitated, swallowing hard, but before Candy could be sure that he had rejected her unspoken plea, Gareth Mason sat down beside her on the sofa.

"Smile, Candace," he said under his breath. "Pretend I'm telling you a hugely funny joke. Pretend you're enjoying yourself mightily, without a care in the world."

She glanced at him in confusion. His thin, sensitive face looked much as usual, pleasant and friendly, his manner relaxed and casual, but she could see the concern in his gray eyes and hear it in his voice.

"Smile," he murmured again. "That's better," he continued as she forced her lips to curve in a parody of a smile. "Don't let any of these people realize you're hurt. Don't concede for a moment that you've done anything wrong. I agree with you, you know. If Parliament passes this Corn Bill, hundreds of thousands of people in this country will go hungry. We landowners made immense profits from agriculture during the war; we should be prepared to tighten our belts a little now."

Candy inhaled deeply. Suddenly she no longer felt like a pariah. "Thank you," she murmured.

Gareth's eyes twinkled. "For what? For being a friend? But don't forget—smile!"

With Gareth's steadying presence beside her, Candy managed to get through the rest of the evening. To her relief, Jack joined her and Gareth, smiling pleasantly and making small talk, drawing other people into the conversation. The unhappy subject of the Corn Bill wasn't mentioned. The atmosphere was so normal that Candy began to conjecture hopefully that perhaps she hadn't blundered quite as badly as she'd originally thought.

She was disillusioned later that evening after she and Jack retired to their bedchamber. Scarcely had the door closed when Jack turned on her, saying angrily, "What could you have been thinking of, Candy? You know nothing of politics, and yet you contradicted a member of Parliament, embarrassing him in front of a roomful of our neighbors. And you were very rude to Papa! You practically accused him and his friends of being greedy and grasping and uncharitable toward the poor!"

Blinking against a rush of tears, Candy muttered, "I'm so sorry. Truly, I didn't mean to offend anyone. It's my wretched tongue—you know what Papa says about me."

Jack gazed at her uncertainly for a few moments. Then, his face softening, he exclaimed, "Oh, the devil! Of course I know you didn't mean any harm. It was just your kind heart speaking." He patted her shoulder. "Let's forget about it, shall we? But for heaven's sake, Candy, do think first in the future before you open your mouth to a member of Parliament!"

True to his word, Jack put the incident behind them, reverting to his normally affectionate, good-natured self. The earl and Charlotte, however, were apparently unable to overlook Candy's faux pas. They remained cool and distant as the weeks went by and spring approached and the time of Candy's lying-in drew near. The earl, in fact, never spoke to her if he could help it. Not even the birth of the baby effected any change in his attitude toward his daughter-in-law. He seemed more interested in the news of Napoleon's escape from Elba than in his grandchild. Candy sometimes wondered if he would have felt different if Amanda had been a boy, a future heir to Brereton Court.

Candy, of course, was unable to understand how the earl, or anyone, could resist Amanda, with her tuft of black curls, Jack's gray eyes, and the enchanting smile that appeared

much earlier, her nurse informed Candy, than babies were
wont to smile. Jack was Amanda's fatuous slave from the
moment of her birth. When Gareth Mason pronounced the
baby a very pretty child, Jack waxed indignant. "Pretty?
Where are your eyes, Mason? Amanda is beautiful!"

Even Charlotte began to show signs of coming under
Amanda's spell. The earl, however, remained cold to mother
and daughter. Whether he would ever have changed his attitude remained a moot point because of an incident that occurred when Amanda was several months old, during a visit
by Sir Roger Percival, an intimate friend of the earl's of many
years standing.

Candy had always retained a soft spot for Betsy, the upstairs maid whose toothache had precipitated Candy's explosive quarrel with Charlotte. Betsy's widowed mother and
siblings lived in straitened circumstances in the village, and
Candy had often sent the family gifts of clothing and food.

One evening during Sir Roger Percival's visit, returning to
her bedchamber before dinner to have her abigail pin up a
loose hem, Candy found Betsy in the upper hall, struggling
to escape the clutches of their houseguest. Betsy caught sight
of Candy over Sir Roger's shoulder and gasped, "Oh—my
lady, please . . ."

Becoming aware of Candy's presence, Sir Roger released
Betsy, who scuttled away without a backward glance. The
baronet cleared his throat, saying, "Very sorry to embarrass
you, my dear Candace. A shame you came along just then.
However, I'm sure you understand my situation. If these servant gals *will* make eyes at their betters, what's a man to do?
Only human, you know!"

Candy said incredulously, "Are you accusing Betsy of
leading you on?"

Percival raised an eyebrow. "Certainly, my dear. The gal's
a taking little morsel, but forward. You can't think I was forcing myself on the chit?"

Candy lost her temper. "I saw you, Sir Roger. Betsy was

doing her best to get away from you. If you must play the loose screw, I suggest you indulge yourself somewhere else, not at Brereton Court!"

Turning a dull red, Sir Roger snapped, "I've never been so insulted in my entire life. Pray inform my dear friend, Lord Linwood, that I will not be dining at Brereton Court tonight, or indeed at any time. I intend to leave here immediately."

He stormed off, leaving Candy with a sinking feeling in the pit of her stomach. She suddenly wished she hadn't been quite so outspoken. Slowly she went down the stairs to the drawing room, where she gave the earl Sir Roger's message.

"Roger is leaving us? Now, at this hour?" the earl exclaimed incredulously. He gave Candy a hard look. "What do you know about this, pray?"

Candy swallowed hard. Her throat felt very dry. She described Sir Roger's encounter with Betsy while her father-in-law's gaze slowly turned venomous. He jumped to his feet and hurried toward the door, pausing on the threshold to say, "I'll do my utmost to persuade Sir Roger not to cut short his visit to Brereton Court. I doubt I'll succeed. *I* wouldn't stay in a house in which I'd been so grossly insulted. If Sir Roger does leave, Candace, you may be sure of one thing: I will never forgive you!"

Jack roused himself from his thoughts of his missing daughter as his tiger inquired plaintively, "I say, gov, were ye planning ter go back ter Lunnon?"

"No. Why do you ask?" Jack glanced around him and discovered to his chagrin that he was passing through the hamlet of Farnborough, well north of Seven Oaks on the road to London, on the same route he had traveled in reverse only that morning. After he had cravenly fled from the village of Millbridge without making any attempt to see Candy, or inquire about Amanda, he had driven aimlessly for several

hours, he now realized, without noticing where he was going.
Now he was well on his way back to London.

"I see there's a post stop here in Farnborough, Tom," he
told the tiger. "We'll change horses, and I'll have a bite to
eat. Have some lunch yourself. Then we'll return to Millbridge."

Tom must think my wits are addled, Jack reflected glumly
a little later as he finished his lunch in a private dining parlor
of the Farnborough Arms. *Perhaps I have gone a little queer
in my attic. Why else am I finding it so hard to confront Candace? In seventeen years she can't have changed too much.
She was never a shrew, or a virago, even if she did leave me
for another man. I've no real reason to think she won't be
cooperative today. After all, she must realize that I'm in the
right. She can't think I'd allow her to kidnap my daughter!*

He hunched over his tankard of ale as memories he had
stubbornly kept at bay for so many years years began to wash
over him.

The last few weeks of his brief year of marriage hadn't
been idyllic. In fact, for the first time since he'd known her,
he had been completely out of charity with Candy. He had
been deeply angered by her rudeness to Sir Roger Percival,
and utterly baffled by her stubborn refusal to admit she was
in the wrong.

"Sir Roger was trying to rape Betsy," she'd declared in-
dignantly. "And then, when I caught him in the act, he tried
to make me believe that Betsy had made advances to him.
Do you mean to say I should have pretended to believe him?
To condone what he'd done, without a word of criticism?"

"Well, of course I don't condone the seduction of housemaids! But yes, you shouldn't have lashed out at Sir Roger.
He was a guest in our house. He and Papa have been friends
since they were boys. I doubt Sir Roger will ever speak to
any of us again after this. I can hardly blame Papa for being
so angry with you. In the fiend's name, Candy, you must

know that gentlemen sometimes have—er—certain weaknesses. Gently bred females learn to ignore such behavior."

Candy had put up her chin at him. "But then, I'm only a farmer's daughter, remember? Perhaps I'll never learn how to behave like a 'gently bred' female!"

It was their first real quarrel, and during the next few days it was never quite made up, causing a growing coldness between them. Nevertheless, the news that Candy had deserted him came as the greatest shock of his life. He could have sworn, up until the very end, that whatever their problems, Candy loved him as much as he loved her.

He returned home from a brief trip to Lincolnshire to purchase a pair of hunters to discover that Candy had left Brereton Court in the dead of night, leaving no message, no explanation. His first guess was that Candy had gone to her old home in Surrey, perhaps to give her, and Jack, too, a little breathing room after their quarrel. But a grieving and shocked Squire Frazier had no knowledge of Candy's whereabouts Eventually Jack's father forced him to recognize the obvious.

"Gareth Mason left his estate, telling his servants he was going to London, on the very day Candace disappeared," the earl informed Jack. "Hardly a coincidence, do you think?"

Jack glared at his father. "I don't know why Candy left me, but I'll never believe it was because she was cuckolding me with Gareth Mason!"

"What an innocent you are, Jack. I've been making some inquiries. Were you aware that—until she was far gone in pregnancy—Candace often joined Mason for early morning rides about the countryside?"

"Yes, I was aware, Father. Candy told me all about those rides. She regarded Mason simply as a friendly older man. I was grateful that she had agreeable company while I was busy learning my future duties with our estate agent!"

The earl shot Jack a sour look. "I repeat, you're an innocent. I can't conceive why you never suspected that those friendly early morning rides had turned into assignations."

He raised his hand against Jack's furious protest. "I realize you won't believe in Candace's misconduct without proof. I intend to produce that proof. Until then, we'll say no more about it."

Results of the earl's initial investigation by the Bow Street Runners was inconclusive, revealing only that Gareth Mason had left England in the company of an unknown female. Later, however, despite the difficulties of communicating with the Continent in wartime, the earl's inquiry agents produced proof sufficient to convince Jack that Candy had indeed fled from Brereton Court in the company of Gareth Mason, and that the pair was living on property owned by Mason in Austria. In his younger days Mason had briefly served as a diplomat in Austria, and still had ties in the country.

"Well, are you satisfied, Jack?" his father had demanded. "I trust you realize now that you should never have married that girl. You must cut your losses and sue Candace immediately for divorce in the House of Lords. You have the grounds, adultery with Gareth Mason."

His pride in shreds, his love betrayed, Jack had been, strongly tempted to punish Candy. In the end he told his father, "No, I can't sue Candy for divorce. She'd be disgraced for life. She could never hold up her head in society again."

"So?" The earl stared at Jack. "Candace doesn't deserve any consideration. Let her lie in the bed she's made. However, there's no reason for you to lie in *your* bed. If you don't divorce your wife, you can never have a legitimate heir."

"I have a legitimate heir. Amanda—"

"I meant a male heir, of course. Amanda can't inherit the Linwood title and estates."

"You have three nephews. They're all decent fellows. Any one of my cousins would make a proper Earl of Linwood. Our line won't die out, Papa. Meanwhile, I'm not willing to ruin Candy and scar Amanda's life with scandal in order to obtain my freedom to marry again. There will be no divorce."

"Jack, for God's sake . . ."

"No, Papa. Leave it be. I've made up my mind. I'll simply let it be known that Candy and I have decided to live apart. Many unhappily married couples solve their problems in that fashion. And if Mason and Candy have the good sense to live quietly and discreetly in Austria, there's little likelihood of scandal."

He'd kept to his resolve not to institute public divorce proceedings against Candy, Jack reflected as he finished his tankard of ale in the parlor of the Farnborough Arms. To this day he didn't quite understand his motives. He hadn't forgiven Candy. His hurt, when he allowed himself to recall it, was still as raw and real as it had been seventeen years before. All he knew was that he hadn't been able to bring himself either to expose his own humiliation to the world or to blacken Candy's reputation.

It had helped, he mused, that over the years he hadn't met another woman he cared to marry. And his love for his daughter Amanda, and hers for him, had largely filled the void left by Candy's flight.

After his father's death several years after Candy's disappearance, he'd settled into a quiet country existence, rarely leaving Leicestershire. He managed his estates with increasing competence, played his part in county affairs, taught Amanda, against his aunt Charlotte's scandalized advice, to become a crack shot and a bruising rider. He would have said, until four days earlier, that he was completely content with his life.

Four days ago his life had fallen apart again. Working at his desk in the library, he'd looked up from his papers at the soft knock on the door. "Come."

Amanda bounded in with her usual energy. Jack smiled. It had often seemed to him that she was in perpetual motion. At seventeen, she was a vivacious beauty, tall and slender, with masses of dark curls, a faultless complexion, speaking gray eyes, and the enchanting, beguiling smile that had charmed family and friends from her cradle.

"There you are, puss," Jack said affectionately. "Are you all packed for our journey to London tomorrow?"

Amanda gave Jack a wary look. "Papa . . . I've decided not to go to London. I don't wish to have a come-out."

Jack stared at his daughter. "What do you mean, you don't wish to have a come-out? Your aunt Charlotte and I have been planning your introduction to society for months."

Bristling, Amanda said, "Papa, you know very well that come-outs have only one purpose, to find girls suitable husbands. Well, I've already found the man I want for my husband. I don't need a come-out."

Jack stiffened, exclaiming, "Oh? Who, pray tell, is your candidate for your future husband? Not young Carlyle, I hope, or Lord Elwyn's cub. They've both been making calf eyes at you, according to Aunt Charlotte, but neither of them is a suitable match for you, not, at least, until you've had an opportunity to sample the London marriage mart. . . ."

"Papa . . . I want to marry Frank Carrington."

"Frank Carrington? Have you gone queer in your attic, Amanda? You can't have thought I'd countenance your marriage to the son of my own tenant!"

"You've always said that Mr. Carrington manages the home farm very capably, Papa."

"What has that to say to anything? I grant you, Frank Carrington and his father are of perfectly respectable yeoman stock. That doesn't mean Frank can aspire to marrying the daughter of the Earl of Linwood!"

Amanda said tightly, "Papa, aren't you being something of a hypocrite? *You* married a farmer's daughter. Why shouldn't I marry a farmer's son?"

Jack caught his breath. For the first time he questioned his forbearance in allowing Amanda to know something of her mother. His father had urged him to conceal all knowledge of Candy from Amanda. "Let Amanda believe that Candace is dead," the earl had urged.

But Jack had considered such concealment cruel. When

Amanda, in early childhood, had questioned him about her mother, Jack had said simply, shading the truth, that he and Candy, unable to live together happily, had chosen to live apart. Later, when Candy had begun writing to Amanda on the occasion of her birthday and at other intervals, Jack had allowed the correspondence. Candy never wrote of anything except her garden and her horses and the quiet routine of the Austrian estate on which she lived. She never mentioned Gareth Mason.

"Well, Papa?" Amanda challenged him now. "You haven't answered my question. You married a farmer's daughter, so why shouldn't I marry a farmer's son?"

Jack opened his mouth to speak and bit off his words before he could betray himself. He'd been about to say that the failure of his own marriage was an excellent reason why Amanda shouldn't marry a man so far below her in station. He had long been convinced that farm-bred Candy's difficulties in adjusting to the more formal ways of Brereton Court had largely been responsible for the discontent that had driven her away from him. But he was loath to say such a thing to Amanda. He had never revealed his and Candy's marital problems to their daughter; he would not start now.

Instead, he said curtly, "Don't be impertinent, Amanda. Your mother's situation and young Carrington's are nothing alike. Candace was the daughter of a substantial landowner, not a tenant farmer. I'll have no more talk about your marrying Frank Carrington. Tomorrow morning we leave for London, where I trust you'll meet a vastly more suitable candidate for your hand."

"Papa, you're not being fair—" Amanda broke off her protest. "Yes, Papa," she said, lowering her eyes. "May I be excused?"

In hindsight, Jack realized he should have known better than to believe that Amanda had meekly given in to his dictum. Meekness had never been a part of his lively daughter's personality. She didn't appear for dinner that evening, but

Jack thought nothing of her absence. He and his aunt Charlotte agreed that Amanda was probably sulking. Next morning, however, while he was at breakfast, Amanda's abigail reported that she was missing. "Her bed not even slept in, my lord!"

Smothering a curse, Jack jumped up from the table, exclaiming to Charlotte, "The brat has persuaded that young fool into an elopement, I'll be bound. I'm off after them. I doubt I'll be too far behind. After all, if Amanda sprang this elopement scheme on young Carrington in the middle of the night, it would have taken him some little time to make the arrangements."

"But, Jack . . ." Charlotte faltered. "If you're not in time—what will we do? Scottish marriages are legal."

"Then I'll drag Amanda back across the Scottish border and decide what to do next," Jack said coolly. "Good-bye, Aunt Charlotte."

Before setting off for Scotland, however, Jack took the precaution of going to the home farm to confirm his suspicion that Amanda had eloped with Frank Carrington. To his profound surprise, he found the young farmer working peacefully beside his father in the fields. Jack's careful questioning satisfied him that Frank knew nothing of Amanda's whereabouts. In fact, he seemed quite surprised that Jack and Amanda hadn't yet left for London.

Somewhat relieved, but still perplexed and concerned, Jack returned to Brereton Court to acquaint his aunt with the new development.

"Where could Amanda have gone if she didn't elope?" wailed Charlotte. She paused, her eyes brightening. "Jack, could she be with your uncle in Yorkshire? She's always been a favorite with him."

Jack interrupted her. "Hold on, Aunt Charlotte. I have an idea where Amanda may have gone."

Leaving his aunt gaping in surprise, he went to his library, where he searched through a pile of papers for a letter he had received several months previously from the inquiry agents he had been employing for years to report to him on Candy's activities. He had never felt guilty about the practice, although he guessed that Candy, should she ever find out about it, might consider the inquiry agents to be no better than spies. But Jack's father had convinced him long ago that he owed it to his position, and Amanda's interests, to know at all times where Candy was, and what she was doing.

The letter from the inquiry agents reported that Mr. Gareth Mason had died at Christmastide of 1814. Rumor had it that he had left a will bequeathing his properties both in England and in Austria to the lady who had shared his life for so many years, the lady who had always been known as "Frau Mason." Early in the new year Frau Mason had closed up the Austrian villa and had traveled across the Continent to Calais, where she had taken ship for England. The inquiry agents had learned that Frau Mason, who had taken the name of "Mrs. Bennett," had bought a modest house in the village of Millbridge, several miles north of Seven Oaks in Kent.

Jack slammed his fist down on the letter. Of course. He didn't doubt for an instant that Candy had notified their daughter about her plans to return to England. In fact, Candy's principal reason for returning must have been her desire to see Amanda at last. She had no other ties in England. Her parents had died many years before, and she had never been close to the cousin who had inherited the farm.

Jack pulled the bellrope. He ordered the servant who answered his ring to inform the stables to prepare his curricle and team for an immediate journey south.

As Candy sat at her dressing table, tidying her hair before she went down to dinner, she heard the sound of carriage wheels rolling along the quiet village street. Her muscles tense, she sat, waiting, until a knock sounded at the door and a trim maid in white cap and starched apron appeared to announce in a rather flustered tone, "If ye please, ma'am, will ye see the gentleman below?" She extended to Candy a tray holding a calling card.

Candy looked at the card. "Show Lord Linwood into the parlor. Tell him I'll be down directly."

Several minutes later Candy paused on the threshold of the parlor to take a steadying breath before entering the room.

"Hello, Jack," she said calmly. She looked at her husband closely. He'd changed so little. He still looked young and vibrant. His carriage was as erect, his figure as trim, his dark hair as abundant and free from gray as ever. But why shouldn't he look young? He was only thirty-six, no, thirty-seven. And she was thirty-five. She put her hand to her face. Did he see many changes in her?

Apparently he wasn't in the least interested in her looks. Not bothering to return her greeting, he said abruptly, "Is Amanda here?"

"Yes. Do you wish to see her?"

His face darkened. "Of course I wish to see her. I've chased halfway across England after her."

Candy crossed the room to ring the bell. "Ask Lady Amanda to come to the parlor," she instructed the maid who answered her ring. To Jack she said, "I've told my servants that Amanda is my niece."

He said coldly, "That was wise of you. It's best there should be as little gossip as possible about Amanda's escapade."

Candy bit her lip. There was no softness at all about him, no indication that there had ever been a spark of affection between them. They might have been complete strangers. Averting her eyes, she waited with Jack in a leaden silence until their daughter entered the parlor.

Amanda's eyes widened. "Papa!" she exclaimed. "How did you—?"

"How did I know where to find you? You must think I'm a real gudgeon, puss. When I discovered you hadn't eloped with young Carrington, I guessed you'd gone to your mother.

Amanda, I've come to take you to London. Your Aunt Charlotte will meet us at the town house. She'll have packed all your belongings and brought them with her."

"I won't go," Amanda declared defiantly. "I refuse to endure a come-out." She turned to Candy. "Mama, you'll let me stay with you until Papa sees reason, won't you?"

Candy hesitated, gazing at her daughter with her heart in her eyes. "Amanda, darling, you know how happy I've been to see you after all these years. It's been a dream come true for me. If I had only my own wishes to consider, I'd invite you to stay as long as you like. But—please don't be angry with me—I can't allow you to remain here against your father's wishes."

"I see how it is," Amanda burst out. "I can't expect support from either of you. You're ruining my life, and you don't care a fig. I hate both of you!" She glared at Candy. "I'll tell you this, Mama. You don't want me here, but Papa will have to use force to drag me away. I won't go otherwise." With one final embittered glance at her parents, she flounced out of the room.

Jack cleared his throat. "Thank you for your—er—support."

"You surely didn't believe I'd encourage Amanda to defy you?"

Looking embarrassed, Jack muttered, "No. Of course not. I did think, however, that you might be sympathetic to Amanda's desire to marry young Carrington."

Candy gave him a level look. "Not at all. I of all people know the pitfalls of marrying outside one's own class." Noting the slow flush that covered Jack's face, she added hastily, "I did my best to dissuade Amanda from rushing into a rash marriage. I told her she was too young at seventeen to think of marrying anybody—to which she replied instantly that *I* was seventeen when I married you!—and I also urged her to return to Brereton Court and talk over her problems with you. Of course, she was in no mood for such advice, and frankly,

I was so happy to see her that I didn't press her." Candy added wistfully, "I hoped that she might stay with me for at least a few days. . . ."

She broke off. After a moment she said, "Well, that's neither here nor there. Amanda is so angry and disappointed with me now that I doubt she would want to stay with me in any event. What are we to do about her, Jack? You can't very well take her out of my house by force without creating a scandal!" She paused, looking at him doubtfully. "Will you stay to dinner? After the meal we could talk about what we should do."

He looked taken aback. "I . . . yes, thank you."

Dinner was a stilted affair. Refraining from speaking of personal affairs while the maid was serving the meal, Candy and Jack could only talk idly. To Candy there was something unreal, almost macabre, about discussing the weather or books or other mundane topics with the husband she hadn't seen for seventeen years. Frequently they simply stopped talking, falling into uncomfortable silences. Once or twice Candy caught Jack looking at her with a curiously intent expression that unnerved her.

Matters were no better in the parlor after dinner. Unable to think of another lame remark, Candy sat down beside the table holding the coffee tray, motioning Jack to a seat, and busied herself with rearranging the cups and pouring the coffee. At length she looked up, cup in hand, to find that Jack was again gazing at her intently.

"Why do you keep staring at me like that?" she said involuntarily.

Jack ignored her question. She doubted he had even heard her. His eyes still fixed on her in that mesmerized stare, Jack muttered, "You haven't changed at all. You're still as beautiful as the day we met on the road near the farm."

Candy could feel the hot color suffusing her cheeks. "Jack . . ."

For a moment he looked completely disconcerted, as if he

himself couldn't believe he had made such a remark. Then the floodgates burst. "Why did you do it, Candy?" he said harshly. "Why did you leave me? Oh, I realized later that you weren't happy those last few weeks, but I could have sworn you loved me."

"I did love you," Candy exclaimed without thinking. "I've always—" She broke off, biting her lip.

Jack said quickly, "You've always what?"

Candy shook her head. "It doesn't matter."

"It does matter. At least, it matters to me. Finish what you started to say, Candy."

She put down the coffee cup and clenched her hands together tightly in her lap. "There's no point to talking about the past."

"Perhaps that's the mistake we made all those years ago, not talking. Let's talk now. Tell me. If you loved me, why did you elope with Gareth Mason?"

Candy looked at him imploringly. "Jack, leave it be. We made a bad marriage. We were never suited. We ended the marriage seventeen years ago. All we have in common now is Amanda."

For a moment Jack sat in a hard-breathing silence, obviously wrestling with his emotions. Then, as though the words were being forced out of him, he said roughly, "For you our marriage may be over, but it isn't for me. Didn't you ever wonder why I didn't sue you for divorce? I told myself that I was too much of a gentleman to drag your name into the mud. But today, the instant I saw you, I realized I'd never stopped loving you, never ceased hoping that you would come back to me. And now I want an answer: Why did you leave me?

"Jack—oh, Jack, my dearest one . . ." Blinking against a sudden rush of stinging tears, Candy buried her face in her hands.

Jack said insistently, "Candy, whatever it is, however painful it is, don't you think it's time you told me?"

She lifted her head, her face drawn and pale. "Perhaps it's more than time." She paused, collecting her thoughts. "Do you remember your trip to Lincolnshire to look at hunters when Amanda was several months old?"

Jack's mouth turned hard. "When I came home from that trip I found you gone."

"Yes. This is why I went away." In disjointed phrases she told him about the night that Jeb, one of the Brereton Court grooms, had stolen into her bedchamber and attempted to force himself on her.

She'd prevented the attack by disabling Jeb with a well-aimed kick to his private parts. Before making his escape, the pain-racked groom had snarled, "Ye needn't think ye're out o' the woods, my fine lady. Yer father-in-law will send someone else ter plant horns on yer husband's head, and then ye'll be out o' Brereton Court in disgrace quicker'n the cat kin lick behind its ears."

"When I heard Jeb say that," Candy told Jack quietly, "I realized your father would stop at nothing to get rid of me. So that very night I left Brereton Court. I went to Gareth Mason for help."

"My God," breathed Jack. His face was twisted with horror. "Why didn't you wait until I got home, Candy? Why didn't you tell me about it?"

"Jack, I couldn't tell you. For one thing, I wasn't sure you would believe me. For another, I couldn't bear to come between you and your father. And finally, I had to admit the earl's instincts were right: You and I *were* mismatched. The longer the marriage continued, the more I would embarrass you and your family. I was afraid you would end up hating me. So I decided to go away. I still think I was right."

Rising, Jack skirted the serving table to pull Candy to her feet. He put his hand to her chin, forcing her to look up at him. His gray eyes darkening with emotion, he said huskily, "Candy, do you love me now?"

"Yes," Candy breathed, her voice a trickle of sound. "Oh, yes. I never stopped loving you. But, Jack . . ."

"No buts. Will you come back to me, my love? Will you be my wife again?"

Candy began to tremble. "It's too late. You know it's too late. What—what about Gareth?"

Jack had turned deathly pale, but his voice was steady as he said, "I don't blame you for turning to Gareth Mason. We—I and my family—drove you away with our blind self-ishness, our refusal to understand your concerns. Whatever happened, whatever you did, it was our fault."

A wave of joyful exultation swept over Candy. Time enough later to tell Jack that she and Gareth had never lived as man and wife, that all Gareth had asked of her was friend-ship. For now she could trust absolutely in Jack's love, and that was all that mattered. She threw her arms around his neck and pressed close to him, reveling in the feel of his hard masculine body against hers, and the intoxicating taste of his lips.

"Mama! Papa!"

Candy and Jack disentangled themselves and whirled to face their daughter.

"I came to tell you I'm sorry," Amanda said uncertainly. "Of course I don't hate you." Her eyes slowly brightened. "You two don't hate each other anymore either, do you?"

Grasping Jack's hand, Candy said simply, "No, Amanda. In fact, your father and I have just discovered that we never stopped loving each other. I'm going home with you and Jack to Brereton Court. We'll be a family again."

Amanda gave her parents a long look. "Tell me: Now that your marriage to a farmer's daughter has turned out so hap-pily, Papa, how can you and Mama object to my marriage to a farmer's son?"

Candy and Jack looked at each other blankly. After a mo-ment Candy said, "Well, Jack?"

The Earl of Linwood turned to his daughter. *"Touché,*

Amanda. I'll make a bargain with you. Promise me you'll come to London with your mother and me to make your come-out. At the end of the Season, if you still wish to marry Frank Carrington, I'll withdraw my objections to the match."

"Fair enough," flashed Amanda. "But I warn you, Papa, at the end of the Season, I'll still love Frank Carrington!"

ELEGANT LOVE STILL FLOURISHES —
Wrap yourself in a Zebra Regency Romance.

A MATCHMAKER'S MATCH   (3783, $3.50/$4.50)
by Nina Porter
To save herself from a loveless marriage, Lady Psyche Veringham pretends to be a bluestocking. Resigned to spinsterhood at twenty-three, Psyche sets her keen mind to snaring a husband for her young charge, Amanda. She sets her cap for long-time bachelor, Justin St. James. This man of the world has had his fill of frothy-headed debutantes and turns the tables on Psyche. Can a bluestocking and a man about town find true love?

FIRES IN THE SNOW   (3809, $3.99/$4.99)
by Janis Laden
Because of an unhappy occurrence, Diana Ruskin knew that a secure marriage was not in her future. She was content to assist her physician father and follow in his footsteps . . . until now. After meeting Adam, Duke of Marchmaine, Diana's precise world is shattered. She would simply have to avoid the temptation of his gentle touch and stunning physique — and by doing so break her own heart!

FIRST SEASON   (3810, $3.50/$4.50)
by Anne Baldwin
When country heiress Laetitia Biddle arrives in London for the Season, she harbors dreams of triumph and applause. Instead, she becomes the laughingstock of drawing rooms and ballrooms, alike. This headstrong miss blames the rakish Lord Wakeford for her miserable debut, and she vows to rise above her many faux pas. Vowing to become an Original, Letty proves that she's more than a match for this eligible, seasoned Lord.

AN UNCOMMON INTRIGUE   (3701, $3.99/$4.99)
by Georgina Devon
Miss Mary Elizabeth Sinclair was rather startled when the British Home Office employed her as a spy. Posing as "Tasha," an exotic fortune-teller, she expected to encounter unforeseen dangers. However, nothing could have prepared her for Lord Eric Stewart, her dashing and infuriating partner. Giving her heart to this haughty rogue would be the most reckless hazard of all.

A MADDENING MINX   (3702, $3.50/$4.50)
by Mary Kingsley
After a curricle accident, Miss Sarah Chadwick is literally thrust into the arms of Philip Thornton. While other women shy away from Thornton's eyepatch and aloof exterior, Sarah finds herself drawn to discover why this man is physically and emotionally scarred.

Available wherever paperbacks are sold, or order direct from the Publisher. Send cover price plus 50¢ per copy for mailing and handling to Penguin USA, P.O. Box 999, c/o Dept. 17109, Bergenfield, NJ 07621. Residents of New York and Tennessee must include sales tax. DO NOT SEND CASH.

ZEBRA REGENCIES
ARE
THE TALK OF THE TON!

A REFORMED RAKE (4499, $3.99)
by Jeanne Savery

After governess Harriet Cole helped her young charge flee to France—and the designs of a despicable suitor, more trouble soon arrived in the person of a London rake. Sir Frederick Carrington insisted on providing safe escort back to England. Harriet deemed Carrington more dangerous than any band of brigands, but secretly relished matching wits with him. But after being taken in his arms for a tender kiss, she found herself wondering— *could* a lady find love with an irresistible rogue?

A SCANDALOUS PROPOSAL (4504, $4.99)
by Teresa DesJardien

After only two weeks into the London season, Lady Pamela Premington has already received her first offer of marriage. If only it hadn't come from the *ton's* most notorious rake, Lord Marchmont. Pamela had already set her sights on the distinguished Lieutenant Penford, who had the heroism and honor that made him the ideal match. Now she had to keep from falling under the spell of the seductive Lord so she could pursue the man more worthy of her love. Or was he?

A LADY'S CHAMPION (4535, $3.99)
by Janice Bennett

Miss Daphne, art mistress of the Selwood Academy for Young Ladies, greeted the notion of ghosts haunting the academy with skepticism. However, to avoid rumors frightening off students, she found herself turning to Mr. Adrian Carstairs, sent by her uncle to be her "protector" against the "ghosts." Although, Daphne would accept no interference in her life, she *would* accept aid in exposing any spectral spirits. What she never expected was for Adrian to expose the secret wishes of her hidden heart . . .

CHARITY'S GAMBIT (4537, $3.99)
by Marcy Stewart

Charity Abercrombie reluctantly embarks on a London season in hopes of making a suitable match. However she cannot forget the mysterious Dominic Castille—and the kiss they shared—when he fell from a tree as she strolled through the woods. Charity does not know that the dark and dashing captain harbors a dangerous secret that will ensnare them both in its web—leaving Charity to risk certain ruin and losing the man she so passionately loves . . .

Available wherever paperbacks are sold, or order direct from the Publisher. Send cover price plus 50¢ per copy for mailing and handling to Penguin USA, P.O. Box 999, c/o Dept. 17109, Bergenfield, NJ 07621. Residents of New York and Tennessee must include sales tax. DO NOT SEND CASH.

Taylor—made Romance From Zebra Books

WHISPERED KISSES   (3830, $4.99/5.99)
Beautiful Texas heiress Laura Leigh Webster never imagined that her biggest worry on her African safari would be the handsome Jace Elliot, her tour guide. Laura's guardian, Lord Chadwick Hamilton, warns her of Jace's dangerous past; she simply cannot resist the lure of his strong arms and the passion of his *Whispered Kisses*.

KISS OF THE NIGHT WIND   (3831, $4.99/$5.99)
Carrie Sue Strover thought she was leaving trouble behind her when she deserted her brother's outlaw gang to live her life as schoolmarm Carolyn Starns. On her journey, her stagecoach was attacked and she was rescued by handsome T.J. Rogue. T.J. plots to have Carrie lead him to her brother's cohorts who murdered his family. T.J., however, soon succumbs to the beautiful runaway's charms and loving caresses.

FORTUNE'S FLAMES   (3825, $4.99/$5.99)
Impatient to begin her journey back home to New Orleans, beautiful Maren James was furious when Captain Hawk delayed the voyage by searching for stowaways. Impatience gave way to uncontrollable desire once the handsome captain searched *her* cabin. He was looking for illegal passengers; what he found was wild passion with a woman he knew was unlike all those he had known before!

PASSIONS WILD AND FREE   (3828, $4.99/$5.99)
After seeing her family and home destroyed by the cruel and hateful Epson gang, Randee Hollis swore revenge. She knew she found the perfect man to help her—gunslinger Marsh Logan. Not only strong and brave, Marsh had the ebony hair and light blue eyes to make Randee forget her hate and seek the love and passion that only he could give her.